VIKING'S PRIZE

TANYA ANNE CROSBY

AVON BOOKS ◆ NEW YORK

VIKING'S PRIZE is an original publication of Avon Books. This work has never before appeared in book form. This work is a novel. Literary license has been taken in regard to circumstances surrounding the battle of Svolde and the battle itself.

AVON BOOKS
A division of
The Hearst Corporation
1350 Avenue of the Americas
New York, New York 10019

First Avon Books Printing: April 1994

AVON TRADEMARK REG. U.S. PAT. OFF. AND IN OTHER COUNTRIES, MARCA REGISTRADA, HECHO EN U.S.A.

Printed in the U.S.A.

RA 10 9 8 7 6 5 4 3 2 1

To Fathers
Because I was fortunate enough to have two.

In loving memory of Jack Vernon Crosby, Sr.
who loved me as though I were his own.
And to my own father
David Oliver Rietz
who's always there when I need him.
I love you Daddy

A special thanks to Frances Whealton, Deputy Director of the Berkeley County Library, along with Dianne Boersma, Michele Bibby, and Madelyne Spann. Also to Kevin Cook, researcher extraordinaire. Thanks for making it your quest to help me recreate the elusive Battle of Svolde.

Chapter 1

At any moment the enemy's castle would emerge from the darkness.

Anticipating the first glimpse with the blood lust of his people, the Viking warlord stood, one foot set imposingly upon the Goldenhawk's prow, and contemplated the task before him. Alarik Trygvason knew full well the risk he took by navigating so far up the river Seine, but the French count deserved this retribution. Never again would the spineless bastard plot to ambush his camp!

Of that Alarik would make certain.

'Twas also the last time Alarik would trust a filthy Franskmann!

He should have realized the ruse the very instant Robert, the French king, offered him native soil in exchange for peace between them. He should have discerned that Count Phillipe, who was forced by his sovereign to relinquish a portion of his own land in the exchange, seethed in fury and would not submit easily. Above all, he should have perceived the true reason Count Phillipe had sent a squat little balding man with the generous gift of French wine.

But he'd been too hungry, too mesmerized by the lush green beauty of French soil. Too enthralled at the prospect of holding a meager parcel of it.

1

Like vipers they'd slithered into his sleeping encampment. And like vipers they had attacked. He'd lost full half his men before any could clear their heads of wine or sleep. Sotted as they'd been, they were ill-prepared to fend off the strike, though thanks to the count's little balding man, Alarik's eyes were now open wide; he knew precisely who to thank for the night's unexpected call.

Phillipe of Brouillard.

His eyes narrowed vengefully. The deceiving fool had thought his plan infallible. Doubtless he'd believed that if he rid himself of Alarik, he would deliver King Robert from the terms of this agreement. But Phillipe had turned over the wrong stone—chosen the wrong man with whom to match wits and might.

And tonight he would pay the price.

So it was that Alarik now kept his angry vigil, his gaze fixed upon the horizon, his expression hard as if molded of unyielding steel. His features were well chiseled like that of his namesake's, the hawk, and his pewter gray eyes were likened to the silver of his sword, *Dragvendil*, for they could slice into the heart of a man with the ease of his fine gilt-edged blade.

The single turret appeared first, standing sentinel alone, its battlements a hungry mouth open to the heavens, jagged teeth exposed and ready to devour the concealing vapors. Gracefully, with little more sound than the lifting and parting of skin-wrapped paddles from the black water, the *drakken* prows slid onward toward shore.

Like a mantle of misty white, the impenetrable fog effectively cloaked his men from the fortress's view, yet Alarik's keen eyes spied the lone figure of a guard atop the stone tower at once, and a prickle raced down his spine as he waited for the man to sound an alarm.

Nothing came.

Mayhap the guard had not spied them, for the mist was thick.

In that instant—as if in approval of their aim— thunder tumbled across the blustery heavens, and someone's ecstatic whisper followed it into the night.

"Thor! 'Tis Thor! He is with us!" the man declared.

"*Ja!*" agreed another, and still others gave grunts of acknowledgment to their predestined victory.

Alarik, no longer believing in the old gods, allowed his men their enthusiasm, but did not share in their triumph. He acknowledged their belief with a deferential nod, but would not accept that a mere rumble of thunder would predetermine the outcome of this battle. Their superior warrior's skill alone, hard earned by the sweat and blood of their bodies, would give them the victory they sought this night. That and nought else. Nevertheless, he was grateful for the camouflaging mist— from whosoever it came, though within moments of that concession, the wind picked up and feathered the haze away, leaving them completely exposed to the watchman's view . . .

Still nothing but silence.

With a calmness that belied the occasion, Alarik listened and waited, his head tilted skyward with no emotion evident in the intense silver of his stare. He eyed the sentry intently for some sign that the alarm had already been sounded . . . that he'd missed it somehow, and then he shook his head, for there was nothing.

Not for an instant did his eyes leave the turret.

And all the while, the current brought them closer . . . closer . . .

With a flick of his hand he motioned for his men to cease their rowing. Their forward momentum alone would complete their glide to shore, and he needed the silence to better determine their position. Even though the oars were abandoned, the night air remained undisturbed, the whispering wind the only sound to reach his ears. Incredibly, there were no shouts of *To arms! To arms!* to be heard from within—despite the fact that Alarik was certain the guard had by now seen them approach. With an absent gesture, he stroked the hilt of his double-edged sword, considering the goal, assessing their options with narrowed eyes.

"A trap, jarl?" By now, every Norseman aboard the three warships had spied the lone figure atop the tower, but it was Sigurd Thorgoodson, Alarik's most loyal warrior, who came forward to voice the concern.

"*Nei,*" Alarik contended, giving the man the briefest glance. Again, his gaze returned to the figure above. The silhouette grew slowly clearer as they neared. "They could not have known we would come—'tis not possible." He shook his head in puzzlement, for none of the count's bumbling mercenaries had lived to carry the tale of the battle. Had even one slipped from his grasp, there would not have been time enough for him to return to warn the count. Alarik had set out forthwith. Truth was, he had no inkling why the witless guard did not alert the castle. "They cannot know we have discovered the hidden portal," he reasoned aloud. "And their best defense would be to fire upon us from the safety of the high walls . . . yet, they do not do so?" The last was a question put to himself. He expected no reply from Sigurd and did not receive one.

Brouillard's thick masonry walls were a deterrent to most in this day when castles were built of timber and so much easier to infiltrate, but Alarik knew its damning secret and his lips twisted with ill-concealed contempt as he thought of the man whose blood he sought to spill this night.

Coward.

Only an incompetent, craven bastard would have such an escape portal. And there was only one thing Alarik despised more than a coward. A *traitor*.

Count Phillipe was both.

Never mind, for while the latter had decreed the count's fate, the former now sealed it. Concealed by the dense trees and bush of the forest beyond lay the means to breach the mist-enshrouded monstrosity—a hidden passage that backed deep into the sheltering woods. He grinned at the thought of it, a slow, merciless smile that swept winter into the silver of his eyes. For that bit of knowledge he could also thank the little balding man, for by it Alarik would return the count's favor tenfold this night. Reflexively, his grip tightened about *Dragvendil's* hilt as he thought of the portal, for 'twas fitting the hidden escape passage should be the count's very downfall this eve.

He had no qualms whatsoever about catching the count unawares. As declared by Phillipe's own Christian God, 'twas fitting to take an eye for an eye, a tooth for a tooth . . . a life for a life. Just as the count had dealt with him, so would he be dealt with himself.

The chill wind rose, swirling the remaining fog in its wake, obscuring the figure upon the turret momentarily before dissipating into the ominous heavens.

And it was then, in that moment, as the ship's prow nudged its keel into the soft muck of the river embankment and ended its journey, that Alarik truly beheld the figure standing above them.

To his absolute shock . . . it was a woman . . . her dark hair long and fluttering wildly in the breeze . . . her light colored kyrtle billowing furiously with the wind, mixing with the swirling vapors.

The very sight of her made the hairs of his nape stand on end.

Elienor braced herself against the buckling of her knees. "It cannot be so," she whispered frantically. "Tell me nay! Tell me nay!" But the dream that had awakened her earlier in the night and had sent her dashing to the tower to disprove it *was*, in truth, unfolding before her! The rising wind buffeted her face, flinging her hair into wild disarray at her back, and sending icy prickles of fear down her spine. "It . . . it cannot be!" Her hand flew to her mouth, stifling a cry of alarm.

She shook her head in denial, yet the proof sailed before her eyes, appearing from mist and shadows like a grim specter from the dark.

Coincidences, Mother Heloise had said. Always when she would dream, and the dream held true, the old abbess would assure her that she was not afflicted with the second sight that cursed her mother's life. And because her visions were few and her desperation great, Elienor had readily believed her. Yet, the sight before her gave testimony to her fears!

So now what was she to do?

Turn and flee down the steps, a voice whispered. Warn the castle!

Her legs would not move. If only her gifts would not mark her for a witch and condemn her to her mother's tragic fate. She shivered as the wind, bitter as ice, lashed her. In the next instant, she saw herself again as a child of four, standing atop the hallowed knoll of graves, the white lily she'd picked for her mother held firmly in her little hands.

In her mind, the voice came back to her with such clarity. "Whatever possessed you to come here at this ungodly hour?"

Hearing Sister Heloise's voice, Elienor had nearly cried her relief. She swung about and hurled herself into the sister's welcoming arms.

"The lily!" she exclaimed, squirming to disentwine herself. The old nun struggled to keep Elienor secured within her embrace to no avail. "The lily!" Elienor insisted.

"Non, non ma petite! 'Tis raining. We must go now! I shall bring you again." she coaxed. "When the rain has—"

Elienor struggled all the more fiercely. "Nay!" she shrieked. Freeing herself abruptly, she scurried to the blossom and hastily scooped up a handful of wet soil from the center of the mound. Handling the lily gingerly, she planted the end of it into the hollow she'd formed, covering it carefully, taking her time whilst Sister Heloise hovered above her and shielded her back from the pattering rain.

Elienor's eyes filled with tears as she turned and thrust herself back into the sister's arms.

Sister Heloise lifted Elienor up, wrapping the blanket about her tiny shoulders. "There, there, now," she soothed. "Sister Heloise will love you now, ma bonne

*petite. I will love you now. Oui! And together we will
care for your maman's lily."*

Elienor nodded into the warmth of Sister Heloise's
shoulder. "Maman loves lilies," she revealed sadly. Her
chin turned up a notch, and a tear slipped defiantly from her dark lashes. "She loves them so much!"
She turned to peer over Sister Heloise's damp shoulder.
With stark violet eyes, she watched the grave recede as
they made their way down the hill. Her words were
broken with emotion as she raised her little hand to
wave farewell.

"Adieu, Mother. Adieu!"

The sound of her own voice brought her back,
and she gulped back a sob of despair. The pain of
her mother's death was still fresh in her heart. To
die so cruelly, for nought more than predicting the
course of a peasant babe's illness—the fates were
cruel, indeed!

Would they question how she'd known to come
to the tower tonight? If only there were some way
to reveal the vision without exposing herself!

She closed her eyes and begged for strength.
Mayhap 'twas still a dream . . . only a dream . . .

But nay, for she felt the bitter wind as surely
as she felt the numbness stealing into her bones.
If only she were not such a coward! Yet even the
merest notion that she might meet the same fate
as did her mother made her knees weak and her
tongue draw into knots.

She bit into her whitening knuckles as she
watched the specter ships advance. Sweet Jesu—
no more time to linger! There was no need to say
what had driven her to the tower, was there? None
need know! She would tell them only that she had
come for air—that she could not sleep, that was all!
Who would think to question her?

Stricken with grief for the fate of Brouillard, Elienor watched an instant longer, needing to be absolutely certain. But she waited no longer than to see the Vikings land their vessels upon the moonlit shores, for little more time could be spared if she were to warn the castle.

She spun about and hurried down the tower stairs, tears brimming in her eyes, her movements stiff with terror and cold.

She should have known 'twas too good to be true! That Count Phillipe had asked for her hand in marriage and her uncle had assented was true enough, but that it would actually come to pass was more than she should have dared to hope for! With assurances from Mother Heloise that Elienor was not beset with her mother's curse, her uncle had withdrawn her from the cloister mere days before she was to make her vows to the church. So long she'd waited and despaired. Tonight marked one full month since she'd first come to Brouillard, and in little more than a fortnight she'd have become its *countess*. She'd been so happy, so very happy! At last she would love and be loved in return! She would bear children into the world, love them, care for them. At last. But it would never be. Despite the fact that Mother Heloise had plainly perjured herself for Elienor's sake. Jesu Christ, even at the peril of her own soul!

Tears welled in her eyes as she rushed down the stairs. Fumbling for the silver ring that hung about her neck from a long leather band, she lifted it out from within the neckline of her *bliaut* and pressed it firmly to her breast. The night was well advanced. She only hoped she could rouse the castle in time.

Yet to what end?

Tears streaked down her pale cheeks, for deep down she knew it mattered not if she were to warn her people.

Their fates were sealed.

The Viking would prevail this night.

Chapter 2

They moved quickly, like soundless shadows creeping through the night. Flattening their war-hardened bodies against the stone walls, they made their way to the hidden portal. Though she was gone now, Alarik could still not wrench his gaze away from the tower above. Even as his men toiled to destroy the wooden portal, his eyes sought her. Once it was breached he could delay no longer, and he shuddered away a prickle of foreboding before turning to his men. 'Twas inconceivable that no alarm had been sounded as of yet, even more so the fact that there was no guard posted at the hidden portal.

"Have eyes to your backs!" he warned them, and then he raised his gilt-edged sword into the night. His eyes glinted with loathing. "May *Dragvendil* spare no man!" he charged. "May your own blades dole no mercy!" And with that, he stooped to lead them through the tiny, well-concealed entry before them.

"To arms! To arms!" Swiping at the tears that blinded her vision, Elienor shouted at the top of her lungs. "To arms!" she called again as she spiraled downward. Her frantic voice carried down before her into the hall below, and she was relieved to hear the ensuing commotion as

11

the men stirred immediately from their slumber.

One man darted up the tower steps, tripping over himself as he rubbed the sleep from his eyes, only to halt when he saw her. "My lady!" he gasped.

"Gaston!" It was the sentinel. He'd come in from the cold to warm himself only to fall asleep at the foot of the stairs. She'd passed him on her way up, had tiptoed around him so as not to wake him— so certain had she been that her dream would not hold true. Had he been at his given post, 'twould have been he who had espied the Viking ships, and not she. She wished, with all her soul, it had been so. Her heart pummeled against her ribs.

For an unbearable instant, neither spoke.

"Thanks be to God!" she exclaimed, finding her voice at last. " 'Tis you! The Northmen are come! I have seen them from the tower. Go quickly—warn the castle!"

The man's eyes widened visibly. "Art certain, my lady?"

"Aye!" she exclaimed. "Aye! Even now they climb the banks! Go!"

Sobered by her revelation, the man did not hesitate to wonder why she'd been in the tower to begin with, nor did he linger to offer explanation as to why he was not, and she said a silent prayer of thanks. She watched as he whirled about and raced back down before her, his gruff voice sounding out alarm.

Knowing there was little time to spare, Elienor followed, praying that she'd not lose her footing on the slippery stone. So intent was she on her descent that she nearly tumbled over Stefan as he came loping noisily up the dimly lit stairwell. Despite the fact that his newly acquired sword clanged

and scraped clumsily against the wall, she did not
discover he was there until she was virtually upon
him.

"My lady!" he reproved. "You will fall to your
death!"

Elienor shrieked as he caught her arm to keep
her from losing her footing. "Stefan!" Sweet Jesu!
How could she have overlooked him? In her hysteria she'd managed to forget him completely! How
could she have? Certainly Stefan had not forsaken
her when first she'd arrived at Brouillard! Despite
the fact that he was no more than a boy of thirteen
summers, he'd been the only one with wisdom
enough to understand her apprehension over coming alone to a strange new household. The rest had
kept themselves apart. 'Twas her duty to save him
if she could!

"My lady? Is it true?" There was a slight trem-
or of excitement to his voice. "Gaston claims you
have spied the Northmen?"

A quiver of fear passed down Elienor's spine,
but she recovered herself, seizing him by the wrist.
Knowing full well that he would feel obliged to
hie to his lord's side, she ignored his question and
tugged him after her. "Quickly, Stefan!" she commanded on impulse. "Follow me!" If his face had
been revealed to her within the tapestry of her
dream, she would have known the futility of alter-
ing its course. But it had not been, and Stefan was
too young to die!

"My lady!" he protested as he spun to face her.
He cringed as the sword Count Phillipe had so
recently presented to him shaved the wall. "My
lord shall be . . ."

"Aye!" Elienor interjected at once. "I spoke to him just now. He said you were to come with me to the chapel!" Inwardly, she recoiled over the lie, but 'twas only a small lie, she reasoned, and she spoke it for Stefan's well-being. Surely God would forgive it.

Stefan's face twisted at the blatant untruth. "My lady?" He tried freeing his arm from her frenzied grip, but Elienor clutched it all the more determinedly. "Did you not realize that my lord has gone to Pa—"

"Please!" Elienor appealed, "do but heed me—if only this once!"

Stefan dug in his heels stubbornly. There were no torches burning in the great hall at this late hour, and the muted light they now used to illuminate their way came from the single torch that graced the stairwell behind them. As Elienor turned to face him, tears shone in her eyes. "Stefan," she cried. "I beg you!"

His shoulders slumped in frustration and his brow furrowed, but he nodded. Elienor nearly wept her relief. Clasping his hand firmly, she drew him at once out of the hall, into the narrow pentice, which provided them with a covered passage from the hall to the kitchens. Once in the kitchen, certain that in scant moments the donjon would be overrun with the Northmen, she ran across the smoke-permeated room, to the far doors. It was the quickest route, she knew, and there was no time to waste. Count Phillipe's small numbers were simply no match for the scourge of the north!

As they left the kitchen and entered another narrow walkway between buildings, she pulled the boy to her protectively. Stefan recoiled at once. "My lady, please! I've no need of such handling.

I am elevated to squire! Aide to my lord!" he protested. "And you would coddle me so? I tell you,
I've no liking for it."

"Hush, Stefan! Instruct me to your heart's content
once we are safe within the chapel, but leave off
just now!" Immediately upon uttering the words,
Elienor grimaced, recalling the enemy. Since when
had the Northmen regarded the Church as hallowed
ground? Had she not learned otherwise? Mother
Heloise had told her that the fiends never spared
castle or monastery alike, whether Roman, French,
or English. It was well renowned, their pillaging of
Grande Bretagne's Jarrow and Wearmouth, as well
as the numerous parishes of her homeland! 'Twas
true that their reign of terror had subsided of late,
but only now that most of northern Francia was at
last under their barbarian rule!

The chapel door stood ajar a scant few feet away,
the dark interior a greater beacon to her now than
the brightest of lights, and she prayed, asking for
God's mercy and aid—not for herself, but for young
Stefan.

Let us reach the chapel—please, please, please!

Tonight, she would live, as the dream had
foretold . . . but Stefan? There was no time even
to make the sign of the cross, or she would have.

Within the chapel it was darker even than it had
first appeared, but having spent so many hours
within its cobbled walls, Elienor had no need of
candle to light the vestibule. Letting her memory
guide her, she snatched up the wooden bar and
placed it within the stout metal rings on either side
of the heavy door, locking them securely within.

"My lady?" Stefan protested again, this time with
an edge of desperation to his voice. He was clearly
growing impatient, yet having no choice, Elienor

continued to ignore him. Taking him by the hand
once more, she led him to a place beyond the crossing, well into the chancel, and finally behind the
altar. There she shoved him with all her might onto
his haunches. She shoved again when he resisted
until he fell back upon his lean little rump.

"Bon dieu!" Stefan exploded. "Enough, I say! Tell
me what goes here! Why do you bar the door when
you know I must—"

From the donjon, shouts of ambush abruptly
could be heard, and after giving Elienor an accusing
glance, Stefan turned and bolted for the door.

Elienor seized him by the wrist. "Nay! You cannot! 'Tis done! 'Tis done, I tell you!"

"My lady! I beg you release me! 'Tis my duty
you would deny me!" Shouts of the wounded and
dying escalated. "Release me, I say!"

"Nay!" The scraping of metal upon stone could
be distinguished beyond the chapel doors. "Nay!"
They heard a bloodcurdling scream. Elienor could
picture it all so vividly, the savage Northmen with
their axes raised high into the air. There was little
use in closing her eyes, for the vision originated
from within, from some accursed second eye within her soul.

"Set me free!" Stefan demanded furiously. Again
he shouted, " 'Tis my duty you would deny me!
My duty, I tell you!" With a final twist, he liberated himself and raced toward the door, his long
legs awkward as he ran.

"Stefan! Nay . . . oh, nay!" He could not go! She
would not allow it! Desperately, Elienor groped
about in the darkness, seeking the means to stop
him. Her hand closed upon the sacred reliquary,
a small copper chest that sheltered a sliver of the
Christ's cross, and she knew at once what she must

do. "Father, forgive me," she whispered fervently, and then she bolted across the nave after Stefan, striking the chest down upon his tender head.

Caught in the process of sliding the bar from the ring, Stefan made some strangled sound and released it, and though she could not see him fall for the darkness, she heard him as he crumpled to the wooden floor, unconscious. As it fell from his grasp, the wooden bar slammed against the door and began to slide cacophonously from the other ring, as well. Without a moment to spare, Elienor seized it, securing it once more.

Chapter 3

The *skali*, or hall, was dark, save for the feeble glow cast by a torch guttering further up the stairwell. Alarik's eyes scanned the shadows, noting with disdain the slain enemy scattered about his feet. What little resistance they put forth, these pathetic French! With a grunt of disgust, he gave the signal for his men to disperse and make use of whatever could be found, be it ale or wench, beast or gems.

He'd never doubted they would prevail, but it had been much too simple a victory, and he decided that tonight his men deserved whatever spoils they desired, for he knew they were not appeased. By the gates of *Hel*, neither was he, for the count he'd come to crush had been conspicuously absent from the fray.

Shouts of revelry followed Alarik as he wandered away in search of the missing count, but the terrified howl of a man found hidden beneath a table in the gloomy light of the *skali* drew him back, and he turned to watch, leaning a thickly muscled shoulder against the arched entryway.

Before him, Sigurd Thorgoodson scampered up the steps to retrieve the torch flitting there and then returned like a maelstrom of fire, sweeping his way 'round the hall, lighting torches as he passed them. He flew by each so quickly that it seemed he lit them with the sparks spilling in his wake.

Alarik understood the haste.

This last kill they would savor fully, terrifying the hefty man with their unappeased blood lust, rendering him senseless with fright. Then, they would offer the poor fool a battle axe. Viking men had little liking for killing the defenseless, for there was no glory to be gotten from that manner of execution. To fight in the face of danger showed one's valor. And if by chance a Viking fell in the enemy's stead, then from *Asgard* would come, donned in shining armor, riding steeds of white, the maidens from *Valholl*, the hall of the slain. Heads held high, solemn and deep in thought, the *Valkyrs* rode, choosers of the slain, and down they would come to the field of battle and swoop up the souls of the dead to join Odin in his great corps, the *Einherjar*. There, only the bravest served.

'Twas the Viking creed, his father's legacy, but no longer his own.

His men encircled the prey, successfully foiling any attempt at escape. Finished with the task of lighting the scattered torches, Sigurd, teeth bared, and growling, elbowed his way back through the pack. Using the pitch torch as his weapon, he lit the man's sparse hair from behind, garnering chuckles and laughter from the others. The Frenchman yowled in pain, and Sigurd at once slapped out the small flame he'd begun, howling hysterically at his own cleverness.

Alarik's brow lifted in droll amusement. Sigurd, ever the jester, was as loyal as they came, but his humor was sadly lacking—though evidently flame-haired Hrolf Kaetilson didn't think so. Red-Hrolf was clutching his belly and howling at the top of his lungs. At once, Ivar Longbeard joined Sigurd in terrorizing the man, taking firm hold of his own long russet whiskers and tugging wildly, looking every bit the demented. And seeing Long Beard ravage the hair of his face, Lars the Fair Head followed suit.

Bjorn, Alarik's younger brother, nut-faced from the sun and too comely for his own good, immediately began the chant, "Die! Die! Die!" The others followed his lead, their voices in the night sounding like a ballad to a Viking's ear.

Suddenly, Sigurd threw an axe at the man's feet and then waited for the fool to grasp it. Sensing his fate, the man instead stood arrested, paralyzed with fright.

To goad the man into lifting up the axe, Sigurd removed and discarded his armor and then his clothing, taunting him all the while, until he was finally nude as the day he was begot.

"Look at me, *Fransk!*" Sigurd goaded in disjointed French. "No breastplate! No shield! And still I'll crush you 'neath my boots!" Hoots of laughter greeted his claim. "Hah! One blade behind my back, even!" With a flourish, he concealed his sword behind his back, and added a lewd pelvic thrust. He then turned to collect grins of approval from the rest. Despite himself, Alarik chuckled, though he shook his head, as well. In that instant the Frenchman sought his gaze . . .

Alarik's flesh prickled as the man stared without blinking. His own eyes narrowed as he reflexively moved nearer. The man shook violently, though his gaze never wavered, and one by one, his men followed the Frenchman's gaze to where Alarik stood behind them, and quieted.

"Tell me French dung," Alarik demanded, when there was silence, "where is your murdering count?" As he continued forward again, the sound of his footfalls echoed against the stone walls.

The man's gaze skidded away, then back.

At long last, Alarik halted before him, allowing a moment longer for his reply. When it was apparent he would not speak, Alarik asked once more, "Your count?"

It was a lengthy moment before the man was able to still his quaking long enough to respond, but when he did, he spat upon the ground before Alarik's boots, proclaiming by that gesture that he would never speak against his lord. Yet, despite the fact that it was meant as an insult, Alarik kept his composure, for there was only one man whose blood he ached to spill this night. This one he would leave to his men. His hand tightened around *Dragvendil's* hilt. "Stupid bastard!" he snarled. He motioned for his men to carry on. "Do with the fool as you will," he allowed them, stepping back out of their way. "I care not what."

The revelry recommenced at once with hoots and laughter, and Sigurd, tired of waiting for the man to pick the axe up, feinted for it. Only then did the Frenchman move to take the weapon, understanding that it was his sole salvation.

Sigurd's claim had not been mere boast, Alarik knew. His men were the finest—the best warriors to be found in all of the North Land. The Frenchman had not a breath of a chance and he knew it. As it was, the man's fate was sealed the very moment his stout fingers closed about the axe's handle.

Abruptly, Alarik turned from the melee, entering what appeared to be the *eldhus*, or kitchen, while behind him an anguished cry spewed forth.

The gruesome sound was followed by the merry roar of laughter. 'Twas over, yet despite his feeling of justification, he was not satisfied—not whilst the gutless count yet lived!

Behind the *eldhus* was an alley leading to a small Christian *kirken*, or church. His mother had been Christian, he mused, as he scrutinized the large ornate doors before him. Fingering the woodwork, he pondered what it was that drew his brother to it, as well, and shook his head over the mystery of it all—so many wars fought.

A muffled sound came from within, and he stiffened. Something clattered thunderously against the door, and he jerked away reflexively. Eager for a confrontation with the count, he anticipated the opening of the door, his sword arm raised and poised to strike. But the only ensuing sound he could discern was a slight shuffling . . . as though someone were dragging an injured leg across the floor.

The count?

Determined not to be robbed of satisfaction, Alarik tried the door, and finding it barred, swore his displeasure. He could well picture the spineless bastard hiding like a coward within his little forsaken chapel—more than willing to let his men fight his battle without him— just as he had before! For his perfidy, Alarik vowed, the man would surely die this night, as cruel a death as he could manage! "Coward!" he snarled at the door, and with a war cry, he lifted his broad axe from the loop in his belt and raised it high. With a savage curse, he brought the gleaming silver inlaid blade crashing down upon the door, shattering it easily with the force of his blow.

*   *   *

At the terrible sound, Elienor bolted from her knees and seized Stefan's arms. She tugged with all her might. *She had to get him behind the altar! Had to hide him!* When the thundering crack of a battle-axe met with the wood of the chapel door a second time, she panicked. Instinctively, she threw herself over Stefan, her heart thumping madly as the barrier between them and the Viking cracked and splintered away. She squeezed her eyes shut, and tried to block out the voice of terror in her mind.

Her heart leapt into her throat as heavy footsteps tromped across the hallowed sanctuary, echoing over the ageless crypt that lay beneath. Stifling the urge to cry out in fear, she clutched Stefan.

She dared not move.

When finally the footsteps ceased before her, she did not perceive it, for her heartbeat thundered in her ears.

Chapter 4

The moon's glow filtered in behind him—
enough to light a goodly portion of the *kirken*,
but Alarik's enormous shadow kept the figure
before him cloaked in darkness. Enshrouded in
shadows as it was, it appeared no more than
a nondescript black form hunkering before him
upon the floor. He stepped aside, and in moving
his body from the moonbeam's path exposed, not
one, but two shapes lying still at his feet. He cocked
his head in curiosity, lifting a speculative brow at
the odd positioning of their bodies.

Were they lovers, then, preferring death by their
own hands rather than meeting with his blade?

Stilling his own breath, he strained to catch some
nuance of life, but no sound was immediately dis-
cernable. "Pathetic French!" he snarled in Norsk.
"May your carcasses rot where you lie!" He booted
the uppermost figure.

It was then he noticed the thick mane of dark
hair that cascaded beneath his boots, and his brows
drew together. In his curiosity, he stepped away
and stooped to fondle the pool of lustrous strands.

Soft. So soft.

Squatting with one arm resting across his thighs,
he lifted the length of hair from the chapel floor. At
once a recollection of the long-haired woman upon
the stone turret, her hair fluttering in the breeze,

materialized within his mind, and another prickle snaked down his spine.

He'd somehow managed to forget her during the fray.

Overwhelmed with curiosity now, he slowly wound the silken strands around his fist, and without a trace of gentility, jerked up the lifeless head.

He fell backward onto his heels, unable to stifle the sudden catch in his breath at what was revealed to him in the silvery light: Dark hair framed a face more lovely than was conceivable. Skin that was almost translucent in the light of the moon beckoned to his fingers that they would revel in the softness of her creamy flesh. Eyes that were so blue they were almost ethereal met his own without fail, and he nigh toppled from his haunched position to see them focused upon him so intently. The scowl that touched his squarely jawed face was violent, for his body's lustful response was immediate and unappreciated under the circumstances.

Those eyes seemed a maelstrom in deep sea waters, a stormy violet blue that glowed in the darkness with the intensity of blue heat from a torrid flame. He'd thought her dead, but it was more than obvious to him now that she was not, not by any stretch of the imagination, for her eyes were vibrant. Reflexively, his fingers moved to the fragile softness of her cheeks, examining the cool satin flesh.

Elienor swallowed with difficulty at the featherlight touch, though in truth she wasn't certain whether it was from fear or something else entirely. Her eyes closed as a quiver sped through her. By the blessed virgin, was it supposed to feel so good to be caressed by one's enemy?

Or was she simply faithless?

At that thought, her eyes flew open once more, and it was then she saw him—truly saw him. That face! Sweet Jesu—that face! She recalled it from her dream and shuddered, though what it was exactly that made her tremble she did not know, for she recalled only the face. Her cry of terror was stifled only by the fierce constriction of her throat, for the tales she'd so oft heard of his kind truly did the man little justice. He was every exaggeration ever told—multiplied a hundredfold!

What had she dreamed of him? She couldn't think. Too acutely was she aware of every stroke of his thumb. Jesu! When would he cease? She tried to find her voice—to plead with him to . . . to stop—but could not speak for the terrible lump in her throat. God help her, but she didn't think she could bear it much longer!

What kind of man was this?—that he could slay her with his gaze, yet touch her as gently as one would a tender babe? In the darkness his eyes were sinister pits that seemed to bore into her very soul. They had to be black as pitch in color, for they were, indeed, blacker than the night that engulfed them. Yet if his eyes appeared overly dark, then the opposite was true of his lion's mane of hair. In the heathery moonlight it appeared ethereal and silvery.

She forced herself to look below his shadowed face and shining hair, and swallowed with difficulty as her gaze took in the rest of him. His shoulders were massive, wider than any man's she'd ever beheld! Reflexively, her scrutiny fell to the laces of his boots, where she found herself staring desperately at the ties that criss-crossed upward toward his leather-protected knee. But if she'd thought it would help to look away from his face in order to regain her self-control, she was mistaken. Jesu Christ—his legs were enormous as well! They reminded her of oak stumps. She commanded herself not to look, but she couldn't keep herself from it. In panic, her gaze skidded upward—to his arms! No doubt he was capable of swatting her dead with the palm of his hand as effortlessly as the tanner could a fly!

God in heaven above, have mercy on their souls!

He chuckled, and her gaze flew to his in alarm.

"We shall see if your God will aid you, little *Fransk*," he said smugly.

Elienor's blood curdled within her veins to hear his husky voice and his words of flawless French. How had he known what she was thinking? She'd not spoken it aloud! Or had she? Sweet Jesu—did he have the sight, as well? *Nay, nay . . . get hold of yourself, Elienor.* She tossed her head back, a defiant gesture that the nuns, admonishing her, said was worldly and proud—not virtues suited to one promised to the cloth. Then again, she'd never felt the calling in her soul—had always fought against her other disobedient self in order to be what the nuns had wished of her. She appraised him contemptuously. "What know you of my God?" she countered before she could stop herself.

Again he chuckled. The sound reverberated within the chapel, unnerving her. "Enough to know he'll not intervene for you this night," he replied evenly. "As of now, little *Fransk* . . ." one finger swept down her cheek, beneath her chin, forcing her gaze up to meet his shadowed eyes, "whether you like it or *nei*," he informed her, "you are mine to do with as I will. And there is no one here who would gainsay me—not you, not your spineless count . . ." He chuckled again, the sound wholly sinister. "Nay . . . not even your God!" He laughed, mocking her.

Elienor gasped at the blasphemy. He would dare scorn her faith! And Count Phillipe, too, in the same breath—when the poor man was like to be dead and could no longer defend himself! Heartless fiend! Her eyes closed with loathing as she shook the Viking's offending fingers from her chin. But his hold only tightened in her hair. Her scalp screamed under the torture, yet Elienor dared not break.

"He was not my count as of yet!" she informed him. Again his fingers tightened. Elienor winced, but would not be cowed. Her chin tilted. "Nor was he craven!" she added. "Count Phillipe was good and kind and true!" It had to be so, for surely her uncle would never have given her to one not worthy. Despite her resolve not to give in to hysteria, her heartbeat quickened, though as difficult as it was to control her traitorous body, she hid her fear. He's but a man, she reasoned wildly, is he not? Aye! her mind argued, a man! and a blood-thirsty Viking as well!

With fingers so warm and gentle they sent quivers down her spine.

Her eyes welled with tears. Nay! she scolded herself. You will not go to pieces in the face of this! If she feared, 'twas only for Stefan—at least that was what she told herself as she felt the trembling work its way through her unsteady limbs.

"Think not?" the Viking countered, his voice husky and full of derision. His brow arched. "But 'tis a fact, wench, that your precious count is as spineless as they come!"

Elienor shivered at the malice in his tone. *"Is?"* she returned contemptuously. "What is he now but

dead? And by your hands! You murdering sav—"
She felt his fingers tighten against her scalp and
cried out in pain.

"I would have a care with that blade of a tongue
if I were you," he advised softly. "If I say he is,
'tis because the bastard yet lives. He scurries from
me like a squeamish maid—fled the castle, I'll warrant." Her eyes narrowed in disbelief and his brows
arched. "Did you not realize, wench? Did you not
realize he'd left you to die at our hands?"

As stunned as Elienor was by his disclosure, she
could do nought but glare at him. In that instant,
Stefan moaned beneath her and her eyes flew to
him fearfully. She prayed fervently that he'd not
wake. If he would die . . . best he not know it! Best
he not feel the cold blade of the barbarian's axe
meet with his tender flesh!

"Mayhap you do," the Viking said, glancing
down meaningfully at Stefan's twisting form. "Mayhap 'tis him you shield even now?" he suggested.
His eyes glinted dangerously.

"Nay!" Elienor shrieked, her heart pummeling
madly. "I swear 'tis not! Leave him be!" The
Viking's gaze never wavered, and Elienor found
her own eyes locked steadfastly with his. Sweet
Jesu! Mercy! she pleaded silently. Mercy! I trust
in you! I do! I do! I swear it, Lord!

Alarik contemplated the wench's reaction to the
boy. It was evident there was some bond between
them. What it was, he wasn't certain, but his curiosity was piqued. Tightening his hold upon the
woman's hair, he rose from his stooped position,
hauling her up against him as he came to his feet,
and the feel of her soft body hardened his more fully. He noted briefly there were no grunts or moans
against the pain he knew he inflicted, and he could

only admire her mettle. "Who is he, then?" he asked, his tone as menacing as the gleaming blade of his axe, "if not your precious count?"

The woman wet her lips. "He . . . Stefan is but a boy . . . please . . . please—leave him be!"

His lips broke into a slow sensual grin as he pressed closer, savoring the feel of her high, round breasts against his chest. Bending to whisper in her ear, his lips brushed her lobe. "Leave him be? You wish me to leave him be?"

She nodded frantically.

"And what prithee will you pledge me if I do?" She closed her eyes, yet he would not be swayed. The feel of her against him so warm and soft and firm in all the right places drove him to shift his pelvis for comfort. Stirring into her, he stifled a groan of pleasure.

"What do you pledge me?" he demanded impatiently.

Chapter 5

Elienor swallowed convulsively, for the look in the Viking's eyes left no doubt as to what he wanted of her. Mother Heloise, in preparing her for Count Phillipe, had enlightened her to the needs of men, and 'twas *that* need she sensed the Viking sought to quench just now.

"I . . . I . . ." Stefan stirred slightly, moaning as he lifted his head. Elienor's gaze flew to him at once.

Scowling suddenly, the Viking turned to observe him, as well.

"Nay!" Elienor exclaimed. Forgetting that her hair was raveled so tightly about the giant's fist, she hurled herself at Stefan, as though to shield him with her body, and with a wounded gasp halted her dive to the floor, turning again to look into the Viking's smoldering silver eyes.

Tears brimmed as once again she locked gazes with him. Hysteria welled within her. For the first time in her life she was well and truly at a loss for words. For what could she say? Barbarian, sir, could you be so kind as to release my hair so that I may warn this kind boy against you? Hah! Likely he'd laugh in her face before plunging his sword into Stefan's heart . . . and then mayhap into her own! Yet, whatever he would do to her, she could not allow him to harm Stefan. At any cost she would save him.

Her eyes closed. She swallowed. "I . . . I have nought of value," she said bitterly. "Please . . ."

The Viking grinned, his teeth flashing white in the shadows. "Truly?" he asked, and then laughed outright.

Elienor shivered at the wicked sound of it. "Nought save myself," she told him honestly. Her eyes misted traitorously, but she held herself rigid and proud.

Alarik's brow lifted as her eyes filled with tell-tale moisture. His lips twisted sardonically. So, she knew the game after all? What woman did not? Again he pondered what bond she and the boy shared that she would protect him so fiercely—even so far as to offer him her body in payment to save him. Did she always contribute so freely? The possibility rankled, though he knew not why it should.

"I see," he said more sharply than he'd intended. "And what makes you think 'tis your body to barter with at any rate, wench? As of this night 'tis mine already," he reminded her pointedly. "Why would I bother to haggle for that which I already possess?" Alarm flared in her blue eyes, and that too, rankled—that she would find the thought of him so repulsive. Yet what else would she feel for him? And why should it concern him? As he gazed into the misty, violet-blue pools of her eyes, he was compelled to release the hold he had upon her hair.

At once she fell to her knees over the boy—and it was a boy, for now he could discern the whiskerless face. A quiver sped through him as the long, dark strands wove their way out of his callused fingers like cool silk over his warm bare skin. The pleasing sensation sent a surge of familiar heat rushing through his veins. A smile curved his lips as he imagined that whispery length tangled about his bare thighs. In that moment, he craved her more than he did revenge over the spineless count, and the realization jarred him. Yet he acknowledged that even more than that, he wanted to know her—that barely subdued passion he could see with such clarity in her eyes. He wanted her acquiescent—and so consumed with desire that she would whimper and sigh beneath him—atop him.

" 'Tis done, then!"

Startled, the woman glanced up at him, her expression confused.

He smiled darkly. "You have yourself a bargain, my little *Fransk*." When she still seemed bewildered, Alarik explained, "Your compliance for the boy's life." He felt no need to point out that he had no intention of harming the lad. He had no taste for slaughtering children, but it would serve him well if she thought he might.

She swallowed visibly, and shuddered, but nodded agreement before returning her attention to the boy. With a quick flip of her hand she removed the length of her dark hair from his pale face.

Feeling a sudden rush of heat and anticipation, Alarik stepped forward to better observe the pair. The woman's nondescript kyrtle covered her form completely, yet even in such a shapeless garment her generous curves were more than apparent as he gazed down upon her, and he felt the burn of his loins intensify. Never, in all his experiences, had he seen her equal—hair as dark as the Byzantine, yet skin and features as fair as the Norse—and he found himself mentally disrobing her, drawing up a luscious picture in his mind. For the first time in his life he was sorely tempted to lie a wench flat and ride her against her will. But he would not. He abhorred such weakness in his men—though now, for once, he could comprehend what drove them to such ends. He watched in silence as she gently lifted up the boy's dirt-smudged face unto her scrutiny.

With her eyes, Elienor warned Stefan to remain silent. With her heart, she prayed that he would understand.

"My lady," Stefan moaned, wincing. "What have you done to me?"

Tears pricked at Elienor's eyes as she envisaged the outcome of the battle. " 'Tis over, Stefan. There . . ." She swallowed. "There is nought to be done now," she told him.

Stefan moaned pitifully. "Then I am shamed!" He lifted himself up and thrust his head into her lap to hide the moistness gathering in his eyes. Elienor felt the telltale wetness even through her layers of clothing. Tears of frustration came to her own eyes as she searched for the words to ease Stefan's conscience, but before she could utter another sound, the Viking giant suddenly gave a fearsome growl of displeasure and lifted her up into his arms, over his hefty shoulder, pinning her there. She gasped, startled. Blood rushed to her head as he swooped down yet again to yank Stefan up, as well.

"Wha—my lady!" Stefan struggled to gain his feet. With scarcely an effort, the Viking hauled them both outside into the clear light of the moon.

As she watched Stefan struggle, Elienor's heart went out to him, and she vowed in that moment that she would die trying to save him. Furious that he would be treated so harshly when they'd already effected a bargain, she demanded at once, "Release him!" The giant said nought, merely kept his pace, and Elienor pounded his back with all her might. "Beast, you made me a bargain!" she reminded him fiercely.

Stefan was suddenly dropped to the ground, though almost as swiftly as he was released, the Viking caught him by the back of his tunic and began to drag him across the empty yard behind them, like a dog by its lead rope.

Elienor's anger intensified. "Brute! Is force the only way of your people?" she accused him. Yet as soon as the question left her lips, she felt a fool for asking it. Of course it was! Wasn't that what she'd always been told? "Barbarian!" she spat.

Abruptly, the Viking lifted Stefan to his feet, urging him to walk, but Stefan only stumbled to his knees. Without hesitation, the giant hauled him up once more, then shoved.

"Walk!" he snarled, "Or you'll find yourself without legs to walk with!"

Thankfully, Stefan did as he was told without balking, though his knees wobbled visibly all the way into the *donjon*. Elienor's heart stung for him. As they approached the now brightly lit hall, her nostrils flared with the overwhelming stench of death. Her eyes widened at the gruesome sight that greeted them; a horde of Vikings frolicked about the hall, partaking of ale and whatever else they encountered. One man, his writhing form as naked as the oak in winter, danced merrily over the body of the dead sentry, Gaston. She cried out, clutching the giant's tunic lest she fall with the wave of nausea that assailed her. Squeezing her eyes shut, she tried to block the sight of it from her mind.

Cheers resounded the moment they were spied coming into the great hall. Viking voices hailed

them—no doubt praising the barbarian that had
carted her in! The din threatened to burst her
eardrums, and she knew in that moment that
the shoulders she'd been irreverently slung over
belonged to none other than the leader, himself.

"Jarl! Jarl! Jarl!" they bellowed, each man louder
than the one before.

One bedraggled beast with hair the color of the
noonday sun came to stand behind Elienor's captor. Roughly, he jerked her up by the hair to see
her better.

Heathen! What she wouldn't give to slap his
face just now, not for herself, but for all the terror
they had wreaked upon Count Phillipe's castle! For
Stefan! For the way that he'd been treated!

Bon dieu, were she not such a peace-loving soul
she'd strike the heinous smirk from his face but
good!

Uncouth, Godless—

Unable to stay her hand, Elienor's palm cracked
along the side of his face.

Abruptly, the hall went silent, and one by one,
every pair of eyes turned toward her.

The flame haired's gaze narrowed upon her, his
eyes fairly sparking with fury.

Her palm stung. Still, she held it in midair, poised
to strike again. She peered up fearfully to see a welt
beginning to form upon the flame haired's cheek.

"Jesu!" she whispered hysterically. Seeing the
ire in his eyes, she regretted her rashness at once,
despite the fact that he deserved worse! 'Twas
merely that she feared provoking his wrath, she
told herself. Beneath her, the Viking's shoulders
began to quiver, then shake, and then rumble, and
she found to her dismay that he was laughing.
Laughing?

How dare he?

The fiend she'd slapped, on the other hand, glared at her, though to her immense relief he responded only by gurgling his ale in her face. When he finished swooshing it, he grinned, letting the sudsy, amber liquid seep from between rotting and missing teeth. She winced as a sprinkling caught her full upon the brow, and resisted the urge to swipe the revolting droplet away.

Beneath her, the golden one's shoulders shook ferociously with mirth. Bracing her palms against her captor's back for support, Elienor willed him to perdition and beyond! Yet even as she struggled for balance and blasphemed him, his husky laughter filled her senses, riveted her, and only belatedly did she realize that Flame Hair had taken another hearty swig from his tankard. He swooshed it again, puffing his cheeks to spew it upon her. Fie! No doubt all would burst into fits of hilarity this time. Uncouth savages! She squeezed her lids closed and braced herself for the deluge.

It never came.

The metallic hiss of a sword being drawn caught every ear.

"Foul heathens!" Stefan's voice resounded off the stone walls, flying upward into the tower. "Leave her be!"

Elienor's eyes flew wide in time to see him charge at the leader's back.

Her mouth formed a scream that never materialized, for what happened next happened so quickly that she would never be entirely certain of the chain of events; Stefan came at them with blood lust in his eyes, his sword rising up. One instant, the Viking leader was empty handed. In the next he held his sword and was facing Stefan, ready to strike. With astounding ease, he'd also managed to snatch her down to hold her by the waist before him. Next she knew, Stefan lay dead by his sword.

"Nay!" she screamed. Hysteria burst through her. "Nay! Nay! We made a bargain!" Frantically, she resisted the Viking leader until he was forced to release her. "You made me a bargain!" she cried as she tumbled to the floor beside Stefan. His face in death was still as sweetly innocent as it had been in life, no fear, no regret—he'd done it for her. "Nay . . . oh, nay!" He was but a boy . . . only a boy . . . and God have mercy, he'd died for her! She seized him, clutching him to her breast, rocking him. "Stefan! I . . ." she whimpered. "I'm so . . . so . . . so, sorry!" 'Twas her fault.

All her fault!

She cried out, her features twisting with horror as she lifted her tear-stained face to take in the chaos about her. Bodies were strewn about the once spotless hall, littering every corner. Tables were toppled. Stools, so beautiful once with carved legs that clawed the ground, were axed into little more than rough-hewn splinters. The only lives that seemed to have been spared were those of the female servants who now screamed for mercy beneath the abusing bodies of the murdering Northmen.

Nay, they were not being raped just now, but how long before they were all defiled? How she wished she could aid them! She released Stefan, and tried to rise, but her vision blackened as blood rushed into her temples. "He . . . he . . . was just a boy," she croaked, her throat constricting. Desperately, she fought another wave of nausea as she rose. Her legs had never felt more unsubstantial.

Anger unlike anything she'd ever known soared within her. She whirled to face the Viking leader abruptly, loathing in her eyes. "You made me a bargain!" she cried furiously. She lifted her fists to strike him and he caught both wrists in midair with a single fluid movement.

Wrenching herself free, Elienor turned abruptly to face the rest of his butchers, all the while shaking her head in denial. "He was just a boy!" she shrieked.

The flame-haired Viking laughed uproariously. Undaunted, she met his gaze without fail, her own eyes vivid with fury. He would laugh? He would rejoice at the death of a child? Too furious to consider the consequences, she lunged at the flame-haired Viking, too desperate to avenge Stefan to consider the consequences.

An arm caught her firmly from behind, about the waist. Elienor screamed, bucking and squirming against the hold.

"Think you a boy cannot deal a death blow?" a husky voice asked at her back.

"As God is my witness, I wish he had!" Elienor told him and meant it with all of her soul. Despite the fact that she knew it was a sin to wish anyone ill, she could not find it within her to feel repentant. "Set me free, you deceiving, misbegotten cur!" Trying in vain to shake herself loose from the leader's grasp, she kicked him. He dropped her at once.

Muttering something that sounded suspiciously like a Norse curse, he spun her about, his expression furious, though he said not another word. Blinding tears welled in Elienor's eyes and trickled down her cheeks, but she lifted her chin, daring him to make her repudiate her words, daring him to say aught more to defend himself. They'd struck a bargain and he'd forsaken it, and she'd not forget it. Ever!

A muscle ticked in his jaw. "Whether boy, or man, in fact," he enlightened her, "it mattered not! By the blade he wielded he declared himself a man!" He spared a quick glance at Flame Hair, and turned back to Elienor with a look that was lethal.

Elienor shook her head. Accursed blade! And Stefan had been so proud of it, she recalled with a pang. Accursed fate! "Beast!" she accused him, and then cast a withering glance at the one he called Red-Hrolf.

The Viking leader snarled and tore his gaze from her abruptly. "Enough!" he commanded his men. His scowl was as cold and fierce as the northern winds. "We go now! Take whatever catches your fancy," he bellowed. "But do so quickly or you get nought from this wretched mound of stones!"

The Viking in the nearest corner snickered wickedly and again tackled the wench he'd pinned to the floor. Red-Hrolf shouted heinously as he turned and dove upon her, as well. Struggling in earnest they squashed the buxom wench beneath their strongplay, causing her to scream in fear and protest.

Another came and tapped the leader upon the shoulder. He smiled meaningfully. "I'd have a taste of this one, too. If it please you," he added more warily when the leader's brow arched in challenge.

"*Nei*, you'll not!" the leader barked. His eyes narrowed in warning. "Take what else you will with my blessing, but do it now, Bjorn. Best you not try me this night!"

The other Viking stood beside him stubbornly, his expression offended and resentful.

"Suit yourself," the leader grumbled, and then still scowling, he turned to yet another—the nude one! "Enough, you bare sapling, dress yourself! We go! And you!" he added to Elienor, "get yourself up and walk!" He pried her away from Stefan, lifting her and nudging her forward.

"Nay!" Elienor refused. She planted her heels. "I'll not leave him!"

He shoved her this time. "You will," he apprised. "Now walk of your own accord, wench, or I shall haul you out myself!" When she wouldn't comply, his fingers dug into her upper arm in warning. "Walk!" he demanded.

There was no doubt in Elienor's mind that he would carry her out as he'd warned, but it was the only way she would leave, she vowed. If he would steal her from her home, she would not go easily! She fought him, kicking and screaming.

Muttering another savage curse, the Viking leader lifted her up, and for the second time this night, flung her over his hefty shoulders.

Chapter 6

Three longships were beached upon the narrow embankment, the largest of them monstrous, over eighty feet long. Spanning more than sixteen feet in the midsection, it held no seating; the oarsmen used great-footed war chests in their stead, their surfaces weather-beaten and smooth from use. Moonlight glinted off the polished wood, casting deep shadows into the planking.

Elienor was dumped unceremoniously into the core of the largest vessel, into the shadows, next to a young woman she recognized by name as Clarisse, Brouillard's *fille de chambre*. And then, cursing roundly, the Viking simply turned his back and stalked away.

"I shall see you rue this day!" she swore tearfully at his back. Never had she felt such loathing for another human being. Indeed, never had she even considered it possible! She might have forgiven him anything—anything! Stealing her away from her home, the raid upon Count Phillipe's castle—anything but the killing of an innocent boy!

"Oh, God . . . Stefan." Her throat tightened. In her mind she could see him again so clearly, his innocent young eyes widening the instant he recognized death. " 'Twas unfair! Unfair, unfair, unfair," she sobbed. Her gaze bore into the Viking's back as he assumed his position at the helm. Curse him—

a thousand times curse him! The Norse fiend had been three times Stefan's size, and likely claimed three times his skill!

Trembling with fear and fury, Elienor sat in bitter silence and watched as the last of the Vikings boarded, seating themselves upon their sea chests. At once they took up their oars.

"M'lady?" the young woman beside her ventured timidly. "Y . . . you should not fault yourself. I . . . I beheld it all . . . 'twas the boy's . . ." She swallowed visibly. " 'Twas Stefan's . . ."

Elienor shook her head adamantly, refusing the comfort offered. She knew without hearing the words what it was Clarisse was trying to say and could not bear to hear them voiced.

"Aye, m'lady!" Clarisse insisted. " 'Tis true!" She began to sob quietly, disconsolately. Elienor thought she might be weeping for Stefan, for she knew they, too, had been close. Impossible not to care for young, lighthearted, sweet, smiling Stefan. " 'Twas his duty to defend you!" Clarisse maintained. "My lord Phillipe would have expected it so!"

"But he was so young!" Elienor cried. "So very young!" Hot tears blurring her vision, she swallowed and met Clarisse's gaze at last. She swiped at the fiery wetness upon her cheeks, and shook her head. " 'Twas mine own fault, Clarisse. If . . . if only . . . if only I'd not struck the demon!" She averted her gaze, unable to continue, grief and remorse wrenching her heart. Through misty eyes she watched as the Vikings launched their dragon ships into the Seine. 'Twas like nought she'd ever seen before. In one fleeting moment the castle was in plain sight, in another 'twas gone, so swiftly did they glide away and vanish into the night mist without a trace.

And with it, their last chance for deliverance.

Would her uncle know where to seek her? Would he bother? And what of Count Phillipe? The Viking had said he yet lived. Might it be true?

She dared to hope.

Against her will, her gaze was drawn again to the helm of the ship, where the King of Demons stood peering out over the waters. Murderer! her heart screamed. His back was to her this instant, but even at this distance, she knew him. Aye, she knew him—never would she forget those silver eyes, so cold and hostile!

The men surrounding him were large of stature, yet he towered over them, his fair hair glowing pale beneath the silvery moonlight. Bound with a braided leather strip about the forehead, its silky length fell well below his nape, catching the light so that it gleamed. The thought occurred to her suddenly, bitterly, as she stared transfixed, that she'd never seen the likes of his hair before, not even the fairest ladies of Francia's court had such beautiful tresses as did he. She found herself wondering over the feel of it.

Would it be as soft to the touch as it appeared?

The instant she considered it, she recoiled. Sweet Jesu, but whose thoughts were those? Surely not hers. She shivered as the breeze swept her hair into her face, and she closed her eyes to pluck away the stinging strands from her lashes. When she opened them again it was to meet the Golden One's dark gaze.

The way he watched her never ceased to send quivers down her spine.

In the chapel . . . Jesu . . . in the chapel!

Faithless was what she was!

But nay, all it took to keep those thoughts at bay was to remember Stefan's face as he'd died. "Murderer," she whispered passionately, and hoped he could read her lips. Still, she could not wrench her gaze away, and so she willed him to know what was in her heart, every last trace of loathing! Yet if her emotions were truly in her eyes, he seemed wholly unaffected by what he saw, for his gaze never wavered. His lips merely curved at one corner, as if to mock her, and then mercifully he turned to address his men, releasing her at last.

With another shudder of her shoulders, Elienor turned to meet Clarisse's probing gaze, and gasped in surprise at being watched so cannily. Chagrined at what thoughts might have been evident in her confused expression, she wrenched her gaze guiltily away. Yet 'twas not of the look that had passed between herself and the Viking that Clarisse inquired.

"M'lady?" Clarisse asked weakly. "What do you suppose they will do with us? W . . . when the destination is reached?"

Elienor's blue eyes were full of torment as she turned to acknowledge the question. She had no notion what to say to allay Clarisse's fears. In truth, she had no inkling what lay in store for either of them; the dream had ended in the chapel, with the screams of the wounded and dying. She shook her head miserably.

Clarisse nodded, bowing her head, and Elienor turned again to watch the men at their rowing. Heathens though they were, they moved gracefully together, in perfect accord with one other. Yet, as beautiful as their motion was, the sound they made was diabolical. Keeping time with the head oarsman's pounding rhythm, the oars groaned eerily as they rolled over wet wood, lifting and plunging again like savage beasts into the murky water. As the three dragon ships soared over the night-blackened waters, the sound only escalated, grating on Elienor's nerves.

For the longest time, neither she nor Clarisse spoke. She simply sat, watching all, seeing nought. Against her will, she kept envisioning the Viking leader . . . the way his eyes had pierced her within the chapel . . . the way he'd touched her . . . caressed her cheek so tenderly . . .

Those eyes.

She saw them again as he'd caressed her within the chapel. Troubled by the image, Elienor nipped at her lip. How could he have touched her so gently, and be so coldhearted? She closed her eyes to ward away the memory and at once it was replaced with another.

Stefan.

"Sweet Jesu!" She moaned. Would she ever forget the look on his face as he'd died? In answer, she shook her head. Tears welled in her eyes. Never! she swore vehemently. "Never!" she whispered.

All too soon, the three longships exited the mouth of the River Seine and entered into the turbulent channel. Water rose up to slap against the dragon vessel like mighty wrathful hands. At once the rowing ceased and the rigging was hastily raised, the sailcloth unfolded and prepared. In short time the red diamond-patterned sails, which struck terror in the hearts of men, women, and children alike, billowed sharply with the strengthening breeze.

Elienor's heart wrenched as the sails filled and the ship punched forward with a terrible fury, leaving the mainland of Francia small in its wake.

Yet she dared not weep. With silent, stoic pride, she watched her homeland vanish before her eyes, then squeezed her eyes shut, even as her heart constricted with grief.

It was her duty to be strong, she told herself. For Clarisse.

Her duty.

Beside her, Clarisse began to weep in earnest. Burying her pallid face into the sleeve of her gown, the girl fell forward against the planking to sob.

Hours later, as the sky began to lighten, Clarisse lay weeping still, though quietly now. Elienor had no notion what to say to comfort the poor girl. Try as she might, the words would not form. She scooted to the maid's side to soothe her the only way she knew how, the way Mother Heloise had so often done for her. She stroked the back of Clarisse's matted hair, and when Clarisse's sobs began to ebb at last, Elienor coaxed the girl's arm away from her face. Clarisse resisted, whimpering, concealing her eyes. She turned her back to Elienor, and it was then Elienor discovered the sticky blood that coated the girl's dark hair behind her head. "Clarisse!" she exclaimed. "You're injured! Jesu, why did you not say?"

Clarisse moaned and shook her head, refusing to bare her face. "I . . . I . . . sorry, m'lady! Sorry . . ." She moaned pathetically. " 'Tis the light!" she complained.

As best she could, Elienor parted the girl's hair to find the gash little more than a graze. The welt beneath, however, was a furious purplish crimson. She hesitated to touch it. "Does it pain you much?" she asked, and then berated herself for the question. Of course it pained her!

Clarisse nodded emphatically, concealing her face protectively into her sleeve, yet the gesture managed to bare her wound more fully to Elienor. Elienor gasped to see the swelling so severe at the base of her skull. She shook her head. "Sweet Jesu . . . what have they done to you?"

Clarisse responded by coiling herself protectively.

"Clarisse, how can I help if you will not speak?"

"H . . . he . . ." Her breast heaved on a great sob. "He s . . . struck m . . . my head against . . . against . . . the stairwell."

There was no need to ask who. In Elienor's heart it wouldn't have mattered *who* the guilty party had been. She knew precisely at whose feet to place the blame.

His.

"I . . . It aches more with every passing moment!" Clarisse whined.

Cautiously, Elienor reached to probe the wound with her fingers, gently, so as not to cause more suffering.

At Elienor's touch, Clarisse wrenched herself away with a shrill cry, rolling out of reach. Once again she began to sob, and Elienor felt utterly helpless, wanting to aid her, yet knowing she had not the means. Elienor looked to the helm, and this time, she rose determinedly, not thinking, only feeling.

The very least these heathens could do was to supply her with cloth and water to cleanse the wound!

Without warning, before she could rise fully to her feet, she was shoved backward by the one called Red-Hrolf. He scowled fiercely at her and began to bellow viciously in his garbled tongue. Elienor knew not a word, yet understood him perfectly. He commanded her to stay—like a dog! Well, she refused to be cowed! Clarisse needed aid and she'd not fail her!

As she'd failed Stefan, a little voice beleaguered.

Resolved as Elienor was, she rose again, only to be thrust backward once more.

"How dare . . ." She halted on a gasp, restraining the angry words, and despite the trembling in her limbs, once more rose to face the irate Viking. "I would speak to your jarl!" she demanded furiously. "I'll not sit idly by and watch this woman die! Have you no mercy at all?" She didn't stop to consider why she felt the jarl would help her any more than the flame-haired one would.

Red-Hrolf continued to bellow, shoving at her arm intermittently, and then abruptly he ceased his tirade to glower over her shoulder.

"Since when do thralls demand aught?"

Elienor gave a startled shriek at the unexpected voice behind her. *His* voice! Her heart flying into her throat, she buckled to her knees. Sweet Jesu! Mary mother of God! She resisted the urge to cross herself, as well, for with only a single harshly spoken word, *he'd* accomplished what Red-Hrolf had not. She dared not rise, nor turn to look at him for fear that her eyes would betray her. Her heart throbbed painfully as she waited for him to speak again, but when he did, it was to address Red-Hrolf in their own tongue.

Red-Hrolf immediately sat down upon his sea chest. Flushed and angry, he took up his oar once more, all the while glaring resentfully at Elienor.

At once she was wrenched about to face the Viking leader.

"And you, Mistress Arrogance! I remember not affording you choices!"

"Arrogance!" Elienor gasped, fury choking her. "Arrogance?" she returned contemptuously, "And what, prithee, my lord *Viking*, could be more arrogant than to steal into a sleeping manor and butcher those within for the sake of glory, or greed?"

The Viking's eyes darkened to coal before her own; they fairly smoldered with ire. "Glory?" he replied sharply. "Greed?" His sneer mocked her. "*Nei*, wench! But I've no inclination to explain myself to you. Best you listen to me well, for I vow I'll not deign to warn you again! From here on you *will* do what is expected of you, or you *will* pay the consequences!"

Elienor met his gaze boldly. Something about this barbarian Viking liberated that wicked part of her she'd repressed for so very long; so many times she'd had to bite her lip to keep her words from spilling free, but not this time, she vowed. "And what might that be?" she dared. "Might I lie down and die for you?" she asked contemptuously.

He shook her briefly, and she choked back a startled cry. His eyes glinted in warning, his jaw working furiously. "What is expected," he paused, battling his raging temper. "What is expected of you, wench, is that you be seated in silence and goad my men no further! As it is, you've caused more than enough unrest this day."

She had caused unrest? She? Where the courage came from, Elienor would never know, for she felt anything but valiant in that moment, but her chin lifted in challenge. "Nay!" she spat, "Not I, my lord *Viking!* 'Tis you, you that have caused so much destruction and depravity this night! And you dare accuse me?"

The angry retort hardened his features, and in answer his other hand flew to her shoulders so quickly that before Elienor knew what he intended he'd lifted her until she stood on the tips of her toes. His jaw working with fury, he shook her furiously, till her teeth jarred. When he spoke again, his lips were so near to her own that she felt the heat and fury of his breath. "Best you realize now, little *Fransk*," he advised in a seething whisper, the endearment anything but tender, "I dare anything I please! Mayhap yesterday you garnered your will with your shrewish ways and biting tongue, but today you belong to me! And so you will *answer* to me! Incite my men to violence once more, I tell you, and I will see you repent it sorely—woman or *nei!* Do not try me again this day!"

Elienor tossed her head back as best she could, her eyes blazing with ire. Belong? He would dare remind her of their bargain! "Nay, Viking!" she returned sourly, spitting the word as though it were the vilest of epitaphs. "You are mistaken. I *belong* to no man!" She dared again to lift her chin, cursing the sinful pride that would impel her to do so. "No man!" she stressed again, flashing him a look of disdain.

His eyes narrowed and his lips thinned in anger. "Aye, my little *Fransk*, but you do," he returned huskily. "For you belong to me—bargain, or *nei!*"

God help her but she could not keep her tongue. "And I would remind you, my lord Viking, that you breached our bargain mere moments after effecting it. You have no claim over me, nor shall I give you anything freely, nought!" Again, she lifted her chin. "Now release me, if you please!"

He grinned suddenly, ruthlessly, pressing her closer. "In such case . . . believe me when I tell you that I shall *deeply* enjoy the taking!" He chuckled nastily. "I am beast," he said, his tone heavy with sarcasm, "a *Viking*, as you so like to point out, and by your own words, force is the only way of our people. Nought—*nought!*" he stressed with relish, "shall give me greater pleasure, I fear, than to take what you will not freely give!"

Elienor's heart flew into her throat, for she doubted him not. "Then by all that is holy, I shall fight you!" she returned, swallowing her fear. To her dismay, she shivered beneath his gaze.

Feeling her tremors, he laughed outright, his expression knowing, his grin widening. "So be it, then! I trust we are understood?"

Elienor averted her eyes, loathing even the sight of him in that instant, loathing the fear that was undoubtedly in her own eyes.

He shook her once more, prodding her. "We are understood?" he repeated. His fingers tightened about her arms when she did not respond.

Her gaze reverted to his suddenly, her eyes shimmering violet fire. "Release me, barbarian! Release me!"

Triumph, that forbidden prideful emotion, flooded through her when he winced at her words. It was a victory, no matter how small, and she savored it fully. And then his expression turned utterly violent. Sweet Jesu, but she was in peril of losing all self-control did he not release her soon. She could not withstand his scrutiny, or his touch, much longer. "Aye!" she spat at once, feeling suddenly weak and vulnerable in the face of his fury. "Aye! We are understood! Release me," she cried. "Release me!"

He complied at once. She collapsed to her knees. With a last shriveling glance and a disgusted shake of his head, he turned to leave.

Kneading the soreness from her arms, Elienor whimpered softly, cursing him for the heartless heathen that he was. How cruel to remind her so viciously that she was no more than his chattel. Yet as much as she loathed him—and aye, feared him, even—she could not allow him to go without requesting aid for Clarisse. "The maid is ill!" she cried out, her voice trembling. She prayed all trace of her tears was gone . . . and her fear.

She prayed for strength.

The Viking stopped abruptly, pivoting to face her, his gaze as deadly as his sword.

With the last vestiges of her pride, Elienor raised her chin. "I would aid her, but have need of water to—"

Without a word, he lifted his skin from his belt and flung it at her, then turned and stalked away. Elienor had no choice but to catch it, for it landed squarely at her breast, snatching her breath away— not from the impact, but because she'd not expected to gain it so easily.

She watched him go without another word. With the skin in her grasp, she dared not speak to prevent him from taking his leave lest he change his mind and seize it away from her. Her gaze fell suddenly to where Clarisse lay. The girl's eyes, focused upon the jarl's massive back, were wide with fright, her cheeks tear stained. Her gaze reverted to Elienor.

"M . . . m'lady, I . . . I fear 'tis not wise to provoke him!" Clarisse fretted. Her eyes closed suddenly and her face contorted with pain.

Desperate to aid her, Elienor knelt beside her, brushing the damp hair away from her forehead. "Your fever rises, Clarisse . . ." She said. "Alas . . . I fear you speak true, yet I find I have no choice." 'Twas more fact than Clarisse could ever know, for whether intent was there or not, Elienor's accursed tongue spoke with a will of its own—this time was no exception. This time particularly, for 'twas joined by her heart. Had she always been so sinful in nature? How had she suppressed it for so long. It shamed her . . . and yet . . . and yet somehow . . . deep, deep down . . . it strengthened her.

Clarisse groaned pitifully. "Aye, m'lady, aye . . . but . . . but—oh, the light!" she exclaimed. "The light . . . it p . . . pains mine eyes!"

Elienor's brow's furrowed. "What of the wound?" She wet her skirt with water from the skin, then wiped Clarisse's brow with it, soothing her. "Where does it pain you most?"

Clarisse shook her head fitfully. "M . . . mine neck . . . and . . . and mine eyes . . . the light, m'lady! 'Tis the light!"

Elienor offered Clarisse the skin of water to drink by.

Clarisse shook her head, refusing it.

Elienor's own mouth felt dryer than sun-dried wool, and her tongue too large, but she held the skin out resolutely for Clarisse to take. "I have no thirst just now," she lied without pause—yet another sin! But God forgive her, she knew the girl would not accept it and knowingly deprive her in order to quench her own thirst. Clarisse's station, regardless that here among enemies they were equal, was not so easily forgotten. Still Clarisse would not accept it. "Go on," Elienor prompted. "I would that you drank from it first."

Still Clarisse hesitated. Elienor nodded encouragement, her eyes pleading. "Take it!" At last Clarisse reached for it, her lean fingers quivering as she lifted it eagerly to her sun-parched lips. She drank deeply, and with desperation, and then finally lowered it from her lips, giving Elienor a look of utmost gratitude.

Elienor set it aside for the time being.

"Why do they not simply kill us and be done with it!" Clarisse cried suddenly.

Elienor knew not what to say, for she'd wondered the same. She shrugged. "Clarisse . . . I . . . I would aid you if you'd allow it. Would you turn for me that I might cleanse the wound?"

Their eyes met and held. Elienor knew she requested the girl's trust unjustly, for she'd failed Stefan, yet for answer Clarisse nodded, rolling slowly to show her back, moaning with misery.

Elienor's eyes were drawn again to the helm, never more full of anguish. Whatever it required of her, she vowed, she would not let them harm Clarisse! She refused to accept that she had not the power to prevent it. Whatever was required of her, she would do.

She could not bear yet another death upon her conscience.

As he took a hefty swig from his flagon, Alarik watched the little *Fransk* offer the skin he'd given her to the ailing girl. He could clearly see the longing in her own eyes, yet she refused it when the girl offered it back. Curse the wench! With a muttered oath, he recapped his own skin. Why had he not left her in Francia? He should have, he acknowledged with a scowl. Whatever madness had possessed him to take her? What could he have been thinking? 'Twould serve her right did she die from lack of water!

And what did he care?

He had the urge to go to her, force the shrew to drink.

Casting an irate glance at Red-Hrolf, he cursed her again. His men would see such a gesture as a weakness in him, especially after their previous confrontation, and that was the one thing he could not risk. In his world, strength alone ruled, now more than ever, for there was much unrest in the Northlands over this new Christian faith.

And it helped matters not that his brother, Olav, would force the people's hearts where they would not. With his own eyes he'd witnessed the iron hand his brother wielded. In anger that one of his own men—his own—would not take the faith, Olav had offered him to Odin before the rest of his men, cut like a sacrificial beast upon the altar stone, making of him an example.

His gaze was drawn again to the girl. She was no more than a thrall, he reminded himself, and not worth risking the loyalty of his men for, and with that he turned his attention to the skies. The wind filled the Goldenhawk's sails adequately for the moment, but 'twas only a matter of time before the weather turned foul. Hopefully they'd be well on their way north by then . . . mayhap even within sight of Friesland's broken coastline.

By the Norns, he cared not a whit for the Frenchwoman, he avowed. He'd taken her only to avenge himself against the count.

Yet he'd be damned if the wench didn't have mettle.

Nonetheless, as intrigued as he was by that fact, it also rankled, for just as surely as the termagant sat there glaring at him, he knew she would bring him grief.

Yet had he to do it all over again . . .

He would take her again.

And that admission made him scowl. For he also knew that, in truth, his decision to take her had little to do with vengeance over Phillipe of Brouillard.

Plainly and simply and with an intensity he'd never conceived possible . . . he wanted her.

Chapter 7

Each hour dragged on longer than the last.

By late afternoon, Elienor could no longer feel the sun's heat upon her flesh, though its glaring brightness assured her it had not fled. She thought she might not bear it if that was how she would pass the remainder of the journey! With a groan, she glanced at Clarisse and found her sleeping fitfully. 'Twas good that she slept, for she seemed only miserable when awake.

Above them, the sails rippled noisily. But down below, where they lay, the air was stagnant, humid, and strangely peaceful, making Elienor feel oddly sedated and dazed. To begin with, it had been colder upon the sea than it had been on land, but now that her body was sun-scorched, she couldn't feel anything but heat. The salt air stung her eyes, and she squeezed them shut to ward away the burn. Still, though she felt a desperation to, she could not succumb to the slumber that beckoned; her thirst was too fierce, her face too burned, her throat too raw, her worry for Clarisse too great. With a sigh, she lay down as near to Clarisse as possible, closing her eyes to rest them, and somehow, she dozed.

But she slept no longer than an hour when she awoke abruptly to the ungodly sound of the sea shattering against the vessel. In such short time the weather had turned foul. Salt water dashed over the gunwales, the mist spraying her flaming cheeks, easing the burn fleetingly until the moisture evaporated, and then her skin blazed twice as tender as the salt cured her flesh.

With a groan of misery, she turned to give the one side of her face respite from the scorching sun and blistering wind and whimpered as her abused flesh met with sea-drenched wood. Sweet Jesu, but it stung! To her dismay, in that instant her eyes met Red-Hrolf's, and the look he directed upon her was sheer malevolence.

Cold fingers fled down her spine as he continued to glare. Hatred, unbridled and fierce, glittered in his Nordic blue eyes. He would kill her, she knew, were the choice his own. Thank heaven above 'twas not! Fear twisting her heart, she glanced hastily away, shocked to find herself thanking God in that instant for the Viking jarl's protection. And though she shuddered at the notion, she recognized the truth of it, and conceded to it.

He *was* the lesser of evils—much as she loathed to acknowledge it.

Beside her, Clarisse moaned pitifully. Reflexively, Elienor sought out the skin of water to give to her. Never taking her eyes from Red-Hrolf, she took two greedy sips for herself, then forced herself to stop. Using as little water as possible, she moistened her skirt, then used it to cool Clarisse's face once more. That done, she lifted Clarisse's head to her lap, and without avail, tried to part the girl's lips to feed her the water. To her dismay the water merely trickled down Clarisse's chin. With a heavy heart, Elienor conceded defeat, recapping the skin, and tucking it beneath her to conserve for later.

Clarisse awoke in that instant, a pained expression on her pale face.

"Clarisse?"

"Aye, m'lady," she croaked.

Elienor brushed black damp wisps of hair from Clarisse's sickly pale face. "Art better?" she asked.

Clarisse's voice was weaker this time, almost a whisper. "Aye, m'lady." She grimaced as another wave struck the ship, pitching it violently. "The light," she croaked pitifully. " 'Tis the light . . ."

Elienor glanced up at the sun and with all her heart wished it away.

Darkness came without warning that evening, spreading shadows over the sea like an enormous black veil, and with it came an unbearable chill that settled into the bones. The winds grew progressively stronger the further north they sailed, and to Elienor it seemed that in the darkness demons railed at them. No matter how she lay, she was ill at ease and found herself shifting every so often to find a new position. No doubt *he* felt perfectly at ease in this infernal clime—fiend that he was!

Not for the first time, her gaze was drawn to the helm.

Only two of the Vikings were left awake, the leader and the nude one. Nay, the one was not unclad now, but Elienor would always see him as she had that first time, nude and dancing merrily over the dead of Count Phillipe's castle. She blinked away a vision of Gaston prone beneath him. Both Vikings were now staring out over the dark waters, their enormous bodies silhouetted by the immense moon. Soft murmurs came to her ears, but she didn't bother trying to eavesdrop, knowing nought of their heathen tongue.

*   *   *

Feeling the woman's overwhelming presence, not for the first time this eve, Alarik turned to slice his rapier gaze through the thick sea mist.

She glanced away the instant his eyes found hers.

Unobserved by his slumbering men, he watched as she curled close to the other, laying her head gently upon the overlapping planking. When she still could not find a suitable position, he watched as she gathered up the length of her dark hair, her movements graceful and sensual despite the stiffening cold in the air, and attempted to employ it as a pillow.

His body hardened as he watched her cozy into that glorious mane. What would it feel like to share that silky pillow along with her? Recalling the softness of the tresses he'd caressed within the chapel, he craved the feel of it fiercely, yet he resisted the urge to walk the distance separating them.

He'd find out soon enough, he told himself, the very instant their feet were on solid ground. And with that resolution, he resumed his vigil over the fickle sea, banishing thoughts of the girl from his mind once and for all.

It served no purpose to think of her now.

The fact that she found it difficult to rest upon the hard planking told him much, for while she'd not complained, neither did she appear at ease with the lot she'd been given. She was no maidservant, he surmised, leading him again to the conclusion that she was, in truth, the count's—what? Whore? Wife?

He didn't give a damn what she was!

A light draft ruffled his cloak, rifled through his hair, as he again glanced at the woman, watching her slumber.

She was shivering.

He continued to stare, his body disobeying as he told himself he was unmoved.

By Odin's lost eye, who wasn't shivering? The night air was frigid!

Why should he concern himself over one measly wench?

He elbowed Sigurd suddenly. "Take the tiller," he charged, and then he stalked away without another word.

With careful precision, Alarik picked his way over the slumbering bodies of his crewmen, halting next to the woman, his hands belligerently at his hips. It surprised him to discover she'd found her way back to sleep for he'd braced himself for another confrontation. Or had he hoped?

Without giving himself time to consider either his actions or his thoughts, he removed his cloak, covering her with it, tucking the ends carefully beneath her. A quick glance over his shoulder revealed that for the moment the sea held Sigurd's undivided attention.

Sigurd Thorgoodson was Alarik's sworn man, had been with him longer than any. He trusted Sigurd with his life, but he had no wish to be watched at this moment, even by one so loyal. Sigurd seemed to understand that, and for his deference Alarik was grateful. The rest of his crew slept on, and knowing this he was unable to stay his hand. The need to touch her was insuppressible. Lifting a loose strand of her hair to his lips, as if to taste of it, he then brought it to his nostrils, breathing deeply of its exhilarating scent: roses, sea, wind. They shouldn't have mixed so well together, but they did.

Exquisitely.

Once again a vision of her standing atop the tower, silhouetted by the heathery moon, her hair fluttering wild and free behind her, appeared to him, and he shivered with anticipation. Never had he craved home more than he did in that instant. The prolonged anticipation was almost intolerable.

"What hold have you upon me, little *Fransk*?" he whispered gruffly. She roused an alien emotion in his hardened heart. Somehow . . . when he'd stared into that ethereal face of hers for the first time . . . 'twas as if he'd lost something of himself. And then, when he had slain the boy, and she'd looked at him with such accusing eyes, he'd had absolutely no notion why he'd felt the need to defend himself. He had taken his first life long before his twelfth year—so had many others, for that matter, but the look in her eyes had drawn the words from his lips nevertheless.

"'Tis but lust!" he swore emphatically, lifting her hair to his nostrils once more. He inhaled the essence of her, and it held him spellbound a full instant.

When she didn't stir, his gaze wandered down the length of her, and abruptly, another vision of her lying prone beneath him with long shapely legs wrapped about his waist assailed him. His body hardened painfully, and he shifted for comfort, cursing softly when he found none. With a muttered curse, he cast aside the lock of her hair as he surged to his feet.

Hel and damnation, he cared nought for the wench!

'Twas but lust and no more, he assured himself, and swore again, for even as he made his way back to the helm, the lie followed him.

Chapter 8

The skies remained downcast the next day.
And the next, as well, though fortunately it didn't rain.

Late in the eve of the fourth day the wind suddenly began to gale as they moved past a string of large islands. In the rising tempest, the ship thrust forward so swiftly that the islands soon vanished in their wake.

Elienor had not eaten at all that fateful first day. On the second she'd been given measly portions of dried fish and water. Clarisse had not eaten a bite, had grown progressively worse, though thankfully, she had sipped some water. At the moment Elienor was not hungry, despite the fact that she'd eaten nothing yet this day. They'd given her more of the dried salmon an hour past, but she'd not eaten it. Instead, she had saved it for Clarisse, in hopes that the girl would try it when she awoke this time. Fervently, she prayed that the storm would abate and the waters would calm, but to her dismay, the storm only intensified.

Willing away her fear, her thoughts focused upon a happier time. The month she'd spent in her uncle's court had been all too brief. For the first time in her life she'd felt a part of something, even if her relation to Robert, King of Francia, was known only by a select few.

As she remembered, her fingers skimmed the ring that lay hidden beneath the neckline of her *bliaut*. If her life before the priory ever seemed unreal, distant, or if she ever doubted the vague memories she had of her noble sire and gentle mother, she needed only to look upon the ring that bore her family crest, the royal crest of Francia. Her uncle had given it to her, the grandest of gifts, for the ring had once belonged to her father.

She cherished it.

With bittersweet memories she recalled the moment her uncle Robert had bestowed it upon her—the day he'd taken her from the Abbey. *Having been summoned to the chapel, she'd found him humming softly, the Latin words too soft to make out. At the sound of her footfalls upon the hollow wood floor, he'd turned from staring at the cross above the altar, and the humming ceased abruptly. He cleared his throat. "You've the look of your mother, child," he croaked.*

"Aye," Elienor answered. "So I have been told, my lord." She was helpless to keep the bitterness from her tone. "But as you can see, I am a child no longer."

"Aye . . . truly . . . and your father would have been proud."

He must have sensed her longing at his words, for afterward, when they had talked awhile, he removed the ring from his finger. "Take it, Elienor, for it belonged to your sire . . ."

Elienor hesitated.

"I understand should you choose not to . . . yet you are as much entitled to it as I."

Still she hesitated.

"Try not to condemn him, Elienor. 'Twas your grandsire who wished him to cloister your mother, not he, for he loved her well. Your father was—as I have been— nought but a pawn in the politics of matrimony."

At last, she took the ring from his grasp. "As am I,"
she reminded him.

He nodded gravely and sighed deeply. "As are you.
But you should know that he refused to repudiate her
at first."

Her heart stumbled at his words, and she gazed at
him hearteningly.

"Alas . . . as you know . . . to no avail," he told her,
and sighed. "I fear it served my father well that your
mother was known to bear the divine sight, for it took
very little goading on his part to rouse the common folk
against her. And though your father was his bastard
son, he would not tolerate her tie to the blood of his
own." He gazed at her pointedly. "At any rate, 'tis
fortunate, indeed, that she did not bequeath to you . . .
her . . . her inauspicious gift."

Elienor's heart turned violently. She dared not meet
his gaze for fear he'd suspect. "Aye," she croaked, " 'tis
fortunate."

He seemed not to note the alarm in her tone, for he
carried on. "Were it not for your father's intercession
with the church," he told her, "she might not even have
been buried on sacred ground. For that at least, you
should offer your father a pardon . . . aye, Elienor, for
he loved you, too."

And so she took the ring.

And she was grateful for it, for with it, her uncle
had given her a sense of belonging. It had meant
much to her to be acknowledged by her family.
She had despaired of ever fulfilling that dream.
She thought she understood why her uncle had
been compelled to reveal it all after so long, for
he indubitably felt at least a twinge of guilt for
what his father had done to Elienor and her mother. Then too, she was a little sad for him; Robert
of Francia knew firsthand the pain and agony of

losing a loved one, for he too had fallen victim to such manipulations. His first marriage had been annulled in much the same manner as was her own father's, and his love thereafter confined to the priory.

As grateful as she was, she could not help but feel a little bitter over all that had been taken from her as a child. Nevertheless 'twas best not to dwell on that, she knew. She tried to focus instead on the good things in her life: She was learned in the scriptures, knew her histories, as well, and could tally her numbers well, for Mother Heloise had been priming her to become abbess in her stead.

With a sigh, she curled her legs into the mantle that had appeared upon her so mysteriously the morning of the second day and wondered again to whom it belonged. It was not Red-Hrolf's, she was certain. Nor did any of the others seem overly concerned with her welfare.

Still, she had a suspicion to whom it belonged, for it smelled of him; an elusive combination of wind, sea, and man. 'Twas insane, she knew, to know his scent, when she knew him not at all, but she did.

The wind howled about her, hissing like a viper through the sails, and Elienor raised herself to make certain Clarisse was covered by the mantle as well. Leaning over her, Elienor tucked the coverlet gently beneath her, and then peered out over the gunwales. Nothing but angry gray swells met her gaze. They were so far from anywhere . . .

The unfathomable depth of the ocean made her shiver abruptly.

She felt so vulnerable out here, almost as vulnerable as she had on that fateful day when her mother had been buried. The sea was so dark—as dark as she'd so oft imagined her mother's grave to be. She shivered again and hugged herself for warmth, cursing her lips, for they burned incessantly—even in the cold, damp darkness, they burned. She raised her fingers to them as if that brief touch might ease them.

She wasn't so much afraid to die, she told herself. Rather she was terrified that if she did, they would toss her body into the sea—to the dreadful creatures that dwelled within it. With a groan, she glanced down at Clarisse. Moonlight glinted off the young maid's face, making her skin seem too pale, her eyes black and eerie. The thought occurred to her suddenly that Clarisse might not survive the sea voyage. She was so weak!

Once again she was failing. Failing! *As she'd failed Stefan.*

Swallowing the thickness in her throat, she tilted her head skyward. Had God truly left them to die? She shook her head, denying the possibility, even as she thought it. Her hand covered her mouth. In the darkness, with no eyes to see her and the rising wind to carry away the sound, she began to sob quietly. Fifteen winters she'd spent within the priory. Fifteen long, lonely winters. And Phillipe? He'd been her greatest hope.

Above her, the sails rippled violently, twisting the mast windward. Shuddering, Elienor crossed herself. What fate was this God had given her? To see Stefan die—and now mayhap to watch Clarisse suffer and do the same? Well, by God, she'd not allow it!

As if her fury had become tangible, the wind suddenly lifted, pitching the ship viciously and jostling those aboard.

"Clarisse?" she cried out. But there was no response from the weak form beside her. Frantically, she shook the girl's shoulder as the ship listed once more. "Clarisse!" she shouted. Still no answer. Clarisse lay unmoving. "Nay! Oh, nay!" Panicking, Elienor felt for a pulse at Clarisse's neck, and finding it fragile, breathed a shaky sigh of relief. With trembling hands she fumbled for the skin of water behind her. 'Twas the fever, she was certain. If she could but cool her somehow. She found the skin instantly, but the moment her fingers lit upon it, the ship listed yet again, sending the skin flying behind her. She turned to catch it and was startled to find Red-Hrolf awake, watching them. Grinning balefully, his boot came down upon the skin, halting its slide across the planking. Fearful to retrieve it on her own, Elienor held out her hand for him to return it, hoping against hope that he would.

His grin only widened, and Elienor's heart twisted. Nevertheless, knowing Clarisse had need of the water, she dared to reach for it now, uncertainly at first, keeping her gaze on Red-Hrolf. Yet to her alarm, before she could grasp it, the ship listed once more, this time violently.

Chaos erupted.

With a terrified shriek, Elienor rolled atop Clarisse, striking her hard enough that she rose up only to bounce down upon the planking, her head landing with a sickening smack that Elienor could hear even above the sound of the wind and the waking shouts of the crewmen. To her horror, Clarisse's body began to convulse beneath her, bucking as though possessed. Elienor screamed, taken aback by the sight and feel of Clarisse twisting and writhing beneath her.

And seeing Clarisse, Red-Hrolf began to shout. He jumped to his feet in revulsion. "The woman's afflicted!"

"Nay!" Elienor denied, "she is but ill!"

Clarisse continued to buck and twist. Elienor couldn't stop her. Her tongue lolled limply from her mouth, and her eyes opened and crossed, the sight appalling enough to terrify even Elienor.

"'Tis a plague from Hella!" Red-Hrolf shouted. "We shall all perish! Shrivel away to bones!"

Fear clawed at Elienor's heart. Before her eyes she saw again her mother's accusers, heard their chanted convictions: *Witch! Kill the witch! God'll strike us dead for her sins! Kill the witch!* She closed her eyes to ward away the bitter vision and prayed for strength. Merciful heaven. She must remain strong!

"Pitch the whore to the sea!" someone interjected, his voice gruff from hours of sleep.

Kill the witch! Aye! Kill them both! The daughter's a filthy witch, too! Send them both to Hades from whence they came! To Hades! "Nay!" Elienor shrieked at the memory. "Nay! Please! Please!"

"Pitch them both to the sea!" another echoed in French, glaring at her.

"Nay!" Elienor shrieked, wild with terror now. "Nay! Nay! Have mercy—I beg of you! Sweet Jesu! Have mercy!" She rose up, clinging to Red-Hrolf's tunic, begging. "Jesu Christ—Mother! Nay!"

Red Hrolf thrust her away in revulsion. "Filthy *Fransk* whore!" He lifted up his oar to frighten her away.

Frantic now, Elienor rose up with him, pleading incoherently with fear. "Please, please, leave her be—oh, please!"

There was no time to avoid the blow, even had she been aware of it.

She screamed as the pinnacle of an oar struck her head. Her eyes widened at the sound of her flesh ripping, so loud it seemed to come from within her.

Had her visions been so wrong?

Was she to die as well?

Something wet and warm blanketed her temple, blood, she thought vaguely. Blood. Before her eyes a hazy blackness settled in, and it seemed an eternity passed as she fought the inevitable. A hollow ringing shrieked in her ears, blocking out all other sound.

And then silence.

The silence of her mother's grave?

In that instant, she felt as though she would retch, so violently ill did she become. She opened her mouth to call for aid, but the words never formed.

Sweet Jesu, who did she expect would aid her? *No one*! a little voice sneered. "No one," she whispered weakly, her vision fading swiftly to gray.

To her shock, the face that swam before her in that instant was not her uncle's, not her mother's, not the kind old abbess's, not Count Phillipe's, nor Stefan's, nor Clarisse's . . . but his . . .

She tried to look toward the helm, to plead for help, but abruptly the world went black.

Accustomed to frequent heated verbal matches amongst his bored crewmen whilst at sea, Alarik had paid the sudden upheaval little mind, until he heard the scream. He turned in time to see her collapse to the planking. With a hoarse cry, he hastened to her side, lifting her face up. Her blood flowed freely into his hands from a gash at her temple. He turned his wrath upon Red-Hrolf, who was the only one near enough to have inflicted the mighty blow. "What need was there for this?"

"She's mad!" Red-Hrolf defended, his expression indignant. And then uneasy over the way Alarik glared at him, he insisted, "She's mad, I tell you! and the other's afflicted!" His face reddened under Alarik's censure, but as he caught an assertive nod from Bjorn, he dared to speak up once more. "At any rate, why should you object to what I've done to the whore, jarl? She's just a filthy *Fransk!* We ought to toss them both overboard and be done!"

As though the Gods of Asgard held their breath for Alarik's response, even the winds abated in that instant, and the uncanny hush that followed Red-Hrolf's inquiry taunted him. In truth, 'twas a question he'd asked of himself. As of yet there was no answer. Still, he'd not have the wench mistreated, and the vehemence with which he said his next words stunned himself more than it did his men.

"I care!" he snarled, "because she is mine. Mine!" He slammed a fist against his chest and shot his brother a contemptuous scowl, cautioning Bjorn to take care, for he'd not missed the encouraging look Bjorn had given Red-Hrolf. Bjorn's eyes widened in startle, and when Alarik was satisfied that his warning had been interpreted correctly, he turned to all within plain view and reiterated. "The *Fransk* is mine to do with as I will! I dare any who thinks otherwise to defy me!" Again he met each of their gazes; one by one heads shook in negation, shrinking from the challenge. No one dared even to speak.

Feeling the warmth of her blood flow over his hands, Alarik glanced down, and with his salt-sprayed tunic, he swiped at the blood streaming so swiftly from the wound, baring the flesh of her temple only momentarily before another rush of her blood covered the open gash. As he'd feared, there was a fairly deep laceration just below the temple, a very delicate spot, he knew. Concerned by the gravity of her injury, he scanned the storm-tossed waters.

The wind was rising once more, but there was little choice to be made if he wished to aid the wench. He was the best navigator aboard, but in light of the circumstances, he felt he could trust no one to minister to the *Fransk*.

Sigurd, he thought, could skillfully guide the ship in such foul clime . . . 'Twas merely that he'd always preferred to sail himself at such times that he couldn't be wholly certain and he cursed himself for that flaw in his character.

Why did he always feel the need to do aught himself?

No matter, those were his choices; to sail himself and let the woman die, or to minister to her and possibly kill them all in the process. In that instant the Goldenhawk pitched to one side. With a muttered curse, Alarik braced himself, but he was too late. He was flung down upon her.

So small.

She was so small beneath him.

He couldn't let her die. His hands tangled in her bloody hair.

He wouldn't let her die!

As long as he lived he'd never comprehend the pull she seemed to have over him, but he made his insane vow nonetheless—to save her life at all cost, even at the risk of his own, and those of his men. Why he would make such a treacherous pact with himself was beyond comprehension. He only knew that something beyond his power of reasoning had compelled him unto it.

As the *drakken* turned its prow into the white-caps once more, he peeled his body from hers, his gaze slicing through the sea-spray and mist to see that the man at the helm was struggling at best.

Sigurd would simply have to attempt it. His decision made, not even Thor himself could have swayed him from it. Not understanding his own motives, Alarik turned to Sigurd. "Replace Ivar at the helm! Quickly!"

Sigurd's jaw dropped with disbelief, his eyes widening. "But jarl—"

"Go!" Alarik roared. "Go!"

Shaking his head gravely, Sigurd went.

Laying the woman's head upon the planking, gently, so as not to cause her further injury, Alarik stood watching him go, his hand reaching for his bone-handled dagger as he came to his feet. The wind battered his tunic as he held the hem within his fist, ready to slash it. He glared at Red-Hrolf as he rent a wide strip of his garment, baring his chest to the biting wind.

Red-Hrolf stood stubbornly, shaking his head frantically, torn between his fear of a watery grave and Alarik's wrath. "You'll kill us all!" he accused.

Hoping Alarik would change his mind, Sigurd halted abruptly, turning to hear Alarik's reply.

In the meantime Bjorn dared to speak his mind. As Alarik's brother, he maintained certain privileges others were deprived of—at least that much was granted him. "Alarik, mine brother, you are the only one who can guide us through this storm!"

Alarik stood silent, his legs braced apart, his eyes gleaming dangerously.

"Think on it, Alarik!" Bjorn's face screwed with disbelief. "You would kill us all over a worthless *Fransk* bitch?" Almost at once, he regretted his boldness. Noting the ire that danced like fiery daggers in Alarik's dark eyes, he shuddered, never having seen his brother so furious.

Clasping his dagger firmly, Alarik slashed another strip of material from his blood-smeared tunic, oblivious now to the numbing chill. He fixed a warning glare upon Sigurd. "Take that helm, Sigurd," he said coldly. "Now." While his warning seemed directed at Sigurd, it was in fact meant for his young brother, and he issued the last of it as he turned to Bjorn. "Or 'tis you I'll toss overboard and not the wench." He turned again to Red-Hrolf and added pointedly, his eyes burning with fury, "With a dagger in your belly, to boot! I'll not have my words questioned—not ever! Do y' heed?"

Knowing Alarik's words were not mere threats, Sigurd immediately took to the helm.

"And you, Bjorn," Alarik warned. "I shall take little more insolence from you—brother or *nei*! Now lower the cursed sails!"

At once, Bjorn leapt to do Alarik's bidding, knowing there was too little time to waste. In this Hel wind it would take very little to devastate the sail cloth.

"Leave the mast raised!" Alarik called after him. He would need it later to raise a shelter. Then too, as soon as the wind abated some he would again hoist the sail and use the drift anchor. Best to make use of it while they were able.

Once more, the Goldenhawk tilted violently. With hoarse shouts and curses, the men braced themselves against it, lest they tumble into the frothy ocean. Alarik stood his ground like an effigy from hell, not wholly real, but paralyzing in his towering might and intensity.

Satisfied that he would have no more resistance from his men, he gave his complete attention to the woman at his feet. Salt spray whipped his face as he knelt beside her once more, working furiously to halt the bleeding.

Chapter 9

"She'll bring unrest," Red-Hrolf said suddenly at Bjorn's back.

Bjorn didn't bother turning. "How so?"

"Because she is Christian," Red-Hrolf declared. "Why else?"

A prickling crept down Bjorn's spine at Red-Hrolf's proclamation. He paused at his task, turning abruptly.

Red Hrolf's expression was filled with scorn. "What else would a Frenchwoman be?"

Shuddering over the notion, Bjorn frowned, returning to the task of lowering the sails. He tugged violently at the lines. "And why should that concern me?" he asked. "You heard as well as I . . . she is mine brother's problem! Speak to him if you would!"

Red-Hrolf's eyes narrowed balefully. "Are you so blind, Bjorn? I say she is a threat to all."

"And I say she's nought but a puny wench!" Bjorn countered.

"You underestimate her!"

"I think not."

"Like a coiled up adder is a woman's bedtalk. If you allow it, she'll work her accursed faith upon you both! Destroy your alliance with the old gods! Mark my words, friend—else you will fall to its force . . . as has Olav . . . *as has Alarik*," he suggested.

Bjorn's face contorted with disgust, and he dismissed Red-Hrolf once and for all. "You lie!" he charged. "Mine brother has not claimed the White Christ! I would know. Never would he keep such a thing from me—nor I from him! No matter what else lies betwixt us, there has always been truth!"

Hrolf's face contorted. "Hah! Do you not see how he risks us to save her? Even so far as to endanger you, his brother! *Nei*, Bjorn, we all see what value he places upon your life."

At once, Bjorn's gaze was drawn to where Alarik knelt over the Frenchwoman. He stood watching a moment, doubts creeping in even against his will.

"*Ja!*" Red-Hrolf said darkly. "Watch them closely," he warned, and with that spun away, leaving Bjorn to mull over his counsel.

As the storm abated, frosty white flakes began fluttering down from the northern skies, sweeping their way into the icy blue sea. Despite the fact that the gale was brief it was fierce and Alarik estimated that it had borne them at least a full day closer to their destination. He'd been concerned for a time because the third and smallest *drakken* had vanished from view, but only moments ago it had been sighted ahead of them, its sails slightly tattered from the winds, but otherwise still intact.

A cool flake lit upon the bridge of his nose, dissipating almost at once. Considering the fact that the temperature had already dropped considerably, he made his way to where the small canvas shelter had been erected utilizing the mast, cursing himself for doing so yet again.

Nor could he discern why he'd spared the other wench's life when 'twas possible his men could have been right. She might, in truth, have carried the pestilence—something he could not have risked at sea. Yet he had.

All because the little *Fransk* had protected her so fiercely.

Why should he be so affected by that accusing glare of hers?

And why, by the thunder of Thor, should he care what she thought of him?

'Twas only meager consolation that the other wench was so much improved, for he had, in truth, risked more than he ought to have in letting her live. Alarik had no idea what malady had possessed her earlier, but she appeared to be recovering now, and Sigurd seemed to have taken to her, as well. The old warrior managed to play nursemaid to her when not otherwise occupied, and Alarik could well see why, for she was a comely little thing.

Reaching for the tent flap, he hesitated before lifting it, torn between his loyalty to his men and that which he'd sworn to the woman within. He should be aiding with the navigation, he knew, but he also knew he could not attend to his command without first seeing to the wench, and his scowl deepened.

What in damnation ailed him?

Surely he'd been bewitched!

With a disgusted shake of his head, he shoved aside the flap and stooped to enter the small cloth-enclosed chamber. Within he straightened to his full height and moved silently toward the figure slumbering so peacefully upon the pallet. At her side, he dropped to his knees, noting that the wet rag he'd left upon her forehead had fallen to the side of her face. Lifting it, he contemplated the milky paleness of her skin.

In the dim light her features were ethereal, the fine bones of her face set in the most perfect arrangement he'd ever beheld on a woman. And her skin . . . as pure and unblemished as freshly fallen winter snow. Nevertheless, 'twas her eyes that drew him most, held him inexplicably spellbound. They were a work of artistry, with the delicate line of her brows arching over bewitching violet irises. Though closed now, Alarik could still see their vivid violet color, startling in its clarity.

To him, she was more beautiful even than the imagined *Valkyrs* of his youth, though he was well aware that few others would share his opinion, for she was darker than the maids of his land.

Retrieving the skin of fresh water that lay discarded atop the coverlets, he uncapped it, dousing the rag once more. He'd watched her do the same for the other maid and had surmised she'd done so to deter the fever. He was well aware that fever induced madness, and wondered that it might have incited the other maid's fits. Recapping the skin, he tossed it carelessly aside, then refolded the dampened cloth, considering the woman lying before him.

She'd slept without waking in the hours since her injury, causing him to wonder. With his own eyes he'd witnessed such a state where the injured fell into the deepest slumber and remained therein for days, weeks, months even, ere waking.

Some were said never to revive at all.

Such was not the case with this one, he assured himself, his mouth curving into an unconscious smile, for the little wench babbled much in her sleep. Indeed, for the better part of her slumber it seemed she'd dwelled in a world of vivid fantasies.

On impulse he moved the coverlet down to view her body beneath.

In removing her wet kyrtle, an undertunic of fine embroidered linen had been revealed, affirming the fact that she was a woman of substance. Discarding the rag, he placed his hand at her ribs, ascertaining whether the garment had dried, and despite himself his body quickened at the feel of her warm, soft flesh beneath the filmy gown. Unable to recall when he'd been so affected by a wench, he shook his head in self-disgust.

His eyes were drawn upward, and he stared, transfixed, his heart hammering like mighty hoof-beats against his ribs. With all his might, he resisted the urge to slide his hand up to cup one luscious breast, squeeze it gently.

God . . . he craved it madly.

What was wrong with him that he was so aroused by an insensate woman?

Was he no better than Red-Hrolf?

Cursing himself, his hand drifted downward, away from that which tempted him so sorely, only to encounter something hard and round beneath her gown. Curious as to what it might be, he slipped his hand quickly within her neckline, his eyes closing with self-restraint as his fingers moved between her bare breasts, skimming her warm flesh.

Surely the Gods taunted him!

He drew from her undertunic a long leather string, and his brows lifted in surprise, for suspended from it was a gleaming silver ring, generously embedded with tiny jewels.

For the longest instant, Alarik merely stared, transfixed, studying the ring thoughtfully. If his memory served him—and it did—the design within the raised border was the same worn by the Frankish King.

Who, then, was this woman to be wearing such a ring as this? A thousand possibilities crossed his mind, none of them acceptable.

"By the jaws of Fenri!" he whispered, removing the ring from about her neck and weighing it speculatively within the palm of his hand. "Who are you, wench?" He caught it suddenly, closing his fist over its hardness, and then with a muttered curse drew it over his own head, dropping the ring beneath his tunic. Taking hold of the discarded rag once more, he raised the cloth to the woman's forehead, smoothing it over her brow. And despite the grim turn of his thoughts, the ache in his groin intensified as he slid the moist rag down her lovely throat . . . so white and soft.

Loki take her!

Was she mistress, or daughter?

He refused to consider that she might have been Phillipe's bride.

She *had* claimed he was not her count as of yet. Mayhap then, she was his betrothed?

He didn't bother trying to convince himself he'd taken her for revenge, for he knew it wasn't true— not when the merest thought of Phillipe touching her left acid burning in his mouth.

As an afterthought, he lifted one hand, inspecting it, noting the calluses that contradicted the noble breeding the rest of her proclaimed. Strange that a highborn woman should bear the hands of a laborer. He considered that an instant, and then released her hand abruptly, letting it drop at her side, lifting his fingers reverently to her lips—such a luscious pink they were, despite the fact that they had been chapped by the wind.

But it was her hair that was her crowning glory, the color of richest sable. This moment, it was spread like a crown of shining velvet about her face, with a wayward lock entwined about her slender neck. Moistened with water from the rag, it clung to her silky flesh like a jealous lover.

The comparison fully aroused him.

Determined now to view all he would lay claim to, he drew the blanket down to her ankles.

His eyes never made it beyond her breasts. Beneath the sheer undergarment her nipples were dark and lovely, hidden only by the gossamer linen, and he resisted the nigh irrepressible urge to touch them, telling himself that he was content to savor them with his eyes as they rose and fell with her gentle breath.

Later he would have his fill of her . . . later when she was healed and able to partake . . . later when he could take pleasure in the passion he knew he could arouse. In his arrogance, he never doubted that he could, but he knew he would need to leave her be for now. Unlike Red-Hrolf, he'd gain no pleasure from this manner of loving.

Flinging the coverlet over her, making certain those parts of her body that would tempt him were covered, he rose abruptly, considering what he would do about Red-Hrolf, for as certain as the wench had beguiled him, he also knew Red-Hrolf would cause dissension among his crew. He might have been distracted with the wench, but he'd not missed the confrontation Red-Hrolf had with Bjorn—nor had he missed Bjorn's agitated expression afterward.

It boded ill.

Raking his hand across his scalp, he moved toward the tent opening, peering out speculatively at his men. All was quiet for the moment, but another tempest was brewing.

He could feel it in his bones.

Chapter 10

Elienor first became aware of the bitter chill seeping through the blankets she wore, and immediately thereafter of the briny scent of the sea.

Where was she?

Such strange, strange dreams she'd had. Ships and warriors. A battle at sea—and that face—*his* face!

The floor beneath her swayed suddenly and she winced against the sharp pang that surged through her head at the unexpected motion. Struggling to sit upright, she brought her hand to her throbbing temple. It was then she saw him.

Everything came rushing back at once. Her voice faltered. "W . . . what have you done with Clarisse?"

He turned abruptly toward her, his brows rising, but if she thought she spied relief in his expression she was sorely mistaken. His lips twisted sardonically as his silver eyes narrowed and met her blue ones. "Last I looked, wench, you were in no position to command answers from me."

Elienor said nothing, only glared at him.

"I take it you recall?"

"Would that I did not!" Elienor exclaimed.

A lethal chill entered his silver-flecked eyes. "Nevertheless," he countered, and the depth of his tone sent shivers down her spine, "what is done, is done." His eyes were alight with challenge and mockery. "Were I you, I would worry now only with covering myself . . . lest it be your aim to tempt the *beast*."

Following his gaze to where the coverlet pooled at her lap, Elienor gasped, seizing it to her bosom, her face burning scarlet. "W . . . where . . . where are my clothes?" She drew her arms defensively within the blanket.

"Wet," he announced matter-of-factly. "I removed them, lest you catch the ague."

"A . . . and what of Clarisse?" Elienor persisted, her chin lifting slightly. When he didn't reply, only lifted a brow at her, she swallowed at the inevitable conclusion she drew. She closed her eyes briefly, resisting bitter tears. When she opened them again, it was to meet his penetrating gaze. God help her, but she had to know for certain. "So tell me, my lord *Viking*," she said trying to sound conversational, but failing miserably. "Did you relish watching her take her last watery breath?"

A muscle ticked at his jaw as he stooped to lift up the skin of water at her side and uncapped it. He drank from it slowly, as though he considered his answer, never taking his eyes from her.

Elienor bristled at his apathy.

Swiping the back of his hand across his lips, he asked, his brow lifting in challenge, "You would have had me instead expose my men to whatever malady she might have carried?"

Elienor's heart twisted violently at the affirmation. Her eyes squeezed shut as hot tears threatened to flow. "Jesu Christ!" she declared in an agonized whisper. "You *are* beasts!" She heard him stir toward her and she averted her face, crying out in fear that he might strike her for the insult she'd dared to fling yet again. But he didn't. There was only silence between them; a massive silence in which the creak of the mast and the drone of voices from beyond the tent opening screeched into her conscious. That and the sound of her heart pounding against her ribs.

"Scorn not what you do not understand," he replied with deceptive calm. " 'Tis the law of the sea, wench . . . survival of the fittest."

Elienor dared open her eyes to look at him. But it was her undoing, for the intensity of his gaze ensnared her.

" 'Tis the law of the land, as well," he disclosed in the same mesmerizing tone.

"To murder the blameless?" He expected her to simply accept such a thing? Not ever! "Not of my land!" Elienor returned miserably.

He lifted a brow. "*Nei?*"

" 'Tis not our way to kill innocents!" Elienor maintained, her eyes averting to the skin of water, and then returning.

"Mayhap," he conceded, his dark eyes growing darker, stealing her breath away.

'Twas ludicrous—inconceivable, even—but he would not release her gaze; 'twas as if he held it physically within his grasp and refused to yield it.

"Then, again . . . I was not born of your land," he disclosed, glancing down at the skin of water in his hand. He took another modest sip and then surprised Elienor by holding it out to her.

Elienor stared at the skin as though it were sin itself he were offering, wetting her lips and cursing her weakness, for as thirsty as she was, she could not even begin to refuse it.

He smiled suddenly, as though he'd read her mind, and thrust it closer. "You don't have to," he said huskily, his dark eyes sparkling with mirth at her expense.

Elienor blinked.

"Do you always speak your thoughts aloud?" he asked her, his brows lifting.

Elienor's color deepened—curse and rot her mouth! "So I've been told," she ceded grudgingly, removing the skin from his hands—enormous hands with long, graceful fingers, she couldn't help but note.

Tipping the flagon to her lips, she remembered the warmth of his touch on her face and sighed. And then she stiffened abruptly, catching his scent.

To her dismay, she found the scent of him lingered—she could swear she tasted him as well—yet 'twas absurd! Her brows drew together, and distressed by the discovery, she drew the skin away from her lips, as though singed, only to find that he watched her still, ruminating, something peculiar in his expression.

"The Northland is cruel to those not hale enough to endure it," he announced suddenly. "Those not up to the trial are best put to rest."

By his expression, Elienor thought he might be trying to justify his decision to murder Clarisse. Let him try—nought could justify it! she reflected bitterly.

As though to escape her accusing eyes, he rose abruptly, moving to peer out of the tarpaulin. There was silence a long moment, and then he countered, "Isn't it more heartless to let the weak live . . . only to see them die yet another day?"

"What say you?" Elienor glared at his back, horrified to remember against her will the firmness of his flesh beneath her palms as he'd carried her out from the *kirken*, and then again to the ship; the refined strength in his every movement, the ease of his stride as he'd walked. She swallowed convulsively.

"Only that I see it as an act of mercy, and not cruelty, to free the weak from misery," he said simply.

"Mercy?" Elienor repeated incredulously. "Mercy?" She shook her head. "How can you think so? 'Tis murder and nought less!"

He glanced over his shoulder at her, as though considering her reply. "Mayhap you think 'tis more merciful to let the sickly child live and thereby allow others to suffer for it? In the Northland food is scarce—oft times 'tis what drives men from their homes to seek another . . ." Again he turned to peer out from the tarpaulin. "And it is what," he said in self-derision, "leads men blindly into slaughter for the mere chance to hold a parcel of fertile land."

"You are right," Elienor said acerbically. "I *don't* understand! How can the one justify the other?"

"Just as surely as the healthy would be deprived of food in meager times, did the sickly child live," he explained without turning, "had the girl carried the pestilence, then all of my crew would have suffered for it." He peered over his shoulder at her, asking pointedly, "Should I have allowed the many to perish for a single wench who'd doubtless die on her own?"

It finally occurred to her what it was he was trying to say. "Do you tell me that you kill innocent babes? That a mother would allow it?" Her own mother had gladly forfeited her own life to save a child not of her blood!

He didn't bother to turn toward her. "As I said . . . scorn not what you cannot possibly understand."

She couldn't believe what he was telling her so dispassionately. No one could be so cruel! "Surely, only God has the right to decide such things!" Elienor exclaimed. When he didn't respond to her charge, her gaze swept the length of him, taking in his massive size once more. "How facile for one so fit to pass judgement on those less fortunate!" she said with anger and contempt. "I'm certain that *you*, my lord *Viking*, would have had nought to fear!"

He turned toward her suddenly, his lips curving, as though her proclamation amused him somehow, and in that moment, Elienor felt a great rush of contempt for him.

His eyes were dark and insolent. "You think not?"

Elienor averted her gaze, flushing clear to her toes.

"From here forth you will cease to refer to me as *my lord Viking*," he told her. "My given name is Alarik . . . it would please me should you use it in future."

Please him? She'd rather think of him as the demon he was! "I'd as soon join Clarisse!" she muttered bitterly.

"That too could be arranged."

Elienor's gaze flew to his, dizzying her with the quickness of the motion. He'd not dare!

His eyes gleaming, he chuckled deeply as he turned and moved toward her.

Jesu—he would. Her heart leapt.

He seemed to read her thoughts, for he halted abruptly at the terrorized look in her eyes.

"The truth is, wench," he told her, perturbed, "mine own father thought to put me out as a babe."

As shocked as Elienor was by the revelation, she tried not to show it. Her lips parted to speak, but nothing came.

" 'Tis true," he assured, his dark eyes sparkling.

Forsooth, and that should amuse him? Anger surged through her, but it was directed more at herself. Why should she have expected more from mere barbarians? Pain flared through her head and she cried out, her hand going to her temple.

He was beside her in mere seconds, stooping before her, his warm palm splayed across her own hand. She recoiled from him, but he held her fast, drawing her hand gently away in his own to peer beneath, and his voice was wrathful, yet oddly tender when he spoke again. "Hrolf Kaetilson will be punished for his savagery," he assured her.

Elienor peered up at him, trying to shake his hold from her hand. "You . . ." Her voice, skeptical, suddenly faltered. "You would condemn your own man for harming me?"

His silver eyes hardened, his long powerful fingers refused to relinquish their hold. "As I would any for defying me," he told her pointedly, squeezing her fingers lightly. Quivers swept down her spine at the gesture.

For defying him? And why else? Elienor asked herself scornfully, wrenching her hand free. "I see," she replied.

She was suddenly aware of his hands upon her arms, sliding up and pressing her backward upon the pallet. "Rest now," he commanded. "You must regain your strength." He pulled the coverlet high about her throat, and his fingers slid the length of her jaw, sending gooseflesh racing down her arms. "I shall bring you nourishment directly."

"I'm not hungry!" she answered petulantly, averting her eyes.

"Nevertheless," he countered, his voice as deep and unfathomable as the sea, "you'll eat what I bring."

Rising abruptly, he stood over her for an uncomfortable moment, looking down at her with ... with ... not concern; it couldn't be! And then he turned to leave. Yet he halted before ducking from the tent, glancing backward, as though suddenly reluctant to go. His eyes narrowed. "The boy ... he called you Elienor?"

Reminded of Stefan, Elienor once again fought the salty burn of tears in her eyes.

"Is that how you are known?"

Curse him, Elienor thought, for he had not even the decency to show compunction when speaking of Stefan! "Aye," she relented, a raw lump forming in her throat. A single tear slid down her cheek, but she swiped it away, vowing to shed no more. "I am known as Elienor," she told him, suddenly feeling so very fatigued, so defeated.

"Elienor," he whispered, as though savoring the sound of it. His eyes bore into her own. "It suits you well," he told her. "From whence do you hail, Elienor?"

Her eyes narrowed with anguish. Another tear slipped silently past her lashes. She blinked it away. "As if you did not know," she cried softly.

Something strange flickered in the gleaming silver depths of his eyes—regret? She didn't want his tenderness, nor his concern. She wanted only to loathe him!

"I mean before. Who was your fath ..."

Realizing what he wished to know, Elienor sought to deter him, uncertain how it would bode her if she revealed her relation to Robert of France. *"Baume-les-Nonnes,"* she supplied.

One brow shot up in surprise. *"Nonnes?* You came from a holy house?"

Elienor nodded, her eyes stinging with tears she refused to shed.

"But I thought you were to be wed to Count Phillipe?" His eyes were sharp, assessing.

"I was." Elienor flashed him a look of contempt. "Until you came!"

"Then you're not . . . ?"

Elienor shook her head in answer, and then shivered, for as she watched, the tiniest smile twisted his lips, spreading deep into his bladelike eyes. She vowed to say no more, not wanting to please him.

As if sensing her withdrawal, he nodded, evidently appeased for the time being, and ducked beneath the tent flap, disappearing into his own world.

God help her—she wanted no part of that world!

Her heart heavy with grief, she watched as the flap swung to and fro an instant, and then tugged the coverlet over her head to hide the tears she could no longer keep.

Chapter 11

Feeling wretched, but refusing to shed another tear, Elienor turned uncomfortably upon the pallet.

Had she truly thought she'd known confinement?

"Forsooth!" Her tiny call at *Baume-les-Nonnes* had never seemed so grand than at the moment. Still, as she had no wish to see any of her barbarian captors ever again—even to breathe fresh air—she remained within the confines of the tent. When they reached dry land would be soon enough to be amongst them. That she had to suffer Alarik, the demon—she couldn't say his name, even mentally, without adding the epithet—was torment enough!

He was the one who brought her food and water, and for the first two days had ministered to her head wound solicitously, yet she felt anything but grateful at the moment.

Some part of her, the part that felt the loss and guilt most keenly, wished only that he would let her die in peace. How could she bear to live with such beasts?

She could have borne it had she had someone to care for, to protect, someone who needed her. But there was no one now. Stefan and Clarisse were gone, and she'd never been more alone in her life, not even when she'd been abandoned to the priory!

Turning away from the tent opening and the starry darkness beyond it, she recalled what Alarik had said to her—that his own father had thought to put him out as a babe. She closed her eyes, and there the image plagued her. Desperately, she tried to free her mind, but 'twas no use.

Why couldn't she stop thinking of him so?

Why couldn't she simply go to sleep?

He was anything but vulnerable, she knew. So why was she foolish enough to see him otherwise?

Tugging the coverlet up, she buried her face in the abrasive wool and managed to coerce herself into a troubled slumber.

In her dream the rain pattered on her back.

"Whatever possessed you to come hither at such an ungodly hour, child?"

Hearing Heloise's voice, Elienor swung about, hurling herself into the old nun's welcoming arms.

"There, there. Sister Heloise will love you now, ma bonne petite. And together we will care for your maman's lily. Oui?"

Elienor nodded into the warmth of Heloise's wool clad shoulder. Scratchy as the fabric was, it felt good to her little cheeks. "Because Maman loves lilies . . . She loves them so much . . ." She sighed. Here she felt so safe . . . so sheltered . . .

Dreamily, she lifted her face, smiling, to gaze into . . .

His face!

And that look! So tender. Alarik was holding her, his arms strong, shielding her from the pattering rain.

She couldn't help herself. She let him, sagging against his coarse mail-clad chest, her arms going around him.

Safe . . . safe . . . yet how could it be so?

The sun was shining, sweet and warm on her face.

But something was wrong.

Something . . . though she knew not what . . .

It was much too bright suddenly, the sun glinting off silver helms and mail. All about her swords clashed with a mighty clang. But she could see no one!

Shields flashed.

Bringing her hand from around from his back . . . she discovered blood.

Betrayed? Had she betrayed him? But how?

How was it possible when she'd never given her loyalty to begin with.

It could not be.

All at once she was torn from Alarik—seized by a man without a face.

Elienor screamed . . .

"Shhhhh, little one," a husky voice whispered. "Shhhhhhh. 'Tis only a dream." A warm palm smoothed her damp hair away from her forehead.

Elienor's eyes flew wide, and her heart leapt into her throat. As her vision adjusted in the darkness, she found him hovering above her, his expression so . . . tender—that same expression she remembered from the church . . . and more recently from the dream. Her breath caught as his hands moved to her shoulders, stroking gently, the gesture oddly soothing yet disturbing in its intimacy.

"You?" she croaked. Reaching out, she seized his hand in a desperate attempt to stop his ministrations.

His hands stilled, but remained where he willed them "Aye," he whispered, his lips hovering so close to her face that she could feel the heat of his breath. "You were dreaming. Again," he added with quiet emphasis.

Again? Elienor's heart somersaulted. Acutely aware of his hands on her shoulders, as well as his lips so near her own, she licked her lips gone dry and swallowed. Each night since her injury she'd dreamed that same distressing dream.

Had he come to comfort her those times as well?

"Again?"

His fingers recommenced massaging her shoulder, undeterred by the nails she dug into the back of his hand.

"Again," he whispered, his warm breath caressing her lips.

A chill raced down Elienor's spine. She whimpered softly, recalling the last time a man, Count Phillipe, had lingered so close. The possibility that Alarik might kiss her made her heartbeat quicken and her breath catch in her throat.

What would she do?

Looking down into her frightened face, Alarik wanted to ask what made her cry out so desperately in her sleep each night, but was loath to hear that her nightmare was of him. For an instant, he tried to imagine how he would see himself through her eyes and cringed at the image. "You were weeping," he told her, his voice strange. "I heard and came."

" 'Twas nought," Elienor protested, her hand drawing his away from her shoulder. "As you said . . . nought but a foolish dream." Desperately, she needed distance between them. How could she think with him hovering so close?

"Aye," he replied huskily, releasing her abruptly. He surged to his feet. "You should go back to sleep." His breath sounded as labored as her own. " 'Tis early yet . . ."

Elienor's heart thrummed in the silence as he gazed down upon her.

Yet he didn't go.

He did not so much as move.

Nor did his expression shift.

The silence between them grew until Elienor thought she would shatter from the tension. Her mind searched desperately for something to say. "Why would your father do such a thing?" she asked impetuously, agitated as much by the way he watched her as with the silence. "To his own son?" She could understand how it could come to pass that a father might abandon his daughter to the clergy, for the sake of greed, because it had happened to her. But murder outright? "Why would any father think to cast aside an innocent babe?"

For an instant, Alarik could not fathom what she was speaking of. He'd altogether forgotten that first conversation. And then, remembering, he nodded, feeling for the first time in so many years those conflicting emotions he'd experienced the first time he'd asked that question himself. He turned from her momentarily, frowning as he went to the tent opening, lifting up the flap to peer out from the tarpaulin, into the quiet night. Only the creak of the wood, adjusting to the movement of the sea, and the snores of his crew broke the silence. "Because I was born too soon," he revealed after a moment of discomfiture. He turned to face her once more, the unwelcome emotions swiftly mastered, tucked away even from himself. "Born too soon," he reiterated without inflection, "and thus too small."

Elienor shook her head in horror. His face, lit only on one side by the night sky, appeared wholly sinister in the deep shadows of the tarpaulin, yet it was his lips that unnerved her. Even at this distance she could still feel their heat near her own lips. "What stopped him?" she wanted to know.

Something in her tone made Alarik flinch.

The last thing he'd intended was to stir her pity. He wanted no one's pity.

He straightened. There was nought to pity. "My mother's weeping," he disclosed matter-of-factly. " 'Tis the way it should have been," he added in a tense, clipped tone that forbade further questioning. The way she looked at him in that instant, full of compassion, set his teeth on edge. " 'Twas my father's given *right*!" he told her, his brows colliding when she continued to look his way in silence, her eyes scrutinizing him through the black shadows. "Damn you—I've no need of your pity, wench—save it for yourself! You seem to wallow in it more than enough!"

"I've not been wallowing in pity."

"*Nei?* Is that why you lie here, day in, day out, staring blindly and mutely at the ceiling?"

Elienor flashed him a look of contempt. "And what would you have me do instead?" she countered icily, her voice rising with her anger. "Rejoice over having been taken captive by a hoard of barbarians?"

Alarik felt a rush of satisfaction at hearing the bite in her tone. If she was angry, at least she was feeling. The more she'd retreated within herself, the more guilt had gnawed at his gut. Yet quick on the heels of his relief came an overwhelming rush of resentment, for once again he mocked himself; why should he care what came of the wench?

He glanced out from the tarpaulin, his scowl as dark as the night without. To his way of thought, no wench was worthy of more than a fleeting thought, and he didn't make it his practice to reflect on them much. Nor did he idle away his time with them, save to quench his body's cravings, and for that there was always a willing body. Aye, there had been a few who with their expert ways and comely faces had set his mind to reeling and his tongue ready to

recount any number of love words but only for the
time, because once his body was sated, cold reality
crept abed.

He'd never spoken the words. Never would.

All it ever took to set his mind straight was
to remember another woman who might have
destroyed so much in his life. Deceit and treachery
was the way with them all.

By damn! he cursed himself. He didn't care!

So why was it he came running to her side at
hearing her cries each night?

Moreover, why did he wait to hear them so that
he could come?

He did, Loki take him if he didn't! He shook his
head in self-disgust, maddened by his conflicting
emotions. Resisting the urge to rip down the tarpaulin where he stood, he turned to face her. "By
the jaws of Fenri, wench, I care not what you do!"
he exploded suddenly. "Go back to sleep—and next
time, be certain to smother your cries lest you rouse
my men! I won't bother to answer them—ungrateful, aggravating, *witch!*" Blaspheming himself next,
he thrust aside the tent flap and ducked out into
the night.

But Elienor heard only the *witch*. Her face paled.
Witch.

The sound of it kindled terror in her heart, as it
never failed to.

She dared not sleep again. Dared not dream.
Closing her eyes, she prayed for morning.

Chapter 12

Take care what you pray for, Elienor thought, recalling Sister Heloise's words of warning. To her dismay, the first bright rays of morning had come much too early, with no regard for her body's fatigue. Yet despite her weariness—or mayhap because of it—she felt restless. She sat abruptly, glaring at the tent opening. She hugged her knees, thinking that more likely 'twas *he* that made her feel so cross. How dare he accuse her of wallowing in self-pity! Especially when she had every cause to do so!

She shivered suddenly, rubbing her arms beneath the blanket, remembering against her will the incredible warmth of his lips.

Don't think of that, she scolded herself.

How could she have felt sympathy for the beast? Amazingly, she had—for the babe he'd been, and for his mother—and along with it, she'd experienced such an incredible urge to comfort—a ridiculous notion, for he'd seemed not at all affected by his declaration. His face had remained an impervious mask, and if anything he'd seemed vexed with her for questioning his murderous father.

Listening to the sounds of the crew rousing without, she wished them all to perdition, their arrogant leader most especially!

She stood, shaking off the blanket in the heat of her ire, and began to pace the confines of the narrow tent, stopping to listen to the ghoulish groans of the mast. She pounded the wooden pillar soundly with her fist, wanting it to cease once and for all.

She couldn't bear this much longer!

And she most certainly was not a witch!

What of the dream? a little voice appealed.

Elienor snorted inelegantly. "What dream?" she countered stubbornly.

Ah, Elienor, you forget so easily—any one of many— last night when he held you . . .

" 'Tis nought but coincidence," Elienor answered petulantly, refusing to acknowledge the other accusation—that she'd allowed him to hold her—regardless that it was merely a dream. "Mother Heloise said it was so!"

And you believe it still? Can you be so blind? Open your eyes at last, bien-aimée.

A shiver passed down her spine. "*Beloved*?" Something about the way the endearment came to her, the way it sounded so clearly in her head, suddenly discomfited her. It brought back memories of her mother's soft gentle voice. She swallowed, glancing about warily. "Mother?"

I have been with you always, bien-aimée. You must heed the warnings.

Elienor's heart raced and a chill passed through her, sending gooseflesh racing down her arms. "Mother!" She whirled suddenly, searching for the face that went with the imagined voice, and shook her head in negation.

Heed them, Elienor.

Again she spun about, facing the rear of the tent, seeing nothing still. Sweet Jesu! Surely not? Surely 'twas only her imagination. 'Twas true that she oft talked to herself—but never like this! "I'm mad!" she exclaimed a little hysterically. Eyeing the blanket she'd discarded upon the pallet, she felt acutely the crispness of the air. Jesu, she'd freeze to death, and 'twas all *his* fault! "Truly, I am mad!" she exclaimed again. Jesu, but it was cold! She started for the blanket suddenly, intending to wrap it about her shoulders. "Mad, mad, mad!"

"I'm inclined to agree."

Elienor practically leapt out of her stockinged feet. She spun about to face the tent opening where Alarik, the demon, stood watching her, his arms crossed, his lips twisted with ill-concealed amusement.

"Don't feel obliged," she replied testily, irritated by the mockery in his tone.

A grin suddenly overtook his features . . . those sensuous lips twisting devilishly. "Who can argue with truth?" he answered arrogantly, his eyes sparkling with rare humor. "Without question, you're unusual, Elienor of *Baume-les-Nonnes*."

Elienor shot him a look of contempt, forcing her gaze from his lips.

Unusual? Precisely *what* was he implying? Unusual, indeed! Nevertheless, she dared not ask, lest he accuse her of witchery again. "Beg pardon if I offend thee, *my lord Viking!*"

"Alarik."

Elienor's eyes narrowed belligerently. "Pardon again! Alarik, the *demon!*" she countered, daring to use her own epithet for him. And emboldened by his silence, she dared even further. "Mighty Norseman, slayer of innocents!"

He stiffened as though she'd physically struck him.

Her voice rose in renewed anger over Clarisse's senseless death. "Alarik, the executioner!"

"Enough!" Alarik snarled at last, his eyes warning her. "Lest you wish to join your friend."

Elienor snorted to cover her moment of fear. "You would!" she plunged on carelessly. Let him do what he wished to her! She refused to forget her pride ever again.

A muscle ticked at his jaw. "Aye, wench, I would . . . never doubt it!" His eyes glittered dangerously.

Yet he did nothing of the sort, Elienor noted. He simply stood glaring at her.

Tossing her head back, she eyed him with cold triumph, daring to challenge him with every fiber of her being. Only the longer he stood, the darker his look became, and the more ominous he seemed, and Elienor began to truly doubt her sanity.

What was wrong with her that she would goad him so?

He said absolutely nothing, merely stood there, his eyes glittering with barely restrained fury, and then he flung her dry kyrtle at her.

Elienor gasped as the garment cuffed her in the face. She fumbled for it, missed it, and then fumbled for it again as it fluttered to the planking. She stared down at it numbly, glancing up in astonishment.

He was gone.

That was it?

She'd pushed and pushed, yet that was all he would do in retaliation? She felt giddy with relief. For a befuddled instant, she stood there gazing down at her saltwater-stained garment, illuminated suddenly by a dazzling shaft of sunlight,

and wondered in horror how she could have forgotten what she was wearing—or rather what she
was not! At once, she fell to her knees, seizing up
her bliaut, her face burning crimson with shame,
and then again glanced at the tent opening.

Sunlight burst onto her face, and she shielded
her eyes, amazed at how much light he kept from
the tarpaulin when he stood in the doorway. With
his departure the shelter was again awash with
light.

Which led her to wonder just how she'd not
sensed him standing there.

Worse, how long had he stood there before
making his presence known?

"The cur!" she muttered, and promptly drew the
ruined gown over her head, smoothing it over her
undertunic.

The man was impossibly arrogant!

Still she couldn't believe he'd done nought more
than swat her with her gown.

Leaving her so she could dress, Alarik vowed to
stay clear of her—vicious wench that she was! So
much for attempting civility. Had he felt bad about
the way he'd spoken to her last night?

No more!

From here on, Sigurd was perfectly capable
of carrying her meals to her—otherwise she could
spend her days in solitude, or content herself with
her biting tongue for company!

Nevertheless, as the day wore on, Alarik couldn't
quite remove from his memory the caged look she'd
had on her face as she'd paced the confines of
the tent. Nor could he erase the image of her
standing there in dishabille, ripe and luscious,
and very likely untouched for all that she'd

disclosed. And Loki take him if that possibility didn't make him burn for her all the hotter.

'Twas unlikely Phillipe would have forced himself upon her with her pious upbringing and her connections—whatever they were—to Robert of Francia.

Yet another thing that bedeviled him.

Leaning back against the prow, he eyed the tent restlessly, shaking his head in disbelief. The stupid wench didn't even have the good sense to stay covered beneath the blanket he'd given her. Anyone could have walked in and spied her standing as she was!

What galled him most, however, was that she still blamed him for Clarisse's death. Mayhap it wouldn't so much if, in truth, he'd tossed the baseborn wench overboard, but he hadn't—though he damned well should have!—and what provoked him most was that the *Fransk* she wolf didn't even realize the truth.

And he couldn't tell her.

Nei, he amended, he wasn't about to tell her.

Let the witch believe what she would of him!

"Have you told her yet that her friend lives?" Sigurd inquired from the helm, as if he'd read Alarik's thoughts.

Alarik gave his old friend a scowl for his prying. His brow rose slightly, yet he made no reply beyond that imputing gesture.

"You could send Clarisse in to keep her company," Sigurd suggested cannily.

"Clarisse?" Alarik asked with lifted brows.

Sigurd ignored the taunt. "Mayhap if you told her . . . she wouldn't feel so confined . . . and her tongue wouldn't be quite so sharp."

"You overstep your bounds, Sigurd," Alarik reminded him.

"Couldn't help but overhear," Sigurd said, defending himself. At Alarik's black look, he shrugged in mock resignation, and returned his attention to the steering of the vessel.

The hush that followed mocked him.

"She has two legs of her own!" Alarik barked. "If she ever bothers to come out, then she'll know. Otherwise she can assume whatever she pleases!" His attention was again drawn to the tarpaulin.

He couldn't make out her silhouette at the moment. 'Twas only at night, highlighted by the light within, that her lithe figure behind the canvas taunted him. And not solely him, he knew, for he'd not missed the looks his men cast her way.

Damn the wench, for within the tent, she had no notion what spell she'd cast over him!

He didn't give a rat's piss that she felt confined. She was his prisoner, after all. In truth, he didn't much care if she starved herself to death either— stubborn, venomous wench!

Truthfully, it'd save him the trouble of strangling her.

Chapter 13

So why was it that he abandoned his duties yet again to serve her like a common slave?

Stooping as he entered the tent, Alarik moved swiftly toward her, heedlessly tossing at her side the wooden platter he'd brought. It settled upon the planking with a hollow clatter. "I don't give a whit if you're not hungry," he snarled at her. "You'll eat regardless—and smile as you swallow!"

Elienor blinked at his ruthless tone, so at odds with his actions. He didn't care . . . yet he brought her food? Some of her outrage dissipated, leaving only confusion in its wake, along with a lingering dose of chagrin for the way that he'd found her this morn. Her eyes dropped to the platter. At the sight of it, her stomach grumbled.

"Don't bother denying it, wench!" He sat back upon the enormous rounded block that supported the mast. "Even your body defies you!" He grinned suddenly. "Forsooth! your belly rumbles louder than Thor's hammer in all its fury."

Elienor glanced up at him through her lashes, her eyes narrowing.

A faint light twinkled in the depths of his eyes as he raised one brow in challenge.

Jesu, he was jesting with her. *What ailed him?* Wrenching her gaze away, she returned her attention to the platter.

He chuckled abruptly, the sound deep and warm. "Not a thing ails me, wench!"

Startled, Elienor's gaze flew to his, and to her dismay she could feel her cheeks heating. She glowered at him for his quip and averted her gaze, grateful that his smile faded, for the sight of it seemed to incite her heart to insurrection. Frowning, she glanced down at the platter, noting the assortment of cheeses and bread; she was grateful for the lack of pungent dried salmon he'd brought every other meal. To her chagrin, her mouth began to water at the sweet odors that wafted to her nostrils. She sat upright, trying to appear indifferent, yet failing miserably. Her stomach grumbled once more, and she cursed it, along with her pounding heart.

He slid down the block to sit upon the planking before her, and her heart turned over violently. Hardly able to understand what his presence aroused within her, Elienor tried her best to ignore him.

"Why is it that you don't realize when you're talking to yourself?" he asked with genuine interest.

Elienor looked at him, shrugging. "How should I know?"

"Has it always been so?"

"As long as I can remember," she relented, trying to still the erratic beating of her heart. Again she cursed her tongue. How many times had she been reprimanded at the cloister? Too many to recount—and always at the hour of prayer. "Mother Heloise said that it was because I have a restless mind." Feeling more agitated by the instant, she tried to discern the demon's purpose in speaking so civilly to her, but could perceive no reason for it.

Surely, there was something he wanted of her?

He nodded, apparently satisfied with her explanation, and reached for a slice of soft white cheese, surprising her by bringing it to her lips.

Elienor's brows lifted. "You would feed me?" she asked, resisting the urge to snatch it whole into her mouth—and bite off his fingers in the process!

Alarik's brow rose at her question. Retrieving the cheese, he tore off a modest bite for himself, popping it in his mouth. "Unless, of course, you're not hungry?" he told her.

Elienor was, but she wasn't about to beg for her supper! Let him eat it all if he would. She watched him chew covertly, fascinated by the strength in his jaw . . . his lips . . . the way they appeared . . . so soft . . . and yet so hard. Her fingers went to her own lips, her brows drawing together, and then catching herself, she startled.

Forsooth, what did he want of her? That she would forget all that had passed between them in the space of an afternoon? Hardly possible.

Seeing her chin jut forward stubbornly, Alarik decided to cease with the jesting lest she starve over her stubbornness—he had not missed the confusion in her face when she'd watched him eat. The way she'd touched her own lips as she'd contemplated his sent talons of desire clawing through him. He held the cheese out once more. "A peace offering," he suggested.

"Peace?" Elienor retorted. "Betwixt us?" Just to make certain there was no confusion as to whom she meant, she gestured between the two of them, her expression clearly disbelieving.

"Aye. I would say 'twas in your best interest," he apprised her, his voice velvet edged.

"Mine?" Doubtless he spoke true, yet that he would concern himself with her best interest was

inconceivable. "Since when do you trouble yourself with such things, my lord?"

My lord. Not *my lord Viking*? Alarik grinned, feeling a small victory at the concession.

His pewter-gray eyes seemed to penetrate her very soul, probing. A quiver swept down Elienor's spine, but she managed an indifferent shrug. Yet she was anything but unaffected. He had a way of looking at her that disconcerted at best.

He offered the cheese again.

"Mayhap," she ceded. "Still . . . I did not realize 'twas how it was done." She eyed the morsel malevolently.

His gaze dropped from her eyes to her shoulders, to the cheese . . . or at least Elienor assumed it was the cheese. Something about the hunger in his eyes seemed more than just a bit carnal.

"How what was done?"

The depth of his tone sent a quiver down her spine. She crossed her arms, rubbing them as though to erase the gooseflesh that prickled her. Her lashes lowered. "The feeding of captives, of course."

"I see . . . and you have been a captive before, perchance, and know the way of it?" His tone mocked her.

"Nay!" Arrogant cur. " 'Tis only . . ." She flashed him a glare, thoroughly disturbed by the incongruity of his words and actions—that they should be sitting here speaking so casually was unimaginable, yet here they were, and it disconcerted her beyond reason. "What does it matter what I thought!" she retorted. "You're surely the authority, having had so many prisoners!" Sensing that her stomach was about to betray her again, she indignantly swiped the cheese from his fingers and fought the urge to shove the tiny mutilated bite into her mouth.

"The truth is, Elienor, that usually I keep no thralls."

"Thralls?" Involuntarily her eyes returned to his lips. As she stared something fluttered deep within the pit of her belly.

His eyes glittered with amusement. "Slaves."

"I see," Elienor said stiffly, her gaze affixed to his face as she nibbled from the cheese in her hand. "So then, what, pray tell, am I?"

Alarik's half-grin faded, for he found himself suddenly at a loss. What was she, indeed? In truth, he rarely took prisoners. Every last one of the steading's servants were freed men, hired for pay. And while slavery was indeed the way for many Norsemen, Alarik had chosen not to employ it. Mayhap it was the circumstances of his birth that kept him from it, for he wanted no bastard children born under him, despite the fact that there was no shame to be had in bastardy. Not when one was accepted by his father.

And he was.

Barely.

No matter.

He was.

He simply had no taste for begetting bastard children who felt less than whole . . . and fancied they had something to prove to the world.

So, then, what the devil *was* the wench to be, if not his slave? His brow rose as he considered her question . . . and then he happened to recall the ring, and his gaze fell to the creamy expanse of her neck. "I believe a more poignant question remains to be asked, wench. What were you to Count Phillipe? Better yet, what were you to Robert of Francia?" he asked, letting her know with certainty that

whatever her title was up to now . . . it was no
more.

Elienor nearly choked on the cheese. Her eyes
widened, her hand flying to her breast. Sweet Jesu!
How could she not have noticed it missing? She
flashed Alarik a look of alarm, but he said nought.
His glittering eyes merely bore into her with silent
expectation.

What did he know?

Provoked by her silence, Alarik gripped her
suddenly by the wrist, jerking her toward him in
warning.

Elienor's breath caught. Panicked by the look in
his eyes, she tried to free her arm, but he only
smiled ruefully. His other hand went to her temple, to her wound, caressing it ever so gently, yet
somehow never touching at all. She tried to look
away, but he yanked her toward him once more,
bringing her so close that she could feel the heat
emanating from his body.

Mistaking the look in her eyes, and the way she
studiously avoided his gaze, Alarik's silver eyes
glittered coldly. "Am I so repulsive to you, Elienor
of *Baume-les-Nonnes,* that you would fly from my
touch? Does my Viking face repulse you even now,
after I've cared for you? Fed you? Protected you,
even? Can you not cease to judge me for who you
think I am—the heartless barbarian Norseman—
and see me differently? In truth, I am not so gentle
as some, but neither am I cruel, I think. Forsooth! I
am but a man," he finished angrily. "I'd not have
you look at me as though I were a fire-breathing
serpent."

Elienor's face paled. She managed to shake her
head. Nay, if the truth be known, she was not
repulsed by him just now, but by herself, and her

body's odd response to his touch—to his very presence.

She thought she might die if he didn't release her at once.

"I'll not harm you, wench," he told her hotly. "You need not shun my touch again."

"Nay?"

The blue flecks in his eyes deepened and his voice was softer, huskier when he next spoke. "I grant you my word that I shall take nought from you that 'tis not freely given."

Her chin lifted. "Which is it, my lord?" she dared to challenge, a note of hysteria in her words, "that you shall deeply enjoy the *taking*? or that you'll take nought unless given freely?"

Her question struck Alarik much as if she'd cracked her palm against his face. She dared to throw his own words back at him? For the longest instant, he was stunned enough to say nothing. "My word!" he declared. "But take care that you do not offend me further," he warned, his eyes narrowing. "You'd do well to remember that 'tis I alone that stand betwixt you and my men. Understand my meaning?" He squeezed her wrist lightly, though not enough to cause pain, his brows lifting in question. When Elienor nodded, he released her at last.

Yet he held her eyes fast.

Ensnared by his gaze, Elienor rubbed her wrist absently.

From beyond the tent came a sudden roar of merriment, diverting their attention.

The sound of it sent a familiar thrill of excitement rushing through Alarik's veins. Instinctively, he understood that the Goldenhawk had finally reached the Gareinger Fjord.

Home.

Chapter 14

When he looked at her, Elienor's face was full of dread.

It was clear she understood the joyous shouts as well, nevertheless, Alarik had no desire to reassure her just now—not with the havoc her beautiful face played upon his mind—not when she looked upon him as though he were some mad beast from the wilds. Never mind that she had a right to fear him. 'Twas true that her life had been nought but chaos since he'd entered it, but it had been his duty to avenge his men.

His duty!

She seemed to realize suddenly that even after he'd released her, she'd remained within a hair's breadth of him, for her eyes widened, and she gasped, thrusting herself backward. Her reaction to him clenched his gut. Avoiding her gaze as he stood, Alarik left without another word. He stepped outside into the bright sunlight, wondering what it was about her bewitching eyes that made him lose all sense and reason.

Had he proposed peace betwixt them? When she obviously preferred his head on a platter instead? What ailed him, indeed!

As the Goldenhawk glided over the sun-brightened waters, light as a gull, the crew shouted hoarse cheers to the two smaller *drakken* sailing in its wake.

Not a single man aboard the three sister ships could suppress their exhilaration over the sight before them. Alarik's mood lightened considerably.

The home soil rose white and proud on either side of the wide, ice-scattered fjord, reaching magnificently into the clouded blue heavens. The drizzle was heavier now, the crisp air smelling of freshly fallen snow. With much pleasure, Alarik took the fresh, cold air into his lungs until they stung from the chill. The scene before him never ceased to overwhelm him, to fill him with satisfaction. There were times the Northland's harsh winters left him aching for the sun and sea, but inasmuch as this was so, it was also true that an interval at sea filled his heart with a fierce longing for the rugged fjord that harbored his home.

His home.

His.

All his life he'd endeavored to prove himself—first to his father, then to his people, and finally to himself. He'd sweat blood, pure and bright, for his right to hold this land. It was his now—all of it—stark as it was in winter, meager as it was in spring—as far as the eye could behold. He'd earned every last grain of soil.

Like a mother that snuggles a hungry babe to her bosom, so did the twin knolls on the horizon give refuge to his steading. As he watched, the end of a snow-peppered dock appeared, and as the Goldenhawk rounded the bend in the fjord, the wooden structure grew in clarity before his eyes, as if stretching in welcome. With a father's pride, Alarik stood, relishing the sight.

No doubt, the red diamond sails of the Goldenhawk had been spied the very moment they'd entered the mouth of the fjord. Long before the first *drakken* glided into dock, the pier was teeming with gleeful kinsmen.

Feeling much as she imagined a caged animal would feel, Elienor paced the confines of the tent, wondering how long it would be before *he* came for her. And though she couldn't possibly have waited longer than fifteen minutes, when Alarik appeared in the doorway, darkening the tent interior with his presence, she was so anxious that she shrieked in startle.

"Gather your belongings. We've arrived."

Elienor bristled at his choice of words. "Pray, do you mean all my many coffers, *my lord Viking*?" she said with a slight smile of defiance.

Alarik frowned at her.

"But there are so many!" she continued flippantly, lifting her chin, meeting his icy gaze straight on. "My, but 'twould take hours to pack them all!"

Without warning, Alarik stalked forward, seizing her by the hand and hauling her out of the tent after him.

Dread shot through her suddenly at the reality of this new world she was entering, so different from her own. The drastic change in weather, the uncanny chill of the air alone was staggering. Nevertheless, she concealed her fear valiantly behind bold words. "Then shall I simply go with the dress on my back?" she asked sarcastically, wincing at the brightness of the sunlight. "Tell me, will we send for the coffers later?"

He said nought, merely tugged at her arm, and she glared at his back. Jesu, but it was cold! All about her there were people, embracing, laughing, joking. How could they? Elienor bristled. Certainly there was nothing joyous about this day!

Alarik stopped and turned, and Elienor gasped as she collided with his leather-clad chest. He'd been about to speak out, but halted abruptly at her cry of pain. And again, that look as he gazed down at her. She couldn't bear to suffer his scrutiny, or his concern! His hand went to her healing scar. "I'm fine!" Elienor snapped, shrinking away from his touch.

His hand froze between them, and at once his look transformed to that of sobering rage. He jerked his gaze away, and without a word to her, immediately began to bellow out orders to his men for the unloading of the three vessels. And then, hauling her after him once more, he led her off the ship and up a narrow pathway that led up the cliff side.

Beneath Elienor's leather shoes, a thin layer of snow sloshed, evidence of the rush of feet that had trod up and down the pathway to the docks this morn. Obviously someone loved these men well, though she couldn't imagine who, or *why*. That they would have families who cared for them was inconceivable.

Halfway up the cliff side, her heart full of misery, Elienor cast a glance over her shoulder at the despised dragon ships that had brought her to this godforsaken place. And to her shock, she spied Clarisse being led onto the docking by the Nude one.

"You lied to me!" Elienor exclaimed at Alarik's back. When he didn't respond to her accusation, she tugged wrathfully upon his arm. "Clarisse lives!"

"So she does," he replied dispassionately.

Again Elienor tugged at his arm, this time with more force. "But you said . . ."

"I said nought," he snapped, glancing backward at her, his eyes dark and smoldering. He tugged her forward. " 'Twas you who said, wench. I simply didn't bother to correct you!" He kept walking, virtually dragging her after him.

"How could you deliberately have misled me?" Elienor exclaimed. She stumbled over her feet, unable to keep pace with his greater stride. "Stop! Stop! Let me speak to her, for the love of God!"

He stopped abruptly, and once again Elienor collided with him. Only this time, she dared not cry out, for the malevolence in his expression when she looked up at him was startling in its intensity. "Misled you?" he asked, his voice low and silky. He shook his head slowly. "*Nei*, Elienor of *Baume-les-Nonnes*, for you were bound and determined to believe the worst of me! I simply chose not to disappoint!"

Elienor blinked, uncertain of what to say in her defense, for in this he spoke truth. She *had* suspected the worst of him. And yet how could she not have?

He turned sharply and continued up the path, again hauling her after him.

"My lord, a word please!"

Startled by the voice so near, Elienor gasped and turned to face the bearer of it—and found herself reeling yet again at the sight that encountered her unbelieving eyes. Struggling not to trip over her blundering feet, she watched in shock as the man passed her by.

A monk? Here?

But nay, it could not be!

Shaking her head in mute disbelief, she once again took in everything, from his frock, tied with braided rope, to his tonsured head.

Elienor's mouth opened to speak, though she was unable to find her voice. And still Alarik would not stop. Curse him! Instead, he seemed to walk all the faster, jerking her after him, as though he did not wish her to acknowledge the monk at all. For his part, the monk seemed as surprised by the sight of Elienor as she was of him, for he stared in return as he attempted to catch up with Alarik. He gave up abruptly, falling back to walk beside Elienor, his chest heaving with exertion.

"Jesu!" Elienor exclaimed at last, trying desperately to keep pace with Alarik and failing miserably. "You *are* a monk!"

"Aye!" Alarik exploded, jerking to a halt. "Loki take you both, for the man is as much a thorn in my side as you are, wench!" Alarik turned and eyed the monk furiously. "What is it, Vernay?"

Vernay prudently ignored Alarik's accusation. Bowing his head slightly to Elienor, he added, "I am Brother Vernay, my la—"

"By God!" Alarik exploded. "Odin's cursed me!"

"My lord!" Vernay reproached, turning to wag a finger at Alarik, the sight so ludicrous—Vernay as small as he was, and Alarik as tall as he was—that Elienor's brows furrowed with incredulity. "You should not speaketh the name of God in the same breath with the other!"

A muscle ticked in Alarik's jaw. "So you've said afore, holy man! I weary of this and have much to do. Best you speak whilst you have my attention, or lose the occasion until it suits me."

At that, Vernay immediately tore his gaze away from Elienor and turned to Alarik. "Aye, m'lord! As to that matter—"

"Alarik!" another voice shouted, a feminine voice this time. Elienor glanced upward in time to catch Alarik rolling his eyes, and then she heard Brother Vernay's answering groan. Scanning the path ahead, Elienor spied the cause: A figure descended toward them, a woman, with her long, golden hair plaited thickly and resting seductively over her left shoulder.

"That, m'lord," Vernay interjected quietly, "is the matter I wished to address."

"Nissa?" Alarik asked, his brows rising.

Brother Vernay nodded, grimacing.

The woman smiled and held her arms outstretched as she came into Alarik's reach. "Finally, you are home!" she declared in a French that was heavy with Norse inflections. Evidently she spoke it for Vernay's sake, for she eyed the monk sharply, yet Elienor found herself grateful that she'd spoken French, for she could hardly have borne the uncertainty of not knowing of what they spoke.

"I have worried so!" Nissa chided sweetly. She halted abruptly as she spied Elienor standing behind Alarik, her ice-blue eyes centering at once upon the hand he held locked within his fist. Her brow furrowed softly. "Of course . . . 'tis a woman's lot to wait and worry, is it not?" She gestured at Elienor. "And who . . ."

"Someone I'll wish for you to tend," Alarik broke in. He drew Elienor forward to stand between them. "I'd have you go and make ready for her in my chamber," he directed.

Elienor's dark lashes flew wide. "Nay!" she shrieked, and tried to shake her wrist free.

"In your chamber!" Nissa cried.

Elienor's gaze flew first to Nissa's; the woman's expression mirrored Elienor's horror. And then twisting free of Alarik's death grip, she whirled to face him.

"In my chamber," Alarik repeated, ignoring Elienor and looking past her at Nissa. "And I'd have you bring her something to sup on, for I'll not be dining in the *eldhus* tonight. I've much I would see to first."

Nissa shook her head, unquestionably flustered by his request. "B . . . but . . ."

"As I will it," Alarik countered, his tone unyielding.

Nissa recovered herself at once, yet Elienor didn't miss the gleam of repressed tears in her eyes as she straightened her spine. "As you will it," Nissa said softly. She averted her gaze. "Sleipnir awaits you at the summit, my lord," she disclosed in a choked voice. "I . . . I . . . I shall walk back."

Alarik nodded in appreciation. "Ride with Bjorn," he advised. He glanced at Vernay. "And you I shall speak to anon!"

Vernay nodded. "Aye, m'lord." He glanced circumspectly at Nissa.

And then Alarik was urging Elienor up the incline once more. She stumbled but acquiesced, knowing she had very little choice in the matter. Vernay followed silently. Yet Nissa didn't stir, and as Elienor glanced backward at the woman, she couldn't help but feel wretched for her. It was clear that Nissa was either mistress or wife—in either case, little esteemed and little loved.

She glanced impulsively up at Alarik, and was shocked to find herself conceding that he was a striking man, in profile even more so. Yet if he thought he would take her virtue without a battle, he was sorely mistaken! "Put me in your chamber as you may—alas I've no choice in the matter—but rest assured nought else will come easily," she swore vehemently.

He glanced down at her, his eyes cold. "I made you a vow, wench. You go to my chamber for your own protection," he told her.

"Protection?" Elienor asked incredulously, yet deep down she knew it was so. Still she could not bear to concede him even that. "Protection from whom?" she asked bitterly.

The beast, of course! she answered silently.

Beast? a little voice countered. Would a beast have spared Clarisse against the wishes of his own men?

Resolutely, Elienor thrust aside the ludicrous question. He was a beast! she asserted, and she'd be best served never to forget!

"Care to extend me the same welcome you planned for my brother, Nissa?"

Nissa was so lost in her thoughts that she didn't see or hear Bjorn approach. She started at his husky whisper in her ear then shrugged out from under the hand he placed upon her shoulder. "Hardly!" she said petulantly.

Both watched as Alarik and his prisoner reached the summit; he placed her at once upon his horse, Sleipnir, and then hauled himself into the saddle behind her.

"I wonder if you wouldn't happen to have my horse saddled and waiting, as well?" he asked her.

At Bjorn's question, Nissa's humor was restored. "I wonder," she replied lightly, her smile returning.

Bjorn grinned, though as he turned to see Alarik and the Frenchwoman disappear from view, he shook his head in disgust. "You should have seen them aboard ship," he told her.

"Oh?" Nissa cocked her head inquiringly.

"He risked us all for that shrew!" Again he shook his head. Red-Hrolf's words had implanted the seed of doubt within his heart, but it was Alarik's inconceivable need to protect her that had nurtured those seeds to root. He still could not credit the change that had come over his brother in such short time.

Nissa's blue eyes narrowed cannily. "How so?"

"It matters not," Bjorn snapped. "All you need know is that he did. At any rate, there is no loss to you, my love, for I've told you before that he has no interest in you, at all."

Nissa snorted, her brow rising slightly. "I believe I'd take offense . . . yet I know what lies beneath your words . . ." She eyed Bjorn astutely, her smile widening. "You would still have me in your bed, Bjorn, Erik's son," she purred. "Would you not?"

Bjorn smiled at her usual frankness. "How canny of you, my love."

She laughed abruptly, trying to sound indifferent. "Well, I'm loathe to disappoint you, but my father would not receive you well at all." She moved closer, whispering into his ear. "Though truth to tell," she relented with a sigh, "were my heart not already given . . . mayhap, then . . ." She shook her head regretfully. "Still, as comely as you are, 'tis the position of Alarik's wife I crave, and none else. My father wishes it so . . ."

"Your father need not agree to your choice of husband," Bjorn reminded her.

"Oh! but my father is not a man to thwart," she countered. "Is he? Besides," she added, laughing as Bjorn's mouth opened yet again to contest her, "you forget that Alarik is the one I desire as well! After all, he is master of his own." She poked at his chest in sport. "And you, Bjorn, cannot claim such an honor, can you?"

Bjorn's eyes narrowed as he returned the playful poke to her breast. "I wonder if you shall open your eyes someday?" he said, his wistful smile reaching into his eyes.

"Doubtless not," Nissa retorted, her hand going to her breast. She narrowed her eyes in censure. "Pardon, now, whilst I go and do *my love's* bidding," she purred, and then turned her gaze up the cliff side, in the direction Alarik had ridden. "I believe I shall have the servants prepare him a grande fare to tempt his palate tomorrow eve. That should indubitably please him. Likely, he's had nought more than scraps for meals aboard that beloved ship of his." She turned to Bjorn, fluttering her lashes coyly. "What do you think?"

Again Bjorn sighed, deeply. "An arrow never lodges in stone," he replied, wisely. "And it oft recoils upon the sender."

Nissa wrinkled her nose at his truthful remark.

"You don't listen, Nissa," he explained. "And you strive for nought. Alarik has never been interested."

Nissa paid him little mind. Bjorn doubted she'd even heard him for she turned, not bothering to acknowledge his counsel, and made her way up the cliff. He watched her go, unable to keep the bitterness from creeping into his heart. Was he always destined to have his brother's leavings?

And in this case, he wouldn't even get that.

Chapter 15

Alarik's bedchamber was crude at best, no more than a large square room with no windows and thus no natural light. Skins were draped everywhere, doubtless to keep what little warmth there was from escaping. Additionally, in the center of the chamber was a small, rectangular, stone-rimmed hearth, where dying embers flickered in defiance of the dark, casting eerie shadows on the walls. Smoke escaped through a small opening in the ceiling above.

After bringing her here, Alarik had abandoned her forthwith, without so much as the courtesy of a single parting explanation—not that Elienor would have cared to share words with the man! She wished she'd never need speak to him again, though 'twas doubtful she'd be so fortunate. It wasn't likely he'd take her back to Francia in the near future—and curse him if he didn't speak the truth. He *was* her only protection against these barbarians.

Shivering at the notion, her gaze settled once again upon the bed—an immense oaken piece, intricately carved with birds of prey—hawks, she thought, though they were much too embellished in form for her to be certain. At the sight of it, she began to pace anew, refusing to consider whether she'd occupy that monstrous berth herself come nightfall.

At that, she glanced about uneasily, wondering if night had yet fallen. With no windows to peer from, it was impossible to judge time, yet there was nought to be gained in fretting over it, and so she dismissed the bed from her thoughts, once and for all. Running her fingers across the rich grain of the oaken walls, she considered that they were natural-colored instead of whitewashed, to which she was accustomed. Wherever there were no skins draped, there were horrifying weapons suspended from pegs, weapons of every ilk: axes, swords, spears. At the sight of them, Elienor couldn't help but shudder—such a passion for violence, these Northmen possessed! Little could she comprehend why. What glory could be had in such a warring life, and death?

Her gaze was drawn across the room, to the coffer of wood that had been carried in earlier by servants. Atop it lay a coat of mail, the same Alarik had worn that first night, she surmised. The links glimmered like brilliant diamonds in the light of the dying fire. And above it, dangling by a peg, hung a rounded shield, painted blood red with a gilded hawk soaring in the middle.

Mesmerized, Elienor stared at the hawk . . . trying to recall what it was about the shield that was so eerily familiar. Had he carried it that first night? Likely so . . . yet it was something else that plagued her . . .

Something from her dream? But what? Sweet Jesu, what could it be? Rubbing her arms for warmth, she shook her head, thrusting her musings away. She couldn't remember, and in truth, didn't want to!

At once, her eyes reverted to the thick oaken door. Tempting as it was, she'd already tried it and found it locked. Yet surely there'd been no need to lock her within. Alas, where would she have gone?

"Home," she murmured wistfully, her eyes burning suddenly.

Mother Heloise would surely have heard by now and would be wringing her poor hands raw with worry. But what of Count Phillipe? Her uncle? Had they forgotten her already? Elienor felt like weeping, for 'twas likely so. Never had anyone exacted judgment upon the Northmen with any measure of success. 'Twas one of the reasons they were so dreaded, for oft there was no worthy recourse to be taken against them. They came swiftly to wreak their brand of terror, and disappeared more swiftly yet, into the unknown. Only this time, Elienor had vanished along with them.

Would anybody care?

"Nay," Elienor whispered softly, achingly. Nobody but Mother Heloise had truly ever cared, she thought mournfully. Hugging herself, her gaze fell to the floor, her eyes stinging. God aid her, but she was unable to stifle the tears that trickled past her lashes. Yet she refused to cry aloud, refused to let *them* hear defeat!

She refused to be defeated!

Her burning eyes reverted to the bed, and she vowed again to fight him to the death if need be! Yet, as fatigued as she was, she refused to cower from it just now. Throwing herself upon it, she buried her face into the mattress to stifle her tears.

She fell asleep fretting over what the Viking would do if he caught her in his bed.

He understood now what it was that Brother Vernay had been trying to tell him. It seemed that from the moment Alarik had walked out of his chamber, he'd been assaulted with a bevy of complaints, requests, and accounts—nearly all concerning Nissa. He shook his head at the thought of speaking with her, for of everyone, she was the one person he never looked forward to seeing.

Ejnar's daughter was a bother at the least, with her ceaseless questions and meaningless banter, and a detriment at worst, for Alarik knew very well the risk he took in permitting her to remain when he had no intention of ever accepting her to wife. But it seemed that every time he'd attempted to inform her father of that fact, Ejnar the Dane found a way to make him reconsider his eldest daughter. And reconsider Alarik had, more times than he cared to count; yet no matter that he did, he still could not stomach the thought of her in his bed—not that she wasn't comely. In truth, she was exceptionally fair to the eyes, but that alone did nought to recommend her, for Nissa was also a terrible shrew who had no qualms over using the artifice of tears when her tongue did not gain her what she wished.

Abruptly, a vision of Elienor as she'd appeared within the chapel came to him. The little vixen had stood proudly while he'd appraised her, with no trace of tears. In comparison, how many times had he cursed Nissa for hers? More times than he could count. And how many tears had he seen her shed over petty things?

Yet Elienor had given him none of the expected.

Nei, Nissa had used every artifice available to her for far too long. His lips screwed with disgust. What age was the shrew now? Twenty? Far too old to be holed up in his home, yet he'd be damned if he could find a single man to take her off his hands. He sighed wearily, raking his hand through his hair as he entered his hall and made his way past the high seat to his chamber.

He was grateful, at least, that until he found someone willing to wed the shrew, she was able to earn her keep by caring for his household. Nevertheless, he'd be damned before he gave the woman control over his house! He'd need to speak to her as soon as possible, for he wasn't about to allow her to continue ordering about free men and women. His people knew their duties well enough, and he'd given her no leave to discipline them, nor to reassign them!

He unlocked the door impatiently and entered his chamber, noting at once that it was dim and growing cold. The fire had evidently long since died, and he frowned, for he'd not meant to leave her so long. His eyes scanned the room and found her at once, nestled within his bed, her tiny form enshrouded by the bulky furs.

Moving silently, so as not to disturb her, he went to the hearth, stirring the embers, but the effort proved fruitless. The fire was cold. From a pile of timber stacked in the corner he chose new wood, placing it within the hearth, and having done that he left the bower momentarily to retrieve a torch from one of the wall braces on the facing wall.

Using the torch to ignite the wood, Alarik waited to be sure the orange-blue flames climbed and licked a path into the new wood. Once he was satisfied the fire would thrive, he returned the torch to its brace and then closed the door behind him as he entered, going to the bed. He stood over her, watching her sleep. She seemed so serene, yet he could still see evidence of her tears. His hand went to her cheek, cupping it delicately. She stirred slightly and the gesture became a caress.

She moaned softly and his body responded with a vengeance, yet he forbade himself even the thought of waking her.

He'd sworn to protect her, had vowed to take nought she'd not freely give . . .

Nevertheless, he'd said nothing about lying down beside her, and that he would not deny himself, for he determined that one day soon, vow or no vow, she'd welcome his loathsome Viking touch.

Again the dream.

Again the same; first Mother Heloise held her in the safety of her arms, then Alarik, so tenderly, gazing down upon her with those steel-gray eyes—confusing eyes, for the emotion nestled within their murky depths was unnamed—like no other her own eyes had e'er beheld.

Then abruptly, the unnamed emotion was fled, and so were the gray eyes. Now they were violet as her own, and sorrowful. There was no face to frame the eyes, still Elienor recognized her mother in them. "What?" she asked desperately, for the eyes seemed to be warning her. But of what?

Again, she withdrew her hand from about Alarik and once again discovered blood.

Betrayed.

The shield . . . she saw it again so clearly, the bright sun striking against the majestic gilded hawk . . . and there was Alarik at the helm of his longship, no longer at her side. Defiantly, he cried out and leapt into the sea. Elienor watched in horror as his shield followed him beneath the surface. With morbid fascination, she watched as the hawk's wings spiraled beneath the waves and then disappeared completely. She glanced at her hand—the blood remained.

All about her were shouts and threats and ships jarring together, hundreds of them. Steel against steel.

Yet in that moment, all sound seemed to pass away, for suddenly Elienor understood.

'Twas war they were at . . .

And Alarik would die.

Chapter 16

"**B**y the hounds—!"

Alarik bolted upright at the scream.

His mind sleep-fogged, it took him a befuddled instant to realize it came from Elienor, another to discern that she slept on, her rest fitful, yet unbroken still.

His heart still hammering, he settled back down, incredulous that she could slumber through such a shriek—regardless that 'twas her own. Hella's curse, it had been shrill enough to wake the dead.

Raking his fingers across his scalp, he wondered with a weary sigh what demons tormented her so ruthlessly that she failed to sleep peacefully even through one night. And in the quiet of the moment, as he considered that question and listened to the sounds of her stirring beside him, he became fiercely aware of his nudity . . . as never before.

Never had it given him such gratification.

Never had the bedsheets seemed so cool.

His skin so hot, despite the chill.

A vow so despised.

She whimpered and his arms reacted of their own will, drawing her into his embrace, soothing her with a hand at her shoulder, the small of her back, caressing her. It was a mistake he realized far too late, for his hand was suddenly upon her thigh where her chemise had ridden up, her skin silky smooth beneath his fingers. His pulse quickened as his fingers caressed her ever so delicately, relishing the feel of her flesh.

Soft . . .

His heart felt as though it would erupt from his chest it thrummed so savagely. Slowly, languorously, his hand slid upward, between them, across her abdomen, his fingers sensuously spanning her belly before moving down to skim over her woman's mound.

Of their own will, his fingers gathered up her gown, until he could feel at long last the soft curls of her womanhood beneath his knuckles.

Was he mad?

Aye, he was—and lost as well! With no will, at all.

He was weak, and worse . . .

He was a liar.

He tried to convince himself he had to cease his foraging, forcing himself to recall his vow. Yet in utter defiance that self-same hand slid to her luscious bottom. He groaned with pleasure at the sensation of her filling his rugged palm. Groaning, he drove her hips forward to crush against his groin, his eyes closing in pleasure, his head thrust backward with carnal relish. Spurred onward by a heady, sleep-induced drunkenness, he found himself undulating softly into the sweet warmth between her thighs.

Elienor felt as though she were wavering between darkness and light, alternately descending through the deep blackness, only to ascend and grasp for the golden stream of light that teased her senses. She tried to lift her heavy lids, failing miserably, and moaned with pleasure, her mind engulfed by a velvety haze.

Somehow, Alarik had returned from the murky depths of the ocean, somehow, he was holding her, cherishing her as she'd never been cherished before . . .

But wasn't it just a dream?

His mouth hovered above her own, ready to kiss her as Count Phillipe had, only she'd felt nothing with Count Phillipe—not like this.

Desperately, she concentrated on those movements beside her that seemed so earthy and tangible and sighed deep in her sleep.

If this was a dream, she never wanted to waken. Never had she known such pleasure! She didn't attempt to deny herself, for it wasn't real.

'Twas nought but a dream . . . a hazy . . . pleasant . . . Dream.

Alarik's hands worked quickly to lift her gown, revealing the dark tips of her breasts against luminous white flesh in the flickering light of the chamber. Reflexively, his lips moved toward them, seeking out their heat, desperate to suckle like a babe of her milky softness.

Feeling himself harden fully, he rolled her backward, and followed, his knee settling between the softness of her legs as his lips suckled her. There he hovered, fighting a fierce battle against his will. Yet even as he vied for control, the hand that had grasped her bottom moved upward to the small of her back, holding her still for his lip's devotion. Feeling the nipple harden upon the tip of his tongue, he groaned and brought it fully within the heat of his mouth.

And in that moment he dared to imagine the woman in his arms awake and aware, eager to let him spend his passion deep within her.

He dared to persuade himself it was so.

Almost feverishly, his lips moved to her neck, nibbling the flesh there as he kneaded one breast with his free hand. He wanted to devour her.

God—was he daft to be loving an insensate woman?

Ah, but what a beautiful one she was.

For the briefest instant he thought he felt her undulate along with him and it gave him the most incredible burst of euphoria.

He thought he would explode in that moment, yet still he burned.

Intensely.

He eased himself down upon her, half-mad with need, beads of perspiration dotting his brow as he worked himself into a gentle but unstoppable rhythm.

Did he truly care that she was unaware of his loving?

Did he care?

She felt so good, and he needed release so badly—it had been too long . . . too long . . .

He muttered unwittingly in answer, for he knew that in truth, it did matter. He could not continue in this without Elienor's awareness at least . . .

Else he was no better than Red-Hrolf.

And that sobering realization discouraged him enough that he shoved away from the woman beneath him and turned onto his back.

By damn, it did matter.

And he didn't like it one whit!

What ailed him anyway?

Sensing that morning was near enough, he heaved himself up from the bed, dressed in the dim light, and stalked from his chamber, delivering himself from the temptation once and for all!

* * *

Stretching beneath the blankets, Elienor wondered dazedly of Clarisse. How did she fare? She wondered if she would have the opportunity to speak with her today, and then suddenly . . . she recalled the dream—all of it, and her face burned crimson with shame.

Sweet Jesu, she'd dreamed of *him* in the most shameful manner! And now in the light of day she could not bear to recall it. She glanced about the chamber suddenly and found it brightly lit, and then spied the reason why and came fully awake, but too late to avoid it. Elienor gasped as frigid water struck her full in the face, cutting off her breath.

"Lazy thrall!" Nissa hissed. "Here we cannot afford to lie abed all day!"

Sputtering, Elienor opened her eyes to find Nissa poised above her, an empty ewer within her clutches, her gaze accusing. She pitched the ewer vehemently, barely missing Elienor's face and striking the wall behind her.

"I said get up! Do you think to lie about like the French whore you are? I vow you will earn your keep if I have to have you beaten!"

Elienor's heart tumbled. From Nissa's expression she could very well believe the woman would do just as she claimed. She scrambled from the furs, trying to comply as quickly as she was able. No sooner had her feet lit upon the wooden floor than Nissa seized her by the arm, jerking her forward.

"Go, bitch!"

Elienor tugged her arm from Nissa's grip. "You need not abuse me!" she muttered. Nissa eyed her balefully but said nothing, and Elienor began walking in the direction indicated, grateful that she was dressed, at least, for the contemptible woman had

not even given her the opportunity to straighten
the wrinkles from her gown—not that it mattered
how she appeared to these barbarians. She cared
not what they thought of her!

Nor did she care how Alarik saw her.

Liar! a little voice mocked.

They found the great hall deserted.

As in the bedchamber, a stone-lined fire pit sat
in the center of the hall where smoke billowed and
curled in an attempt to escape through a narrow
shaft in the wooden ceiling. Flanking the pit were
tremendous wooden tables, lined with benches
that were carved with small heathen figures. At
the furthest end of the chamber sat the dais, with
its great high seat. She imagined Alarik there, and
paled when she saw for the briefest instant . . . the
image of herself sitting there beside him.

Nissa didn't linger in the hall. She hurried
through, booting a runty pup from under foot.
It wailed pitifully and scurried beneath a table
with its tail tucked between its legs, its eyes sad
and somehow looking as desperate as Elienor felt.
Resisting the urge to stop and soothe it, Elienor
wondered at Nissa's skittishness, for if Elienor
didn't know better, it seemed Nissa was glancing
about as though afraid to be caught.

The kitchens, Elienor found, were located in
a separate building, not unlike the kitchens at
Brouillard—likely in safety against fire. Also like
the kitchen at Brouillard, it was crowded and
overheated. At the largest table Nissa released
her, shoving her forward.

"You will work here today," Nissa informed her
curtly, lifting up a large kitchen blade and burying it into an unplucked hen. Elienor swallowed,

stepping away. Her eyes must have betrayed her apprehension, for Nissa smiled thinly. After a lengthy moment, she gestured toward the table. "I told you. Here everyone must earn their keep! You will pluck hens, and if you manage to finish—"she sneered as though she doubted the possibility— "then you will go to Alva. She will know where to send you next." She gestured toward a plump, dark-haired, older woman, who wore the strangest expression as she glanced in Elienor's direction. "Do you understand?"

Elienor nodded, her gaze reverting to Alva. The older woman shook her head at them, made a face, and sighed.

"Good," Nissa said, and satisfied that Elienor would comply with her wishes, she left to supervise other duties. Elienor felt only relief watching her go. At once she set about the task assigned to her, lifting up the hen.

"She's a haughty one, indeed!" a voice declared. Elienor glanced up to see the one called Alva ambling to her side. "Thank goodness the jarl has returned!" Alva exclaimed. "Surely, he will return the shrew swiftly to her place."

Elienor couldn't help but flash a smile at that very accurate description of Nissa. "Set her in her place?" she ventured. "Who is she, then . . . if not his wife?" She ignored the tiny jolt in her breast as she asked the question. She knew better than to be so intrusive, yet if this was to be her home, she would know her situation.

It had absolutely nought to do with her curiosity over whether the jarl had a wife.

She didn't care.

Liar!

Besides, she doubted Nissa was his wife . . . unless here men and women didn't share the marriage bed.

"She's Ejnar the Dane's daughter," Alva revealed, peering up at the door where Nissa had departed. "Her father has long sought a union betwixt the jarl and his daughter, yet the jarl has never shown the least interest in her. Still, her father is a powerful man and 'tis best not to make discord with Nissa."

Elienor glanced at the door as well. "She's not his mistress, then?"

"Humph!" Alva exclaimed, gratefully overlooking the unseemliness of the question. "Not his mistress, nor his bedmate—though certainly not for her lack of trying! The woman's as ceaseless as the sea! Still," Alva relented, "one must grant her allowances, for I believe she's not so bad deep down. Mind you, you wouldn't know it to speak with her, yet I fear she is as vulnerable as you are, my dear."

As vulnerable as she? Snatched from her home—forced to share a bed with a man not her husband. Unlikely! "How so?"

Alva shook her head a little sadly. "She seeks so desperately to please her father—and to no avail. The man is cruel!"

"Why do you tell me this?" Elienor asked.

The woman glanced at her slyly, and said cryptically, "The jarl has never brought a woman home before."

"I'm his captive, and nothing more!"

The woman raised her brows, nodding. "Of course you are, my dear." She chuckled, glancing down abruptly at the chicken upon the table. "Here," she said, seizing the hen from Elienor to demonstrate what to do with it. "I would venture to say you've never done such a chore as this before. 'Tis really not so difficult—"

"But I have," Elienor broke in. The woman looked at her a little skeptically. "It has been a time," she ceded. "Still, I remember only too well how 'tis done."

Alva raised both brows. She drew Elienor's hands into her own, turning them for her appraisal. "I see," she said approvingly, "well, then, 'tis best to busy yourself. Until the jarl can speak to Ejnar's daughter, she will make your life miserable lest you comply with her wishes!"

Elienor glanced at the door and was momentarily surprised to see Clarisse being led in by Nissa. Nissa pointed the girl in Alva's direction, and then watched to be certain Clarisse obeyed. In that instant, Elienor met Nissa's gaze. At once she looked away, unwilling to provoke the woman further. 'Twas obvious Nissa liked her not at all. "How is it that Nissa has the right to remain unwed in Alarik's household?" Elienor asked Alva.

"Alarik?" Alva smiled knowingly at the way Elienor addressed him. "Nissa abides with her eldest sister who is wed to Ivar Longbeard, one of the jarl's men," she explained, when Elienor's brows drew together. "She came here to Gryting years ago to help with her sister's birthing, and stayed—to everyone's dismay!"

"A . . . Alva?" a soft voice inquired.

Elienor set the hen she was working on down upon the table and glanced up at Clarisse, heartened to see that the girl was truly well.

" 'Tis I!" Alva exclaimed merrily, "I, and none other!" She turned toward a white-faced Clarisse. "You are to work with me, I presume?"

"Aye, madame," Clarisse replied quietly, her gaze shifting uneasily between Alva and Elienor. "M'lady!" Clarisse cried out suddenly, her face screwing pitifully as her eyes pleaded with Elienor to understand. "Verily, I am sorry to have caused you so much ill!" She hung her head in shame. "I'm sorry!"

Elienor resisted the inclination to embrace the girl, for she knew Clarisse would feel ill at ease to accept it. Alva watched them. "Oh, nay, Clarisse! I'm pleased that—" She glanced at Alva.

Alva nodded that they continue. "Don't mind me!" she said cheerfully, yet she kept her gaze locked on them, willing to miss nothing of their conversation.

Annoyed at the prospect that her life might never again be her own, Elienor's gaze reverted to Clarisse. Unable to keep herself from it, she placed a consoling hand upon the maid's forearm. "Truly, I'm only pleased that you're well. I worried so!"

Clarisse's face lifted, her expression remorseful. "I'm sorry, m'lady! I awoke to find you ensconced within the tent, and I wanted so desperately to go to you, but Sigurd would not allow it."

"Sigurd?" Alva clucked, her brows rising higher. "Truly this discourse grows more interesting by the instant—yet," she advised in a high whisper, "if you value yourselves you will work all the while you gossip." She gestured toward Nissa, who was watching them intently. "Snatch yourself a hen! Clarisse, you say?" Clarisse nodded quickly, fearing she'd overstepped herself. "Come, come— don't just stand there, my dear. Choose yourself a hen and set yourself to work!" Alva offered a smile. "Go on!" she prompted.

"Aye, madame!" Clarisse exclaimed, and complied at once. "Verily, I'm sorry!"

"Humph! You are much too sorry!" Alva clucked reprovingly. She glanced sidelong at Nissa. "Yet won't we all be," she said with a sigh, "if we do not busy ourselves at once. Come, come now! Work—work—both of you!"

Chapter 17

If Elienor had thought the kitchen simply warm when she'd first set foot within, she was sorely mistaken. Hades couldn't be so torrid! Wet strands of hair clung to her face and nape as she worked. She brushed them aside, smearing her face with the chicken grime from her fingertips. Blinking to give her eyes respite from the heat, she glanced longingly at the walls, unable to believe there were no windows at all. Simple vented openings in the ceiling sucked up what smoke would be freed, and in this building, unlike the other, the walls were made of stone, trapping every last bit of heat.

The only wood to be found were the work tables, and those were set as far from the ovens as possible in precaution of fire. Yet despite the distance, Elienor felt utterly consumed by the intense heat. Hours later she felt near to swooning from the stress of it, yet she dared not rest under Nissa's watchful eye.

She glanced at Clarisse and heaved a weary sigh. She'd spoken only sparingly to the girl, despite the fact that Alva seemed not to mind, and in truth seemed to encourage it. As Elienor watched, the older woman meandered from table to table, supervising, giving guidance, and laughing merrily with the women while they worked. From the way they all looked after her when she departed their table for another, 'twas obvious they regarded

155

her highly, unlike the abhorring glances they sent Nissa's way.

Yet, if Alva seemed overly friendly, no one else ventured near them. They proffered glances now and again, some amicable, others not; still Elienor made an effort to befriend them all from afar— if not for her own sake, then for Clarisse's, for 'twas evident Clarisse would not smooth the way for herself.

At any rate, Elienor had long since decided that she'd be best served to concede to her circumstances, for despicable as it was, this was now her new home, much as she resented it, much as she wished it elsewise. Aside from that, 'twas best she showed a good example for Clarisse. Lamenting their circumstances at this point could do nought to ease either of their lots.

'Twas only in the one matter Elienor swore she would never yield—despite her traitorous mind and body. Sweet Jesu, how dare she dream of him so shamefully!

And how dare she contemplate his kiss! If possible, her face burned hotter at the recollection of her dream. Against her will, she compared Count Phillipe's clumsy attempts, the way his tongue had nearly gagged her. He had disgusted her—her husband to be!—yet in her dream, she had dared to crave her enemy's lips!

Her enemy.

Bones of the saints! What was wrong with her?

" 'Tis but natural, m'lady," Clarisse ventured. "You should not blame yourself for being attracted to the jarl."

Startled, Elienor glanced up at Clarisse. Again she cursed her tongue, and shook her head. "I . . .

I don't know what you mean," Elienor replied, her face coloring traitorously. She glanced down at her hen, working zealously to remove the feathers.

"He's a fine looking man," Clarisse stated matter-of-factly. " 'Tis the truth that I berated myself, too . . . at first . . ."

Elienor's eyes widened as she met Clarisse's gaze. "You don't mean . . ."

"Sigurd," Clarisse replied, without regret, nodding timidly. "He cares for me well, m'lady—in truth, better then I was treated at Brouillard. Verily, I am sorry for you . . . but for me . . ." Her eyes pleaded for understanding. "I can feel nought but glad they came."

Elienor knew not what to say in response. How could Clarisse so easily forget? She sighed as her thoughts turned to Mother Heloise. Likely only the gentle Abbess would continue to fret, for the old woman had been the closest thing to a family to which Elienor could lay claim. Heloise had taken her under the folds of her habit the instant Elienor had arrived at the priory . . . at little more than four summers . . . after her mother's death.

Elienor closed her eyes with pain over the memory of her mother's execution and burial, and inadvertently, her fingers went to the place where the ring had lain against her breast. She wanted it back so desperately, but was afraid to bring it up to Alarik lest he ask its origin. She sighed, feeling an incredible emptiness over its loss, and made the mistake of glancing at Nissa in that instant. The animosity in the woman's eyes snatched Elienor's breath away. She reverted her gaze at once to the bald hen in her hand, not wishing to provoke the woman any more than she seemed to have done already.

"She does not like you much, I think," Clarisse gambled.

'Twas more than obvious, Elienor thought as she plucked the final feathers, and she cursed Alarik yet again, for her fingers were growing rawer by the instant.

Alarik stood in the doorway of the *eldhus*, one hand braced above him on the door frame, as he tempered his anger. He'd left the steading early to seek out Ejnar the Dane, only the harder he'd ridden, the more fiercely thoughts of the little *Fransk* had nipped at his heels. As it was, he'd failed to locate Ejnar, but was more resolved than ever to rid himself of Nissa—especially now that he could see to what extent she was willing to go.

She dared to counter his command that Elienor be left in solitude?

After finding Elienor missing from his chamber, he'd searched everywhere only to find her here, under Nissa's watchful eye. The hair at the back of his nape prickled in anger as he stepped into the kitchen and made his way toward Elienor, giving Nissa a look of warning as he passed her.

"Who has set you to work here?"

Startled, Elienor glanced up to see Alarik advancing upon her, his gait menacing. She bit her lip nervously as she glanced about and found everyone staring. What? What had she done now? She set the hen upon the table and took a step backward in defense.

"Who?" Alarik demanded once more.

He wore a black kyrtle and leather-skinned breeches that hugged his legs indecently. Even his boots left nought to the imagination, for they were made of the softest leather and were nought more than laces that bound his well-muscled calves. Elienor could not help but stare. "N . . . Nissa," she answered, unsure whether it was the right thing to say.

Nissa had followed Alarik and now halted behind him, watching.

Alarik turned to her, somehow sensing she was there. "*You* have put her to work here?"

"*Ya,*" Nissa admitted, backing away warily. "I did wrong?"

"Who gave you the order to do so?"

"Why . . . why, n . . . no one," she stammered.

"From here on," he informed her, "you will give no orders at all, Nissa. In fact, you will gather your belongings. As soon as I may speak with your sire, you will leave Gryting once and for all!"

"Why? What have I done?"

The instant fear in Nissa's expression gave him pause. "You've overstepped yourself," he said somewhat less harshly, though still unyielding. "You've gone too far, Nissa," he told her. "Aside from that . . . 'tis time you made yourself a home . . ."

"But—"

"Elsewhere," he told her firmly, his eyes spearing her.

Nissa shook her head, her hand flying to her mouth. The color draining from her face and her eyes burning with shame, she turned, but not before giving one last hateful look at Elienor. Without another word she fled the kitchen.

Elienor's gaze reverted to Alarik. She was wide-eyed with fear, for if he could banish one of his own, what would he do to her? She still had no notion what she might have done for him to look so wrathful.

"Come," Alarik demanded of her, his gaze fore-boding, and without another word, he led Elienor out from the kitchens and across to the great hall, now filled with boisterous men at drink and sport.

The moment they entered the hall, Elienor's eyes focused upon his chamber door, behind the dais. Every step brought her closer, and with every step her heart felt as though it would fail.

What could she have done?

She could think of nought.

From somewhere within the hall came a pup's wail. Elienor's eyes scanned the proximity at once, searching for the whimpering animal. She found it caught by the hind legs like a rabbit after the hunt, hanging from a strong pair of arms. Her gaze flew from the man's arms to the man's face, and to her dismay she recognized him straightway—Flame Hair. Her breath quickened painfully, her heart twisting with terror.

Sweet Jesu, how could she have managed to for-get him?

His coarse red hair was a fright, one side of it standing upright while the other laid reluctantly flat. His tunic was stained with foodstuffs and his breeches rode up one leg, caught near to the knee by untidy cross leggings. The other pant leg was laced neatly down in perfect order. He'd merely been sporting with the mongrel previously, but he smiled cruelly when Elienor met his gaze and crushed the small pup's legs within his fist. Elienor cringed, for his meaning was clear. He would have preferred those legs to have been hers!

Suddenly the hand upon her shoulder tightened. She'd not even realized it was there, but she looked up and was startled to see the fury that danced in Alarik's eyes as he gazed down at her.

"Red-Hrolf!" Alarik snarled, his gaze returning to the flame-haired man. The hall fell immediately silent. Drinking horns settled onto the tables. Some arrested in midair.

Alarik had not missed the warning meant for Elienor, and intended to put an end to this situation once and for all. "Come forward!" he commanded.

After a long awkward moment, Red-Hrolf sauntered toward them, staggering every few feet. He stopped at one of the lower tables, seizing a man's drinking horn, gulping from it deeply before slamming it down. That done, he again made his way toward them, leering at Elienor.

"You dare to defy me yet again?"

There was no response from Red-Hrolf save to turn his head disrespectfully and spit the ale he'd retained within his cheeks upon the floor at Alarik's feet. Beads of ale caught in his beard and dripped slowly through the coarse strands, alighting in tiny droplets upon the tip of one boot. His eyes narrowed wrathfully as they returned to meet Alarik's. "I've been awaiting this moment," he admitted finally. "I dare!"

Alarik's eyes narrowed ominously, furious that Red-Hrolf would dare force his tolerance beyond the threshold, cursing the fact that he would now lose a good warrior because of it. Red-Hrolf knew very well that he could not deliver such challenge without requital. It was a point of pride to a Viking man to be led only by the strong. As jarl, he could not afford to lose the respect of his men. He'd not planned to match with Red-Hrolf, but Red-Hrolf had set the method of his punishment with his open challenge and Alarik was determined to carry it out.

He nodded, and from his war belt he released *Dragvendil*. The metallic hiss as it cleared his scabbard seemed a death knell in the silence of the hall. He stretched the shimmering tip of the fine Frankish blade close to the rising knob in Red-Hrolf's throat as he whispered in low tones, "Because I fear the drink may have addled your brain, I grant you one last occasion to ask my pardon."

Red-Hrolf raised a mocking brow, emboldened by the pardon Alarik offered. "Ho, now!" he taunted. "Does my mighty jarl quiver like the feeble maid at his side at the thought of matching blades with Red-Hrolf?"

Alarik glanced briefly at Elienor, who though not cowering, was indeed wide-eyed with fear, and then turned to lower the tip of his longsword from Red-Hrolf's throat to his distended chest, forcing it to penetrate the fine wool tunic until it pricked blood. His eyes smoldering with fury, he turned once more to Elienor. "Get you to my chamber," he said slowly, softly, his eyes gleaming with warning. "Now!" he asserted, when she did not move quickly enough to suit him. And then he turned abruptly to Red-Hrolf and declared, "By your words, then, so be it, Red-Hrolf! You would do well to prepare yourself for *Valholl!*"

From the corner of his eye, Alarik saw Elienor back away from them, slowly at first, her expression that of horror and disgust; then she turned, and he was keenly aware of her feet racing across the *skali*. His chamber door opened and shut, the unspoken flag for the battle to be joined.

He gave not a whit that she thought him barbaric!

She simply did not understand the precarious hold a jarl had upon his people. There were many who were fiercely loyal to him, but there were always a few who would test the boundaries, who craved the high seat. Alarik had striven too long and hard to gain it—never would he yield it!

Hrolf's gaze returned to Alarik's and he backed away cautiously. As he retreated, he drew his weapon of choice, his trusty axe, and swung it menacingly, snickering.

"If you were sober," Alarik vowed. "I would cut the heart from your treasonous body, here and now."

Red-Hrolf's eyes glazed with drunken malice. "*Ja*? Well, I'm sober enough, let us all see you try!" He swung his axe at Alarik.

Alarik dodged it too easily, and that fact enraged him all the more. His face contorted with disgust. "I thought to only punish you lightly," he called out angrily, parrying with his sword. "But . . ." He stalked Red-Hrolf, letting his threat hang menacingly in the air between them a long moment, aware that all eyes were fixed upon them by now.

Suddenly Red-Hrolf lunged at him, clutching his axe with both hands as it sliced through the air. Instead of dodging it, Alarik snarled and with a war cry leapt at him, striking the side of the axe blade so violently and unexpectedly with his left arm that the axe flew out of Hrolf's grasp, the battle ended before it had begun.

At once, Hrolf bent to retrieve his axe from the ground, but Alarik's enraged bellow halted him. "Leave it! You're no longer worthy." He shook his head in revulsion. "You cannot even meet me in combat like a man of honor. Drop it!" he snarled, when Red-Hrolf's fingers closed about its handle.

The axe clanged noisily as it dropped to the floor. Red-Hrolf straightened, his eyes blazing with animosity.

His jaw twitching in anger, Alarik thrust his blade in the locale of Red-Hrolf's heart, holding it just shy of his tunic as he spoke. "You shame me, Hrolf Kaetilson. Can you no longer even fight long enough to break a sweat?" His eyes darkened wrathfully. Slicing his blade across Red-Hrolf's tunic suddenly, he rent it, though he scarcely penetrated the surface of his flesh. "Go with this!" he charged. "My reminder to you! My warning to those you would serve! Get out of my sight!"

Red-Hrolf's look was that of outrage, yet he'd barely flinched when he'd received the gash that now marred his chest.

"If ever I see your treacherous face again," Alarik snarled, "I would take great pleasure in carving the blood-eagle from your useless body!"

Reflexively, Red-Hrolf placed a hand to his half-bared chest. " 'Tis not yet done betwixt us, Alarik! *Bastard son of Trygvi's French whore!*" He turned to go, making certain to meet Alarik's angry eyes one last time before turning and stalking from the *skali*.

Alarik went at once to the symbolic high seat, but he did not seat himself. He stood behind it, his legs spread apart in challenge, his sword still in hand. "First Nissa," he said, barely more than a hiss, "then Hrolf—does anyone else have a mind to challenge me this day?"

A few shook their heads in negation. More sat arrested, gawking at their drinking horns in contemplative silence. The *skali* remained deathly silent as Alarik anticipated who else might dare betray him.

No one dared move.

No one met his gaze.

Chapter 18

Sigurd burst into the hall and paused, disconcerted at the uncanny silence he encountered upon his entrance. Having no notion why Alarik scowled so darkly, he nevertheless perceived the gravity of the situation and said nought; instead he stood waiting anxiously until Alarik turned to acknowledge him with a nod. "Riders approach by way of the fjord!" he blurted.

Impatient to speak with Elienor, Alarik's irritation multiplied tenfold. "How many?" he barked.

"Too many to count, my lord! It appears to be Olav," Sigurd revealed. "Yet we cannot be certain. What would you have us do?"

Alarik sheathed his sword, muttering silent curses. Just what he needed this moment—Olav, the very individual at the heart of everyone's discontent. As if he didn't have enough discord already. Regardless, Olav was his brother and he would make him welcome. "Let them come," he declared with a sigh, and stepping down from the dais, he followed Sigurd from the hall to await his half-brother's arrival.

Outside, snow fell as dry and light as whispers. Against the stark white landscape, the shapes and colors of the approaching forces grew in clarity. After a long moment, Alarik was able to identify his brother's sorrel from the immense party that accompanied him.

The animal, with its pure white mane and tail, had a regal prance all of its own, and Alarik would know it anywhere. He'd long admired the beast. With Olav's consent, he'd bred the horse with one of his own two years past. As of yet, there was only another puny mare for the effort—exquisite in form, yet much too diminutive to be of much service to Alarik. Like as not, he'd fall flat on his back if he so much as attempted to mount the beast.

Contemplating the animal, he was unable to prevent his thoughts from straying to Elienor. Proportionately, she was just right for the mare. He found himself envisioning her upon the sorrel— her long chestnut hair fluttering in the breeze, the sun in her face . . . perhaps in the spring he would present the animal to her as a gift. Aye, that's what he would do . . . when came the spring . . . perhaps by then she would have grown accustomed to his home.

To him. A shuddering coursed through him at the thought.

He was completely unaware of the long minutes that elapsed until Olav and his men had entered the compound and dismounted before him, bringing him out of his reverie.

Olav's arms flew out at once to embrace Alarik. "Mine *bror!*" he bellowed cheerfully.

Alarik grunted, returning the embrace.

Olav punctuated his greeting with a number of whacks upon Alarik's back.

Not to be outdone, Alarik whacked him back, none too softly, then embraced him more heartily, conceding with a grumble that he was glad to see his brother—even if Olav's timing was ever poor.

"Come, old man, let us go in ere we die of exposure," he suggested.

"Old man?" Olav exclaimed. "You've more years on that body of yours than I can claim."

As they walked together, Alarik awarded Olav a disgruntled glance. "Just tell me, Olav, how is it you always seem know when I'm newly arrived? And why is it," he wondered aloud, giving vent to his frustration, "that you always show up in time to usurp mine bed?"

Olav placed a hand upon Alarik's shoulder, grinning. "I couldn't wait to see you, of course," he exclaimed with a hearty chuckle.

Alarik offered him a dubious glance, his eyes sharp and assessing. "That so?" he challenged.

Olav chuckled and ceded, "The truth is that while I never miss the opportunity to see mine faithful *bror*, I was, indeed, looking for your ships to arrive." He cleared his throat. "I rather hoped you would join me in a small voyage. Tyri wishes—"

Alarik snorted. "And how is your lovely wife?" His eyes glinted with sarcasm.

Olav scowled at him for the quip and then conceded. "I'm afraid time finds her more bitter than ever," he grumbled. He heaved a hearty sigh. "She would have her lands in the Dane's mark returned to her and has pressed me to retrieve them. I should say . . . she's immensely displeased not to have holdings in the Northland as befits a queen of her station, and I find myself wondering if, mayhap, she might be right." He lifted his brows in question, and Alarik knew full well he sought concordance.

Alarik refused to give it.

His own brows knit in disbelief. "As your wife, Olav, Tyri wants for nought and still she whines

for more?" He shook his head and cautioned, "You
know where I stand where she's concerned—let us
not find reason to quarrel this night. I take it,"
he said, shifting the topic, "that this *voyage* you
wish me to consider is significant enough to you
that I should consider leaving the comfort of mine
steading mere days after arriving?"

Olav sighed. "It is," he assured, looking weary.

Alarik shook his head, thinking that Tyri once
again led his brother on a merry chase. Yet better Olav than him. He shuddered to think how
close he'd come to binding himself to the harri-
dan himself. "Then I shall consider it," he yielded.
"However . . . until I decide, I'll not be giving up
mine bed to you!" In truth, he'd been able to think
of nought other than the sweet torture he'd experienced the night before. Why he should seek to
subject himself to it again, he couldn't fathom, yet
in time, he determined, she would learn to accept
him . . .

Aye, he'd sworn not to force her—and he'd keep
that vow.

Still . . . there were ways . . .

"You won't?"

Alarik glanced at Olav, his brows lifting. "Won't
what?"

Olav cocked his head curiously, wondering what
had Alarik so preoccupied. "Give up your bed?"

"*Nei*," he asserted, once and for all shaking his
mind free of the little vixen awaiting him in his
chamber. "Not this time. You'll need find yourself
another bed to snore in, for I'll not be giving up
mine."

"But I did not ask you to!" Olav protested. "Not
for your kin—nor your king!" he added plaintively. "Even if I did gift the accursed thing to you!"

Alarik's lips twisted wryly. "As of *yet*, you've not," he asserted, giving Olav a narrow-eyed glance. "And in truth, the only reason you gave me that accursed bed was that your precious Tyri would not take her rest where you'd bedded your mistresses."

Olav placed a hand to his heart, yet he grinned shrewdly. "Ever you wound me, mine *bror*! I tell you I was not going to ask that you give up your bed. Tyri is not with me, as you can see, and so I shan't be imposing."

Alarik's eyes sparkled with mischief. "I didn't notice the virago was missing," he said lightly.

Olav's brow furrowed. "She'd not like to hear you say such things. As it is, she believes you'll never forgive her."

" 'Tis likely she's right," he allowed.

Olav's face contorted suspiciously. "But you no longer care for her?"

"*Nei*," Alarik answered without hesitation.

"Yet still you won't forgive her?" Olav asked, beginning to take offense. "I'm not certain I relish hearing what I think I'm hearing from your lips," he said tightly.

Alarik heaved a weary sigh and offered his brother a frown. "*Nei*, Olav, 'tis not what you think. I believe you know very well that I care little that Tyri chose your miserable hide over mine. In truth, I thank Odin at every opportunity that she did!"

Olav winced at Alarik's choice of deities. "Aye, well! Thank the God of Abraham instead."

"Whomever. What I do care about is that she gave not a thought about coming betwixt brothers."

"I see," Olav said, and then teased, "so then you will always dislike Tyri because you cherish me so much?" His brows rose.

Alarik chuckled. "Cherish?" He shook his head. " 'Tis your word, old dog, not mine!" Yet he was forced to concede to himself that he valued both his brothers more highly than he did any other living soul. It was simply not his way to acknowledge such things aloud.

Olav chuckled heartily, his sense of humor returning. "Well . . . 'tis more likely Tyri did not feel a mere half-brother worthy. You know mine bride—only the finest of aught!" He stole a look at Alarik. "In fact I've oft wondered how she even considered you at all?"

Alarik lifted his brows, grinning, thinking that it was more likely the other way around.

"At any rate, 'tis the truth that she did not expect we would be so close," Olav revealed. "I don't believe she meant to come between us, at all. She simply did not realize, is all."

Alarik gave him a dubious glance. His own opinion of Tyri was not so benevolent. Like Nissa, while she wasn't malicious outright, she had no qualms over using whatever means necessary to gain her purpose.

Olav placed an arm about his shoulders as they entered the enlivened hall. "At any rate, mine *bror* . . . I've heard a rumor . . . won't you tell me about this wench you've brought with you from Francia . . ."

Chapter 19

Elienor had been eager enough to comply.

Why she'd felt a momentary qualm over leaving Alarik's side she had no notion, but she was grateful now he'd ordered her to his chamber. She had no wish to witness their barbarous contest. Still the temptation to listen at the door had been much too great.

What if he lost? What would become of her then?

She shuddered to think of herself at Flame Hair's mercy, and couldn't help but say a fervent prayer that Alarik win. It was appalling that she should be compelled to pray for such a thing, yet here she was, reduced to it nonetheless! She told herself firmly that it was only for her own protection that she cared who won, or that she'd hesitated to leave him to begin with, for otherwise, he could take himself off to Viking purgatory for all it concerned her!

Unaware that she held her breath, until the sound of the scuffle was over and her vision blackened at the edges, she slumped against the door, sighing in relief, hardly able to explain what had just happened.

Jesu Christ—her head ached!

Had he truly banished his man? For her? Surely not.

After an interval, she sat upon the bed to wait, pondering his motives. Yet half an hour later, he still had not appeared, and Elienor's nerves were fraying fast; she had expected to see his scowling face come bursting into the chamber at any moment.

A female servant arrived to stir the fire and serve supper, and then she left without a word, and still there was no sign of him. Lying back upon the bed, Elienor dared to hope that she would be spared his appearance . . . and thus his fury, for she still could not discern what had angered him so.

Eventually he would need to come to his bed, though, and 'twas that she dreaded most. She'd been fortunate so far in that he'd not defiled her, yet how long would he leave her be?

She refused to think about it just now.

At any rate, mayhap he'd spent his anger upon the flame-haired one and no longer need to abuse her.

He's not abused you yet! a little voice argued.

"Yet!" she whispered, and then sighed, for he'd truly not abused her . . . not precisely—his men had, and then he had been the one to abduct her . . .

Still, he's kept his word. He's not violated you, has he? You lie at his mercy and still he does nought but tend you, feed you . . .

"Hush!" she commanded her wayward thoughts.

What was an abduction if not a violation of her freedom, at the very least? She closed her eyes with a sigh, wondering if she might not indeed be a little mad? And then her face heated suddenly— after the shameless way she'd dreamed of him last eve, she doubtless was!

At once, she envisioned his lips hovering above hers, so close, daring her to yield, and again she could not help but compare Count Phillipe's wet kisses. In deference to her uncle, Count Phillipe had never done more than simply kiss her, but sweet Jesu, deny it all she may, never with him had she felt such . . . such . . . anticipation? Even now she felt a strange fluttering deep down at the merest thought—and Alarik had yet to even touch her in any manner at all—much less an intimate kiss! In truth, he'd not so much as looked at her as though he would kiss her. And still she could not expunge the vision of his lips from her mind.

Forsooth! Did she require further evidence of her insanity?

"I shall make it right," Bjorn crooned, thrusting his fingers into Nissa's disheveled hair. Leaning against the storage building, he drew her gently into his embrace.

"But mine father!" she cried, resisting him. "Oh, Bjorn, I'm so ashamed! I've failed him!" She shook her head woefully, her eyes swollen with tears, the crown of her head covered with icy flakes. "He'll be so displeased with me! So angry!"

Stroking her quaking back with his fingers, Bjorn compelled her to lay her cold cheek against his pounding chest. Reaching up to brush the snow from her hair, he closed his eyes in quivering pleasure and laid his own head back against the rough timber, allowing the fresh snow to sprinkle down upon his face. He couldn't be more exhilarated by the turn of events—despite the fact that the woman he loved was weeping in fear and pain. He truly believed Nissa loved him too—had always loved him, as he had her. 'Twas only her driving need to satisfy her unpleasable father that made her think otherwise.

"I'll speak to Ejnar, myself, Nissa. You'll see . . .

everything will work out for the best. You don't love Alarik!" he told her. Finally, something sweet would come his way. He intended to convince Ejnar the Dane to award him his youngest daughter, and then he would spend the rest of his life building her a home. "I swear it!"

Nissa turned her tear-stained face up to look at him. "I swear it!" he whispered again, more fervently, and his body jolted with elation as she returned his embrace. He stared at her a long moment, trying to discern whether he'd understood correctly.

Nissa stared back, nodding. Bjorn needed no more encouragement. At once he hoisted her up into his arms to carry her within the reserve hut, at last to make her his.

From the high seat, Alarik watched as the runty pup Red-Hrolf had tormented lifted its curious head, then stood and stretched before limping toward the high table. He tossed the pup a scrap from his own plate, and recalled the way Elienor, at hearing its whimper, had been prepared to leap to its defense. She seemed to have a propensity for mothering both man and beast alike—seemed to need to protect—and, in fact, leapt at every opportunity.

Olav slammed his fist upon the wooden table suddenly, arresting his attention.

"I tell you no matter how hard I try, those cursed rebels will not give! They protest that Christianity will weaken them—turn them into whimpering fearful little creatures who flee at their own shadows. Bah! I say to them, for they need only look at me to know 'tis not so. How much more strength need I show?"

Alarik glanced at his brother, his face impassive, for he recognized the mood. "Mayhap that instead is the issue, Olav. Mayhap a lighter hand will gain you more?" he suggested, and then sighed when Olav shook his head adamantly. "If I know you . . . you did not take their refusal lightly."

"*Nei—nei*! I did not. Most assuredly I did not!" Olav leaned forward upon his elbows to stare into his tankard. "Can they not comprehend how much it would profit us if we united with the empire?"

"Have you explained as much?"

"The fools will not listen!" Olav responded defensively.

"And what *did* you tell them?"

Olav said nothing, merely continued to stare into his tankard.

"I must know if I am to support you, Olav."

Olav's head jerked up and his canny green eyes locked with Alarik's. "Then you have decided?"

In truth, Alarik had decided months before to accept the Christian faith as his own, yet he would not admit as much to Olav, nor would he allow himself to be baptized as a public profession, for he knew only too well that he was the only thing standing between Olav and his own people. Olav would not force them so long as Alarik did not convert, and Alarik did not relish the thought of seeing them manipulated as Olav would. Very few had come forward as of yet to profess a change in faith, and until they all did, of their own will, Alarik refused to concede his own. "*Nei*," Alarik said with a sigh. "I have not. Yet you know I would back you regardless, for you are mine brother. What did you tell them?"

Olav's face reddened with remembered fury. "I commanded that they acknowledge the Christian

God by baptism . . . or be sacrificed to Odin!"

Alarik winced. "And?"

"None of the fools accepted my challenge, of course," Olav gloated.

"Well . . . what is done is done, but I'd be willing to wager that none will take your challenge lightly. Guard yourself," he advised, for neither a jarl's nor a king's power was absolute if he was not backed by the masses. Leadership was not simply gifted to a man for his birth status; rather, the position of jarl or kingship was exacted by the most able and revered, otherwise Alarik would not have achieved half of what he had, for as a bastard, his bloodline was far from noble.

Olav threw a hand up in condemnation. "Bah! Let them perish in the offal of their heathen gods, then! Now . . . tell me more of the girl," Olav demanded, shifting the subject drastically. "You say she was raised in a nunnery?"

Alarik nodded, lifting his tankard to his lips. He glanced backward at his chamber door. They'd come into the *skali* long hours ago—had been here so long he'd finally had to send repast in to Elienor—and he was rapidly growing impatient with the company at hand. Curse Olav and his rotten timing! "So she claims," he muttered, drinking deeply of his ale.

It did not escape Olav that Alarik continued to peer back at his chamber door, and he suspected he understood why, yet he did not relent. His brows collided, and he heaved a ponderous sigh, considering the repercussions of Alarik's abducting the woman in question. "You know I do not wish discord with the church. Alarik, are you listening?"

Alarik swung back toward his brother. "Mmhhh." He wondered what she was doing. He'd not set eyes upon her since ordering her to his chamber.

"I've simply come too far to risk contention over a wench, of all things." Olav placed his hand upon Alarik's shoulder in appeal. "Mayhap, if you did not care for her overmuch?"

Alarik's scowl darkened, for the last thing he wanted was to become a beleaguered husband. He shuddered suddenly at the turn of his thoughts. *Husband?* Since when would he even have considered a thrall as a candidate for wife? Since when had he considered a wife at all? "I don't," he muttered.

Olav's mood lightened, satisfied as he was with the expected response. "Well, ho—I didn't think so! At any rate," he continued, "mayhap for the sake of peace with the church, for me, you will return her to . . ."

Alarik slammed his tankard down, shrugging Olav's hand from his shoulder. "She stays!"

Olav scratched his chin, tilting his head in stupefaction. "Yet you don't care for her?"

"*Nei*," Alarik maintained, his jaw taut.

Olav chuckled suddenly, his green eyes dancing. "I see."

Alarik glowered at him and shoved his tankard away. "You see nought, you pompous old dog!" He rose abruptly from the table. "I'm going to bed," he said irascibly.

To that declaration, Olav merely threw his head back and roared with laughter. "And he says he does not care for her?" He turned to elbow Brother Vernay.

At Olav's unexpected jab in the ribs, Brother Vernay choked upon his ale, uncomfortable at taking his meal with so many hostile eyes upon him. Yet it was only when Olav called that he was forced to, and so he simply endured and listened . . . and learned.

Alarik ignored the quip, shoving away from the table determinedly.

Brother Vernay cleared his throat. "Er . . . my lords?" He raked his chair backward and stood along with Alarik. "If I might be so bold?"

Alarik turned from Olav, to the pestering monk his brother had cast into his life, his face contorting with impatience. 'Twas the bane of his existence that Olav adhered to the one extreme, Bjorn to the other. "Go on," he prompted, his brow furrowing suddenly as he scanned the hall. Bjorn was nowhere to be found, and he wondered idly that he'd not missed his youngest brother ere now. Nevertheless, Bjorn's absence surprised him not, for the animosity between he and Olav was palpable, oft splitting Alarik between the two.

"You did say the demoiselle was raised in a nunnery?" Vernay asked.

"Aye," Alarik affirmed. "If her word is true."

"Well, then—if I may be so bold to advise—I believe I know a way we might appease everyone."

Both men stared expectantly.

"Aye, well!" Vernay continued. "My lord, Olav, I know how much you would like for me to record for you l' ecriture sainte, and if the demoiselle can copy, then she might be the answer to our quandary!" Both men continued to stare blankly, unaware there was a quandary. Brother Vernay cleared his throat and tried again. "You know I cannot write," he reasoned. "And the demoiselle would be perfectly suited to the task. Surely they would have taught her letters at the priory. And jarl?" he prompted, appealing to Alarik's desire to keep the girl. "Wouldn't that be the perfect persuasion? If she thought this were God's will for her? Having been raised in the priory, she couldn't possibly disagree. If only she were to realize how much she was needed here!"

Alarik nodded, considering.

"And my lord, Olav . . ." He searched for a way to phrase what followed so that Olav would understand and Alarik would not take offense. "I believe the demoiselle might even prove to be a suitable . . . er . . . influence, shall we say, for . . . ," he inclined his head subtly toward Alarik, " . . . us all?"

"Aye!" Olav exclaimed, warming finally to Brother Vernay's meaning. "Aye! I believe she would in fact be the perfect solution! 'Tis settled then!" he said excitedly.

"Er . . . not quite, my lords," Brother Vernay broke in once more. His brows rose apprehensively. "There are those who would need to be appeased—her family for instance—but I would be delighted to speak in your behalf!"

"Very good!" Olav exclaimed.

"I dare say, we should hear no objections from the church," Vernay added. "And I'm certain that in itself will hold tremendous sway with her family. Surely they can have no objections when informed by the church of the exceptional task set before her? Know you who they might be, my lord?"

Alarik's gaze riveted on the monk as he considered the ring. He glanced at his brother and knew without a doubt that Olav would be less inclined to approve of his keeping Elienor if he suspected that a man as influential and pious as Robert of Francia was her kin. "*Nei*," he said after a moment, averting his eyes. "She has not said." Again, his gaze returned to spear the monk. "And your only interest in the wench is merely to guide her in copying the holy writ?"

Brother Vernay's lids lifted, and his eyes widened in stunned surprise as he caught Alarik's meaning. "Of course, my lord! I assure you my passion is in God alone!"

Alarik nodded. "Very well then, she can begin on the morrow . . ." He turned to consider his brother. "If Olav has no objections."

Olav shook his head, his mouth contorting as he considered the way Alarik had so easily yielded to his request. Never had he so easily. "Not at all," he assured. "In truth, it would please me greatly." He ran a speculative hand across his jaw and reclined further within his chair, considering what had just transpired.

Brother Vernay, on the other hand, beamed. "Well then! Will you summon her now and speak to her, jarl, or would you have me appeal to her in your stead? She could not deny me, I assure you!"

Alarik's scowl returned, for he disliked being manipulated. He grunted with irritation and said sharply, "I shall speak to her, myself, though not just now. I grow weary and would seek mine bed!"

"Then I look forward unto the morrow." Olav proclaimed, straightening as Alarik turned to leave. "Oh, and Alarik?"

Alarik turned, beginning to think it a conspiracy to keep him from his chamber. He tried to keep the impatience from his face and tone, but felt as agitated as a stallion in a brood mare's stall, separated from his obsession by mere walls and the will of others. He stole a look over his shoulder at his chamber door.

As the stallion with the mare, he was keenly aware she was there.

"What might be the name of this wench I've not yet met?"

"Elienor," Alarik answered on a sigh, "of *Baume-les-Nonnes*." He turned to go, vowing no one would keep him from his destination this time. "*God natt*, Olav!"

"Rest well, mine *bror*," Olav returned.

Brother Vernay nodded approvingly. "*Baume-les-Nonnes!*" he murmured. "My lord! Somebody must have valued her highly, for it took good coin, I warrant, to ensconce her within those walls."

"Aye," Olav agreed, settling back as he watched Alarik stoop to pick up a small yapping pup before continuing on to his chamber. "Aye."

"My lord?" Vernay said more quietly. "I believe we may finally have found the perfect way to persuade your brother!"

Olav nodded, again smoothing his hand along his jaw, watching shrewdly as Alarik carried the animal within his chamber. "Mayhap," he agreed. "Mayhap we do, at that."

Chapter 20

Elienor awoke in the midst of the nightmare, uncertain whether the sound that had roused her was her own whimper or that of the door opening. She made an effort to orient herself, for the chamber had grown dim with the fire's waning, and after an instant she could discern the sound of footsteps. She knew it would be Alarik, yet she dared not move in hopes that he would think her asleep and leave her in peace.

He made his way across the chamber, and Elienor watched through her lashes as his dark form stooped along the way to set something upon the floor.

Alarik had no notion why he'd carried the accursed animal in, only that the image of Elienor with her anguished expression when Red-Hrolf had abused it had prompted him unto it. He watched a moment as the pup sniffed its way around the dark chamber, settling near the dying fire, and then he turned to contemplate the woman lying in his bed.

He sensed at once she was awake.

Elienor watched with bated breath as he came nearer, his silhouette dark and forbidding against the dull orange glow of the firelight.

He stared down at her for an interminable moment.

"Did you dream again?" he asked softly.

Elienor averted her gaze, terrified that despite the darkness, he would discern that she had, and worse, he would inquire of it. How could she tell him? And yet how could she not? Her fingers twisted the bedsheets. She understood now what the dream revealed—had dreamt it so often that she could recall every vivid detail.

According to her divination, Alarik would die, betrayed, though that part of it she could not yet make out.

In truth, she should have been elated at the notion, yet God aid her, she wasn't.

She was terrified.

He hovered silently above her, waiting for her to reply. Swallowing, Elienor avoided his question, distracting him with another. "You . . . you banished them?"

" 'Tis none of your concern!" he declared, his tone harsher than he'd intended, his body grown rigid. Because of her, he had, and that simple fact provoked him more than the deed itself.

Why was it that his response seemed to deflate her spirit somehow? And why had she thought he'd banished them for her? Because he'd held her so tenderly in her dream—silly fool! she berated herself. It had been no more than a dream, after all. There was nought between them. Nought.

Nought!

"Tell me, Elienor . . ."

Elienor swallowed, averting her eyes, sensing what he was about to ask yet again. She turned to her side, clutching the blankets to her breast.

"What demons haunt you so that you cannot sleep through the night?"

Elienor's grip upon the bedsheets tightened. She balled it within her fist, daring to say nothing, not trusting her voice. His shadowed eyes seemed to peer directly into her soul.

"Surely something?" he demanded.

"Nay," she croaked, swallowing. "I . . . I merely dream of my mother," she improvised. Not wholly a lie, yet not the truth, either. She reminded herself that it was a sin to lie, yet rationalized that the truth might very well find her burned at the stake.

And she was a coward.

"Your mother?"

"Her death," Elienor murmured in explanation. "'Twas senseless." Guilt plagued her. How could she, in all good conscience, let a man perish when God, or Lucifer, had seen fit to forewarn her of his death? Shouldn't she use her gift to the good of mankind?

Mayhap 'twould be for the good of mankind did he die, she argued.

Yet was she much better than he was if she simply allowed him to perish without a single, solitary warning?

Her heart leapt in confusion and growing desperation. Her mother had been courageous enough to speak freely of her visions. Why couldn't she?

Because you're a coward! a little voice plagued.

She glanced up to be certain she'd not spoken the self-depreciating accusation aloud. His expression was unchanged, brooding, and she couldn't help but wonder if he sensed her lie.

She suddenly heard a faint whimper, and her brows knit as she watched Alarik bend to the floor and lift something up. To her surprise, he placed a whining pup upon the bed, and her eyes widened as she recognized it as the same one Nissa had booted and Red-Hrolf had abused. She peered up at him in surprise.

"I thought you might like to have it," he disclosed in a husky whisper, his eyes spearing her through the shadows.

Her heart hammering, Elienor said nought, yet the hand that clutched the bedsheets suddenly released their hold and reached out to accept the pup. She drew it into her arms protectively and sat up to examine each leg for injury, finding none.

Alarik watched, wholly satisfied with her response to the animal, for it confirmed his suspicions about her maternal nature. It was her response to him that he couldn't bear to see. "Do you loathe me so much?" he asked.

Elienor's heart turned over, her breath choking her. He could not know, she assured herself—could not know of the dream—could not know that she'd chosen to deny him the knowledge that might save him! In reality, how could she even be certain that her dreams were anything more than her own fancy, she reasoned.

Mayhap 'twas only coincidence, after all?

The silence between them lengthened.

"How is it you came to be raised in a nunnery?"

Elienor dared not look at him. His presence beside her was becoming much too disconcerting. Releasing the dog, she raised the bedsheet and scooted backward in self-preservation—not that she supposed he might harm her. They'd been alone enough that she knew he'd not. She simply felt undone with him so near, that was all. The dog followed her, whining as it reached up to lap at her lips, begging for affection. Elienor couldn't suppress a soft giggle at its effort, and at once she recommenced stroking its head and back.

Her unexpected laughter jolting him, Alarik watched Elienor's fingers move gently over the pup, his body quickening as he imagined those same fingers moving just so over his own flesh. Keeping him lucid was the simple fact that she would not even look at him—and that if she did, her smiling expression would revert at once to that of loathing. No matter how he treated her, how he spoke to her . . . that he kept his vow, she saw him only as she saw fit—as a demon, butcher, slayer of innocents. No matter how he strove to, he could not banish the sound of her accusing voice from his thoughts . . . and now her laughter lingered, as well; the two sounds were incongruous, yet equally tormenting.

"Why do you wish to know of my days in the priory?" Elienor wanted to know.

"Simple curiosity."

"I entered the priory when my mother died," she relented.

"And you say 'tis her death you dream of?"

"Aye," Elienor replied, disgusted with herself. Not only was she a coward, but she was a liar, too!

Nevertheless, wasn't his death just penance for all that he'd done? she asked herself once more.

"You need not speak of it . . . if it pains you," he yielded.

Elienor nodded, grateful that he would interrogate her no further, guilty that he would choose this moment to consider her feelings—particularly so since she'd only just convinced herself he deserved to die.

"Yet . . . there *is* something I would have you tell me," he prompted, settling upon the edge of the bed. Her violet eyes watched him warily. "I would know your relation to Robert of Francia."

"He's my uncle," Elienor yielded with a sigh, too weary to conjure another lie, and too repelled by her cowardice to care that he might hold it against her.

Without realizing he did so, Alarik exhaled in relief. The tension in his body eased.

Again the uncomfortable silence.

"Would it please you to know that we have a *kirken* here," he asked suddenly.

Her brows knit. "A *kirken?*"

"A church."

Elienor snorted. "A heathen church!"

"*Nei*, Elienor, not a heathen church . . . a Christian church." He was silent a long moment, weighing his words, and then continued. "You will discover it soon enough . . . mine brother is Christian."

Her eyes widened at the revelation, but she seemed to recover herself at once and inquired, "Your brother? And not you?"

Alarik grunted. Elienor took it to be a denial. "He was converted by a soothsayer in the Scilly Isles," he explained, "and was confirmed with the English king Ethelred as his godfather." His eyes seemed to smolder as he looked down upon her, assessing her reaction to his disclosure.

She didn't intend to give him a reaction—not a positive one at least. "I see," she said stiffly, raising her brows. "Am I supposed to feel at ease now that you've revealed this to me? Because I cannot! You've taken me far from everyone I've loved, everything I've—"

"Did you love Count Phillipe?" he asked sharply, his eyes piercing her through the shadows.

"Nay," Elienor snapped, glaring back at him. She shrugged. "How could I? I did not know him long enough to love him. You saw fit to that!"

Sensing that further interrogation would gain him nought and stir up much discord, Alarik decided to forego further questioning. Instead, he informed her of Brother Vernay and the holy writ to be copied for Olav. Elienor was so astounded by the request to aid the monk that she remained speechless, gawking at him, her lovely face flustered.

Elienor shook her head as though in disbelief. "You wish me to copy for you?"

"For Olav," Alarik amended. "Know you how?"

"Aye," she murmured softly, still shaking her head, confused . . . "but . . ."

"Should you agree to the request, then you'll spend the majority of each day with Brother Vernay . . . at the *kirken*," he revealed. "The rest of the time you will spend with me, tending mine needs."

Elienor's chin lifted, heartened by the knowledge that he could argue all day 'twas God's will she comply, but if she chose not to assist Brother Vernay, then he could never force her. Besides, she doubted God would bring suffering to the guiltless for such a thing as this! Mayhap Alarik had spared Clarisse, but she could not forget Stefan. "And if I do not agree?"

His lips twisted wryly, scarcely amused that he needed to use himself as a threat. "Then you'll spend the majority of each waking day tending me, instead."

Elienor quivered. "I shall be delighted to assist Brother Vernay!" she relented at once, choking on her pride. "May it never be said I resisted the course of God's will," she ceded ruefully.

" 'Tis settled then. You shall begin in the morning," he told her. Something about his tone made her feel that he was somehow displeased with her reply . . . yet he'd gotten what he wished of her, hadn't he? He withdrew her ring from about his neck, his look sullen. "You'll be wanting this back, I think," he said, offering it to her.

When Elienor merely stared at it, stupefied, he dropped it over her head and watched it settled at her bosom. Her fingers went to it at once. "Did your uncle give it to you?"

Elienor closed her fist about it, her eyes locking with his. "Aye," she murmured.

"An acknowledgment of your kinship?"

"In a manner of speaking," she ceded, glancing down at the ring in question. "For my eyes alone," she clarified with a sigh. "I can never be acknowledged as my father's issue." She glanced up, assessing his expression.

"Why?"

"Because I was disinherited at the age of four in the eyes of both church and state—my mother as well—so that my father might take to wife an heiress more suitable to his needs."

Her lashes lowered, black as midnight against her pale flesh, and once again Alarik wondered that one so dark could be so fair. At her forlorn expression, he felt an overwhelming compassion for her, a kinship even, separate from any carnal emotions he'd possessed before; yet he couldn't afford those sentiments and so he dismissed them, severing the moment abruptly.

"You should go back to sleep," he suggested, commencing to undress at once. " 'Tis late." He lifted his tunic up over his head and tossed it upon a coffer. At once, he began to unlace his breeches.

Elienor gasped, averting her eyes. "And where shall you slee . . ."

The aversion in her voice twisted his gut. "Atop you if you don't move yourself over!"

he said impatiently, and his stomach turned as she propelled herself to the far side of the bed, going so far as to place the pup between them.

Chapter 21

In her dream Elienor endured Phillipe's sloppy kiss. 'Twas her duty, she told herself. Her body grew taut, and she endeavored not to cry out in disgust, counting herself fortunate that he never did more than this. Still, it sickened her and she worried how she would abide it when they were wed. She'd find a way, she was determined.

She'd find a way . . .

It was a long befuddled moment before she could rouse herself sufficiently to realize it was not a human tongue at all, for 'twas much too large— and wet!

Her eyes flew open to find an eager pink tongue lapping at her face. Sputtering in surprise, she sprang upward, grappling with the clumsy animal that seemed suddenly all the more determined to devour her face!

A soft chuckle reached her ears. "I wondered how long it would take you to rouse," a husky voice remarked.

Elienor's eyes found him at once, leaning casually, arms crossed, against the chamber door. To her alarm her first emotion was relief—relief that it was him, and not Count Phillipe.

Yet that was ludicrous, was it not?

He was dressed, though scarcely, wearing mere linen breeches and a tunic thrown over one shoulder, and she caught her breath at the sight of his bare chest, so immense. Seeing him thus was unsettling, to say the least, as well as uncouth on his part!

Not to mention unseemly . . .

An arrogant smile curved his lips as he noted the direction of her gaze, and his silver eyes gleamed. The thought of him standing there, scrutinizing her in sleep while she was entirely unaware of it, unnerved her. Elienor nudged the pup aside peevishly. "Why didn't you simply waken me?"

"Because you needed rest," he said simply.

Elienor's brows knit. Just how was she supposed to continue to loathe him when he continued to say such things? Worse, how was she supposed to forget her nightmares, or the simple fact that she'd decided to let him reap his well-deserved reward? She couldn't be certain the dream was prophesy, she reminded herself, and so she hadn't *truly* dispensed him to die. 'Twas more self-preservation that kept her silent. The memory of her mother's persecution, for so much less, plagued her. She met his gaze boldly, trying to seem unaffected by him. "I'd have thought you'd have better things to do with your time, *my lord Viking*," she said with easy defiance, "than to watch your prisoners slumber?"

"The name is Alarik," he asserted, his sensuous lips curling as though on the edge of laughter. "And *nei*, I've nought better to do at present, Elienor . . . though you do," he disclosed. He broke into a smile at her confused expression, but said only, "You're filth-ridden."

Unnerved by his brilliant gaze, not to mention his insult, Elienor lifted the coverlet to her breast. " 'Twas not my choice to be abducted . . . or abused," she threw back at him icily, shifting her gaze to the bed once more and then back.

He tensed visibly, but ignored her accusation. A muscle quivered in his forearm as he unconsciously closed one fist in response, and Elienor tried not to notice the bridled power in his arms. "I thought mayhap you'd like to bathe before meeting with Brother Vernay?"

Elienor regarded him suspiciously. "A bath? You're offering me a bath?" Against her will, her eyes returned to his bared chest, and she swallowed, feeling a new wash of shame as she stared at the satiny smooth flesh there. Like the hair upon his head, the hair of his chest was so pale against his sun-bronzed skin that it glistened. "Aye," she croaked, disconcerted that a mere glance could make her feel things she ought not feel. She swallowed, trying to speak past the lump in her throat. "I . . . I would very much appreciate a bath ordered."

Amusement flickered in the eyes that met hers. "Ordered? Here we do not order tubs brought into our chambers, Elienor."

Elienor shivered at the dark sensuality of his tone. "Oh?" she choked out, trying to control her erratic heartbeat. She hoped she sounded scornful and not distressed. "Just how *is* it done, then, *my lord Viking?*" she asked, her voice breaking. She swallowed.

"You'll soon see," he told her silkily. He suspected she would balk at what he intended, but he determined to deal with her objections later and not now when she could dispute him and be overheard. In the bathhouse, he'd simply shut the door, and then she could rail to her heart's content.

"Come," he demanded softly, shoving away from the door abruptly.

Had Elienor any choice but to obey? As she thrust away the covers and stepped out of the bed, he opened a small coffer, lifting out a crimson mantle. "You'll be needing something more than your simple kyrtle," he disclosed, wrapping it about her shoulders. And than without bothering to cloak himself, he snatched her by the elbow, leading her out of the bedchamber and through the *skali*.

To her surprise, he led her outside, and from there to a small outbuilding where smoke drifted up through the rooftop. He opened the door revealing a well-lit chamber within and an immense sunken tub in its center, grand enough for at least six people to sit and bathe. Eight flickering torches, each set in beautiful ornate iron braces, illuminated the chamber. On the right wall, two torches flanked an enormous hearth, and dancing beneath the smoke-blackened kettle in its gaping mouth burned a torrid fire. Elienor surmised the kettle was there to warm the bath water. Additionally, luxuriant furs were strewn about the floor and fresh drying rags were stacked upon a single wooden stool.

Elienor shook her head, awestruck by the sight. "I've never seen the likes!" she whispered, forgetting for an instant that they were supposed to be bitter foes. She knelt by the tub, shrugging the cloak off and thrusting her hand within the water to test it. As she suspected, it was heated. Turning to catch Alarik's amused expression, she told him, "In the priory we did not bathe . . ."

His tawny brows shot up in surprise.

"Oh aye, we did!" Elienor amended, "though certainly not in such luxury!" She flushed suddenly, chagrined by her impetuousness. "The church does not sanction such . . . such . . . opulence." She glanced down hastily into the misty water, swaying softly, blaming her sudden dizziness on the heat of the chamber and not the way he stared at her.

His eyes glowed with a savage inner fire as intense as that within the hearth. "A private bathing chamber is also an extravagance in the Northland," he assured her, his tone silky. "The design is merely one of many I've encountered in mine voyages to the east. In fact, most steadings do have but a single bathhouse for all to share . . . but then, this is not most steadings . . . 'tis mine."

Elienor inhaled deeply in an attempt to harness the fluttering in her breast. "I see," she replied, swallowing the lump in her throat. Suddenly anxious to be within the cleansing water, she straightened her shoulders and waved a hand toward the door. "And now that you've enlightened me, you may leave. Certainly, I can manage adequately!"

Alarik's good humor spread clear into his lively silver eyes.

"I see nought so amusing!" Elienor replied at once, her hackles rising.

To her dismay, he merely chuckled softly. "Wench. You're bold to order me out of mine own bath chamber," he remarked blithely.

Elienor stiffened, bracing herself for the upcoming confrontation.

" 'Tis the truth that you never cease to amaze me, Elienor of *Baume-les-Nonnes*," he said, huskiness deepening his tone.

Elienor merely glared at him, unnerved by the way he said her name, with so much dark promise. "Surely you realize, my lord . . ." She repressed the epithet that by now came automatically to her lips, determined to master her tongue for once. "Surely, you know," she began again, her tone bordering on hysteria, "that I cannot bathe with you present?"

Once again he chuckled, the sound wholly disarming. "Oh, but you can," he disagreed softly, "and you shall, for I do plan to stay." He watched with unconcealed amusement as her eyes widened abruptly. "Trust me, Elienor—" He averted his eyes momentarily, but his gaze returned with startling intensity. "I made you a vow," he continued grimly, "and I shall keep it. I'll not force myself upon you."

Elienor lifted her chin, emboldened by the shred of guilt she detected in his countenance. "Aye, but you've made me vows a'fore," she reminded him, "and you've broken them as easily!"

He flinched visibly, his jaw taut. "I said I'd not touch you," he assured, trying to keep the agitation from his voice. Anger would gain him nought, he apprised himself. Still, he couldn't keep himself from baiting her, wounding him so easily as she had. "Unless, of course, you desire it to be so?"

Elienor snorted, rising abruptly to her feet. As dirty as she knew she must be after so long at sea with no bath, and wearing the same garments as she had, she refused to bathe in his presence! He'd have to force her. "You are the last thing I would ever desire, I assure you!" she told him.

Liar! her conscience accused her.

"Regardless!" Alarik thundered, losing his composure for the briefest instant. He took a moment, tempering his tone, if not his words. "I told you last eve that I would require your services, and I'll not forego that dictate simply because you're too squeamish to undress in mine presence. If you wish not to, then simply do not, but assist me, you will," he avowed. "Within the tub," he explained. "Alas, 'tis your gown to ruin if you please."

With that declaration, he jerked the tunic from his shoulders, tossing it atop the stack of towels upon the stool. The force of the impact toppled the heap to the furs. His gaze piercing her, he remarked, "At any rate, 'tis not as though I've not seen you unclothed, is it my little *Fransk*? Nor is it likely you would have been spared this task, even had you wed your precious count. As mistress to Brouillard," he reasoned, "would you not have been expected to bathe your lord's guests?" His eyes glittered coldly. "Think of this just so," he said huskily.

Elienor took a step backward even before he took his first forward, sensing his determination. She knew without a doubt that arguing her point would gain her little. The demon before her would simply do as he pleased and nought less—yet she could not in all good conscience simply disrobe and bathe before him! Nor could she bear the thought of looking upon his intimidating nakedness—regardless that it was a duty she readily would have embraced as mistress of Brouillard.

Retreating another step as he unlaced his breeches, she stumbled backward into the tub.

He chuckled deeply, his eyes shimmering like molten silver. "Does the sight of me affect you so?"

Elienor straightened to her feet at once. "The sight of you does nought but offend me," she denied hotly. But her face heated with the lie. About her limbs the water was fiery, yet she dared not extract herself from the bath. Lifting her skirts as much as she dared in a futile attempt to save them from ruin, she raised her chin proudly. To her dismay, he continued to disrobe, discarding his breeches with conviction and ease, his silver eyes sharp and confidant.

"I cannot bathe you!" Elienor declared with growing hysteria, shifting indignantly from foot to foot. Her gaze darted about the room.

His lips parted, displaying straight, white teeth. "Can you not?" he asked, and then suddenly he was fully revealed before her. Elienor didn't wait to see whether he would follow her within. She turned and raced toward the far side of the tub, foundering in her haste. To her horror, the further she went, the deeper the water became and the slower she moved. She shrieked as she heard water splash behind her and could almost feel the strength and purpose of his stride. Abruptly she was caught by the arm and was whirled about to face him. She squeezed her eyes shut, vowing that if he would force her hand in this, then at least she'd not look. He could not force her in that!

He chuckled low in his throat, and the unholy sound sent a ripple of alarm tearing through her. Elienor's heart felt near to bursting.

It took every ounce of will Alarik possessed not to rent her clothes from her back, so revealing was her wet gown. She had fine hips and shapely thighs, and at the glimpse of them desire, like molten iron, slid through his veins, arousing him at once. Partly because she seemed so frantic at the thought of seeing him unclothed and partly because the state of his body dictated at least a modicum of modesty, he did not coerce her to open her eyes. "Have it your way, little *Fransk*," he murmured.

To Elienor, it seemed every nerve in her body came to life. "Were I to have it mine own way," she hissed, " 'tis you who would be skewered instead of Stefan!" Her heart raced as his strong fingers closed about her arm. She gasped as they slid down to her wrist. Turning her palm up, he pressed something small and hard within her hand, and then in the other . . . a cloth? Soap? Jesu! she swore silently, quivering anew at the thought of touching him. "I . . . I . . ."

Her protest ended with a gasp as he hauled her blindly toward him. With deliberate precision, he placed her hands upon his chest, and a terrible jolt burst through her. "Wash me!" he hissed.

She tried once more to voice a protest, opening her mouth. Nothing came. Her chest constricted as he began to guide her hand, along with the soap, across his satiny smooth flesh. Tiny hairs sprang at her touch, and to her horror she imagined them wet and gold and glistening beneath her fingertips. That image made her quiver where she stood.

Dear God, but she was warm! She could actually feel wisps of steam waft by her face, could almost smell the heat. And him. Sweet Jesu, she thought she might swoon! His flesh must surely be made of steel not to be affected by the heat? Yet it didn't feel like steel at all; it was disconcertingly soft to the touch . . . yet solid.

Her fingers, scalding and soft, set fire to Alarik's flesh wherever they touched. It took him a staggering moment to discern that she'd begun to wash him of her own accord, her movements progressively slower with each stroke; when he did he released her, dropping his fists to his sides. Her heart might loathe him still, he concluded with satisfaction, but her body reacted with a will of its own, and her body did not loathe him, at all. He knew she was not conscious of the instant when her scrubbing became exploration, but he was. Acutely. His breath quickened as she turned her face up instinctively, and the profound expression she wore took hold of him and clenched his gut. Lust, in its most guileless form. She had no notion, he was certain, what it was that she was experiencing, for her countenance wavered between innocent desire and utter confusion.

Her face was arresting, irregular for the willful chin he'd come to know, her cheeks flushed rose, her lashes long and sooty. She had no notion how beautiful she appeared with her face upturned and her hair dragging the water behind her, her slender white neck arching with passion. His fingers traced the scar at her temple—even it failed to detract from her beauty.

Mingled with the steam, the feminine scent of her was utterly intoxicating. Reflexively, he drew her closer, his heart leaping a little when he realized she did not resist him. He began to stroke her back, though lightly, not wishing to break her concentration. He could almost imagine her garments vanished, for clinging to her as they did, they left little to the imagination.

Elienor groaned in dismay. The feel of him . . . 'twas just as she had dreamed, frighteningly pleasing and strangely reassuring. How could that be? She was vaguely aware that her hands continued to glide of their own accord, over his chest, shoulders, his arms—so immense! Yet she was unaware of the incredible silence of the bathhouse, for the roar of the fire and the pounding of her heart seemed to overwhelm her senses.

Alarik's breath came more labored with each delicious stroke of her hands, his reasoning more convoluted. His better judgment warned him to resist the need that clawed him like a wild unreasonable beast, yet his body could not concur.

Would not.

His goal today had been merely to initiate Elienor into her duties with the most intimate of tasks—to make her as familiar with his body as he craved to be with hers. He was sick unto death of seeing the revulsion in her eyes and wanted merely to force her to bear the sight of him.

But he'd gotten much more . . .

His head fell back with a groan as her hands flitted, light as feathers, down his too sensitive sides, halting at his waist. And then suddenly, they began a new descent, and he moaned, a mixture of torment and pleasure, unable to stop her.

If she desired it, then who was he to interfere?

His hands slid to the small of her back, forcing her into closer contact, relishing the feel of her cool wet garments against his burning flesh, and then he bent to cup his palms around her luscious bottom, pressing her up into his throbbing loins. His body jerked when her fingers lit upon his own buttocks, emulating him, and then she suddenly stiffened and made some choked sound in the back of her throat, as though only just realizing.

Her eyes flew wide, the vivid violet piercing him with their anguish, yet he refused to release her. They stood in that bent position, their bodies arcing so close they might have been one, their faces intimate . . .

Just as it had been in her dream . . . Elienor closed the distance between them, boldly touching her lips to his. God forgive her but she could not keep herself from it. She was faithless, and wanton, and . . . and she didn't care in that instant that her body had betrayed her!

Never had she imagined she would desire this joining of mouths.

Never had Count Phillipe's sloppy kisses made her feel so brazen, so exquisite.

The shocking contact sent the pit of her stomach in a wild tumult. Alarik returned the touch, caressing her mouth more than kissing it, and shivers of delight assailed her at once. In that mindless instant, Elienor returned the kiss with reckless abandon, her blood leaping from her heart and pounding into her head.

She dropped the soap, the rag, and her hands slid up, her arms winding themselves about his neck of their own accord. Moaning, she sought more of him and felt his knees weaken as his fingers kneaded her bottom, sending delicious spasms through her entire being. Desperately, she clung for support, afraid that if she released him, she would drown in her own passion!

Never could she have imagined when Phillipe was kissing her that it might be so blissful. Would that she had known, yet she sensed somehow that it wouldn't have been the same at all. There was a dreamy quality to the moment, and at once recollecting what came next, she followed Phillipe's example, sliding her tongue along Alarik's firm, sensual lips. He groaned, and emboldened, she offered her tongue into his mouth, pleased that she had recalled correctly.

For the briefest instant, she thought she would die from the titillating pleasure. It didn't matter that they were enemies. She found to her dismay that her traitorous body didn't care at all!

It took Alarik a full instant to realize what she'd done, so lost was he to the carnal pleasure—that the invasion of his mouth was forged by none other than her eager little tongue—but the instant he did, he growled, thrusting her away in startled offense. He spat, wiping his mouth with the back of his hand, spitting again.

Elienor landed on her backside, splashing down into the bath with a shriek of surprise, and then came up sputtering.

"Forsooth, wench!" he swore. "Spend one cursed night with the little mongrel and you respond in kind!"

Elienor was so staggered by his unanticipated response to her kiss that she said nothing, only stared, her eyes wide, her lips burning where his had been.

Certainly with Phillipe it had never ended this way.

To her dismay, he turned from her abruptly and lifted himself up from the tub. As he did, water cascaded from his husky form, falling in rushing streams all about him. Despite the horror of the moment, Elienor allowed herself to look upon him fully; his backside was rosy from the warmth of the water, his golden skin glistened with moisture.

Sweet Jesu! How could she have been so wanton? Her face burned, yet try as she might, she could not avert her eyes. She still didn't comprehend what had happened, could not fathom what she'd done wrong. Only belatedly did she realize she was ogling him, and averted her eyes, instantly ashamed.

He seized a towel from the furs and briskly rubbed it over his scalp, and then throwing the towel across his wide shoulders, he tugged on his breeches and stalked out, not bothering to speak as he departed.

As the door slammed, Elienor's fingers went to her mouth where the heat and the taste of him lingered still. She licked her lips, her face heating in shock at the memory of her own eager response to his touch. By the heavens, she could not even claim he'd forced her, because he'd merely asked to be washed.

'Twas she who had given so much more!

Chapter 22

Her face burning fiercely, Elienor completed her bath, not bothering to remove her gown. 'Twas ruined already.

Aside from that, she had no notion whether Alarik would return, and she'd reacted shamefully enough as it was! She preferred not to be discovered exposed, as well.

As she finished soaping her hair, the door opened, and she glanced up to find Alva clucking disapproval.

"You've ruined your gown—all for silly modesty!"

"I fell in." Elienor lied, refusing to admit what had so shamefully transpired within the bath chamber only moments before.

"Well!" Alva determined, the cheer returning to her voice, "what is done, is done, and the jarl has sent you another, and a fine one it is, I might add."

Resisting the urge to seize the gown in question and rip it to shreds, Elienor averted her eyes and said instead, "I've no wish to don someone else's garments, Alva." Her chin lifted as she met Alva's twinkling eyes. "You may return it to your demon master, and tell him I said . . ."

"But the jarl is not my master," Alva demurred, politely disregarding the epithet Elienor had given him in anger.

Elienor's brows lifted, curiosity overcoming her anger. Still, she couldn't quite keep the contempt from her tone. "Nay?"

"*Nei*," Alva avowed. "He is my nephew. And this gown," she added saucily, "well, it belongs to none, save yourself. 'Tis true," she swore at Elienor's skeptical look. "He came to me yesterday and bid me fashion something of his good Byzantine silk."

"Silk?" Elienor asked in startle. Her gaze returned to the blue cloth, scrutinizing it for the first time. "He would clothe a mere slave in silk?" she asked tartly.

Alva chuckled. "It would seem so." Her shrewd eyes crinkled with merriment.

In that instant it wasn't difficult for Elienor to see the kinship between them. That irritating smile! "So Alarik is your nephew?"

Alva nodded, setting the rich blue cloth down upon the stool. She then proceeded, without being asked, to help Elienor rinse her hair. "His mother and Bjorn's perished of fever four years past," she revealed. "But whilst she lived, there could have been no finer son than Alarik. He was good to my sister Mathilde unto her dying breath."

Elienor said nothing.

Was she supposed to think of him differently with that revelation? Hardly!

"Would that Bjorn had cared so much," Alva declared, sighing a little sadly. "I'm afeared Bjorn was my sister's greatest sorrow. She oft worried that he did not possess Alarik's strength of character, and alas, 'tis true!" she confessed, "for while Alarik has long overcome his birth circumstances and has gone on to forge his way to become jarl over his people, Bjorn has never done aught but grumble over his station in life. He bears such bitterness in his heart for what he lacks, and resents both Olav and Alarik for it as well—Olav more so!"

"I see," Elienor replied softly, having gained more insight into the three than she'd ever cared to own. Still, she couldn't help but be curious. "Did all three share the same mother?"

"*Nei*," Alva disclosed. "Mathilde was Trygvi Olavson's slave—freed upon his death. As you were, she and I were begot in Francia."

Elienor's eyes widened at the revelation.

"'Tis the only reason I know the tongue, of course," Alva declared. "We were both taken during a sacking there."

"How long now?" Elienor asked in horror. The testimony shouldn't have surprised her, she told herself, but it did.

"Too many years for this old memory to recount! They took Mathilde because she was too fair and beautiful to resist . . . and I, alas, as dark as I am . . . well, because Mathilde would not abandon me with our mother and father both slain. Now, Astrid," she continued, returning to the previous topic, "she was Olav's mother and Trygvi's rightful wife—and Bjorn . . . well, he shares no kinship at all with Olav, save through Alarik. He and Olav share neither the same mother nor the same father, for while my sister was Bjorn's birth mother, his father was not Trygvi Olavson, at all. 'Tis confusing, I know," she said apologetically.

Dazed by the muddled history Alva had so quickly recounted, Elienor focused on the one thing she'd heard clearly. "I did not realize 'twas a sin to be dark," she said crossly, offended not for herself but for Alva.

Alva sighed a little sadly. "Ahh, well, for you 'tis not, for you are fair enough in other ways. For me 'tis different." She nodded. "Nevertheless, sorrow not for me, my dear girl, for I have been content."

Elienor was too stunned by all that Alva had disclosed to reply. 'Twas inconceivable that she could be so content when she'd been brought to the Northland under such similar circumstances as had Elienor.

Wouldn't acceptance of her lot have been a betrayal of her mother and sire?

Elienor pondered that a time, and once her hair was rinsed, Alva assisted her out of the tub, wrapped a towel around her head, and then again, without being asked, proceeded to strip her of her wet gown. "I can manage!" Elienor declared at once.

"Nonsense!" Alva rebuked. "I came to assist at the jarl's request, and assist I will! Besides, look at you. You've a fine figure," she announced. Her brow furrowed in reproach as she lifted the wet gown up and over Elienor's head. Elienor crossed her arms, unaccustomed to being tended so. "No need to conceal yourself, my dear!" Alva rebuked. "Why," she said with a chortle, "I can no doubt see why the jarl hoards you for himself. You should be proud 'tis so," she proclaimed with a nod. "The jarl is a fine specimen of a man—aye, he is," she asserted, when Elienor's brows collided. "That, and gentle besides, I'm told."

"Gentle?" Elienor scoffed, unwilling to grant him a single redeeming quality, nor was she willing to consider what had very nearly tran-spired in this accursed bath chamber—and her own shameful part in it! She shivered, uncertain whether 'twas the cold, or the memory of the kiss she and the demon had shared . . . his lips so soft . . .

"More gentle than most," Alva maintained, giving Elienor a curious look.

"Mayhap so," Elienor ceded ruefully, "but I cannot say as I've known his gentleness."

Alva's brows furrowed.

"The man took me per force, for the love of God! And upon his ship . . . he caged me within his tent, ne'er to see the light of day! Moreover, he allowed his men to slay an innocent boy before my own eyes—aye, he did—and then led me to believe that he'd tossed the maid Clarisse into the ocean—alive! To be devoured by the creatures of the sea ! Not once did he bother to relate the fact that Clarisse was alive and well, even knowing full well that I loathed him for it."

Alva cocked her head curiously, staring up unabashedly into Elienor's angry violet eyes. "Nothing more?" she asked in surprise.

The question struck Elienor as impudent. Her brows rose as she tilted her head in challenge. "Should I require aught more to despise him?"

Alva made some choked sound, her hand covering her mouth. "Could it be?"

Elienor's face flamed under the older woman's scrutiny.

"You mean to tell me that he's taken no . . . that he's not . . . Nay! Well, 'tis no wonder his mood is so black!" she declared aghast.

'Twas not that it had been such an unpleasant thing, this sparring of tongues, Alarik mused.

Merely unorthodox.

In truth, he'd shoved Elienor away more in surprise than in disgust, for the lingering taste of her teased his senses still.

As a man, 'twas his place to lead, and she'd mentally unbalanced him. That she'd made the initial gesture had been enticing in itself, but she'd somehow usurped his self-control with her brazenness, and that was not so easily dealt with.

Moreover, it led him to wonder where she'd learned such whore's tricks, and 'twas that which disturbed him most. Though he'd heard talk of such tongue kissing, it was the first time he'd encountered it himself.

That Elienor would know of it burned at his gut.

He'd needed distance from her, to think. And to that end, he'd saddled Sleipnir, as he was wont to do when his mood was black, and had ridden half the morn in pursuit of peace. Yet, returning now, he found that his mood was no lighter for the endeavor.

Nor had he been able to discover anything about Ejnar's whereabouts, and he was more determined than ever to remove Nissa from his keep. Truthfully, he was beginning to wonder if Ejnar had determined his intent and had resolved not to be found, for he was well aware that Hrolf had found him easily enough when he'd looked. He'd received word already this morn that the flame-haired Hrolf had joined with Ejnar's band—another reason for the color of his mood.

"I wish you to give Nissa consent to remain at Gryting!" Bjorn appealed at his back. Alarik had not heard his approach, and that fact only irritated him more. Damn, he couldn't afford to lose his faculties. In these times there were many who would gladly cleave his back in two for the honor of his high seat alone—not to mention his kinship with Olav. He didn't bother turning; Bjorn quickly overtook Sleipnir's sluggish gait.

Alarik hauled back on the reins, bringing Sleipnir to a halt. "I cannot."

Bjorn glared up at him. "Cannot . . . or will not?"

Alarik shrugged. "Makes no difference. Will not, if you would."

"Loki take you, then!"

"She oversteps her boundaries much too far already," Alarik contended. "And the blame falls to me for not removing her sooner. Forsooth, Bjorn, Nissa creates discontent where'er she goes! Already she tries to usurp Alva's authority, and Brother Vernay—"

"She cannot abide Brother Vernay!" Bjorn interjected in her defense. "He assumes—and not so subtly either—he will convert every last soul to Olav's accursed Christian faith! 'Tis for that reason Nissa did not allow him within the hall whilst you were gone."

Alarik eyed his youngest brother irascibly. "I would remind you, mine *bror*, that it is not Nissa's hall to banish him from," he pointed out, his eyes gleaming. " 'Tis mine, as you seem to forget, yet I understand she also kept Vernay near imprisoned within the *kirken* during mine absence. I ask you now . . . what right had she to assume such a thing? 'Tis little wonder Vernay did not take his complaint directly to Olav rather than wait to address it with me."

"And since when do you concern yourself with Olav?" Bjorn raged. "Ever have you walked your own path. Might Hrolf be right? Might you have fallen for that witch and her spine-weakening

Christian faith? It seems to me you have changed." he accused, and without waiting for a reply—knowing he would get none if Alarik chose not to give it—he stalked away.

Alarik whirled his mount about. He sat rigid in the saddle. "Wed with her, then, Bjorn!"

Bjorn halted, his back stiffening, and turned, his hands on his hips, his legs spread insolently.

"Wed with the shrew—take her off mine hands—and then I just may consider your request."

The brothers stared at each other, at an impasse; Alarik because he could not afford to relent more than he had, and Bjorn because he knew Nissa would stay only did Alarik request it. She would not wed with him so easily as that, and they both knew it. And he could not woo her once she was back under her father's thumb; she craved her sire's approval too much to walk against him, nor would Ejnar so simply accept Bjorn's suit. Bjorn had little to offer Ejnar's daughter. Olav was king to a nation, Alarik master of his own, but what did he have to claim?

Nought. Not a cursed thing!

"There you are!" Olav bellowed as he approached them.

Both Alarik and Bjorn turned at the sound of his voice. "I wonder if you two bickering old women might join me in a jaunt to the *kirken*? I wish to meet this Elienor, at last!"

Alarik's eyes narrowed.

"Alas, you cannot fault me for being curious," Olav defended.

"By your leave?" Bjorn interjected, the courtesy anything but. His eyes were wild with resentment and anger. He and Olav had never embraced as brothers, and he wasn't about to begin now simply because Olav chose to include him for once. Pivoting, he made his way toward the longhouse, declaring, "I believe I shall decline."

With furrowed brow, Olav regarded Bjorn's retreating back an instant, and then his gaze returned to Alarik. "You see that I try, to no avail," he complained. "What ails the whelp this time, at any rate?"

Alarik's silver eyes shadowed. "The same as which drove you to wed Tyri, mine brother, and Longbeard to Nissa's sister . . . our sire to Astrid," Alarik suggested, failing to add himself to the despicable list. He'd sworn he would never be led by his groin, yet here he sat, striving not to appear overly eager at Olav's request to meet with Elienor. He'd been trying to come up with viable excuses to stop in at the *kirken* to no avail. What possible reason could he have conjured up when everyone, including Vernay, knew fair well that he took great pains to keep his distance from the little church he'd erected merely to appease Olav?

The only possible reason was that he wished to see Elienor, and *that* he was unwilling to cede.

Even to himself.

Especially to himself.

Chapter 23

"Dominus vobiscum."
"The Lord be with you."
"Et cum spiritu tuo."

Elienor was silent a moment, not because she could not recall the meaning of the phrase, but because she was tiring of Brother Vernay's ceaseless interrogation—at least that was what she felt it to be. She took in a fortifying breath. "And with your spirit," she replied wearily. "Brother Vernay!" she protested, her eyes pleading. "I assure you I know this! How much longer must we go on?"

After her bath, Alva had dressed Elienor and plaited her hair and then had escorted her the short distance to the vale where the small church of which Alarik had spoken was erected. Dressed now in the exquisite sapphire silk Alva had brought her, Elienor felt more like a Jezebel than a servant of God. In truth, never had she felt so distant from her spiritual self, and though at the moment she longed for the simplicity of her flowing white novice's garb, and the safety of the cloister, she resented her presence in this mockery of a church!

Brother Vernay shook his head apologetically. "I beg your pardon, my sister. 'Tis but that I cannot read much myself, and I *must* be certain you fully comprehend the tongue before we can begin transcribing. You see, I cannot be certain I can verify all your letters," he explained gravely. "And I could not allow you to copy erroneously—'twould be a sin to alter scripture so. I, for one, would not relish burning in the fires of hell for such an avoidable transgression, and alas, neither could I bear the thought of you consumed by those flames!" he stated emphatically. "Alas, we must continue!" He lifted up the volume he'd been reciting from, opening it to a familiar page—Elienor could tell by the comfortable expression upon his face. Then he set the tome down on the bureau before Elienor. "Read to me here," he demanded, indicating with his finger.

Put so Elienor could not refuse him. She sighed, scrutinizing the page before her a long moment, her vision slightly blurred for the hours she'd spent staring at the *papier 'a lettres. "Domine Deus . . ."* Her voice faltered with fatigue. She rubbed her temples. *". . . Agnus Dei, Filius Patris: qui tollis peccata mundi, miserere nobis."* She lifted her gaze to find that Brother Vernay had moved behind her and was now peering over her shoulder.

"Very good," he commended. "Now do you perceive what it means?"

Elienor nodded, and translated without bothering to reexamine the paragraph, " 'Oh, Lord, Lamb of God, Son of the Father: who takest away the sins of the world, have mercy on us.' 'Tis from the Gospel of John, I know it well. How is it, Brother Vernay," she expressed with exasperation, "that you can recite from memory—can even know where each can be found in your volume—yet you claim you cannot read?"

Brother Vernay moved away from her, his face reddening. He turned his back to her. "I *can* read," he disclosed softly, hesitantly, turning to face her somewhat diffidently. " 'Tis that I sometimes confuse my letters, is all. They do not always appear the same to mine eyes," he added plaintively. "And so, because it confuses me . . . I read little and remember much."

"Oh?" Elienor replied, chagrined over the accusation that had darkened her tone. "*Je m'excuse* for questioning so discourteously," she said softly, running nervous fingers across the page; she could almost feel the letters rising up from the hallowed parchment. "There was a time when I made these words my life," she told him pensively, her voice distant. "I suppose 'tis that I take exception to being forced to read them now." She lowered her head meekly. "I . . . I ask your forgiveness for the impertinence I've shown you." She lifted stark violet eyes to find Brother Vernay staring, his head cocked in compassion.

"God doth have his own plan, my sister," he said cryptically, studying her a long moment. "Alas, you must listen to your heart. 'Twill not mislead you, I think."

Her eyes were shadowed, filled with torment. She shook her head miserably. "I wish it were so," she replied softly, blinking away the sudden sting in her eyes, "but I fear did I listen to my heart, Brother Vernay, then I would perceive nought but hatred." And did she listen to her treacherous body, she amended silently, averting her eyes in shame, she would be nothing but the Jezebel she felt to be in this leman's gown!

Elienor was confused. She could not comprehend what it was she was supposed to be, to feel. Everything had been so clear . . . until this morn. And now she was afeared of she knew nought, she trusted nought. Nevertheless, there was some comfort to be had in the familiar scriptures, and she vowed to put her heart into it from here forth.

If nought more, it would save her from foolishly giving it elsewhere.

The door opened suddenly, startling both Elienor and Brother Vernay, though upon seeing Alarik, Vernay at once eased and smiled in welcome. Elienor's face flushed at the sight of him, yet she did not avert her eyes in shame. She dared not, for Brother Vernay had turned toward her and was watching them curiously. She tilted her chin up deliberately, fighting the urge to turn away as Alarik's tawny brow rose. He said nothing as he removed his crimson cloak, this one not so fine as the one he'd given her to wear. Behind him entered another man who Elienor sensed watched them both, as well. For a disconcerting instant, the silence of the chapel was interminable as she and Alarik stared at each other.

And then the stranger spoke. "Do we make progress?" he asked of Vernay. Elienor turned to regard the man at once, and at the sight of him her heart vaulted into her throat. To her shock, he was near the image of Alarik—like him in most every detail but for the darker shade of hair and his startling green eyes. She shook her head, doubting her sight, and blinked. When the pair did not unify, she squeezed her lids shut until she was certain the vision had vanished.

"Why," the man said. "I've not seen one so dark and yet so fair since mine days in the Danelaw!"

Elienor opened her eyes, her face growing more pallid with each second.

The man laughed. "Forsooth, *bror*! I've seen many

a look accorded us for our semblance, but never one so terrorized! What have you done to the poor girl?" he chuckled. "She looks as though she might perish at the notion that there are two of you."

Hours later, as Elienor paced the length of Alarik's chamber, she still could not compose herself.

Sweet Jesu, but the likeness between them amazed her! And now she was more confounded than ever—the dream; who, then, would die? Mayhap 'twas not Alarik, after all. Mayhap 'twas Olav instead? And then mayhap neither?

She fumbled for her ring at once, holding it desperately within her fist, grateful that Alarik had thought to return it. "Mother." She whispered miserably. "How did you bear it?"

As if in response to her question, a mournful whine came from the vicinity of her toes. Elienor glanced down to spy the pup sniffing bashfully at her feet. No sooner had she stooped to stroke it behind its ears then the door clicked opened. Alva entered. Startled, Elienor sprang to her feet, leaving the pup to paw at her soft leather shoes in protest.

"I've brought you another garment along with your own clean ones," the older woman announced, coming forward to offer the neat stack of finery into Elienor's arms. "The silk is splendid, to be certain, but 'twill hardly keep you warm enough in this clime."

Sighing, Elienor accepted them, her reply no more than a cheerless nod.

"I understand you met Olav today?"

"Aye," Elienor replied. "And the likeness between them is remarkable indeed."

" 'Tis true," Alva agreed. " 'Tis said that it is why Olav could not deny Alarik as his blood kin the first time they met, yet there are many differences betwixt them if you'll but see them," she suggested. "Oooh, what a vexing mongrel!" she declared, spotting the stubborn pup at Elienor's feet. "Always into aught. Away!" She shooed it, waving her hands indignantly. "I've not an inkling what possessed the jarl to bring the mongrel into his bedchamber!"

Elienor had wondered the same, yet she had been pleased he had, for she felt a bond with the poor beast.

As if discerning that he was the cause of Alva's tirade, the pup scrambled away, secreting himself beneath the bed. As Elienor watched its ears droop unhappily, she felt more than a touch of kinship with the animal—not that Alva was unkind. Elienor had found her anything but, yet this was not her home, and she did not feel especially welcome. Save for Alva and Brother Vernay—and Clarisse, of course—no one was overly welcoming. And Clarisse, she understood, would be leaving the steading before long, for Alarik had given her to Sigurd. Still, Elienor sensed that the time had come for her to forget the past and make the most of the situation at hand.

Like it or nay, this was her future.

"I suggest you change for bed," advised Alva. "I heard the jarl saying that he and Olav were to leave early in the morn—something about gathering men for Olav's voyage. If 'tis so, he'll be in directly, I think, for he'll be wanting his sleep." Having revealed this, Alva took her leave, though not before imparting one last bit of advice. "Best you hie to it lest he comes and you be forced to undress before him." She stifled a giggle as she closed the door, for Elienor immediately thrust the bundle from her arms to the bed.

Having been forewarned, she quickly divested herself of the loathsome silk over and undertunic. And then, after snatching her own garments from the pile upon the bed, she donned them hastily, leaving herself concealed only by the frail linen undertunic. Before she could scurry into the sanctuary of the furs, however, the door clicked opened once more.

"Do mine eyes deceive me?" a husky voice remarked. "Or are you truly so eager to share mine bed this night?"

Elienor froze, her heart beating frantically as she turned to face him. She crossed her arms as Alarik closed the door, concealing herself. Her face flamed under his scrutiny. He took a step forward and she instinctively took one backward, reassuring herself with the simple fact that he'd yet to force himself upon her.

'Twas unlikely he would begin now, she told herself.

And in truth, after this morn, she wasn't certain he wasn't as repulsed of her as she claimed to be of him.

Her brows knit suddenly. Claimed?

Nay, she amended silently, *was*!

She *was* repulsed of him!

So why did she feel so strangely excited by the possibility that he might desire her? Averting her eyes to the floor, she stammered, "A . . . Alva advised me—sh . . . she said you planned to seek your bed. I . . . I only thought to . . ."

"Conceal yourself before I arrived?" Alarik asked dryly, his gaze rivetted, despite her lack of dress, upon her lips. To his annoyance he'd been able to think of nothing else all day, even in the face of Olav's political concerns. Hella's curse, even now he remained in a state of painful arousal with the merest thought of those warm, sweet lips upon his own.

Her gaze returned to him, and the deep violet pools lured him closer. He took another step forward, diminishing the distance between them, fearing he'd finally reached the point of madness, for his reason had all but fled now that he was in her presence once more. "Have I given you so much cause to fear me?" he asked huskily, his eyes brilliant with intent.

Elienor swallowed, her heart turning violently at his question, but she managed to shake her head in response. His eyes, like shards of molten silver, impaled her as he took another step forward.

"Have I taken the slightest liberties with you?"

Again Elienor shook her head, for in truth, he'd not.

She had been the one to take them, for he'd asked only to be washed this morn. Nought more. Her breath quickened, for his eyes impaled her still, burning with something wholly carnal as he came even closer.

"In certainty, who forced whom this morn?" he challenged, as though he'd read her thoughts.

Or had she spoken them aloud? She couldn't discern. " 'Tis you who forced me!" Elienor replied a little hysterically, retreating until the back of her legs encountered the bed. The look of purpose in his wintry eyes alarmed her. "I . . . I did not ask to bathe you," she asserted. "Nor did I . . ."

He stopped before her, reaching out casually

to lift her thick plait into his palm, and Elienor gave a little shriek. He slid his hand up the length of it and back, admiring the healthful shine, holding her gaze. "Elienor of *Baume-les-Nonnes*," he murmured silkily, a quiver snaking through him as his eyes finally acknowledged the rest of her. "I vow, you've bewitched me," he said softly. His fingers slid to the end of her plait, and at once commenced to unraveling it.

Elienor shivered at the charge, closing her eyes to steady herself, suddenly feeling so light-headed and weak-kneed that she feared she might swoon before his eyes.

'Twas said that her mother had bewitched her father . . .

She refused to tread in her mother's shoes—refused, for she could not abide the repercussions!

Did he know? The way he stared at her made her feel he did. She began to quake where she stood.

"Tell me who taught you to use your tongue so," Alarik demanded, his whisper faint but warm upon her face.

Her heart racing, Elienor opened her eyes to find him staring intently at her lips.

Sweet Jesu, did he wish to kiss her now? After spurning her this morn? Surely not?

"Answer me."

Elienor swallowed, trying desperately to think what it was he was asking. "I . . . I . . ." She could not compose her thoughts, yet she sensed it had something to do with the kiss by the way he stared so intently at her mouth. "I . . . I did not mean to!" she cried suddenly, shaking her head. "I . . ." Her voice faltered. "I swear, I . . ." Her mouth snapped shut, for his face was suddenly so close to her own that she feared even to breathe lest they vie for the same breath.

"Who taught you to use your lips so?" he demanded once more.

"Ph . . . Phillipe," Elienor replied honestly, her chin lifting. "I . . . in my country 'tis the custom for lovers to . . ."

His fingers gripped her plait and he rocked backward upon his heels, as though buffeted. "Lovers?" His eyes slitted. "Were you lovers, Elienor?"

His look unnerved her, yet Elienor could not wrench her own gaze away to save her life.

Nor could she calm her raging heartbeat.

Or the sudden heat that flared within her at the memory of his powerful body beneath her fingertips. The fact that he was fully dressed now did little to banish the sultry image of his smooth chest, glistening bronze with sweat and steam from the bath chamber.

A muscle twitched in his jaw as he anticipated her response. "Were you lovers?" he demanded yet again, his tone soft but ruthless, nonetheless. Elienor glanced at his hand uneasily, her heart quickening, for with her plait unraveled, he stroked a lock of her hair between his fingers. If she angered him, what would prevent him from using it to subdue her? She shook her head in answer.

A look of fierce satisfaction came over his harsh features. He brought the lock he was caressing to his nose, breathing deeply of its scent. "That pleases me," he told her, his gaze softening considerably. His fingers moved to tangle deep into her hair, and a quiver swept Elienor's spine as she felt them curl about her nape. Had she wanted to flee him, she couldn't have, for he held her firm now. His other hand lit upon her hip, and she started with a gasp of surprise. He smiled, squeezing gently before sliding his arm about her waist. She cried out as in the next moment she found herself hauled forward and crushed against the incredible heat of his body.

"I've known kisses afore," Alarik said bluntly, his eyes glittering strangely. "Kisses of homage betwixt men . . ." He touched his warm lips to each side of her face, lingering as if to savor the scent and taste of her skin. Elienor's blood rushed into her head at the delicious sensation. Instinctively she knew that never were those kisses he spoke of so lingering and spine tingling as this one had been.

"Kisses of promise," he continued gruffly, "those meted behind the backs of fathers . . . or between lovers," he added pointedly, pecking her lips softly. When their lips parted an eternity later, Elienor felt a heart pang over his disclosure. Yet why should she object that he'd shared such kisses with others, she asked herself scornfully. He was her enemy, she reminded herself.

His smile deepened. "Never," he revealed fervently, his molten silver eyes penetrating her defenses, "have I thought to taste so deeply."

Elienor looked up at him questioningly, and he shook his head slowly, his provocative mouth stirring closer, his lips brushing hers as he spoke. Elienor whimpered softly at the soft caress, and his grip firmed upon the back of her neck as though to keep her from escaping him. "Never have I considered it, even," he told her, "for 'tis not our way. Yet I find the flavor of you lingers, Elienor of *Baume-les-Nonnes*. Lingers," he whispered, "like exquisite *Fransk* wine—strange to the palate, intoxicating nonetheless."

Mesmerized by the heady sensation of his lips so close to her mouth, Elienor's limbs weakened, yet as his lips pressed into her own, her sanity returned enough that she shoved at his leather-garbed chest in confusion.

Alarik merely grinned. "I've had babes give more of an effort," he told her bluntly. "Mayhap you are undecided?" His silver eyes mocked her.

A quiver raced down Elienor's spine, yet she managed to lift her chin as best she could. "Unhand me!" she cried softly.

"Elienor," he whispered, relishing the sound of her name on his lips. His brows flickered a little, his eyes growing openly amused. He chuckled deeply, and the sound made Elienor's senses scatter. "Ever you amaze me, my little nun. Men tremble before me, yet you seem not to fear me at all." He crushed her to him once more, a demonic smile curving his lips. "Still, you cannot think to entice me," he advised, a glint of wonder in his eyes, "only to deny me after."

Elienor felt a flush rise to her face. She opened her mouth to protest, but nothing came. Suddenly, and without warning, he swooped to take her mouth as though he were famished for the taste of her.

Alarik groaned in gratification as Elienor allowed his tongue to sweep across the soft fullness of her lips. Resistance came only when he attempted to enter the silky warmth of her mouth. She whimpered and pressed her lips together to deny him entrance—a last dire effort, he knew, but he refused to be denied.

His body quickening with the feel of her in his arms, he reveled in the taste of her sweet lips, nipped them, lapped them, feasted upon them, coaxed her to open unto him. When that failed, he lifted her abruptly to the level of his face. Too long he'd waited, and now there was no more patience, no more reason. "Open for me, Elienor!" he demanded harshly, his breath ragged. By the blood of his father, he'd sworn to take nought she did not freely give, but he couldn't be certain what he would do if she refused to yield!

Elienor cried out, her heart leaping into her throat. She clung to Alarik for support, her eyes closing in desperation, and obeyed at once, her lips parting softly.

God forgive her, but she found she could not help herself, could not deny him.

At once Alarik reclaimed her lips. Half-insane with the desire to taste her, his tongue drove in at once to explore the velvety recesses of her mouth. His heart hammered.

Loki take him! She was more delectable than he remembered.

The pit of Elienor's stomach responded with a tumultuous swirl as his moist, firm mouth demanded a response. To her horror, even as she called herself wanton, fool, and shameless, she reveled in the kiss.

Like liquid fire his tongue stabbed into the warmth of her mouth, drinking of her as though his soul demanded it . . . and the saints protect her, she delighted in it, radiated with it. The thought crossed her mind in that instant that she'd never been cut of holy cloth, for surely no bride of Christ would respond so eagerly to a mortal man.

Much less her sworn enemy!

Her heart twisted.

He was her enemy.

Alarik nearly erupted where he stood as Elienor offered her soft little tongue. Yet he thrust it back savagely with his own, determined to retain control this time. And then suddenly he paused and drew away.

To her shame, Elienor whimpered deep in her throat, wanting only to draw him back, yet before she could open her eyes, she felt his lips touch her brow and her heart turned over. She opened her eyes, looking up at him, half-dazed.

"I..." Alarik swallowed, unaccustomed to asking for aught. Nevertheless, he would have her willing, or not at all. "Elienor...I would show you what else these lips...this tongue of mine can do." His eyes, slivers of smoky gray, entreated her.

Elienor's heart flew into her throat. She said nothing—dared say nothing, for she feared that if she spoke, the answer would come forth as aye, when she knew it should be nay. It had to be nay! She could not, in all good conscience, simply give herself to her enemy!

"Elienor!" he implored, plunging her to the bed abruptly.

Elienor felt a scream catch in her throat as he trapped her between his arms. Yet his lips did nothing more than to seek out hers and brush them in a surprisingly gentle kiss—hot and persistent, coaxing, tormenting, burning.

"Elienor?" he hissed between her lips.

All thought of protest vanished when his tongue slipped into her mouth once more, this time finding easy entrance.

Was she so faithless? So wanton?

Her heart ached at the thought. She gasped as Alarik lowered his body to cover hers. This time she managed a whimper of protest, and turned her face in vain.

It stopped him not at all. His lips sought her neck instead, nibbling feverishly, consuming her . . . and to her shame, Elienor found herself responding in ways she'd never conceived possible.

Her body became a separate entity, arching of its own will. Desire, like molten fire, flowed through her, coloring her cheeks with mortification. Yet to her dismay, she simply moaned in pleasure as his hands cupped her face and he sought her mouth once more, his tongue stabbing in, and out, then in, out, in, the rhythm mesmerizing. With each thrust her heart leapt higher.

With an oblivious groan, Alarik suckled Elienor's tongue, greedily taking everything she would give. His body hardened more fully with each taste of her, and so did his resolve; he would have her—tonight, by Odin! He *must* have her.

Or grow mad.

Her passionate whimpers melded with his groans of desire until that sweet melody was the only sound to fill his ears, spurring him onward, exciting his senses.

All the while, her hands stroked him unconsciously. He doubted she was aware of that, nor that her body writhed beneath him in virginal frustration. When her pelvis careened into his instinctively, he rocked forward ruthlessly in answer, eagerly pursuing what she so naively offered.

More than aught else, he yearned to bury himself deep within her—she was so soft . . . so soft and supple in his arms.

He swore beneath his breath.

She tilted her pelvis once more, and the desire he'd harnessed for so long erupted violently within him. Need clawed him like a wild beast, stealing reason. Yet despite his instant of oblivion he found a moment to lift himself, to remove his boots, discarding them hastily upon the floor beside the bed. At the same time, before she could regain her senses enough to protest, his fingers slipped up her gown, until he found her, and he quivered with anticipation when he felt her wet to the touch.

Elienor cried out, starting at the unexpected sensation of his warm fingers in her most intimate place. Yet startling as it was, his stroking sent jolts of pleasure bursting through her.

Slowly, seductively, his head thrusting backward in sheer pleasure as he discovered her, he stroked her, wanting nought more than to rip the gown from her body and feel her more intimately beneath him. Yet he restrained himself, knowing patience and cunning would gain him more. A sheen of perspiration broke forth, bathing his flesh with the salt of his body as he drove his finger once more into the depths of her, stroking the nectar within, preparing her for the size of him. When she closed her legs instinctively, he nudged them apart with hands that trembled, so potent was his lust.

Elienor moaned, her body twisting. She cried out at the almost painful pleasure.

Did he realize the confusion his touch evoked upon her body? Upon her mind? She opened her eyes, the turmoil clear in her eyes.

Indisputably, those eyes were the most bewitching Alarik had ever beheld. He stared, mesmerized by the violet-blue pools. "Truly, truly, you art lovely," he whispered huskily, teasing her still. He watched her breast rising and falling, her breathing quickening as she gazed at him, and in that moment he understood that she acquiesced with her startling blue eyes . . . and her silence. The knowledge filled him. His body quickening, he parted her once more and slowly inserted a finger. She cried out, tilting for him, her eyes glazing with passion.

He smiled mercilessly, shuddering.

Elienor whimpered, a helpless sound deep in the back of her throat and twisted in frustration. "You . . . you . . . promised not . . . not to force me!" she cried feverishly.

"So I did," he admitted. "So I did." His eyes glittered. "You wish me to stop, then?" His eyes flickered knowingly and his lips curved slightly when her eyes widened.

She forced herself to speak. "Aye!" she cried out, uncertainly, twisting on the bed.

There was something amiss within her soul, something she could not comprehend.

He withdrew, smiling devilishly.

Elienor's heart plummeted. Her face flushed, for rather than feel relief that he had adhered to her wishes, she yearned only for the return of his touch. She berated herself that it was a sin to lie with a man without benefit of matrimony, yet at this moment she feared she craved just that.

Mayhap it was the simple fact that Francia, Phillipe, Mother Heloise, and the priory were so far away, or mayhap, if she could be honest with herself, 'twas simply because she desperately wanted that certain something his kisses tendered, the promise of fulfillment.

Was it so wrong to seek it?

She'd despaired that she would ever know a man—indeed, had never dared to consider it until Phillipe. Yet now . . .

She feared she craved it with a madness that was shameful.

There was absolutely no guile to his little nun at all, Alarik acknowledged. Her eyes indisputably asked him to continue, yet he would hear it from her own lips. His own eyes narrowed ruthlessly. "Say it, Elienor." She'd given him a taste of her passion, had shown him how sweet it could be.

He wanted her willing.

Or not at all.

Elienor shook her head.

"Say it!" he hissed, his knuckle returning to graze her curls. She cried out at the shock of his touch. "You want this," he whispered huskily. The gray of his eyes smoldered as he looked down upon her.

The beat of Elienor's heart quickened.

The shame of it! She could not—would not look into his knowing eyes! Squeezing her lids shut in surrender, her traitorous body tilted into his fingers.

Alarik shuddered as he watched her respond, his male flesh straining at his breeches. Swiftly, he unlaced his ties with his free hand, easing the confining garment downward. "Elienor," he murmured thickly. "Lovely, lovely, Elienor."

Elienor trembled softly as she opened her eyes to see him peeling his tunic up and over his head. He flung it aside, his eyes scrutinizing her, yet she knew she would not protest when he lowered his body to hers once more, touching his hardness to her softness. Aware only that the pressure now was different in *that* place, she whimpered in the back of her throat, and her eyes fluttered closed.

Slowly, so slowly, he entered her, and so easily, Elienor was lost once more.

His heart thrumming in his ears, Alarik shifted, making certain not to penetrate any deeper than was necessary as he pressed her down into the furs.

He withdrew slightly, and drove forward gently, knowing he would need go slowly, for he wished to cause her no pain.

Yet whereas he managed to harness his passion in the one sense, it erupted fiercely elsewise. His hands took hold of her filmy linen undertunic, and in one tug, rent it impatiently from her breast. His lips curled with satisfaction as before his eyes the rosy peaks grew to pebble hardness.

For an instant he could only look, for she was perfection.

And she was his.

Startled by the ferocity of the gesture, Elienor stiffened, her eyes flying open.

Alarik vowed to give her no chance to protest. He was glad she watched, for he wanted her aware of everything he would do to her.

"As I promised," he murmured, his eyes brilliant with purpose as his lips lowered to her breast. He seized both her wrists, pinning them above her head as his lips continued their descent. He relished the sound of Elienor's gasp as his teeth gently closed about the tip of one nipple, tugging delicately. He felt her arch beneath him . . . and heard her whimper as he penetrated a little deeper.

Alarik fought to regain control as he felt the barrier of her maidenhead. His hand trembled as he thrust it behind Elienor's back to keep her steady. He suckled fleetingly at her breast, and then glanced up at her through dark lashes, his eyes shadowed. He blew softly upon the wetness he'd laved upon her breast.

She shuddered, closing her eyes, and Alarik had no inkling whether it was a reaction to his loving, or fear. Yet fear would only hinder the passion he so wished to taste of her, and so he held himself steady within her. Lifting himself slightly to look into her beautiful face, he braced his weight upon his elbows and waited.

When she opened her eyes, he grinned, for the war in her soul was there for him to see.

And the tide was turning.

"Now," he whispered, "to show you those pleasures I promised . . ."

Chapter 24

Elienor gasped as his lips again found her breast.

For the longest moment it seemed she ceased to breathe as tendrils of heat spread through her loins . . . along with every wicked sensation she'd never imagined. Her flesh burned wherever his fingers and lips stroked her, and still her body yearned for . . .

What?

"More," she whispered.

She closed her eyes to fight her fear, for even through the haze of pleasure she could not forget what Mother Heloise had told her about the pain that would come with her first coupling.

Suddenly he ceased.

Elienor opened her eyes to find him staring down at her, his dark eyes fixed upon her, scrutinizing. Curse him! she thought, for his face showed nothing of his thoughts. Surely there had to be more? Something left undone?

Her eyes filled with confusion, for she'd not felt the pain, or neither the pleasure! Even as she called herself wanton, she lifted her chin, willing him to touch her again, willing his lips to return to her flesh, but they did not. He merely chuckled deep in the back of his throat, the unholy sound sending a thousand quivers down her spine.

Outrage flowed through her suddenly, stripping her of the last of her reserve—outrage that he could play her like a lyre, so skillfully, and then leave her to quiver in frustration—outrage that he would bring her so far only to leave her thwarted—outrage that she would allow it!

Well, she thought, her eyes narrowing wrathfully . . . two could play at this game as easily as one. He was not immune to her, she now knew. Her lips curved with a secret smile as she reached out to mimic the way that he'd touched her, her fingers alighting upon his chest, soft as butterflies. She stroked the crisp golden hair, her own body quickening at the feel of his warm flesh beneath her fingertips. As she watched, his eyes darkened, flickering with amusement, yet Elienor continued, vowing to show him what it felt like to be left unfulfilled. He shuddered and groaned as she searched out and found the tiny nubs concealed within the mat of gleaming hair upon his chest, his dark lashes fluttering closed, then open. She smiled in victory, and continuing as he watched, lifted herself to replace her fingers with her lips. She cried out as her own maneuvering drove him deeper still, the thickness both aching and delicious—though not painful enough that she didn't crave him deeper still.

Elienor's fingers clutched at his shoulders as she arched her head backward instinctively. As if in a vision, she felt her hips undulate shamelessly, impaling herself deeper still, though slowly, her heart pulsing wildly, for it was beginning to grow tender. Sensing there was more, she willed him deeper yet.

The gentle sliding motion filled her with heat that consumed her.

It seemed she would die from the pleasure.

Even aware that 'twas she alone that moved, her hips continued to undulate of their own accord, seeking something . . .

More.

"Please!" she beseeched of him, her head thrusting to one side. "Give me . . ."

"What, Elienor?"

She gasped. "I . . . I don't know!"

Alarik had fully intended to let her set the pace, but now he feared he could not. He'd held himself back, but succumbing to her pleas, he rolled his pelvis slowly, gently, taking over the rhythm where she left off.

"This," he ground out, his voice thick with restraint, "is what your tongue-kiss recalls me to." He continued to fill her, withdrawing, teasing, and filling her again, deeper each time.

Elienor's fingers tangled in his hair, urging him forward, drawing his head to her lips. She raised her hips suggestively and moved restlessly against him, drawing him deeper.

Alarik's heart pounded with the knowledge that he had won her surrender. Reveling in her body's unabashed response to him, he groaned, at once sliding his hand down to cup her full bottom. He lifted her hips.

At the same instant that he bent forward to thrust his tongue into her mouth, he thrust forward ruthlessly, fusing their bodies at long last. His own body convulsed with pleasure at the incredible virginal tightness of her.

Elienor responded with an outcry of her own. She arched from the bed, quivering, her eyes darkened with passion. It seemed every last trace of Alarik's will exploded in that instant.

Like a man gone mad, he drove forth again, and again, and again, burying himself deep within her, and deeper still.

She was sweet.

She was passion.

She was his!

His!

His arms encircled her, and his tongue stabbed her mouth with the same furor and rhythm he created with his body.

The feelings that exploded within Elienor were inexpressibly delicious, and she held on for dear life, losing her soul in the tempest.

To her shock there had been only pleasure, intense pleasure—no pain at all.

Her fingers clawing his arms, she gave back full measure as his hands stroked her body and his tongue stroked her mouth. Mindlessly, she tried to return the caress, her hands gliding along the length of his back, but she grew too delirious with the pleasure he was giving her. She reveled in the breadth of his arms, the strong tendons in the back of his neck, and all the while her body responded with an ardor of its own.

"And this!" he rasped, moving swift as lightning within her, "is what your kiss evokes me to!"

As though spurred by his words, something shattered within her. Elienor cried out, her body convulsing madly.

With a last powerful thrust and a savage cry, Alarik spilled himself with a deeper gratification than he'd ever known. Yet even when 'twas done, he could not stir from atop her, so great was the need to stay joined. He buried his face into her nape, smelling her hair, smelling her flesh, and groaning his pleasure.

After a moment, when his breathing returned to normal, he rolled to lay beside her, drawing her into his arms. She didn't resist, and unable to deny himself, he pecked her nose, her eyes, her brow, smoothed her hair back away from her lovely face.

He understood nothing of the bond that joined them, and though he'd never feared anything before, he was unnerved by the powerful sensation that filled him suddenly.

Love was for fools, he knew, and so he gave his emotion the name of desire . . . calling it safely by its baser name of lust.

Yet he was, at least, honest with himself in admitting that he lusted for no one else.

Elienor haunted his every waking moment, his every dream, and only when he was with her did her image cease to torment him.

Too spent to worry over the consequences of what she'd just experienced, and feeling too languid even to care, Elienor snuggled into Alarik's embrace.

Her breathing slowed, and in the instant before she drifted into sleep, the thought occurred to her that she'd never again think of kisses in the same way.

And never again in connection with Phillipe of Brouillard!

She was forever branded.

Alarik lay wide awake listening to Elienor's faint breathing. She'd given him all he'd hoped she would, and more, and now she slept as sweetly as a babe in his arms. He didn't dare move and wake her, so he kept his vigil and waited for the candles to snuff themselves.

And still he could not sleep.

There was, in his heart, a strange sensation he'd never known ere now. Was it possible to lose one's heart so quickly and completely, even against one's will?

He thought so, for if not—then there was no explanation for the way that he felt—no explanation for why he seemed to need to guard her.

Why he burned for her.

And only her.

In her dreams, Elienor saw the majestic dragon ship once more, cloaked in mist. Alarik, or mayhap Olav, stood at the prow, his foot propped upon the wooden serpent—serpent, not hawk? his sword held firmly in his hand. From the mist came another dragon prow, and then another . . . and another . . .

Gasping for breath, Elienor struggled to free herself.

Alarik had only just drifted and was roused by Elienor's outcry. He drew her into his arms and still she struggled.

"Let me soothe you," he insisted.

At once she ceased, but instantly began to weep, and his heart pricked him.

And then his lips thinned as he acknowledged the irony of his request, for *he* was very likely the terror of her dreams.

He was her nightmare.

Moonlight reflected upon the pallid snow, giving Bjorn ample light to find his way. He dared not carry a torch lest it be detected from the manor. Nor did he dare go mounted, for he needed no telltale prints exposing him. Grateful to Thor and to Odin that snow still fell to cover his tracks, for 'twas late in the season for snow, he plodded onward, looking over his shoulder every so oft. Caution served, though without a doubt he knew that the gods were with him this night—after all, 'twas his summons that had brought Ejnar the Dane.

Not Alarik's.

The messenger had come to him in private, had bid him meet with Ejnar in the vale, and it was there Bjorn made his way now. Bitter laughter escaped him suddenly, for the thought occurred to him that he would always have Alarik's leavings and nought more. Never more.

Yet soothing at least was the fact that Nissa shared in his anger. Still, in the back of his mind simmered the fact that she had, in reality, preferred his brother to him. He'd not been her first choice, and he could not quite obliterate that truth from his mind, regardless that Nissa had agreed to wed him if her father chanced to condone it.

Once he reached the concealment of the pine and birch trees, he used their cover to make his way to the sacrificial stone, a runic inscribed altar where sacrifices were made to Thor, the God of thunder—his patron. No matter that Olav would have it otherwise! By Thor, his faith was the only thing in his life he retained control of, and Olav could blind himself before Bjorn converted!

And that was another thorn in his side, for he was well aware that his sole protection from Olav's iron fist was Alarik, the brother whose shadow ever obscured him. For this one thing, at least, Bjorn was indebted. So long as Alarik kept the old faith, Olav would not risk forcing him, despite the fact that Olav would coerce his own mother for his accursed Christian cause.

Arriving in time to see the last of the rites performed, Bjorn stepped boldly into the group of waiting men.

"What took you so long?" a voice snarled. A russet-haired man stepped forward from the gathering, making himself known. He was Ejnar the Red, blood cousin to jarl Haakon. Beside him stood Hrolf Kaetilson.

Bjorn acknowledged Hrolf with a slight tilt of his head and then turned to meet Ejnar's shrewd gaze. "I could not come in the broad light of day and chance being followed," he explained. "Mine brother seeks you—did you not know?"

Ejnar peered over Bjorn's shoulder. "So I've been told," he remarked with an indifferent shrug, glancing briefly at Hrolf. "He will not find me, I think." He turned back to Bjorn, smirking. "You are certain you were not followed?"

"Very certain," Bjorn declared, his gaze distracted momentarily by the two men removing from the old stone an animal carcass that had been sacrificed. "Mine brother is blind to all save his French whore," he confided. He gestured toward the stone. "You are bold, Ejnar, to sacrifice under Olav's very nose. Did you not realize he was in residence as well?"

Ejnar nodded, his eyes boring into Bjorn's. "I did. Why else do you presume 'twas done? You mayhap have a qualm with it?"

Bjorn shook his head.

"'Tis good," Ejnar asserted, pleased with the anger and envy he perceived in Bjorn. "What is it you wish of me, then?"

"Nissa," Bjorn replied bluntly. "I wish to make her mine wife and she refuses me lest I should gain your approval."

Ejnar's red brow arched. He shrugged and opened his mouth to speak.

"I would have that consent!" Bjorn avowed before he could be refused. "Whatever it takes!"

Ejnar's brows shot up. He nodded, contorting his mouth, considering. "Whatever it takes?" he asked, cocking his head in newfound interest. He rubbed his chin. "Mayhap *something* could be arranged, after all. But go now, ere we are discovered. I shall advise you soon of my decision."

Bjorn stiffened. "When?"

"When it suits me," Ejnar declared, taking a rigid stance. "Go on, now, and I will summon you when 'tis time."

Bjorn nodded, elated with the way the meeting had gone. He turned to go, his lips curving into a smile.

"Oh, but, Bjorn?"

Bjorn's shoulders straightened as he turned once more to face Nissa's father.

"Touch mine daughter in the interim and I will lay *you* next upon that stone." He waved casually at the stone in question. "Understand?"

Bjorn's smile faded. "I do," he said resentfully.

Ejnar nodded, and Bjorn spun on his heels, making his way back to the longhouse.

What he wouldn't give, just once—just once!— to have the advantage.

Chapter 25

⌒◯◯⌒

Squeezing her eyes shut, Elienor refused to waken.

Jesu, she'd given herself—willingly—to her enemy! Shame tore at her, and she would have cried in misery, but she was determined to feign sleep in hopes that Alarik would leave before she was forced to open her eyes and face him.

Sweet Jesu, how could she?

'Twas unthinkable!

What excuse that—simply to lose oneself in the heat of the moment? She was faithless! Wanton! Wicked!

"Aaaarghhh!"

The angry snarl roused Elienor at once.

With a startled shriek, she bolted upright, and any shame she'd felt over the night before vanished at the sight of Alarik springing from a stool like a demon enraged. With a cry of surprise, she ducked under the furs as he suddenly hurled the boot he held in his hand. It missed her, striking the floor somewhere near the bed.

"Flea ridden mongrel!"

It took Elienor an instant to discern that he was speaking of the pup, not of her, and that furthermore the pup was racing toward the bed, whimpering as it skid under the bed. Petrified for the animal, Elienor scrambled toward the edge, and

249

poking her head out, thrust her hands down to snatch the pup into her arms as it tried to bury itself beneath the bed.

"Did you see what the little cur did to mine good boots?" Alarik bellowed.

Blinking at the question, Elienor drew the cowering pup under the covers beside her. Both stared out from beneath the covers. Alarik continued to stare expectantly, and she shook her head in answer.

"Damned witless beast!" He bent, retrieving the boot from the floor where it landed. "I'd like to return the favor—chew his accursed hide!"

He waved the boot lividly at the pair huddled together beneath his furs—his furs!—though he was appeased somewhat by the way the pup trembled at the sound of his voice. Elienor, on the other hand, merely stared at the mangled boot sheepishly.

He snarled as he glanced again at his ruined boot, tossing it aside in frustration. Like as not, the pup had gnawed all night to have ravaged it so completely.

And he'd slept soundly like the exceptionally sated.

He pivoted abruptly, heading for the coffer across the chamber.

Elienor gave the pup a reproachful glance. "Look what you've gone and done!" she whispered.

Muttering, Alarik jerked open the coffer. The wooden lid struck the wall so violently that it bounced back, catching his fingers. "By the jaws of Fenri!" he exploded, snatching his fingers out of the way and waving his hand in pain.

Elienor gnawed at her lower lip to keep from giggling, for in that instant, rather than appearing threatening as he had so oft, he seemed more like a sullen boy who'd lost his favorite toy. Strange that during his moments of cold ire and calculating aloofness, she'd dreaded this explosion of tempers, yet to see him in the throes of it now did nought more than amuse her.

"I'll skewer the cursed beast!" he threatened, thrusting a hand into the coffer, yet somehow, as Elienor glanced down at the calming pup, now lapping at her hands in gratitude, she didn't believe him. Her brows drew together. He wouldn't harm the dog . . . she sensed that as strongly as she did the knowledge that something more than mere coupling had occurred between them last night. He would rant and he would rave, but he wouldn't harm the pup . . . or her.

The realization jarred her.

He would threaten, and he would frighten . . . but he had kept his promise.

As much as it shamed her to acknowledge it, he'd taken nothing from her without her consent.

Nay, he wouldn't harm her.

He'd protected her all along.

Hadn't he spared Clarisse by her word alone? Banished his man because of her, after all?

As she stared in wonder, he snatched out another pair of boots and sat upon the stool to lace them on, all the while continuing to curse the dog . . . nevertheless accepting her protection of it . . . despite the fact that he could easily have taken the dog from her.

With his boots donned, he stood, giving them both a black look before stalking from the chamber without another word.

Elienor glanced from the door as it slammed, to the boots, to the dog, and never felt more bewildered.

So now what was she supposed to feel?

*   *   *

As the days wore on, so did the uncommon cold.

The manor fell into a routine; Elienor, as well. Slowly, she was becoming accustomed to the Norse habits. For one, they ate only twice a day instead of three times. As she was accustomed, they broke their fast with *dagver*, the morning meal, but then ate only once more during the day. That mealtime they referred to as *nattver*. Yet she found to her surprise that this new schedule suited her just as well. Be it the clime or the strange hours they kept, she never experienced hunger pangs between meals.

Alarik spent most of his time with unresolved domestic issues. Yet that suited her as well, for she'd yet to determine what her feelings were for this enigmatic man. Olav, on the other hand, spent much time in the *kirken* with her and Brother Vernay, sometimes merely listening as Vernay dictated and Elienor transcribed. Other times, he asked Elienor about her past, her life in the priory, and such.

Elienor thought she liked him, though she sensed in him a fever raging nigh out of control. He was impassioned when he spoke of Christ and the church, yet his eyes held little compassion for those who renounced it.

The combination did not bode well.

Elienor listened quietly, trying to determine what, if aught this quest had to do with her terrible vision.

Something, she knew . . . but what? She'd discover it soon, she was certain, for it seemed to be hovering just out of sight.

She only hoped it was not too late.

Too late for what? a voice censured. *Didn't you determine that Alarik deserved to die? Have you changed your mind so soon?*

"Nay," she muttered to herself. Frost billowed about her face. This, she thought, was one thing she'd never become acclimated to—the incredible chill! Had she truly thought Francia cold? Forsooth, even within the heated manor house it was unbearably frigid. 'Twas no wonder Alarik risked the possibility of fire to have heat within his own chamber. A simple brazier would never have sufficed!

Snow fell so incessantly that men were forced to scoop away mounds of it periodically in order to excavate the entryway, lest they be trapped indoors. Only the servants dared brave the storm, for with the storehouses set apart from the manor, they had no choice.

Nor did Elienor.

Bundled tightly in Alarik's mantle, each day she walked the short distance to the vale. Not a soul ever spoke to her along the way. 'Twas as though they saw in her something vile, for the look in their eyes spoke volumes as she passed them by. They blamed her for something . . . yet *what*?

'Twas she who had the right to cast blame, after all.

She might have felt bad, but these were not her people—let them despise her if 'twas their bent! While she no longer had Clarisse, she did have Alva, as well as Brother Vernay—and God. He was with her, she was certain.

And then there was Mischief.

A smile trembled at her lips as she drew the mantle more securely about herself and the pup snuggled within her arms. She giggled, thinking that he'd surely earned his name. No sooner had Alarik left the bedchamber the day his boots had been ravaged than the pup was once again into devilment. Elienor had risen to dress and had been preoccupied only a moment before she'd found him excavating the fire pit! Already clothed in the blue silk, Elienor had hoisted up her skirts and had coerced herself into the pit to clean up Mischief's mess before Alarik might return and find ashes and earth scattered to the four corners.

And now, with the little church in sight, she again lifted her skirts, and holding the pup close, ran the distance to it, eager to be out of the cold. As she opened the door, her breath coming in white puffs, Brother Vernay smiled brightly in welcome. She liked him, she'd decided. He tested her sorely, but she liked him, for he reminded her in many ways of Mother Heloise. Olav, too, was present today. He came forward to take her mantle as she removed it, chuckling heartily as the pup bounded out to the floor, rolling clumsily.

Upon inspection of the fjords, 'twas evident no one would be sailing before spring thaw. In mere days, the ice had begun to thicken again, so that the ships were now forced aground. Yet despite the fact that Alarik had not relished the thought of setting out so soon after returning, the knowledge that he could not, even if he'd wished to, set his teeth on edge.

Or mayhap it was more the fact that once again he was lured to the *kirken* like metal to a cursed lodestone!

That, along with the probability that he would find Olav there before him, spurred his black humor.

Having abandoned his men at the manor, he rode with the fury of a maelstrom toward the confounded little building that had caused him so much strife, his crimson mantle swirling behind him with a wrath like unto Hel itself.

" '*Neither do men light a candle, and put it under a bushel, but on a candlestick; and it giveth light unto all that are in the house,*' " Vernay announced.

Elienor blinked. "What say you?"

Vernay waved a hand in admonition. "Copy! copy, *ma petite*! '*Let your light so shine before men*!' "

Elienor blinked again, in puzzlement. "Let my light—"

"Nay, nay! Again from the beginning, '*Neither do men light—*' "

Her gaze fell. "*Je m'excuse*, Brother Vernay—I simply cannot think to copy today," she apologized.

"You are so unhappy, Elienor?"

Elienor turned toward the sound of Olav's voice, her blue eyes growing suddenly liquid. Alarik's zealous brother sat in the shadows, upon a small bench, his hands linked before him. "What think you, my lord?" she asked softly, her eyes beseeching him to understand. "Having been taken against your will . . . to a strange land not of your choosing . . . could *you* be content?" Her heart twisted even as she voiced her predicament, for it made it all the more substantial.

Olav shrugged, his hand going to the hilt of his sword in an absent gesture as he stood. "Alarik's mother came to the Northland just so," he pointed out. "She sorrowed not," he claimed, and in further encouragement, he offered, "as I understand it . . . she even came to love my father."

Elienor's gaze fell momentarily. "My lord . . . surely I cannot speak for Alarik's mother," she told him. "But for me . . ."

Olav held up a hand to stop her. "You need not say it," he told her, coming forward. Sighing, he placed a comforting hand upon her shoulder, patting her, and then moved behind her to peer at the parchments spread before her upon the small writing table. "I suppose I understand." He scrutinized the pages a long moment, immensely pleased by what he saw, despite the fact that he'd yet to truly learn the Latin tongue. Feeling as though he should repay her somehow, he announced suddenly, "I tell you what I would do. Grant me your word you will copy until all is complete here, and then mayhap I could persuade mine brother to release you."

Hope flared within her breast—hope that she refused to dampen by acknowledging the immediate pang of loss she felt at the thought of leaving Alarik. She peered over her shoulder at Olav. "You would do such a thing?" she asked, stunned.

"I would . . . though I can promise nothing save that I will speak to him. I fear mine brother has a mind and will of his own. The truth is I cannot force him where he will not."

"My lord!" Elienor exclaimed. "That is all I could ask of you!" For her conscience, for her soul, she needed to go home.

"Tell me," Olav prodded. "Have you someone to take you in . . . if you were to return to Francia?"

"My uncle!" Elienor proclaimed at once. She fumbled for the leather string about her neck, lifting her beloved ring up out of her gown. She then raised it over her head and handed it to Olav. Olav accepted it, examining it.

"If you give my Uncle Robert that ring . . . he will know, at least, that you tell him true."

Olav stared at the ring a moment longer and then his gaze returned to Elienor. "And if mine brother refuses to set you free?"

Elienor's gaze dropped to the parchments. "Still . . . if you would somehow give that ring to mine uncle . . ." she entreated, "I would be so grateful." She glanced up at him suddenly, her eyes pleading. "By it, my lord, he would know that I live . . . that I am well. I beg of you . . ."

Olav nodded, moved by the melancholy in her tone. "Very well," he relented. "So it shall be done. I shall speak to him soon."

Vernay cleared his throat suddenly. "Er . . . my lord?"

"Mmmhhh?"

"The day escapes us. Shall we continue now?"

"Hmmm? Oh! Aye!" Olav yielded, giving Vernay an apologetic glance. He stepped away just as the door burst open, whisking in a swirl of snowflakes. The cold blast scattered pages before Elienor, yet she could not move to retrieve them. Mischief bounded up from his comfortable spot on the floor at her feet, and upon seeing Alarik, began to snarl.

Brother Vernay sighed in defeat. "My lord?" he said, somewhat less than enthusiastically. "Have you come to watch, too? I assure you all is in hand. The demoiselle copies very well, if we but had the time . . ."

Alarik didn't bother to reply. He glanced briefly at Olav, his brows colliding with displeasure at finding him present, and then his wintry eyes sought out Elienor's violet-blue ones, holding them fast.

Elienor's breath caught in her throat as she waited for Alarik to speak, though she prayed he would leave before doing so.

Did he not know what his presence did to her? That she hated herself for what her body wanted of him? He'd not touched her since that night, and she never wanted him to touch her again. She had no wish to feel this way.

She wanted peace. Her mind and body simply would not give it with him so near.

Nor even with him far, she berated herself.

'Twas wrong to submit to his loving, wrong to crave it, yet she could think only of that as she gazed into his stormy dark eyes. She tried to cast the memory of his touch from her mind, but could not. Lowering her gaze to the bureau, she wished she could vanish from the face of the earth.

Truly, she was shameless.

How many years were wasted in the cloister?

None wasted, bien aimée.

Elienor's gaze flew up at the words spoken so clearly in her mind, meeting Alarik's piercing silver eyes. Was she mad? Was she truly mad, then?

How could she allow herself to love her enemy? A man possibly fated to die if her dreams held true.

If she allowed herself to yield to it, would she be compelled to tell him aught?

And would she die for it?

For the longest moment, there was silence.

Alarik flung his mantle behind him in an agitated gesture, telling himself he cared not a whit for the woman whose stark violet eyes slashed into his soul.

'Twas merely lust.

Lust that tore at his gut.

Lust that made her face haunt his thoughts.

Lust that made him want her in every moment of his life.

Lust. And no more.

She was a woman, he reminded himself, and he refused to lose his mind and command over any female—Bjorn being a perfect example of the former for he seemed unable to think clearly for love of Nissa, and Olav of the latter, for Tyri seemed to rule his every decision.

The hard glint in his eyes held a shred of caution as he turned to Vernay, ignoring Olav. "Your work is concluded for the day," he informed the monk curtly.

"Not precis—"

"*It is*," he maintained, his eyes gleaming.

"Er . . . well . . . yes, my lord. Very well . . . if 'tis your wish."

Appeased, Alarik pivoted toward Elienor, his expression veiled. He refused to concede that he needed to be with her. Refused to concede anything at all! He straightened to his full height and took a step toward the woman who bedeviled his every waking thought. Yet before he could speak his intent, Mischief bounded upon his boot, growling insanely, nipping as though possessed. "Hel's hounds!" Alarik exploded in surprise, rocking backward upon his heels. "Demon dog!"

Olav hooted with laughter.

Elienor gasped, springing from her chair to restrain the dog.

" 'Tis as though he abhors you, my lord!" Vernay exclaimed, stifling a chuckle.

Elienor went to her knees at Alarik's feet, prying Mischief away from his boots. "Nay! Mischief!" she reproached when he twisted loose and charged at Alarik's boots once more. It never ceased to amaze her, the vehemence with which Mischief raged at him, particularly since Alarik did nothing but curse at the dog—ever. Never had he laid a finger upon it in brutality—not ever! Nevertheless, she believed Mischief sensed Alarik's aversion toward him, and responded accordingly. Nor did he seem to relish Alarik's boots!

With no small measure of envy, Alarik observed the way Elienor soothed the animal. Would that she would touch him so sweetly . . . of her own will . . . instead of with such disaffection. He wondered how it would feel if just once she would look upon him in pleasure—not in fear, or bitterness . . . or defiance. "It does seem so," he conceded to Vernay.

"You'd think the cur would bear him *some* small measure of affection," Olav declared, chuckling heartily. "Its mother was the man's favorite hound, after all."

With the pup secure in her arms, Elienor peered up at Alarik. "Was?" she whispered, her expression anxious.

Intuitively, Alarik understood what she asked of him. "Is," he assured, giving Olav an admonishing look. His gaze returned to Elienor. "She *is* mine favorite hound, Elienor."

Elienor's brows drew together. "Then where is she? Why does she spurn him? 'Tis my guess that the poor mite is scarcely past the age of suckling."

Alarik's brow lifted. "Poor mite?" he debated. His jaw tightened in remembrance of their discourse over his own birth circumstances. "I've told you, Elienor, the Northland is ruthless. Only the strong survive. The pup's mother lives only because she knows this, and she fends for herself."

Brother Vernay came forward to deliver the unruly dog from Elienor's arms. " 'Tis the truth the jarl tells you, my sister. This land is harsh to those not hale enough to endure it." He nodded when she glanced at him. Olav nodded as well.

Nevertheless, Elienor took exception to those words flung at her once again. She glared at Vernay, letting him know that she considered his siding with Alarik a betrayal of sorts—regardless that she likely had no right to feel so. Vernay might be her own countryman, and a brother in Christ, but like aught else in this forlorn place—including herself—he belonged to Alarik. Her eyes narrowed as they returned to Alarik. "Mayhap instead of casting each other off, as though life were no more precious than offal from a refuse pit," she suggested, meeting Alarik's gaze boldly, "the strong might be wiser to aid the weak. You, my lord, above all men, should realize that ofttimes the weak become the strong . . . and the strong become the weak. God and fate are the only two things truly hale enough to endure."

Alarik's jaw tightened as he gazed down into Elienor's eyes. He was quickly coming to regret telling her aught about his life, yet despite her renewed vehemence against him, the sight of her kneeling before him ignited him, heated his blood until white-hot desire ripped through his veins. He glanced at the pup, safely ensconced within Vernay's arms—it yelped at him, curse its mangy hide!—and then back to Elienor, uncertain of what to say to restore the frail bond that had only begun to form between them. "You named him . . .," he fought the urge to blaspheme the ungracious mutt, "Mischief?"

"Aye," Elienor replied tonelessly.

He cleared his throat, but the hoarseness lingered in his voice. "The name suits him."

"Aye," Elienor answered once more, though this time somewhat warily, for she was stirred by the husky timber of his voice more than she would like to acknowledge. Her heart quickened as he continued to stare down at her.

She held his gaze.

In that moment, as they stared at each other, Alarik forgot where he stood, forgot Vernay, forgot everything and everyone but the intensity of his own hunger and the woman kneeling at his feet.

Did she know she brought such turmoil to his senses?

He quivered, disturbed that a mere look of hers could make him lose so much composure.

'Twas as though she bewitched him with those magnificent violet eyes.

A rush of feeling overtook him suddenly, a wanting like he'd never experienced in all his days, and along with it panic and fear—he who'd never felt such weakness—fear that Elienor held him in a grip from which he could never escape. He fell to one knee, his hand going to her arm in an attempt to regain his edge, his reason. His fingers closed about the soft silk of her gown. As he stared into her stark, violet-blue eyes, his own eyes darkened.

Elienor averted her gaze, her heart skipping a beat at the intensity of his stare. She could not let it happen again. Sweet Jesu, she could not live with herself if it did! Yet she shook her head at her own foolishness, for it 'twas his bent, how could she deny him, when her own Judas body cried out that he lift her up and sweep her away?

That he take the decision from her hands.

"Tell me, Elienor," Alarik said softly, gruffly, his gaze unrelenting, "does Mischief's lady abhor me, as well?" She lowered her face. He forced her chin up with a finger, but her lashes remained stubbornly upon her cheeks. "Does she?" he demanded. "Even after?"

Elienor's lashes flew up, her eyes misting. Especially after! her heart cried out in agony—*especially* after, for now she could not even console herself with the fact that she'd been forced. She'd not been. Shameless as it was, she'd given herself freely and of her own accord. To her enemy. She shook her head miserably, resenting the truth with all her heart, yet unable to deny him the answer he sought.

At her reply, the harsh lines softened in his face. A shuddering took him. "You please me," he told her gruffly. He rose abruptly, drawing her up with him. Elienor cried out as he drew her against the hard strength of his body. His face lowered to hers. "What can I do, Elienor of *Baume-les-Nonnes*," he murmured silkily, "to please you in return?"

Vernay cleared his throat discreetly, afeared that the situation would advance in an unseemly manner. "My lord?" he objected softly, his eyes remaining downcast.

Mortified, Elienor's gaze flew to the monk—the pate of his head shone back at her—and then to Olav. Olav looked pensive, saying nothing. She spun back to Alarik, her spine stiffening in humiliation to have been spied in such a shameless embrace—by a man of the cloth, no less! Olav, she could bear, for he and Alarik were two of the same, but Brother Vernay—'twas miserable! "You could take me home," she appealed brokenly, her eyes stinging with tears. "Take me back to Francia." Before I lose my soul, she appended silently.

Alarik shook his head, his eyes narrowing in displeasure at her suggestion, for it made him consider himself without her—empty, less than whole. And damn him, for he could less bear the thought of being without her than he could the debilitating fact that he should need her at all. "*Nei*, Elienor!" he cried out. His fingers gripped her arm in frustration. He shook her. "Damn you, ask of me something I can give! I wish to please you!"

"I want nought else!" Elienor declared fervently. "Please, let me go!"

"My lord?" Vernay interjected, rubbing his own arm as he observed the possessive way Alarik held her.

Still Olav said nothing, only watched the scene unfold, tucking everything away for later.

Alarik glared at Vernay, then at his brother, who sat silently across the room, his expression strange. He straightened suddenly, as though checking himself, and his expression was guarded as he released Elienor's arm. "You say your work is complete for this day?" he asked Vernay without meeting the monk's gaze, nor Elienor's, but still looking directly at Olav, warning his brother without words to stay away from the *kirken* . . . from Elienor.

"If 'tis your wish, my lord."

"It is," Alarik asserted. The fine line of his control redrawn, his gaze returned to Elienor, his eyes shadowed with a hunger no amount of self-control could dispel. "Fetch your mantle, my lovely little nun . . . I find I'm in sore need of a bath," he told her bluntly.

Olav fair roared with laughter.

Vernay choked.

Alarik's gaze returned to the monk, disregarding his brother completely. From the corner of his eye he noted with satisfaction that Elienor hurried to recover her cape as he bid of her. "You have objections?" he asked Vernay.

Vernay's brows clashed, but he shook his head quickly. "Nay, my lord! 'Tis but that . . ."

"Good!" Alarik declared, cutting him off. When Elienor returned, he snatched the cape from her hands impatiently, placing it about her shoulders. That done, he opened the door and ushered her out, assuring Vernay that she would return at her appointed hour on the morrow.

He said nothing to Olav.

"Mischief!" Elienor exclaimed, remembering the pup as Alarik drew the door closed behind them.

"Vernay will see that he makes it safely to the manor. He won't be able to keep up."

Elienor made no more objection as he led her to his horse, lifting her upon its back. And then, in one fluid motion, he mounted behind her, driving his heel into Sleipnir's flank.

In a little time they reined in before the bath house, and all Elienor could think was that Mischief truly wouldn't have been able to keep pace.

Alarik had ridden as though demons cleaved at his heels.

The realization swept over her suddenly that she wasn't going to be able to halt this.

She wasn't even certain she wanted to!

Dismounting hastily, Alarik drew her down to her feet. Elienor's knees faltered, but he steadied her, and then opening the door to the bath house, he ushered her into the shadowy interior. He'd not even taken the time to have Alva restore the fire, and the dying embers glowed eerily.

"My lord!" she protested, in panic. " 'Tis day yet! There are people about!"

He kicked the door closed, his lips curving diabolically. "We'll not be disturbed," he told her with certainty. Taking her by the arm, he swung her about sharply, until her back was to him, and then proceeded to undo the brooch at her right shoulder, not needing to see it to undo it, his fingers deft at their work.

Her gown slid down on the right side. Crying out, Elienor clutched the silk to her breast, halting its descent. " 'Tis cold!" she protested.

"Not for long," Alarik promised at her nape, his breath warm as it hissed across her flesh. The determination in his voice sent a quiver down her spine. He unfastened the twin brooch at her left shoulder, and with a gentleness that belied his strength, drew the gown down.

Elienor whimpered, her eyes squeezing shut as the silk was pulled out of her grasp. But he wasn't satisfied, for no sooner was the silk overgown discarded than he began to undo the laces of the matching undergown. That done, he drew it up over her head and tossed it aside, baring her wholly to his hungry gaze.

It settled with a whisper upon the furs.

With a sigh of intense pleasure, Alarik traced a finger down her spine, content for the moment merely to gaze at her perfect form. The flush of her skin was perceptible even in the shadows of the dying firelight. She gave a startled whimper and stumbled back against him, and his heart somersaulted like that of an unseasoned youth with the unexpected contact.

"Elienor," he said through clenched teeth, his eyes closing. He shuddered with pleasure at the feel of her bare skin against him. "Do you know what you do to me, my little nun?"

Do you know what you do to me? her heart cried out.

He chuckled suddenly, as though pleased, and his arms encircled her waist. He embraced her a moment, and then his hands drifted upward to seize the prize he'd exposed, his fingers lightly skimming her ribs.

"Please," Elienor moaned. "I . . . I . . ."

Alarik tensed in anticipation of her protest. Although after her whispered declaration, he knew it would take little to sway her—she seemed to have little, or no control of her wayward tongue—at times, this time, it played to his advantage. He bent to place a long lingering kiss upon the delicate swell that crested her shoulder. She said nothing, only whimpered softly in the back of her throat, and he inhaled deeply in satisfaction.

The sweet, heady fragrance of her hair accosted him, lingering in the air, enshrouding him. He found it near as potent a potion as the sound of his name on her lips. With an oblivious groan, he buried his lips within the softness of her hair, and hearing her faint exhale only heated his senses more.

"Elienor," he moaned. "Elienor . . . Elienor . . . Elienor . . ."

Elienor ceased to breathe at the intensity with which he spoke her name. She dared not turn to face him—lest he see the hunger in her own eyes— dared not speak, lest her words and voice betray her.

She fought a fierce battle with her conscience as he held and caressed her body. It felt so right, so right, yet she knew it to be wrong!

As his hands slid beneath her breasts, cupping them with hard but sensitive palms, her body exposed her for the wanton she was. She shivered expectantly as rugged hands fondled her and inflamed her senses, made her burn. She swallowed, her heart leaping into her throat as his lips touched her bare shoulder once more. "I . . . I thought . . . I thought you wanted me to aid you with your bath?" she stammered.

Alarik smiled at the uncertainty in her voice. "I do wish you to aid me," he told her provocatively, bending to whisper into her ear. "But I fear the bath will have to wait, my exquisite little *Fransk*."

Elienor gasped as she became aware of the hardness of him pressing her back. Her heart pounded violently as she fought a battle with her will. Gently, he swept the length of her hair aside, placing a kiss upon her other shoulder.

She trembled, feeling herself losing, losing—not just the battle, but the war itself.

Her resolution to deny herself the pleasure he could give ebbed with every expert touch of his masterful hands and lips. As his fingers gently kneaded her bosom, her head fell backward helplessly, allowing him his will. As though pleased with her response, his breath hissed over the curve of her neck, and she felt her knees go instantly weak.

His body quickened when she went limp in his arms. He steadied her. "Art sweet," he whispered. "So very . . . very . . . sweet." He heard her sharp intake of breath as he nipped her neck, tasting the sheen of desire upon her flesh.

The coppery firelight caressed her creamy white flesh. As though compelled, his hands stroked her wherever the light revealed her, and perceiving that she was at last his for the taking, he groaned deep in the back of his throat, a sound of victory. Impatiently, he tore at the laces of his breeches, undoing them swiftly and with ease. He shuddered with exhilaration as he freed himself. Then, holding her steady, he stepped away to discard the restrictive clothing.

Trembling where she stood, Elienor closed her eyes, listening to the telltale sounds behind her— the rustling of garments as they melted from Alarik's body.

With every part of her, she willed herself to cry out and flee.

And then he was behind her once more, the naked heat of his flesh searing her clear unto her soul. Her heart pounded within her breast, drowning out everything but its wild beating, yet arrested completely as Alarik enfolded her within the warmth of his arms once more.

And then her blood swept into her head and her heart began to pound violently once more as he rocked her, unabashedly, from behind.

Lord have mercy upon her soul. She would die!

Gently, he brought his right hand down and splayed it across her abdomen, holding her steady while he rocked her.

Alarik's arms dropped to her waist as he went to his knees, compelling her downward with him. His heart hammered and his breath became labored as he anticipated how he would take her this time— with all the primitive fury of the Northland! Once she was firmly upon her knees on the soft furs, he molded his body over hers until he was able to settle himself between her legs, shuddering over the exhilarating sensation. In that instant, he knew an incredible desire to please her, as well. He brought his hand around to stroke her, all the while kissing her back, breathing deeply of the scent of her hair.

His eyes closed as he guided himself into her, groaning unconsciously.

Elienor gasped, her head arching backward.

With his chin, Alarik nudged her hair from her back and tasted her warm, velvety skin with his lips. He savored her with his tongue, committing the taste and feel of her to his mind, all the while disregarding his own body's demands; he stroked her until she cried out beneath him, and then he lifted himself, and holding her hips steady for his pleasure, he gave himself up to his own dark passions.

Elienor whimpered in ecstasy at his every thrust, crying out when heat exploded within her once more, wracking her body with delicious spasms. She was helpless to arrest the cry of his name that came to her lips.

The whispered name exploded within his head.

With an incredible rush of pleasure, Alarik gripped her hips tighter, and with one last powerful thrust, poured his life and soul into her.

He remained pressed into her until he was certain his seed was buried so deeply within her womb that she would assuredly conceive his babe.

He quivered almost violently then, separating from her, and collapsing to the furs. Rolling to his back, he took her with him, and holding her close, stroked the length of her hair until he could feel the smooth even rhythm of her slumbering breath. He stroked her until his own breathing settled and his heartbeat tempered.

And still he caressed her, for she felt so right beneath his fingers.

The last thing he thought before closing his eyes was that he was tired of fighting what he felt for her.

He could no longer deny it.

Whatever the bond, it was too powerful. If it was his destiny to love her, then so be it—to hell with the part of him that warned him not to succumb!

The pull was irresistible. Yet, he would, in fact, resist.

As he'd long ago discovered, the heart was a powerful weapon. He could not so freely give his.

He wouldn't make the same mistake twice.

Chapter 26

Elienor came to expect Alarik earlier and earlier each afternoon, and so it came as no shock when, a week later, the door to the *kirken* burst open a mere hour after she'd left the manor house.

Brother Vernay cleared his throat, lifting his brows. "Er . . . you'll be needing a bath, my lord?" he ventured.

Alarik gave the monk a frown. "Among other things," he ceded. His lips curved into a satisfied smile as Elienor straightaway rose to retrieve her cape, displacing the demon dog from her lap in the process. His mood was so high that he felt it no hardship to ignore the yapping pup and the fiendish way that it once again attacked his boots. He gave it no more than a mildly disgruntled glance, shaking it off.

Vernay's cheeks reddened as he came forward to lift up the seething animal, embarrassed by the jarl's frankness, nevertheless pleased at what he sensed between them. "I fear we shall never finish at this rate," he said disapprovingly, though with little insistence.

Alarik grinned. "Mayhap not," he relented, smiling at Elienor as she returned to him. The monk was forgotten completely when she returned his smile, though tentatively.

Yet it was a beginning.

Impatiently, he drew her outside, leading her at once to where Sleipnir stood tethered. He lifted her up onto Sleipnir's back, then untied the horse, bounding up behind her. Only this time, instead of directing the animal toward the manor, he led it away.

"Where are we going?" Elienor asked in surprise.

"For a ride," Alarik replied bluntly. And without further warning, he turned her about to face him, cursing himself even as he did so, for he couldn't even wait until he had her alone. "I burn for you Elienor," he told her huskily, unlacing his breeches as she watched.

Elienor's eyes widened. A quiver burst through her, both from the cold and the sheer determination in Alarik's gaze.

"You can't!"

"You're like ambrosia," he whispered, ignoring her protest. "The more I savor . . . the more I crave."

He felt her shiver and smiled knowingly.

"We can't simply . . ." her voice broke. Her heart skipped its normal beat, for he watched her with that covetous, heavy lidded gaze that stoked the embers of that treacherous fire within her. "Not here!"

"I need you, Elienor," he murmured, grinning. Drawing up her gown, he left no doubt as to his meaning. And with the gown out of the way, he lifted her suddenly, seating her upon his lap. Elienor gasped as he eased into her right there in the broad light of day, under the gray-blue heavens, and atop his steed, for God and all the world to see.

She clung to him.

Alarik groaned, closing his eyes at the incredible feel of her, his arousal grown violent in its intensity. "Wrap your legs about mine waist," he demanded. She did, at once placing them behind him as he'd asked, and he hooked his feet about hers, anchoring her, then bent his head to murmur his plea into her ear, "Now quench me, my little nun."

Elienor closed her eyes, his bold words setting her body awash with color and fire. Yet some small part of her clung to a shred of reason.

The tiniest shred.

"Alarik," she protested.

"Shhhhhh . . . let me please you. Odin's eye!" he swore. "As I live and breathe, wench, I've never desired anything or anyone more!"

Elienor stifled the tears that threatened to flow. She sagged against him in defeat, bracing her hands upon his chest. "Not here," she pleaded again, brokenly, her heart screaming something else entirely: *Desire? Desire? Why can you not love me?* "Why?" she whispered. "Why? Why?"

"Because I need you!" Alarik murmured, misinterpreting her question. He wrapped his mantle about them both, forming a warm cocoon around the two of them, his desire rearing itself like a fire: breathing serpent in his veins. He was overtaken with the need to impale her so deeply that she could never flee.

The need to brand her, to hear her whisper his name in rapture once more, was inexorable.

Elienor's fingers dug into Alarik's flesh. Regardless that she so desperately wished to, she could not control her body's treacherous response to him. Yet at the moment she didn't care, for she feared she loved him.

She gave in to the impulse and slid her arms around his chest, revelling in its size and sinew, as if to unite them together forever. She felt him quiver at her gesture, and his response emboldened her. She buried her lips into his neck, tasting the salt of his flesh, her heart crying her love, even as her lips refused to give it voice.

Instead, she whispered his name.

"God's mercy!"

Elienor stiffened in surprise at his outcry.

"*Which* God?" she asked.

"Damn you! It doesn't matter! Odin's fury, woman, but you feel so right!"

Disappointment burst through her, but she thrust it aside. He was right. It didn't matter. It didn't matter. It didn't matter. She repeated the words until they became a litany.

Only this moment mattered.

"Like this," he urged, guiding her hips slowly with his hands.

Elienor undulated as Alarik commanded, and his head thrust backward in response, the cords of his neck taut. He moaned, and she soon found her hips moving of their own accord in the same deliciously slow rhythm he'd created. His arms embraced her firmly, searing her skin even through her gown, making her burn, until the very slowness of their rhythm was a torment. Once again his name erupted from her lips.

It drove him to the edge.

Alarik held her possessively as the landscape momentarily blurred. Were it not for the death grip his legs held about Sleipnir's flanks, they would both have spiraled to the ground. Within the instant, she muffled her own cries into his shoulder, and then, sighing blissfully, she closed her eyes and lay against him. At once, Alarik turned her about and gathered his mantle about her.

Physically spent from their loving—that and the fact that she'd slept little the night before—Elienor allowed herself to drowse in his arms.

Snuggled securely within his embrace as she was, she didn't see the way that he gazed down at her; he stared, as though by the intensity of that gesture he could see into her soul, searching, probing, questioning, for while their loving, as always, satiated his body's hunger, he was left still wanting.

Placing his lips to the crown of her head, he tangled his fingers into her hair and rode on. And for the briefest instant, as he held her, it seemed as though she accepted him, at last. He found himself wishing he'd never be forced to turn back.

Nevertheless, even as he thought it, he redirected Sleipnir, and it wasn't long before he discerned that they'd somehow ridden past the grove that was his original destination. His lips curved ruefully at the realization. So much for privacy.

Yet they hadn't needed it, he acknowledged with a smug grin. His little sleepy nun had forgotten everything in the heat of her passion.

As had he.

Despite that fact, as they made their way back to the steading he continued to brood, for while he'd indisputably won Elienor's surrender . . .

He couldn't help but feel something lacking still.

"I come with news you'll not relish," Hrolf said with a smirk, leaping down from his mount. He tossed the reins over its withers and then leaned his back against the nearest tree to catch his breath.

Bjorn clenched his teeth, crossing his arms. Hrolf had sent a man to his bed well before daybreak with a message that Bjorn wanted to meet him in the grove this afternoon, and Bjorn had come out of curiosity. Impatiently, he waited for Hrolf to explain himself now.

Hrolf merely grinned, bracing his foot against the tree. He unsheathed the dagger from his boot and then swiped at the sweat upon his upper lip with his sleeve. "I suppose you wonder why I've called you?"

Bjorn tilted his head irritably.

Hrolf's brows lifted. "It seems Ejnar has decided you are not worthy of his daughter," he said at last. Satisfied with the look he'd gleaned from Bjorn, he picked his teeth with the tip of his blade. Again his brow lifted as he eagerly awaited Bjorn's reaction to his revelation.

Bjorn's chin jutted forward. "You summon me in broad daylight? I risk myself to come—to hear this? *Nei*, Hrolf, I think not. If Ejnar had decided not to deal with me, then 'tis his way to simply ignore me. 'Tis my guess you have a proposition for me."

Hrolf nodded. "You always were a shrewd one," he answered. His gaze averted momentarily to the blade in his hand, and then returned to Bjorn, again measuring, his eyes brilliant with purpose. "I wonder what might have been were you to have held Alarik's high seat instead," he suggested slyly.

Bjorn's hands fell to his sword, unsheathing it. The metal hissed as it left his scabbard. "I have never coveted Alarik's seat," he denied hotly.

Hrolf poised himself with dagger in hand, anticipating Bjorn's attack. When none came, he laughed, taunting, "You lie!"

Bjorn lunged at him, but Hrolf dodged him and stood ready once more, dagger in hand. His eyes narrowed, his lips curled viciously. "Still, Ejnar perceives Alarik as the best match for his daughter," he revealed. "He's convinced that if he kills the Frenchwoman, Alarik's interest will return to Nissa."

"Return to her?" Bjorn snarled, striking his sword against the tree. "Mine fool brother has never wanted her for aught! Damn him! Damn mine brother!" He turned to face Hrolf, ready to listen.

Hrolf agreed with a nod. "My sentiments wholly. You and I perceive thus much, but Ejnar refuses to acknowledge it. Then again . . . he can be a very persuasive man." He allowed Bjorn a moment to digest his meaning. "Nevertheless, 'tis none of my concern whether Alarik accepts the bitch, or *nei*. My concern is only that the *Fransk*, along with Olav and the holy man, are poisoning Alarik's mind . . . that soon Alarik will turn from the old faith as has Olav. Were he to join with Ejnar's daughter, I fear to think of the power he would have at his hands. Consider it, Bjorn."

"I've said afore," Bjorn argued, though with less passion, "Alarik has never shown signs of succumbing to that spine-weakening faith. I've told you. I should know, for he is mine brother."

"*Ja*, well . . ." Without warning, Hrolf heaved his knife at the tree behind Bjorn. The bone hilt quivered portentously. "We both know what value he's placed on that of late." He raised a challenging brow. "Don't we, Bjorn?"

" 'Tis none of your—"

"I wonder why he's so often spied at the *kirken* these days?" Hrolf interjected harshly. "He seemed to have little regard for the place before."

" 'Tis no secret that he burns for the Frenchwoman!"

"*Nei*, but mark mine words—'tis merely a matter of time before he begins to employ the same harsh tactics Olav adheres to." Hrolf snatched up his blade, glaring at Bjorn wrathfully. He resheathed it within his boot. "At any rate, I came to relate only this . . . if you should find yourself wishing to oppose your *brother*, you have mine support . . . as well as that of others, for neither am I pleased to be with Ejnar. There is nought for me to gain in remaining with the Dane."

Bjorn straightened, one tawny brow raised. "What you propose is treason."

"What I propose is freedom from Olav's persecution!" Hrolf countered. "Think on it, Bjorn . . . you could have both the high seat . . . and Nissa as well. Consider it, at least," he suggested. "And then let me know what you decide." Having said all he wished to, he turned and seized his reins, then leapt back into the saddle.

Bjorn watched him, saying nothing, his brows knit.

"You won't hear from Ejnar again—not specifically," Hrolf told him. "As you so aptly speculated, he *has* determined it beneath himself to acknowledge your request. So . . . you should consider my counsel carefully." With that he turned his mount about, but swung back to add, "Oh, and Bjorn . . . you should keep in mind that once Alarik has joined Ejnar by ties of wedlock, all will be lost to you. Apprise me soon, if you would." With that, he turned again, riding out of the grove, leaving Bjorn feeling more impotent than ever.

In truth, Bjorn prized his brother—despite the fact that they had so little in common. But what if what Hrolf said was truth? He would not be forced—he refused to cleave to this new faith!

And then there was Nissa . . .

Peering up at the glowing orb of fire that was the
waning sun, he watched Hrolf go, and then turned
and started back toward the steading, Hrolf's words
simmering like a potion in his head.

Alarik reined in suddenly at the sight of the lone
rider racing away from the grove. Even from this
distance, he recognized the sun-fire bright hair.

Hrolf Kaetilson.

He stiffened, for moments later Bjorn rode out
as well, racing toward the steading, clearly so preoccupied that he failed to notice he had an audience.

Alarik's eyes darkened as he watched his youngest brother's flight, his emotions wavering between
fury and regret, and then he swore beneath his
breath and spurred his own mount after him.

Chapter 27

Alarik and Elienor arrived at the steading mere moments after Bjorn. Perceiving that Bjorn would have ridden directly to the stables, Alarik reined in before the longhouse, shaking Elienor awake. "Elienor," he said hoarsely.

Sleepily, she lifted up her head.

"Wake yourself!" he demanded, and the brusque edge to his voice instantly alerted her to his dark mood. She straightened and he dismounted, hauling her down after him. "I would have you go to the *eldhus*," he directed.

Elienor had no notion what she might have done to make him sound so furious. Disoriented from her nap, she asked, "The kitchens?"

Alarik gave her a curt nod. A muscle ticked in his jaw. "Tell Alva to delay the serving of *nattver*!"

Elienor nodded, puzzled by his change in mood, and turned to go.

He watched only an instant to be certain that she complied, and then he sought out Olav. He found his brother in the *skali*, seated at the high table, drinking horn in hand. As he made his way to where his half-brother sat, his look was blacker than the deepest night, causing Olav's horn to arrest in midair.

Making certain that Bjorn was not present, he bellowed a dismissal to everyone within the hall,

283

ordering them not to return until the meal was ready to be served. Only when he stood before the high table did he speak. "Backbiting, sniveling fool!" he declared, ripping off his mantle and hurling it across the table into his empty chair at Olav's side.

"I?"

Alarik's face contorted with cold fury. "*Nei*. Bjorn! A week ago I was told he sent a messenger from Gryting. The man was followed well into Dane territory." A string of oaths erupted from his tongue. "This afternoon he met with Hrolf Kaetilson. Loki take the boy!" he exploded. "He's never wanted for aught under mine hand!"

Olav dropped his horn to the table. "Can he not have come upon Hrolf unintentionally?"

Alarik struck the table with his fist in bitter rage, not caring that he risked his sword hand in the angry gesture. "*Nei!*" he bellowed. "Curse him— a thousand times, curse him!"

"What do you propose to do?" Olav asked quietly. He well understood Alarik's outrage, for Alarik had long coddled the boy—going so far as to soothe Bjorn's wounded pride when he'd felt threatened simply because Olav had appeared in their lives.

Olav had never known his sire, for he'd had the misfortune to be born in the year after his father's death. Directly thereafter his mother, fearing for her son's life at the hands of those eager to claim his father's seat, took Olav and fled to safety. He alone had returned, a man grown. It was incredible to look at the brothers, for other than the color of their eyes and hair, there was little disparity between them.

There were times when Olav envied Alarik that he *had* known their sire, yet not enough to cross his half-brother, for Alarik was, in more ways than not, his kindred spirit.

Bjorn was another matter entirely.

Olav and Bjorn bore no blood relation to each other, save through Alarik, nor did they bear each other much affection. From the very beginning Bjorn had resented Olav coming between him and Alarik, for Bjorn had been a youth in awe of his elder brother. Olav's arrival had driven a wedge between them, yet Olav could no longer bring himself to care, for Bjorn had rebuffed every attempt Olav had ever made to befriend him.

Still, Olav would have saved Alarik the pain of betrayal. "Perhaps my little errand with Burislav could be useful in some manner?"

Alarik heaved a weary sigh, leaning heavily upon the table. He peered up at Olav, his eyes red rimmed and glazed. And then his gaze settled upon the ring about Olav's neck. A rage as he'd never experienced in all his life erupted within him as he stared at that ring. King, or *nei*, brother, or *nei*, he wanted to leap over the table and strangle Olav with the leather that bore it. "I've no idea what to do," he ceded, his voice tense. "But 'twould be wise to keep this to ourselves . . . for now . . . until I can at least ascertain what he intends." Again, he slammed the table and spat another oath.

Olav nodded " 'Tis agreed, then. We shall wait—"

"Where did you get that ring?" Alarik demanded, his voice strained. A thousand possibilities raced through his mind, none of them bearable, for Elienor wore the ring always, well secreted beneath her gown. His eyes blazed.

Olav's brows lifted, his hand going to the band. He opened his mouth to speak, but then he peered over Alarik's shoulder, a motion beyond the door catching his eye. His shrewd green eyes met Bjorn's blue ones, and then Alarik's iron gray ones. "Speak of the beast," he said quietly.

Alarik pivoted about to face his youngest brother, willing himself to remain composed. Damn the fool boy! Some part of him wanted only to tear out Bjorn's heart—carve the blood eagle upon his back—rip out his lungs! Controlling his features to conceal his ire, he attempted a smile. He clasped Bjorn's arm as it was proffered.

"Mine brother?" Bjorn said warily. Alarik nodded, and Bjorn winced at the unyielding grip maintained upon his arm. Bjorn turned to Olav, his mouth twitching as he noted Olav's grave expression. Olav watched as though he expected something dire to occur any moment. "Alarik!" Bjorn protested when Alarik failed to release his arm. He slapped a hand over Alarik's fist, easing Alarik's fingers from his flesh. "Mine arm," he appealed. "Forsooth, mine *bror*, at times I believe you forget your own strength."

Alarik's lips curved only slightly as he released Bjorn; it was all the smile he could muster. "We missed your company today," he said softly, too softly. "Where have you been?"

The silence within the hall was palpable.

Bjorn peered again at Olav, noting the ill-at-ease way that Olav drummed the tips of his fingers upon the table, his eyes fixed upon Alarik.

"Alarik?" Olav prompted. "Mayhap Bjorn would care to join us."

Alarik's gaze narrowed upon Bjorn, his brows lifting. He made no move to reply to Olav. "Holed up with some wench no doubt?" he asked of Bjorn.

His eyes flickered when Bjorn gave him a nod. "Well, then, I do hope she was worth it."

"Indeed, she was!" Bjorn replied.

Alarik gestured toward the high table. "Won't you join us, then, mine brother?"

Bjorn's brows drew together, sensing Alarik's request was more a command. Awkwardly he made his way around the table, taking his seat upon the bench directly at Alarik's left, away from Olav, sending Olav a resentful glance as he sat. He felt a twinge of regret over the decision he'd come to as he rode home—though merely a twinge, for in his heart he felt that what he'd decided was for the best of the steading.

Hrolf was right.

Alarik was not thinking rationally—not if he was thinking like Olav.

The very air within the hall seemed to crackle with tension as Elienor entered. She felt the unease tangibly. When Alarik motioned her to the high table, she resisted the urge to flee past him into his bedchamber—his bedchamber, for she still could not claim it despite the fact that she spent her nights there within his arms.

It was his.

As was she, in more ways than she cared to acknowledge.

As she made her way to the dais, Alarik elbowed Bjorn, and spoke to him softly. Elienor heard not a word, but she had no need to guess what had been said, for Bjorn stood suddenly, toppling his bench backward. His legs were braced apart, his eyes blazing hatred at Elienor. "You displace me for *her*?" His voice rose. "For her! I'll not move!"

"You will," Alarik returned softly.

"I'll not!" Bjorn exploded

Alarik stood, raking his chair backward. His hand went to the hilt of his sword. "You will! And you will do so now," he said with deadly menace.

Bjorn's ire exploded with an appalling string of oaths. Elienor had never heard such words. "Take it then—give it to the whore!" And with that, he kicked the bench away. He stalked off without a backward glance at Alarik. Elienor's face paled at the look he shot her in passing. She glanced at Olav. Then Alarik. Then Olav. Olav's green eyes missed nothing. He lifted a brow in silent question, and something in his look triggered a memory, something in the intensity of his gaze. Something . . . something . . .

She felt dizzy suddenly and reached out to steady herself. The room swam before her and then her vision went momentarily black. She saw him again standing at the prow—Olav. 'Twas him, she knew, for the eyes were green. Green. The ship's prow twisted before her eyes into the head of a serpent. One instant Olav was holding it, the next he was in the water, his crimson cloak swirling downward after him, into the deep blue sea.

"Elienor?" It was Alarik's voice that penetrated her dazed senses.

Yet she couldn't come back. Something held her still. Vaguely, she was aware that he came toward her, and the vision solidified before her eyes. She saw him upon his own ship, watching, too, as Olav plummeted into the ocean. And then again she saw Alarik's face torn. He was torn, uncertain whether to come for her . . . or to go after his brother. In a split second he made his decision—to come for her. Like a hawk, he soared the distance over the churning water. At the same instant, a gleaming axe was hurled through the air, toward his back.

Elienor cried out. Her legs went weak.

"Elienor?" Alarik shook her firmly, the sting of his grip upon her arm bringing her back. "Elienor?"

Aware suddenly that he was supporting her, she steadied herself, shaking her head, but she swayed, giving no substance to her words. "I . . . I . . . fine," she said much too quickly, breaking away. She glanced down at her hands, her heart beating erratically.

No blood.

There was no blood.

She glanced back up at him in dazed shock.

Alarik stood there before her, his brows drawn together in confusion. Yet her dream foretold of his death. Her gaze went to Olav, who sat still at the table, and then returned to Alarik. She shivered. Both! Both would die—not one! She felt suddenly ill with the revelation. "I . . . I . . . I'm not hungry!" she exclaimed, bolting past him.

Desperate to be away from so many pairs of eyes, she thrust open the door to Alarik's chamber and escaped within, slamming it behind her in desperation.

Alarik shrugged at Olav. He had no inkling what had come over Elienor so suddenly, but whatever it was he would discover it, by God!

She'd looked at him with such dazed terror once too often!

He followed her into his chamber and found her lying abed. As he opened the door, she bolted upright, her face pallid.

Elienor could not stop trembling. " 'Twas Olav," she murmured full of anguish, tears welling in the corners of her eyes.

"What did he do?" He took her hands. They

were damp and sticky with cold sweat. He thought he'd kill his brother if he'd harmed her in anyway.

Still the possibility that she might *not* have given him the ring of her own volition filled him with a reckless hope.

He hung his head suddenly, confounded. Guilt ridden. By Odin's breath, he knew not what to feel. Olav was his brother, by the blood of their sire. His brother!

"H . . . he jumped," Elienor stammered. "A . . . and then you came, a . . . and there was blood!" She peered up at him a little wildly. "But there wasn't . . . there wasn't," she said, suddenly pensive. She nibbled her lip.

"You speak in riddles." Alarik accused her, kneeling before her now. "Elienor?" He took her hand in his. "Are you unwell? Did Olav do aught to harm you? Tell me!"

Elienor shook his hand away. How could she explain when it could mean her life? Her gaze returned to his face, his handsome, troubled face.

How could she not at least attempt it? She couldn't simply let him die.

Could she?

He looked at her as though she were mad, and a quiver raced down her spine as she recalled the way her mother had been persecuted, and therein lay the awful truth—she was cursed if she told him, cursed if she didn't! Her mother had been murdered for nought more than predicting the course of an infant's illness.

Nay, she could not tell him. He would never understand.

Besides, she didn't fully comprehend the vision

herself. Despite the fact that it came to her exactly the same each time, it was much too chaotic to comprehend fully. She only knew that there would be no happily ever after for her.

Take what happiness you can, bien aimée . . . while you can.

She didn't even blink at the words spoken so clearly in her head, accepting them unquestioningly. Would it be so wrong? she asked herself. Nay, she determined. She took a breath, calming herself, and assured, " 'Twas nought . . . I'm fine." She became aware of his hands in her hair, stroking the length of it, the look in his eyes peculiar.

"Mayhap you should rest," Alarik suggested, noting the pallor of her skin.

Elienor nodded, and he rose from his knees. Still, he peered down upon her, as though searching her soul.

The back of his fingers grazed her cheek. "Sleep then. Alva will bring supper later."

Elienor nodded again, lying back upon the immense bed. She closed her eyes so that Alarik would see that she was ready to comply, and was surprised by the languor that came over her so swiftly.

Mayhap she was simply overtired.

Mayhap this time her dreams would not hold true.

As she lay there, considering that, daring to hope, she drifted . . .

Alarik watched over her a moment longer, contemplating the terrorized look she'd had in her eyes as she'd looked upon him in the *skali*, and then he lifted the furs to her chin, tucking her within, noting that she shivered still. In fear of him? In loathing? He remained only until he was certain she slept, and then he left to seek out Alva.

If anyone knew how to glean information from reluctant souls, 'twas she, and the woman lying so serenely within his bed had secrets to withhold.

By the rood of her God, he intended to find out just what they were.

Chapter 28

Elienor awoke to find the chamber bathed in shadows. She wondered at once where Alarik was—wondered, too, if it were day or night. With no windows to peer from, it was difficult to judge. Stretching to ease the stiffness in her bones, she rose, yawning, and no sooner had she thrust her feet over the edge of the bed than Alva cracked the door open, peering in.

"Oh! You're awake?" Entering, she bore in her hands a small tray. "I've brought bread and cheese," she revealed in a cheery tone. "You're ravenous, I'm certain!"

Surprised to find it was so and wondering why, Elienor nodded that she was, and concealed another yawn, and then recalled that she'd not partaken of *nattver*. "Thank you," she said when she could.

Alva placed the tray next to Elienor upon the bed. "The jarl said you were feeling unwell?"

"A little," Elienor concurred. "But 'tis passed now. How long have I slept?"

"Not very long." Alva sighed. "The jarl said you came here directly from the *eldhus*."

"I did," Elienor acknowledged, cocking her head in curiosity. "Alva . . . why do you call him jarl . . . instead of Alarik?"

Alva shrugged. "I suppose 'tis because he *is* jarl," she pointed out matter-of-factly. "I've never considered addressing him by his given name. Why?" She took up a poker and proceeded to stir the fire pit back to life.

Elienor chose a hunk of bread from the tray, shrugging. "I simply wondered, is all." She took a bite, and watched curiously as Alva lingered over her task. "And what did you call him before he became jarl?"

"Nephew," Alva answered, with an indifferent shrug. "The jarl has never been one for familiarities," she assured Elienor.

"I see," Elienor replied, though truly she didn't. Her brows knit as she recalled the way Alarik had demanded she use his given name.

"Tell me, Elienor . . ."

"Hmmm?"

"Was it your belly that ached?"

"Oh, nay," Elienor replied softly, wishing it were so simple. Nevertheless, she felt it unwise to elaborate. "Where's Alarik?" she asked, changing the subject.

"I'm not certain," Alva said quickly. "Tell me . . . was it your head?"

Elienor sighed deeply. Her head, indeed. "Aye," she admitted, setting down the unfinished chunk of bread. " 'Twas my head that ached." Suddenly, she didn't feel so hungry. "Alva . . . have you by chance . . . a sprig of rosemary?" she asked cautiously.

Alva ceased her task suddenly, peering at Elienor over the rekindled fire, her brows knitting. "Rosemary?"

"Rosemary," Elienor affirmed with a nod. Mother Heloise had sworn the herb warded away nightmares, and though it oft failed to perform, this time she was desperate. "To put under my pillow . . ."

Alva's round face contorted. "Strange cure for an aching head!" she declared, and then seeing Elienor's dismal expression, she relented. "But if it will ease you, then I shall see." She wagged her head. "Mayhap 'tis that wound of yours still plaguing you," she suggested.

Elienor's fingers went to her temple. All that remained was a thin raised scar. It hurt nought at all. "Mayhap," she lied.

A faraway scream caught her attention suddenly.

Her brow furrowed. "Alva . . . did you hear that?"

Alva cocked her head. "I . . . I'm not certain. I did hear something . . ."

All at once it sounded as though a stampede of wild beasts burst through the hall beyond. Without a word, Alva raced to the door, throwing it wide. She watched, shocked, as every last soul hurried from the *skali*, and then she turned to Elienor, her face pale. "Fire," she said softly, swaying as though she would swoon.

"The *kirken* is afire!"

Alarik burst from the hall, grateful to see that Sleipnir remained where he'd been abandoned. Bounding into the saddle, he didn't wait to see whether he was followed.

Already, the eerie orange brightness of fire blazed into the night sky.

The sound of its roar intensified as Sleipnir flung behind them earth and snow, racing the distance toward the vale. Fury burned at Alarik's gut, as he urged his mount faster—not that he feared the fire would spread. The remote little church sat too far from the rest of the steading to endanger any but itself, and the remaining snow upon the ground would further arrest it. Reaching the raging inferno well before the others, he leapt from his mount, swearing profusely.

They were too late.

The small structure was completely engulfed.

Olav reined in, slipping from his saddle, muttering in anger, and Brother Vernay, who had run nearly back to the manorhouse after Alarik, came staggering behind.

After him hurried his people, many shouldering buckets hastily filled.

"My lord!" Vernay panted, his face scarlet in the raging reflection of the fire. " 'Twas Hrolf! I . . ." He paused to catch his breath, and looked as though he would weep. "I . . . I could not stop them! Lost!" he lamented, his breath a white mist against the frosty fire-lit night. "All lost!" He threw a hand skyward. "All our precious labors!"

"Heathen pigs!" Olav shouted wrathfully, staggering backward as the roof exploded into glowing fragments.

Helpless in his rage, Alarik swore again, batting the fiery flakes away from his face and hair as they rained down upon him.

"My . . . my lord," Vernay continued, still breathless. Alarik turned toward the monk, his gaze burning hotter than the fire at his back. Vernay fell to his knees. "They dispatched me with a message for you. Hrolf said . . . he said to tell you that if you value what you hold . . . you will not rebuild the *kirken!*"

A staggered murmur erupted from those gathered, yet all fell immediately silent as Alarik advanced upon Vernay.

Vernay stumbled backward at the look in Alarik's eyes. "M . . . my lord?" he appealed. "I am but the messenger! This little church bore my own hopes, as well! My lord!"

"No one!" Alarik bellowed, seizing Vernay by his frock in frustration, "no one tells me what I can—or what I cannot build upon mine own land!"

At his declaration, Bjorn elbowed his way to the fore. "I thought you cared not for the *kirken*, mine brother?" he challenged. "I thought you built it simply to appease Olav? Why should you care now that it lies in ruin?"

Only silence met his imputing questions. Alarik released the trembling monk. Vernay fell at his feet. For the briefest instant, Alarik's wrathful gaze sought out Olav's, sharing Olav's question: Had Bjorn been party to the fire?

The evidence seemed weighted against him, for he'd left the *skali* earlier and had never returned . . .

Until now.

And he had met with Hrolf.

Still, some part of him could not accept the possibility. He turned to his youngest brother, holding his rage in check. Yet Bjorn would not let it go.

"Let it lie in its filthy ashes!" Bjorn persisted. "Mayhap then you would send the *Fransk* shrew back whence she came!"

A feeling of hysteria unlike anything Alarik had ever experienced swept over him at the merest thought of Elienor leaving. "*Nei!*" he exploded, lunging at Bjorn. He seized Bjorn by his woollen tunic, nigh renting it in his wrath. He shook his brother violently. "I'll not! Do y' hear? I'll not! The *kirken shall* be reerected!" He glanced about at his wide-eyed people. They shrank back from him, never having seen him in such a fury. "Any man who thinks to oppose me," he roared, meeting their gazes one by one. "Any man!—including you, Bjorn—"

his gaze returned to his brother, and he shook him once more, "will taste of *Dragvendil*, by *God!*"

Bjorn's eyes accused him. "*Which* god, mine brother?" he asked softly. Even dangling by his tunic, and under the heat of Alarik's gaze, he dared ask once more, "*Which* god?"

Alarik fair shook with fury. "It matters not!" he snarled. "What I believe in mine own soul concerns me, and none other! As it is so with any one of you," he declared, meeting his people's gazes once more. He swallowed as his burning eyes returned to Bjorn—eyes that stung from smoke, and tears he could not shed—would not shed. He wanted to accuse Bjorn in that moment, wanted to ask him what demons had possessed him that he would betray his only brother.

He wanted to fall to his knees and weep with sorrow for the brother he'd loved and would have died for. But he said nought of those things. His face grew red with silent fury, and then he shoved Bjorn back into the melting snow, with a violence barely suppressed. "I would have plucked out mine eyes, *brother*—" he said the word with contempt, and a touch of melancholy, "and handed them to you . . . had you only asked!" And with that declaration, he turned, bellowing out orders for the dousing of the fire.

It was daybreak when Alarik returned.

As had the rest of the steading, Elienor witnessed the scene at the *kirken*, but with tempers so high, Alarik had ordered her at once back to the longhouse, fearing for her safety. He was well aware that some followed Bjorn's way of thought . . . though unlike Bjorn, they wouldn't have betrayed him. Unlike Bjorn, they seemed to know he would never force their hearts, for if he'd intended to, he'd have done it long ago, back when Olav had first taken up the cross.

He stormed into his chamber, soot blackened and sodden with sweat and melted snow. He found Elienor sitting upon his bed, wringing her hands. She gasped in surprise at the sight of him, leaping up as he entered the room.

He looked like a demon, his face covered in ashes and soot, his fine tunic tattered and blackened, yet Elienor had to fight the incredible urge to fling herself into his arms. She'd feared for his safety.

Dear God, how she'd feared for him.

He tore his gaze away and slammed the door behind him. "Olav awaits me in the stables!" he told her more sharply than he'd intended, for he still could not vanquish the image of her ring about Olav's neck.

Elienor wrung her hands. "You will seek out Hrolf?" she asked tentatively.

Grimacing, Alarik peeled off his tunic, hurling it to the floor. "I will," he said, meeting her gaze.

Elienor's heart turned over at the pain nestled in his piercing silver eyes. Confused, she averted her own gaze, her heart twisting . . . in dread? Her vision came back to her swiftly, and she feared for his safety. More than anything, she wanted to tell him of it, but she knew better.

It would be a fool thing to do, for he'd not believe her . . . even if he chose not to persecute her for it.

He moved toward her in silence, lifting her chin with a finger. "Tears?" he asked in astonishment. "Elienor . . ." He narrowed his eyes. "Why do you cry?"

Elienor tore her gaze away. She shook her head unable to speak.

"The *kirken*?"

She nodded the lie, swiping away the tears that rolled so shamefully down her cheeks.

Disappointed, Alarik sighed wearily, and nevertheless drew her within his embrace. "The church shall be restored," he assured her. "That I pledge you."

Elienor raised her tear-stained face to his, fighting back a new flood of tears. "You . . . you will take care?"

He blinked at her question, as though startled by it, and then his eyes lit with rare emotion as he gazed down upon her, stunned by her behest. He opened his mouth to speak, but knew not what to say. He swallowed, afeared to hope. Cupping Elienor's chin within his palm, he nodded. He bent to kiss her lips, those lips that had made him burn from the first, those lips that shocked and plagued him still. "You take care as well, my little nun," he whispered, lifting his mouth from hers. He bent once more, unable to resist. Her delicate lids closed as he kissed them too. He wrapped his arms about her, holding her close. "To be certain . . . I shall leave my best man, Sigurd Thorgoodson, to watch over you."

The tender spell of the moment shattered. A vivid picture of Sigurd, dancing nude over the bodies at Phillipe's castle, was conjured within Elienor's mind, and her eyes widened in alarm. "Nay!" she gasped, breaking free of him.

A shadow passed over his features. "I trust him more than I do mine own kin," he assured her, his tone somewhat strained.

Sensing the pain beneath his words, Elienor nodded her acquiescence, her gaze dropping against her will to his bare chest. The sight of it made the blood course through her, and she stared as though transfixed.

His answering chuckle was low and rich. It sent quiver after quiver through her.

Gratified with the way she gazed upon him in that moment, Alarik drew her into his arms, and bent to kiss her, unable to take his leave without partaking once more of the sweetness she offered. With a hand to the small of her back, he coaxed her forward, parting her lips with gentle pressure. Elienor opened willingly unto him, arching to accept his hunger, and his body quickened in response.

He reveled in the taste of her. Never would he have imagined he'd enjoy such a thing so well.

Alas, it seemed the *Fransk* were good for more than swords and wine.

By God, it would be so easy to lose himself . . . so easy to stay. Shuddering over the need that coursed through his veins like terrible jolts of thunder, he crushed her to him, devouring her mouth without mercy.

Her hands entwined about his neck and he groaned his torment, knowing he could not have her just now.

Damn him, he was loath to leave, but he could not linger . . . lest the filthy culprits escape him in the meantime.

Now he had yet one more reason to kill Hrolf Kaetilson.

"Elienor," he murmured huskily. He took a deep breath, tempering himself. His heart hammered like that of a fresh-faced youth. "If only you knew what you do to me . . ." He groaned in regret. "Later," he promised, and bent to nip her gown where it cloaked the tip of her breast, a guarantee of his word.

To Elienor's shame, she delighted in his wicked promise. Leaving her weak-kneed with anticipation, he turned his back on her, and she watched as he strode to his chest, lifted up the lid, and removed from it a fresh tunic. After it, his mail, laying it aside as he donned his tunic, and then, kneeling, he beckoned her to him with a wriggle of his finger. "I cannot arm myself alone," he told her, a ghost of a smile twisting his lips. "Come aid me, Elienor."

Elienor didn't hesitate at his command. Alarik observed her advance in silence, smiling when she struggled to lift his heavy mailed tunic.

Elienor's cheeks flushed. "I did not think it would be so heavy!" she justified.

" 'Tis larger than most, I'll warrant." His dark eyes twinkled.

Together, they guided the mail *brynie* over his head, and once it was in place, she sat again upon the bed to watch as he positioned his scabbard across his hips. Lifting up from the coffer his crimson mantle, he drew it on, placing it carelessly over his shoulders, and then he fastened it with a brooch that was fashioned to look like a blazing sun with a hawk in its center. Finally, he retrieved his sword, inspecting it painstakingly, running his hand over the runes carved so meticulously into its gleaming blade.

"What do they mean?" Elienor asked, cocking her head in ill-suppressed curiosity.

Alarik followed her gaze to his blade, and gave a nod of comprehension. His silver eyes met her violet-blue ones. "*Dragvendil*," he told her. " 'Tis the name of mine sword. it means *readily drawn*—" he gave her a meaningful sideways glance—"as is another blade I own." He ignored the way she shivered at his disclosure, the way she averted her widened eyes, telling himself he didn't give a damn if she feared him still.

But he did.

Mayhap by the time he returned . . . Alva would have something to tell him.

If not, then mayhap he didn't wish to know what haunted the wench.

After all, no matter what . . .

She was his. And would remain so evermore.

He'd not give her up—her uncle be damned, the church be damned, Bjorn be damned . . .

Olav be damned!

With a foreboding hiss, *Dragvendil* was sheathed within his scabbard. The thought of Elienor's ring deposited about his brother's neck clenched at his gut. Without a word, he procured his shield—he wasn't certain he trusted himself to speak—and with a final glance at Elienor, seized his helm and started for the door.

Nothing in his gait suggested he would pause to bid her farewell, but he spun abruptly in the doorway to face her, and stood an unending moment, saying nothing, his visage dark. Their gazes interlocked, clung to one another, and there was some longing perceptible within the silver glint of his eyes . . . as though he anticipated something more of her, Elienor knew not what, and then a momentary sadness in them, when nothing was spoken between them.

His gaze narrowed to shadowy slivers. "Take care, my little nun," he whispered sullenly, "for I vow I *shall* return."

And with that promise he departed.

Chapter 29

Lost.
　Everything had been lost. All her long hours of copying.
　Everything.
　Nevertheless, the *kirken* itself, having been made almost solely of cobbled stone and pitch, stood solid. Blackened with soot, it took nigh a sennight to scrub clean, and still Alarik did not return.
　Each day Elienor watched, along with Brother Vernay, as the *kirken* was further restored. It dismayed her that she'd dedicated so much of herself to the copying.
　They would begin anew, Brother Vernay had said hearteningly, come spring.
　Yet spring came to the steading in elusive glimpses, the snow melting and the greenery stealing timidly forth. And still Alarik did not return. Elienor's dread for him multiplied with each passing day. At night she could sleep not at all. She lay there, berating herself for being such a coward that she would allow men to die unnecessarily. She told herself it was simple dread over what would become of herself were Alarik to perish. But she knew better. 'Twas for him she feared, and each morn the circles that darkened her eyes deepened.
　Nevertheless during the light of day, she labored wherever Alva bid her to, all the while spurning

her heart and her conscience, both. It was, she told herself, the only way to endure.

One late spring morn, as she served within the *eldhus*, kneading and pounding bread, Alva came to her.

"You love him, do you not?"

Elienor refused to confess it. She said nothing, although the way she pummeled the dough gave lie to her silence.

Alva sighed. "My dear . . . one need only look at you to know."

Elienor's eyes misted and she lowered them in shame.

"Hmmmph, now! Why the weeping? Rejoice in it, my dear, for I believe he loves you too."

Elienor swallowed, shaking her head. Why did that possibility, remote as it was, make her feel infinitely worse?

Doubtless because she'd made the decision not to forewarn him . . . and now she could lose him—not that she'd ever truly had him, she promptly reminded herself. Jesu . . . she was so confused. She swallowed once more, fighting back angry tears, unable to look into Alva's knowing eyes. God curse her, for not only was she a liar . . . she was indisputably a coward of the worst breed!

"Something else troubles you, Elienor? Perhaps if you spoke of it?"

Elienor peered up into Alva's concerned blue eyes. Why shouldn't she tell? What mattered it now if Alarik did not come back? she told herself. She could not bear it! Guilt and pain knotted inside her. Mayhap there was time to undo what she'd been too cowardly to face ere now. At any rate, what had she to lose?

Her very life, she reminded herself bleakly.

Yet what life was this to live . . .

Without him?

Fighting back the tears, Elienor confided everything unto Alva, quietly, so as not to be overheard. Alva, she trusted implicitly, but Nissa was present, watching them, and Nissa she trusted not at all. When she finished, she waited anxiously for Alva's reaction.

"Elienor!" Alva rebuked. "*This* is what you've kept tucked away so long?"

Elienor's brow furrowed. That was all? Nothing more? In Francia they put her mother to death—cast her as a babe into a nunnery for the better part of her life—and Alva did nothing more than scold her? She cocked her head. "I don't think you quite perceive what I'm telling you."

Alva gave her a fretful look. "Certainly I do! In the Northland 'tis no crime to be gifted, Elienor! Why, along with the *skalds*, those capable of the sight are well honored! 'Tis the truth," she persisted, when Elienor merely gaped incredulously. "In verity, 'tis the soothsayers, who are most revered, for they are so very scarce." Her brow furrowed suddenly. "Nevertheless, I do hope you are mistaken about this vision of yours . . . you did say you were present during this . . . this battle?"

Elienor nodded hopefully.

"Then mayhap there is time to alter its course. Let us pray 'tis so."

Elienor choked upon Alva's suggestion. She shook her head at once. Mayhap she was forced to make this land her own, but never would she embrace their pagan gods. "I . . . I don't . . ."

Alva smiled knowingly, her brows furrowing. "The God of Abraham," she clarified in a whisper, and then she couldn't suppress a chuckle at

Elienor's look. "Be not so appalled!" she chastised. She wagged a finger at Elienor. "My dear . . . years alone cannot change the bent of one's heart, you realize. At any rate, there are many here who worship the Christian God—and then again many more who do not." She shrugged, giving Elienor a judicious glance. " 'Tis wisest to keep your heart unto yourself. You understand my meaning?" She nodded her chin subtly toward Nissa.

Elienor followed Alva's glance, and met Nissa's Nordic blue eyes. A shiver of foreboding raced down her spine. "I wish now I'd come to you sooner," she whispered softly.

Alva sighed. "What is done, is done," she declared fatalistically, tearing her gaze from Nissa to look into Elienor's overtired eyes. "You must pay her no mind," she stressed. "As for me, I cannot wait for the jarl to rid his home of Ejnar's daughter—the viper! I tell you, she's been nought but trouble since the day she arrived!" And then her eyes suddenly lit with mirth. "I declare a wager!" She unhooked one of the brooches that secured her overgown and offered it to Elienor, grinning mischievously. Her frock hung precariously on one side, but she seemed not to notice. "If the jarl does not acknowledge his love for you upon his return, I believe I shall aid him in the endeavor, but for now . . . I wager you this brooch he's already lost his heart to you. Go on . . . take it!"

Elienor thrust Alva's hand away, shaking her head. "I could not!"

Alva merely smiled as she pressed the brooch insistently into Elienor's palm. "You can," she whispered. "And you shall. Keep it, for I fear I've long since lost the gamble!" Her tone bore that of a young maid silly with her own first love.

Elienor said nothing, only clasped the brooch to her breast. Dare she? Dare she hope?

Alva chuckled and spun away, ambling off to look in on a cluster of chattering women. Rather than scold them, she at once joined in their conversation, tittering cheerfully over something one of them said. Elienor marveled that she accepted these people so easily . . . and they her. Never would she have guessed Alva's tragic past . . . had she not been told. She shook her head in admiration of Alva's fortitude, and observing Alva so intently, she was unaware that Nissa came to her. Elienor started with a gasp at Nissa's hand gently placed upon her shoulder.

"I do hope we can manage to put the past aside," Nissa said, her eyes bright with purpose.

Elienor's hands stilled upon the dough. Having anticipated Nissa's venom instead, she blinked in surprise at the amiable declaration.

"Bjorn has asked me to wed with him," Nissa explained, "and so mayhap . . . mayhap I'll be staying at Gryting after all!"

"Bjorn?" Elienor echoed, momentarily addled. "I . . . I'm pleased for you—truly!" she avowed, and found she meant it. She smiled tentatively. Mayhap Alva was mistaken about Nissa. Mayhap Nissa was as much a pawn of life as anyone else? By her smile, she seemed pleased enough with Bjorn.

Confusion shone momentarily in Nissa's beautiful blue eyes. "Th . . . thank you." She glanced away uneasily, her expression shadowing, as though with regret, and then she again met Elienor's questioning gaze. "At any rate," she continued on a brighter note, "Brother Vernay has asked me to tell you he has need of you at the *kirken*. I'll finish for you," she offered, gathering the dough from beneath Elienor's hands. She glanced up to see that Elienor was standing in contemplative silence. "Hurry now!" she prodded. "I fear I've waited too long already to pass on the message." When Elienor seemed leery, she shrugged a little sheepishly, adding, "Brother Vernay and I don't quite cherish one other, I'm afeared . . ."

Elienor eased a little, stifling a smile at the euphemism, for 'twas more as though they despised one other. "No harm done," she relented, wiping her hands upon a rag. "I shall find him."

Nissa returned a wan smile, nodding, and Elienor turned to snatch her cloak from a peg before rushing out of the kitchen. She only hoped Brother Vernay had not tired of waiting.

As she left the *eldhus*, Mischief launched himself from the spot he'd been chastised to, bounding after her happily, yapping with relish. Elienor bent to stroke his head. He evaded her, baiting her to pursue him, to play, and she laughed. "Nay, Mischief!" She giggled again when his bark propelled him into the air. "Brother Vernay awaits me!" she told him, and then she started off again toward the vale, resolutely ignoring the dog yapping at her heels.

What could Brother Vernay possibly need of her she wondered as she lifted up her skirts, succumbing to a quick race against Mischief. They were weeks away from being able to return to the copying of *l'ecriture sainte*.

Ahhh, well, she sighed, the walk would do her good. She desperately needed fresh air after the stifling heat of the *eldhus*. Forsooth, even in the height of winter the kitchens were sweltering!

To her surprise, Mischief suddenly skidded to a halt. Clumsy as the pup was yet, it tumbled over itself, and then sat firmly upon its backside and began to bark, sniffing at the air. She smiled, for if she didn't know better, she'd vow the dog was ordering her back. Indignant pup! Elienor shook her head in amusement, disregarding Mischief's relentless barking. As it was, Brother Vernay had been left waiting much too long. "Pardon, Mischief!" she called after her. "Later!" she promised, "after I speak with Brother Vernay." A quiver sped through her as she recalled Alarik telling her just the same, and again she thrust it out of her mind once more, lifting up her skirts to run the distance.

The sooner she spoke with Brother Vernay, the sooner she would be back to the steading.

She found the newly hung *kirken* door ajar. With a gentle shove, Elienor opened it wide enough to allow entrance, but lingered in the portal to examine the new door. Admiring it, she smoothed her palm across the rich wood, thinking that Sigurd's workmanship was extraordinary. He seemed to work well with wood. 'Twas fortunate he had talents other than those of bloodshed, she thought a little bitterly.

A prickle raced down her spine, a chill of foreboding that swept through her like a winter gale.

Something here was not quite right.

She stepped into the church apprehensively, calling out softly for Brother Vernay, and couldn't help but note that the walls were still charred black in places.

Another prickle.

Mayhap 'twas simply the ominous appearance of the place. Some things could not so easily be washed away, she mused. Sins and memories both had a way of flooding back to haunt you. So did prophetic visions.

The rush of bird's wings startled her. With a shriek of surprise, she glanced up to spy a small flock taking flight. As of yet there was no roof, and likely she'd frightened them from their perches, yet their cries only added to her sense of unease. Bolstering herself, she reasoned 'twas merely her dismal frame of mind that agitated her so, and thrusting away her brooding thoughts once and for all, she called again for Brother Vernay, thinking it wouldn't be long before the church was fully restored . . . mayhap better than before.

"Alarik will be pleased," she said on a sigh, hugging the cloak to herself.

She hadn't realized she'd spoken aloud.

And neither did she note the shadow that fell across the altar in that instant.

"Will he, indeed?"

Elienor recognized the voice at once and turned to face him, swallowing her fear.

Hrolf Kaetilson laughed hideously as he lifted his weight from the door frame. "You look as though you've seen a *spokelse*," he said, grinning venomously. "A ghost," he supplied at her look. His teeth flashed behind his red beard as he came toward her. "Now, now . . . are you not pleased to see me?"

Chapter 30

His instincts had seldom failed him.

Yet failed him they had.

Wholly.

Cursing roundly beneath his breath for allowing himself to be so recklessly distracted, Alarik gripped the reins in anger, his knuckles fading white with the suppressed violence in his hold, yet his treatment of Sleipnir remained gentle and sure. Heedless of any risk to himself, he rode near a league ahead of his men, impatient to be back at the steading.

Backed by Olav's available forces, they'd pursued Hrolf and Ejnar well into the Dane's mark only to find that somehow the whole lot of them had managed to double back without any visible trace. By the time it had been discovered, it had been much too late to overtake them, and now fury clenched his gut as he contemplated Hrolf's destination.

There was little doubt now as to their intent, for the steading lay no more than another furlong ahead, and the tracks they were now following led directly there. Odin curse him! He knew enough to discern that their change in course boded his people no good.

He only hoped he didn't arrive overlate.

To his relief, when the steading materialized in

the distance, it appeared untouched. Yet the closer he rode, the less assured he felt . . .

Before his manor house his people congregated—an ominous sign, he knew. They chattered anxiously, hands waving excitedly, until his approach, and then each and every one fell deathly silent . . . and stiller yet.

Despite their uncanny hush, Alarik sensed the rise in their apprehension the instant he reined in before them. Sleipnir felt it as well, for he reared slightly only to fall back on prancing hooves. Brother Vernay alone broke from their midst, hurrying forward. Alarik watched his approach with an unease that magnified with each diffident step the monk took.

Vernay shook his head. "My lord!" he bemoaned. "The *demoiselle* . . . she . . . she . . ."

A prickling snaked down Alarik's spine. "She what?"

"She's gone, my lord!"

Alarik was unprepared for the jolt that ran through his gut at the declaration. "What do you mean gone? *Where* has she gone?" He'd expected to be told the storehouses had been burned, that the church had once again been demolished, but not this.

"Simply that, my lord—gone!" the old priest maintained. "One instant she was in the *eldhus* working with the women, and the next . . . well . . . simple vanished, is all!"

His fury barely restrained, Alarik swung down from Sleipnir's back, nodding for one of the youngest lads to come forward. He handed the reins to the youth. "When Bjorn and Olav arrive," he charged the lad, "send them both in at once!" The boy nodded vigorously that he would.

"Oh! My lord!" Vernay called after him again as he stormed into the *skali*, but Alarik continued as though he'd not heard. Still Vernay followed, for though he'd feared Alarik's wrath, as had the rest, his rational calm reassured. "My lord!" he called again. "I very nearly forgot!" He raced after Alarik. "I thought it important to recount that the pup . . . Mischief . . ."

Alarik turned, and the expression on his face choked the remaining words from Vernay's throat. For the longest instant he could not speak, paralyzed by the barely leashed violence that emanated from the jarl's steely gray eyes, nevertheless 'twas the jarl's other emotion unveiled that wrested the words from his mouth.

Alarik threw his shoulders back stalwartly, defying the pain in his heart that the monk had perceived. Still, his voice was hoarse when he spoke. "Where . . ." Despite himself, his voice faltered. "Where was the dog found?"

"Betwixt here and the *kirken*, my lord. Mayhap that is where the demoiselle was bound?"

Awareness came slowly, painfully.

The smell of earth—and of something else vile—accosted Elienor's senses. She rolled, wincing against the sharp pain that burst through her head. Her poor, poor head . . . Her lips met damp soil, and she sputtered at once, swiping her mouth in disgust. Sweet Jesu! It tasted of spoils!

Her eyes flew wide in the darkness. Mercy . . . where was she *this* time? She groaned as bits of memory besieged her: Hrolf standing in the portal, Hrolf striking her with the hilt of his sword.

"Nay," she murmured in agony.

Not again? Bones of the saints, but she should

have remained in the priory. How many times must she endure this? If she wasn't so afeared to draw her captor's attention, she might have laughed hysterically over the absurdness of it all.

And her mouth, it was so dry it lacked wetness to spit with. She tried to swallow and couldn't, tried to moisten her lips and couldn't. Her mouth felt as though it had been filled with thick, furry wool. Closing her eyes she struggled to think through the haze of pain.

Where was she?

Lifting her head slightly—her neck was so stiff—she reexamined her cell. It was nearly too dark to see anything at all, but by a flickering light somewhere up above she finally made out the dirt walls ... dirt floor ...

Her heartbeat quickened, and she swallowed—nevermind that there was nought to swallow—and tried to stifle the deafening bawl of hysteria in her mind. God in heaven above, have mercy!

Nay! she told herself. She would be fine ... she would be fine ... if only she remained calm ... she would be fine ...

Shuddering with fear, she scooted backward, propping herself semi-upright, her breath coming in short pants.

Sweet Jesu, it felt as though she were lying within her own grave!

But 'twas not her grave, she reassured herself. Closing her eyes, she opened them again slowly. 'Twas a cell, a simple cell—a barbarous and torturous cell, but a cell nonetheless. The oversmall pit was dug into the floor of a larger chamber, and was barely high enough to allow a soul to sit upright. Certainly, she could not even attempt to stand. From the upper chamber could be heard voices, faint but increasingly louder. One of those Elienor recognized at once and her heart pummelled faster as it grew closer.

Within seconds, Hrolf's repulsive face peered down through the thick bars. He grinned, a grin that sent a shuddering down her spine. "Well, now . . . you didn't believe I'd forget you?" he asked her, his grin widening at the terror in her expression.

Another face appeared, peering down over Hrolf's shoulder, this one older, more weathered, though less harsh. Still, the ice-blue eyes spewed as much hatred as those of Hrolf's. "You've a soft head," the man muttered, cracking a smile. "Thought you might never waken."

Elienor wished she hadn't.

"Witch! If I'd known she'd fare so well," Hrolf lamented, "I'd have struck her harder!" He spat down at her. His saliva pelted her face and Elienor cried out, swiping it away. "I should have cracked your skull wider upon the Goldenhawk, when first I had occasion!"

"P . . . please," Elienor appealed, battling hysteria and tears. She reached up to seize the wooden bars in sheer desperation, appealing to the man at Hrolf's back. "Please, please, hold me elsewhere . . . I . . ." Hrolf smashed her fingers and she cried out in pain, wresting them from beneath his boot.

Silent tears coursed down her cheeks.

The man laughed, clapping Hrolf upon the back. "*I've* no more use for the darkling," he said arrogantly. "Mine tastes run fairer than she. Do with her now what you will, Red. For certain . . . you two seem to have unfinished matters at hand."

Hrolf tossed a look behind him, grunting in agreement, and then he turned to glare down into the pit. He waited for the man's footsteps to recede completely before he whispered, "Indeed we do . . . indeed we do . . . for you shall gain me back mine honor, witch! Mayhap Ejnar wishes nothing more than to eliminate his daughter's rival, but I shall not be appeased until you give me Trygvi's bastard son into the palm of mine hand!"

Crippling fear swept over Elienor, though this time not for herself. Unbidden, the image of Alarik leaping into the churning sea from the Goldenhawk, the gleaming axe blade hurling through the air at his back, assailed her. In that moment, she knew how very hopelessly she loved him. "H . . . he won't come," she whispered miserably. Averting her gaze, she prayed with all her heart that it was the truth. But even as she prayed . . . she knew . . . whether he came for her, or nay . . .

The dream would hold true.

"*Ya*," Hrolf said. "He will . . . for you've bewitched the fool—though I know not how! Nevertheless, he will come . . . and when he does . . . mine blade will find his back!" His chuckle was malicious. "Mark mine words for true, you black-haired *witch*! And when he's done with, I shall then deal with you," he promised darkly.

Witch.

Elienor's heart wrenched, for Hrolf was closer to the truth than he realized. Her own people had named her so and then had cast her aside for it. Even so, she'd been fortunate 'twas all they had done after her mother's fate. Sweet Jesu above . . . her mother . . . her poor mother had been valiant enough to speak her mind, at least. And she, Elienor, daughter of her womb, was born and would die nought more than a coward. Her eyes closed.

How could she not have warned Alarik? In that moment, she thought of Alva and Vernay, and all who would suffer without him, and wondered how she could be so selfish. She wanted to weep. Wanted to scream. Wanted to die. She sat numbly, hot tears slipping past her lashes. When finally she opened her eyes and glanced upward again, Hrolf had gone.

Chapter 31

After days of relentless searching there was still no sign of Ejnar's camp—despite the fact that Alarik had searched hill and vale for it. He knew without a doubt 'twas they who held Elienor, for within the *kirken* they'd discovered Hrolf's dagger violently skewered through the fine gold brooch Alva had sworn she'd given Elienor only moments before Elienor's disappearance. The infamous dagger had been driven into the brooch's center with such force that it had disfigured and severed the delicate filigreed ornamentation adorning the jewel. Within plain sight, the brooch had been pegged upon the newly hung door, an arrogant missive to Alarik, for by it Hrolf declared that he cared not who knew of his perfidy.

Yet, his wordless declaration seemed not to match his deeds, for the man was becoming a master of evasion, secreting himself more adeptly than an adder in the woods and striking just as venomously and swiftly. Since Elienor's disappearance they'd discovered evidence of sacrifices within the nearby groves—a message to Olav no doubt, and likely to Alarik as well, for though no one knew of his inclination, many suspected.

Furthermore, it aided them not at all in their search that the people seemed to be growing discontent with Olav as their king. In truth, Alarik was even beginning to suspect that Olav had remained with him throughout the winter for his own protection, for Alarik's own people were proving more loyal than his. And it struck Alarik as ill-boding that the steadings they'd inquired at were so reluctant to aid them in their quest. Nevertheless, most *had* complied, if reluctantly so, and still Ejnar and Hrolf eluded them. 'Twas for that reason he'd determined to employ their last recourse.

Bjorn.

His sigh was deep and pensive as he regarded both his brothers at table with him, for he was well aware that Bjorn had found Ejnar easily enough when he'd sought him out the first time.

Mayhap now, with a little manipulation on his own part, the misled fool could draw the Dane out for him.

All else had failed.

The thought of his brother forsaking him sat like acid in his gut, yet even as he hoped his youngest brother would remain steadfast in this . . . he prayed Bjorn would conspire to betray him . . .

One final time.

He wanted Elienor restored to him that desperately.

Loki take him, he no longer cared that it might seem a weakness in him. He was damned weary of being strong. He was weary, period. Too long he'd gone without sleep, or bath, or leisure. By Hella's curse, if it meant the return of Elienor . . . let him be weak. If it meant losing everything . . . let him fall. He wanted nothing at all . . . if he wasn't with her.

And so it was he proceeded with the discourse he and Olav had intended for Bjorn to overhear. Leaning forward, he raked tense fingers over the stubble of his golden beard, and giving Bjorn a covert sideways glance, he turned to Olav and said a mite too loudly, "I've considered your proposal, mine *bror* . . ."

Behind him Bjorn fell silent, concluding the conversation he carried on with Sigurd. Alarik resisted the temptation to turn and be certain he was listening.

Perceiving the cause for Alarik's pause, Olav nodded discreetly for him to continue. "And?"

"I believe I shall join you in your quest to retrieve Tyri's lands from Burislav, after all."

"What?" Olav exclaimed, taking an irritated tone as planned. It would serve them both well if Bjorn believed they'd quarrelled over this. "And spare one instant in your search for the *Fransk* in order that you might aid your own flesh and blood? To what do I owe this honor, at last?"

"Spare me Olav!" Alarik snapped, his eyes reverting to Elienor's ring that still encircled Olav's neck. No matter that he tried, he could not forget the accursed thing. "I'll agree on one condition . . ." The silence behind them thickened; even Sigurd stopped speaking to listen.

The clash of Olav's brows told Alarik that Olav sensed his anger was more than feigned. "And that is . . ."

Alarik shuttered his expression, his soul too chaotic to be glimpsed even by Olav. "That you procure for me from Burislav the Pole at least ten well-manned vessels so that I might launch mine own attack upon the Dane . . . and with him Hrolf Kaetilson. I'll not rest until my blade does as well . . . in his treacherous heart." He sighed wearily. "For now it seems we've exhausted every other avenue," he continued truthfully. "But I *intend* to find them eventually . . . and when I do I want good men at my back."

Olav's gaze followed Alarik's to the ring about his own neck, and his brow flinched in consideration. "And what of me and mine?" he asked abruptly, puzzled by Alarik's unexpected show of vehemence toward him. It seemed of late, he'd spied that look once too oft. "Will you want us at your back, as well?"

Alarik waited a moment before replying, weighing his words. Somehow, the conversation had digressed from that which they'd rehearsed. When he spoke again his tone was more resigned than angry. "Seems to me, mine brother . . . you have your own battle to fight. You have no time for mine." Their gazes locked. In the silence of the moment, Alarik swallowed his resentment, for no matter how infuriated he was with Olav . . . Olav *was* his brother . . . and more than that . . . he was his king. "Nevertheless," he began, when Olav failed to be soothed, "if you would care to make mine battle your own . . . then I will always . . . *always* welcome you at my back." He nodded. "As I, in faith, hope you would have me at yours?"

Olav returned the nod, satisfied. "Very well, then . . . if 'tis possible . . . I shall procure those men of the Pole for you . . . and then I shall add to them mine own. I would be there to see you skewer that red-haired heathen!" There was a lapse in conversation abruptly, a silence that was endless, for it seemed every man within the *skali* was intent on their conversation. "Shall we leave, let us say . . . within the fortnight?"

Alarik nodded. "Within the fortnight," he agreed, and it was then he sensed more than heard Bjorn rising from table. Again, he didn't bother to look to be certain. Somehow, he knew. Pain knifed through him. Closing his eyes, he listened as Bjorn gave his excuses. He felt his brother brush by his shoulder, and opened his eyes, his gaze remaining upon Bjorn as he passed by him and made his way through the *skali*, looking more light-hearted than he had in weeks. A muscle ticked at his jaw, for on the way out, Bjorn stopped briefly to banter with Ivar Longbeard—nothing significant, the two merely shared a snicker—in truth, 'twas as though Bjorn had suddenly been given a new fate . . .

And mayhap he had.

Mayhap this day they all had.

"Think you he took the bait?" Olav had bent to whisper the question at his ear.

Alarik watched a moment longer, until Bjorn departed at last, and then his gaze returned to the ring Olav wore. He said quietly, enigmatically, without emotion, "I feel the blade twisting already."

"Good, then . . . mayhap you will reclaim the *Fransk* before long."

"Mayhap," Alarik concurred.

"Alarik?"

Alarik met Olav's gaze at last. He nodded sullenly.

"It seemed to me that for an instant . . . for the slightest instant . . . there was sincerity in your anger. Is there aught you would speak to me of?"

Alarik considered briefly asking of the ring, but knew he would not. He could not quite bring himself to disclose his weakness for Elienor to such a length. Suffice it that everyone assumed he liked not being thwarted, that he liked not being deprived of that which he owned. Why should any know of the bleakness that had settled into his soul and heart?—verily, even into his bones!

Still, there was something that concerned him just as deeply. "Olav . . . mine, brother . . ." He swallowed, for 'twas doubtless the most difficult thing he'd ever said to his brother. "I know you say you have a passion for this Christian faith . . . that for the love of it you would die . . . but can you not love it somewhat less . . . and practice it more?"

Olav's visage twisted suddenly with outrage. "What say you, Alarik? Do you denounce mine faith?" he raged, his face mottling.

Alarik's expression did not so much as change. "*Nei*, Olav. But if I were to . . . would you then treat me with the same heavy hand you lend to the others when they do not fall to your demands?"

Olav's face reddened. "I'll not answer such an impudent question!"

Alarik shook his head. "You cannot sway the people through force." His eyes fixed upon his brother, unyielding. "Can you not take a single backward step?"

"And you! Can you so easily discard the wench?"

Silence.

"Never!" Alarik replied, his eyes sharp as daggers. "Never." And 'twas God's truth, for even if Bjorn failed to flush Ejnar and Hrolf out, he'd not stop searching until his dying breath!

"Hah! Trygvi's bastard'll not find you, lest I will it!" Hrolf taunted, having overheard Elienor's prayers.

Filthy and reeking from the prison pit she'd been cast into, Elienor struggled to keep her dignity. She'd not deign to reply, she told herself, for every time she did, Hrolf committed some atrocious act upon her person such as spitting down at her through the bars. The man was vile! Jesu, but it felt as though she'd been imprisoned for years. Hell had nothing in store for her after this!

The hours passed so slowly by. There was nought for her to do but sit and listen to the grating sound of Hrolf's voice. Her legs and backside ached from inactivity. But at least they fed her well enough—small consolation though it was.

"Olav, the fool . . . he's turned every man against him with his oppression and his threats!" Hrolf declared. "For truth, there is no one who would betray us to him now—none that I know of! Though there are some who would betray him," he said cryptically, and then snickered. "As you shall soon see . . ."

Still Elienor refused to respond. Instead she listened, for in the last days she'd gleaned much information from Hrolf in just such a manner. Braggart that he was, Hrolf seemed pleased to goad her night and day, and through his prattling she'd managed to discover that her pit graced the hall of an old abandoned steading located on an isle in the middle of a marsh—thus accounting for the sour smelling soil.

"Even those who might have followed the Christian faith will not now because Olav will not suffer them to choose of their own will! He shovels his own grave, I tell you, and he'll pull his bastard brother down with him when he plunges down into it. Alarik, the fool, he's simply too loyal for his own good . . . and you, witch, will insure me his ruin, and then shall you watch as I shovel putrid soil over them both!"

Elienor covered her ears and prayed for strength, forcing herself to ignore Hrolf's mockery of Alarik and his horrifying prophecy. *Dear God*, she prayed, *bear me through this* . . .

Even through her hands, she heard the rise of voices and uncovered her ears, trying to make them out.

"Your God will not aid you!" Hrolf scoffed, snickering nastily.

A quiver raced down Elienor's spine at the all too familiar declaration. Her heart pounded frantically as the muffled voices grew in clarity, finally catching Hrolf's notice, as well. He quieted, pivoting to face the men that entered, and then howled wildly with glee. Walking out of her sight to greet the newcomers, he laughed again and declared, "At last . . . at last! But then I knew you'd come!"

"Dispense with the crowing, Hrolf!"

Elienor cried out softly, recognizing the voice.

"The information I bring comes with a price . . ."

A long silence.

"What price?" Ejnar's gruff voice asked.

There was another pause and then Bjorn declared, "Your daughter, Ejnar . . . your daughter and land of mine own if you should depose him . . ."

Ejnar guffawed. "Bastard!" he said, without animosity. "You'll bed her yet, will you not? Persistent . . . bold . . . I like that . . . very well, Bjorn, Erik's son. If the information you've borne me today proves worthy, I shall indeed grant you my daughter at long last! What say you to that?"

Elienor heard a grunt and ensuing sigh, and imagined Bjorn relieved.

Was this then the betrayal she'd dreamed of?

"If she'll have you," Ejnar added sagely.

"She'll have me!" Bjorn avowed.

Ejnar laughed once more. " 'Tis baffling is it not . . . that a man's weakness should eternally lie betwixt the legs of a woman? Some day, I warrant, the crafty bitches shall rule all the lands!" And with that declaration, all three roared with laughter. "Come," Ejnar charged. "Let us hear what you have to say . . . ," and with that, they moved out of hearing distance.

When Hrolf swaggered into view moments later, his eyes were alight with unholy mirth. Snickering, he bent, unlocked the grate excitedly, and swung the cell door wide. "Come out, come out!" he beckoned ominously. " 'Tis time at last!" And with that, an anticipatory grin split his red beard and face.

And in that instant, a dark foreboding swept over Elienor, a presentiment more sinister than any she'd ever known.

The time *had* come, she knew, and the realization chilled her to the bone.

Chapter 32

Alarik was beginning to wonder that mayhap he'd been mistaken.

They'd made the journey to Vendland to meet with Burislav the Pole entirely without incident, and now upon their return there was yet no sign of Ejnar, or Hrolf. His gut twisted with the thought, for it had been weeks now since he'd seen Elienor.

For the first time he considered that he might not see her again.

Nei, he would find her, by God! If it took the remainder of his days, he would find her.

Altogether they sailed with nearly seventy-one vessels in their entourage, and men enough to crush the life from any army Ejnar could amass upon his own.

And crush him they would . . .

If they could find him.

Along with sixty of their own well-manned warships, they'd managed to recruit another eleven of the Jomsborg Viking's. Still, something beleaguered him now . . .

Something . . .

Above them, the sun shone bright as the Golden-hawk glided over the waves, its proud hawk's head soaring majestically before them, but the breeze swept dark clouds directly into their path. The

331

threat of a storm gave rise again to his feeling of foreboding.

About them the air was calm . . .

Too calm . . .

Instinct told him something was amiss, and he hadn't lived so many years by disregarding intuition.

The gut feeling had begun when first their departure from Vendland had been delayed, but he'd attributed his unease to his agitation over recovering Elienor. Now he found cause to wonder whether it had been a planned conspiracy. Scanning the waters ahead, he spied their escort, the Jomsvikings—they'd granted their ships much too easily, he thought, and his sense of unease intensified.

And now that he considered it . . . Burislav, too, had handed over the lands Olav had requested much too promptly . . . with nary a protest . . .

An hour past, the lead Jomsviking ship had bid them follow, saying that they knew well the safest route through the island sounds . . . that the water was too shallow in places for the Longserpent and the Goldenhawk to pass through. At the time it had sounded reasonable enough . . . though now . . .

His hand went to the hilt of his sword as he inspected Svolth's chalky coastline rising in the distance. It appeared forsaken and deserted, but something wasn't right . . .

Something . . .

And then he spied them and cursed roundly.

In that instant, the clouds moved over them and the skies darkened forbiddingly as he motioned across the frothy waters to Olav upon the Longserpent.

Before he could speak, from another ship, the Shortserpent, came an anxious shout. "My king! Do you see them?"

An undeterminable number of ships made their way swiftly forward, coming like hungry rats from behind their refuge. Even as they advanced, the Jomsviking ships fell back from their midst.

"Betrayed!" Alarik roared to Olav. "We are betrayed! Lower the sails!" he commanded his men at the top of his lungs. "Secure the ships!"

"But there are so many!" someone bellowed from upon the Crane.

Olav's gaze snapped about. "Let not my men think of fleeing!" he warned. "Never have I fled in battle! May God reclaim my soul, but we'll not flee now!" He pivoted to Alarik. "Know you who commands the fleet that sails against us?"

Alarik squinted as the sun burst through the clouds once more, its brightness blinding. He shook his head, turning to Olav, his hand shielding his eyes. "Appears to be Svein Forkbeard with his bloody Danes!"

"Humph! We should have no fear from that quarter! There is no courage in those Danes! Who else dares challenge us this day?"

"The Swedes!" Sigurd bellowed with contempt at Alarik's back.

"Hah!" Olav scoffed. "Better it would have been for them to stay home and lap their sacrificial bowls than to attack the Longserpent and encounter our weapons!"

"My lord!" someone interjected from upon the Longserpent. "Haconson the jarl sails beside them, as well!"

Olav, his visage dark, turned to regard the man who'd spoken, and then focused once again on the approaching ships. "Now there," he remarked, brooding suddenly, "we would be wise to keep our guard!" He turned to Alarik, shouting across the water. "Very likely he considers he has a bone to pick with us. We might expect a smart fight with that force. They are as Norse as we!"

Alarik tipped his head, his gaze returning to the approaching bulwark of ships. He'd known Olav would turn people against him with his heavy hand, but he'd never have guessed so many.

They were far outnumbered.

With his foot propped imposingly upon his prow, he shouted brisk commands to his warriors, urging them to make ready their weapons. Men scurried about, lashing ships together, readying themselves for battle at sea. Alarik merely stood scrutinizing the approaching ships . . . searching . . . searching . . . and then he saw them . . . Ejnar's twin *skeids*, vessels made on specially fine lines and thereby swifter than most other ships, and his gut twisted. A shuddering coursed through him as he gazed at the twin set of striped sails. It was not fright that caused it, for he had no fear of dying should it be his destiny. It was every man's fate to die someday . . . rather it was the thought of dying without telling Elienor what was in his heart.

He didn't want to die without seeing her once more, didn't want to live without her, and the realization struck him like lightning and thunder . . . not only did he love her . . .

He *needed* her.

The glitter of Olav's armor caught his eye suddenly as he glanced toward the Longserpent. As Olav had, most of the men had worn their full armor for this treacherous sea voyage, but Olav's mail was made of a new and thicker weight. No mere arrow could pierce it. A most peculiar presentiment came over him as he watched Olav riding his dragon prow, his magnificent gold helm shining in the sun and his gilded shield and sword held ready in his grasp. Alarik was driven to call out to his kin across the churning water.

Olav turned to face him.

"Take care, mine brother," Alarik charged.

The smile Olav returned was arrogant. "*Nei*, mine *bror*, 'tis you who needs must take care!" he countered, his eyes sparkling mischievously, and then suddenly there was no more time for talk.

As the legion of *drakken* approached, arrows flew—some ignited—and fell like lethal rain from the sky.

Within another moment *drakken* prows collided fiercely. Grappling hooks were hurled both ways, securing the enemy ships to their own, allowing men easy passage from ship to ship.

The whoosh of arrows was a merciless roar in Elienor's ears. She'd been bound hastily with ropes to the mast. And still Hrolf taunted her.

"I cannot wait to see the bastard's face when he spies you!" he told her. Reaching high, he ignited the sailcloth above her with the lighted pitch torch he held in his fist. The billowing fabric caught at once, and the flame licked swiftly upward with the sweeping breeze. He laughed hideously. "Now to seek out the bastard!" he informed her, snickering. "And I shall cleave him in two with mine blade as he watches you burn!" He sniggered malevolently. "Tell, me, *Fransk* witch . . . will you watch each other die? How poetic an ending!" He laughed again. " 'Tis one for the *skalds*, I'll warrant!" And with that he left her, leaping over the gunwale, onto the nearest vessel, forsaking her to the flames.

Elienor watched him make his way from ship to ship, knowing it would be futile to scream out a warning. Over the clamor of war nothing would be heard. And with so many ships surrounding them, she had no inkling where Alarik might be. She could only pray . . . and continue to manipulate the ropes, for she'd managed to loosen them already . . .

Sweet Jesu—she had to free herself!

This was her nightmare come true!

She had to save him.

Furiously, she worked at the ropes, bruising and chafing her tender wrists with her efforts. But she didn't care.

She had to warn him!

Or die trying.

When the first ship collided with the Goldenhawk, Alarik knew not to give his opponent time enough to board. In a battle at sea 'twas common practice to board a vessel, clear it, then take it for one's own. He took the offensive, and with a fierce battle cry that sent shivers down the spines of many, he leapt aboard the smaller vessel, keeping his eyes upon the striped sails of Ejnar's *skeids* that were his destination. When before his eyes one of the ship's sails caught flame, erupting with the wind, reason fled him entirely. He fought feverishly, with the insanity attributed to the berserkers, whose legendary lust for killing drove them into veritable madness in the heat of battle.

By God, he'd not let either Hrolf or Ejnar perish—not before he was able to discover Elienor's whereabouts!

And if by chance they'd harmed her . . . he'd rip the entrails from whomever was directly responsible and feed them to both Ejnar and Hrolf!

Faced with his fury, the first two men to confront him were felled at once. The third, the black-haired leader of the vessel, swung an axe at his head. Alarik dodged it, parrying with his sword. Like thunder, metal clashed against metal, and the mighty force of Alarik's blow hurled the man backward against the gunwale, his spine cracking with the impact.

Yet another Dane rushed at him.

Alarik moved toward the man with deadly purpose. *Dragvendil* sliced swiftly to wrest the life from him—there was no mercy to be shown, for if he did so, he'd not survive the day. With a muttered curse, Alarik shook the man free of his weapon, feeling no satisfaction as the Dane tumbled back over the gunwale into the ocean to swim with the beasts of the sea.

By God, he'd not be satisfied until every last Dane and Swede that had sailed against them this day was slain!

Nor would he rest until Elienor was again in his arms and Hrolf's blood blackened his sword!

Chapter 33

With the last vessel cleared, Alarik made his way one ship closer to his destination. Behind him, blood ran in rivulets. The fighting had been so intense, his mind so centered upon Elienor, that he was completely unaware of the moment the tide turned against them.

At long last, he was near enough to leap the distance unto Ejnar's burning *skeid*, but he froze abruptly. At the shock of seeing her, his chest felt as though 'twould rend in too.

He watched, paralyzed, as Elienor, bound to the burning mast, struggled to free herself. He violet eyes pleaded with him across the distance. His gut twisted, and for the longest instant, he could not move.

And then he made his way toward her once more.

Though Elienor shouted, Alarik seemed not to hear her.

He fought his way toward her, leaping gunwales as though they were nonexistent. She shook her head frantically. "Nay!" she screamed. "Nay!"

With a terrible crack a ship collided against Ejnar's *skeid*. Jolted by the impact, Elienor screamed.

Spying Olav clinging to the serpent head upon its prow, her chest constricted painfully. No time—dear God, no time! Even as she burst into hopeless tears, she wriggled one hand free of its bindings, and without a moment to spare, she began at once to release the other.

As she worked the loops, the vision before her transformed to the smoky scene of her nightmares—it was smoke, not mist, she realized with mounting fear.

Fire raged about her.

More horrible a death she could not imagine! Not even her mother's compared, for after having spent so long confined within what amounted to no more than an open grave, Elienor could no longer feel afeared of that particular nightmare any longer. In the last month she'd faced every horror possible . . . or so she'd thought.

Her chest constricted as sheer panic assailed her.

Aboard the Longserpent, Olav fought savagely. As Elienor watched with bated breath, arrows converged upon his ship. At once his men scattered for the gunwales, shouting and leaping over them into the sea.

As her gaze was drawn again to Alarik, her binding fell free. Her heart twisting, she broke away, screaming that Alarik go, that he leave her and save himself. Desperately, she tried to find a path through the flames, but could not, and she screamed again as arrows and spears flew past her head.

Alarik watched, his mind refusing to accept what his eyes beheld. Even in peril as she was, Elienor screamed fearing for him, shouting that he leave her. All about her, Ejnar's ship was ablaze, burning with Elienor trapped upon it. He'd never reach her in time, nor did she seem to want him to. Helpless to do aught, he watched as the mast splintered and groaned, collapsing sideways upon the Longserpent beside it.

Damn her, he cared not what she wanted.

He'd be damned if he'd simply let her die!

Flames burst and scattered.

In the confusion more men clamored over the Longserpent's gunwales. Olav himself scaled to the highest point of his dragon prow, shouting at the top of his lungs. Torn between wanting to aid him and to save Elienor, Alarik chose Elienor, knowing that his brother could hold his own well enough. Elienor could not. 'Twas up to him to help her or watch her be consumed before his very eyes. The fire was spreading too rapidly. He only hoped Olav would last until he was able to return to aid him. Yet even as he made the decision to leap the distance to Ejnar's *skeid*, his blood turned cold.

As he watched, Olav raised his shield unto the heavens. "I surrender this battle to you, filthy Danes, for 'tis all but lost to me!"

Alarik could not believe his ears. Confusion and outrage erupted within him. "*Nei*, Olav! *Nei!*" he shouted furiously. In his mind, his brother was taking the coward's way out. "*Nei!*" he bellowed.

Olav spared him not a glance. His mind set, he continued at the top of his lungs, "I stand, as God is my witness, at no man's mercy, but at God's instead! Thus I curse your heathen souls! May you rot in hell!" Having said that, he finally turned to smile ruefully at Alarik, letting loose his grip upon the dragon head. Plummeting into the sea feet first, he sheltered his head with his shield to escape the arrows that flew at him. An explosion of bubbles burst from beneath the shield as he fell and then the shield shifted and slid into the murky water as his mail carried him downward. His crimson mantle snagged free. It billowed on top of the water, a grim, silent marker.

*   *   *

Her heart twisting, Elienor watched as Alarik cast down his precious sword. She knew an instant of inconceivable panic as he peeled off his mail, flinging it wrathfully down upon the deck. He glared down into the water where Olav had vanished mere seconds before, and then, letting out an angry roar, turned to face her once more, his eyes locking with hers across the flames, his chest heaving in fury. Elienor could see, even at this distance, the blinding emotion burning within him.

In the next instant, he was running, leaping, hurtling over the churning water toward her.

Just as in her dream.

And in that instant, she heard the unholy laughter, and her eyes followed the sound. As in her dream, she found Hrolf upon yet another ship, with his hand poised in midair. Time stood still as his arm reared backward, then forward, the handle cocked in his tight grasp, the axe aimed . . .

Directly at Alarik.

In the same instant she saw Hrolf heave the weapon through the air, she watched as another blade was embedded within Hrolf's back. Sigurd. Elienor could discern the look of thwarted surprise on Hrolf's face even as he toppled forward into the churning water.

Yet there was no time to feel vindicated, nor even relieved.

God help her, but she knew what she must do. She took a fortifying breath and propelled herself through the flames, screaming, running, and like Alarik, she hurled herself through the air, her skirt ablaze, trying to deflect the blow of the axe from him.

In the instant before they collided in midair, she saw Alarik's look of stunned surprise, and then they hit, their bodies twisting together violently.

With a hoarse shout, Alarik attempted to catch Elienor to him, failing. In the next instant, an axe handle came from nowhere, striking her aside the head. With a soft gasp of pain, she closed her eyes.

And then they were both within the water.

Saltwater stung his eyes, but he kept them wide, desperate to locate her . . . her kyrtle . . . her hair . . . anything . . . anything to seize hold of.

He twisted wildly within the water, bubbles exploding all about, blinding his vision. His weight carried him down . . . down, until at last he caught sight, not of Elienor's, but of Olav's billowing red-gold hair. Instinctively, he seized a handful and propelled himself back toward the surface to recover Elienor.

Olav had been holding his breath, trying in vain against the weight of his mail to resurface. His lungs near to bursting he clawed at his *brynie* with a frenzy born of panic.

Alarik, his lungs beginning to ache as well, fought desperately to regain the surface. Saltwater stung his eyes, and he closed them a mere instant to ward away the burn, then reopened them to find Olav kicking him away.

Alarik shook his head, angrily denying the unspoken command, and again tried to resurface, clutching Olav's hair tight within his fist.

It was then that he caught sight of Elienor above him, her tattered sapphire silk gown blending with the sea itself. Light as she was, she drifted down past him, her body lifeless, and in a sudden panic, Alarik reached out to seize her, releasing Olav momentarily to snatch her about the waist, and then he drove again to regain hold of his brother. Grasping blindly, his fingers secured a hold on the gleaming ring that bobbed around Olav's neck.

Alarik tried in vain, once more to resurface, in one hand holding the brother he'd served so long—in his other, the woman he loved. Christ, how he loved her!

He needed them both.

And by God, he'd save them both!

Resigned to his fate, Olav shook his head furiously, waving Alarik away in desperation, urging him to save himself and Elienor while he could.

Alarik's lungs pained him beyond anything he'd ever known, but he dared not give in, nor even loosen his grip upon the mortal weight he clutched.

He peered up wretchedly at the fading halo of light. It grew more distant with each passing second. How could he simply let go? How could he choose to release his brother—his blood?

Yet in his arms Elienor remained lifeless and he knew he must decide.

With no hands to swim with, and only his feet to propel himself he sank down further still, until he faced Olav in the darkening water.

Olav's cheeks were bloated, his eyes bulging, set in the deepest scowl Alarik had ever beheld. He struggled against Alarik's hold. "Go!" he exploded, and the command erupted with a profusion of angry bubbles. By the time the single life-ending word reached Alarik, it sounded no more than a faint rumbling to his ears. Below him, Olav thrashed wildly as he took the burning saltwater into his lungs, and with his last coherent gesture, he jerked his body violently.

Through the fist that held the leather cord around Olav's neck Alarik felt the spasms that coursed through his brother's body, and then abruptly Olav, too, became limp and grew heavier, carrying him down ... further down ...

Still Alarik could not release him, but his strength ebbed, and his fingers went numb about the cold metal ring, and there came a final instant when he knew he could delay no longer. If he didn't release Olav, Elienor would die for certain.

He could choose life, or he could choose death.

But 'twas not his destiny to choose at all, for just then Olav slipped from the leather neckband that held him imprisoned in Alarik's grip.

Pain knifed through Alarik's chest as he felt the sudden weightlessness—yet he could delay no longer.

His breath exploding from his lungs, he struggled toward the faded light above, leaving a trail of urgent bubbles in his wake.

He only hoped he was not too late for Elienor!

By the blood of the White Christ—what if he were?

His chest burned until it seemed his lungs would burst.

Odin help him—God help him—anybody—the light was too far!

God, he'd sell his soul to reach it.

He'd take Elienor home, to her uncle, if she wished ... if only ...

Too far!

His vision faded black momentarily, and then, when it seemed he could hold no longer, he broke through the spume and was breathing once more, gasping for life-saving air.

He'd held Elienor so tightly that even had she come to and been able to take a breath, it wouldn't have reached her lungs, and he let out a guttural cry as with the last of his strength he hoisted her up into the air.

Vaguely, he was aware she didn't come back down—and then hands reached down mercifully, seizing him, dragging him from the sea, Elienor's ring held in a death-grip within his fist.

The impact to her belly as Elienor was hoisted up and down against the ship's gunwale drove the water from her lungs. She coughed, spewing saltwater. Gasping and choking, she struggled for breath. For the briefest instant, she opened her eyes, saw him not, and cried his name before succumbing again to the blackness that waited to claim her.

Chapter 34

With everyone so preoccupied over defeating Olav, they had somehow managed to escape the battle without notice. Fools! For mere hours now the battle had been ended and already there were rumors bandied about that Olav had been spied making away in one of the Jomsviking's ships.

Alarik knew better.

They'd come straightaway to the steading. For his part, he'd never felt emptier than he did at this moment. And the Gods curse him! He'd never loathed himself more.

Elienor had yet to waken, and for that too he could only blame himself. His chest heaved with emotions he could not express.

If only he'd left her in Francia.

He'd had no right to her then—nor did he have a right to her now!

God—she'd risked her life for him! He could still see the image of her bursting through the flames at him, and the vision would haunt him every last day of his life. She'd taken the blow meant for him, he realized. Had she not leapt at him, shunting his course, twisting his body with the impact of her own, so that it had struck her instead, that axe would have embedded itself between his shoulder blades.

And he would have lain eternally with Olav.

His eyes stinging, he made his way into the dark but familiar *skali* with Elienor's unconscious, battered body draped across his weary arms. Alva led the way before him with torch in hand. Sigurd and then Brother Vernay followed solemnly, along with Nissa, her face grave and distressed. Within his chamber he laid her gently down upon his bed, and then turned to Nissa, feeling an anger toward her he could not define. All he could think in that moment was that she'd been the last to see Elienor before her abduction. "Leave us!" he commanded, his voice hoarse.

Nodding anxiously, Nissa fled the chamber.

Elienor lay so quietly and unmoving upon his bed, as pale as death itself, that Alarik's gut twisted violently at the sight of her.

"For what it's worth, jarl," Sigurd proffered, "I faith she'll heal." Alarik peered up at him, his dark eyes glittering. "You know how many broken bodies I've tended after battle. Her flesh has not the taint of death about it." He nodded hearteningly, and seeing the longing in his jarl's eyes, hoped it was so.

Alva shook her head. " 'Tis the truth he tells you," she added, though with less certainty.

Alarik's jaw tightened. Closing his eyes, he shut out the raging emotions that battled within him. He could little bear the thought of losing her now—now that he finally knew the depth of his love for her.

Aye, *love*, he cursed himself! Fool that he was, he would not see it! He'd not lose her now, by God!

Not before he was given the opportunity to make it up to her. He would give her her heart's desire . . . send her back to Francia if 'twas her wish—anything she requested of him.

Anything!

If only she would come back.

Looking into her slumbering face, Alarik felt the moisture well in his eyes. He covered his face with his hands, growing angry with this unwanted turn of fate. His massive hands slid down to shadow his quivering mouth as he demanded between clenched teeth, "Is there aught more you could do for her this eve?" His gaze turned from Sigurd to Alva to Vernay. "Any of you?"

Sigurd shook his head, as did Alva and Brother Vernay. "Nay, my lord," Vernay replied softly, his own eyes watering shamelessly. "Unless she were to . . . to . . ."

"Then leave me!" Alarik demanded, refusing to hear the monk out. She'd not die. He'd not let her, by God! "Go!" he shouted when they were too slow to comply. He had no wish to disgrace himself further by weeping like a woman before them. Keeping his tone completely devoid of emotion, he added, "And Sigurd . . ."

Sigurd turned, though Alva and Brother Vernay did not. The two of them hurried away to give privacy.

Alarik's voice was gruff. He waited until both had left them and then said, "I'd have you take the watch. I've no idea what will come of the battle, but for certain I'll not let any usurp what is mine."

Sigurd nodded, his expression as sullen as his lord's, for though Alarik's words held every trace of their former strength and determination, they lacked the passion. Never before had he beheld him so crestfallen. "Very well, my lord," he avowed and again turned to go.

"Apprise me the instant you see Bjorn, will you?" Alarik added grimly. "If he dares show his deceiving face."

"Would you have me tell him aught?" Sigurd asked, turning at the door to look over his shoulder at him.

Alarik shook his head, trying to think coherently, unable to do so. "Tell him . . ." He shook his head again. "Tell him nothing. Merely send the bastard to me when he comes—if he comes . . ."

Sigurd nodded, departing at last, closing the heavy door behind him.

Alone, Alarik knelt at the bedside, his eyes closed in anguish.

Elienor had been through all this because of him. Only God knew what she'd endured in the last weeks under Hrolf's hand. "You shall live!" he demanded arrogantly. "You shall!" His gaze softened, moisture burning at his eyes. He squeezed his lids shut and touched his brow, awkwardly beginning the sign of the cross as he'd seen Brother Vernay do so oft.

Odd how he found solace in the ritual when it was done.

After a long moment, he found his voice again, gruff as it was. "I am, Elienor . . ." He shook his head in self derision. "A stubborn, arrogant, fool! Too long have I felt the need to be as mine sire . . . so much so that I've done as he did to the last; I've denied the love of my heart . . . as did he . . . as it was his way to deny all emotions not manly." His voice faltered. "Christ . . . fool that I am, I believed him. I believed his way was the true way of men. God . . . I was mistaken, Elienor . . . forgive me." He laid his head against her breast. "In the name of your God, open your eyes!" he cried hoarsely.

Elienor remained unmoving, and he lifted his face, vaguely aware that a tear, the first he'd ever

shed, rolled down his cheek and fell upon her ash-
en face. Blinking, he touched the crystalline droplet
with a finger, stunned unto death to see it, his
heart hammering, unsure what to do next. With
a low cry, he swiped it away, and bent to kiss her
lips. Taking her head in his big hands, he whispered hoarsely, "Come back to me, Elienor—oh,
God, come back!"

For the longest time, he merely gazed down at
her angelic face, so pale in the dim, flickering light
of the single torch. He felt like cursing. He felt like
howling. He felt like committing murder. He did
none of those. Instead, there, upon his knees, he
kept a silent vigil, and cursed Hrolf Kaetilson to a
death without a place in his precious *Valholl!* He'd
not been able to avenge himself, for he'd not seen
Hrolf again, and he prayed Hrolf had died without
a weapon in his traitorous clutches.

Losing track of the hours he spent at Elienor's
side, he thought of everything Elienor had endured
at his hands, at his men's hands, and knew that
never again would he take man or woman against
their will. 'Twas wrong, and looking at her too
still form, the wound on her forehead—his finger
gently traced the scar that had completely healed,
and then moved into her hair to search out the
lump caused by the axe handle. There was no open
wound, but it could have killed her—might *still*
kill her. And then there were the burns on her legs,
not grave, for they'd plummeted into the water
well before her dress could fully ignite, yet still
there, a loathsome reminder of all she'd suffered
for his indulgence.

Every moment, he prayed for her recovery, but
with the light of the new day, it still had not come.
In its stead came utter exhaustion. The physical toll

of battle and his raw emotions drained him, but he refused to close his eyes.

Nearly asleep upon his knees, he removed his boots and blood-stained shirt, and clad in nought more than his breeches, crawled into the bed beside Elienor.

And still he fought exhaustion as he watched her every unconscious gesture. Reaching out, he grasped a lock of her beautiful hair, and feeling it between his fingers, he again imagined Olav's red-gold hair within his fist. Felt again the moment his brother's body slipped from his grasp to the sea, and a hoarse cry escaped him.

More tears.

But he didn't care.

He'd lost too much to care.

When Elienor had not roused by the following morn, he felt like shaking her awake. His endurance was near to the breaking point. He felt helpless as a babe simply staring. There had to be something he could do to aid her . . . something . . .

With that notion he felt compelled to go to the *kirken*. Elienor had spent so much time within the small building—mayhap there he would find answers. He didn't bother changing his clothing. Restless as he was, he left his chamber dressed in nought more than his leather breeches.

The instant he walked out of the *skali*, Nissa hurried within, toward his chamber.

Alarik didn't note it. And he didn't bother with his mount.

Instead he ran the distance, releasing his frustrations in the course of it. Midway there, he let out a tormented cry and fell to his knees, pounding the ground with his fists in outrage.

"Damn you, Olav!" he shouted to the heavens. "Damn me! Damn your obsession with your Christian God!"

Loki take him, not even Svein Forkbeard, who was well on his way to converting the Danemark, employed such harsh persuasion as had Olav! So absorbed was Alarik in his wrath that he did not hear the approaching footfalls.

He did note the shadow that fell over him, and swung about . . . to face his brother.

Bjorn's face was pale, his eyes wide. " 'Tis true," he declared, shaking his head as though disbelieving his eyes. "You do live?"

"Aye!" Alarik snarled. "Does it gall you, bastard?" He surged to his feet to face him. Anger and disillusionment burned in his dark visage.

If Bjorn had been relieved at seeing Alarik, his relief faded in the flaring of his anger. "*Ya!*" he exploded. "By Odin! I am bastard—as you've so often reminded me!"

Alarik was momentarily stunned by the accusation, for he'd never used the term in reference to Bjorn before. He'd done so this time only in anger.

"You've not heard that cry from my lips," Alarik denied. His fists clenched at his sides. "If you have been reminded . . . 'tis by your own self alone, for you will recall that I am bastard, too!"

"*Ya?* And what ills has your bastardy brought you, mine brother?" Bjorn countered. "You have had aught in life you've desired. I!—*I* am the one who has had nought all my years! Nought!—do y' heed? And for once I had opportunity, can you not see that?"

"I see only a sniveling fool," Alarik broke in, stalking him now. Bjorn retreated slowly. "A fool

who has betrayed kin and country, *both!* In the
same breath—a fool, Bjorn, and nought more! Know
you what price you have paid for your treachery?
Your honor! Kinship! The Northland's future—not
to mention its king!" He stopped before Bjorn, his
stance deathly still yet bespeaking the violence in
his heart. "And the knowledge that you carry the
blood of brothers on your treacherous hands!"
Alarik laughed then, but there was little mirth in
the sound.

"You live!" Bjorn pointed out, and the declaration sounded more an accusation. "As for Olav—"
His brows furrowed, and he shook his head.

"Olav was never mine brother!" Bjorn said vehemently. "Only yours!"

"Spoiled whelp!" Alarik lunged at him, his fury
too violent to contain any longer. The two wrestled
fiercely, until Alarik, exhausted as he was, could
exert no more. He fell atop Bjorn, pinning him
beneath him with an arm to his neck, his face crimson with anger. "You think he was not, bastard!" he
shouted. "You think not? Is that why he defended
your filthy heathen hide to the last? Even in the
face of mine anger and accusations, even when I
condemned you with proof. Aye, Bjorn, Erik's son,
I know well you met with Hrolf, for I spied you
with mine own eyes coming out of the grove! Olav
defended you even then!" His voice broke. "*Nei*,
Bjorn, Erik's son, art mistaken, for Olav was more
your brother than ever you allowed. 'Twas always
you who kept the distance! You, by God!" Slowly
his anger tempered, mellowed by the sight of his
only remaining male kin lying gasping for breath
beneath him, tempered by sorrow for what might
have been and now would never be. "You and no
one else," he ground out miserably. "Think on that

when the nights grow long and you lie brooding in your bed—and you will brood, brother, for 'tis your way!" He shook his head, removing his arm from Bjorn's throat.

"What have you to know of my ways?" Bjorn spat, scrambling out from under him to his feet.

Alarik's sigh was deep and full of pain as he rose again to face his brother. "More than you know . . . more than you know . . . think on my words if you will—" His eyes were melancholy as he turned his back to Bjorn, again making his way to the *kirken*. "Choke on them, if you would!" he called out after him. "But leave me be—leave Gryting—take Nissa and go. The sight of you sickens me!"

Bjorn stood rooted to the spot. "I wish to stay!" he announced at Alarik's back.

Alarik stiffened, turning.

Bjorn had sounded as defenseless as the little boy he'd once been, and Alarik found himself remembering wistfully the bragging youth who had followed him so faithfully. When had it ceased to be so? For the life of him, he couldn't recall. Bjorn had been a shadow to him all of his days. But no more; he'd managed to sever the ties completely with his betrayal. He'd thought his heart could grow no heavier but it did, yet he found he could not hate one who shared his blood.

Mayhap . . . mayhap still they could find a way back.

"I . . . I did not intend it to end as it did," Bjorn appealed. "I . . ."

"How else could it have ended, Bjorn?" Alarik shook his head morosely. "I cannot decide this now," he announced before Bjorn could reply. He didn't wish to hear bloody excuses—could think only of Elienor. There was nothing left to be done for Olav. "Stay for the time," he allowed with a weary sigh, and then he turned abruptly, again making his way to the *kirken*.

Chapter 35

Mercy, *she'd done this before, had she not?*
Elienor groaned as pain erupted through
her head. She rolled and endeavored to open her
eyes, but the light was too strong, and she closed
them once more.

And sweet Jesu, but her body felt so tender ...
her legs ... 'Twas as though her ribs and chest were
bruised. Nevertheless, she welcomed the pain, for
it bespoke life. Precious life!

Taking in a long draught of air, she knew
an instant of serenity she'd never experienced
before—despite her soreness, despite her confusion—for she sensed the nightmare was ended
at last.

"Elienor," a voice called softly.

Still disoriented, Elienor's eyes opened, focusing
after an interminable moment upon Nissa's face
hovering just above her own. With a startled gasp,
she tried to rise.

Nissa was quick to aid her. "Allow me!" she
exclaimed, placing her arms behind Elienor for
support. Her expression seemed genuinely troubled, but Elienor could only think that Nissa had
been the one to lure her to the *kirken*. She stiffened
at the touch.

"W ... where ... where is Alarik?" Elienor asked,
swallowing for fear that she would hear what she
wished not to ... that he had perished at sea. If

357

such was the case, her heart would perish along with him.

Nissa released Elienor at once, sensing her mistrust, but unable to blame her for feeling it. Her lashes fell. "Only now has he gone from your bedside," she revealed softly. "He worried much," she disclosed, her gaze returning to Elienor, and it seemed to Elienor her eyes were filled with worry as well as regret. "D . . . does your head pain you overmuch?" she asked.

"A little," Elienor ceded. Her lips twisted wryly. "Though 'tis a wonder I've any head at all with the abuse it has received!"

Nissa smiled uncertainly. She shook her head. "I . . . I am sorry," she said again.

"Where has Alarik gone?" Elienor asked quietly.

"I'm certain he'll return soon," Nissa announced. "I . . . I hoped you would hear me before then . . . I'm so sorry!" she rushed on when Elienor did not at once refuse her. "I meant to cause you no harm. 'Tis simply that mine father . . . well, he wanted so much that I should wed Alarik. Oh, Elienor—can you forgive me?"

Elienor's emotions reverted from giddy relief at knowing that Alarik was close by to her former wariness. "Why should you suddenly wish my forgiveness?" she asked skeptically.

Only silence answered her question.

"Nissa?"

"Because I wish to stay at Gryting!" Nissa revealed in desperation. "With mine sister! And . . . and Bjorn," she said more softly, her lashes lowering. "I . . . I believe I've loved him from the first," she admitted brokenly, and there was a wistful note in her voice. Once again her sky-blue eyes returned to Elienor and they shimmered with unshed tears. "I've given myself to him, Elienor . . . and now I carry his babe. He wants so badly that our child be born here. Gryting is his home!" she appealed once more.

"And what of your father?" Elienor asked.

Nissa shook her head in sorrow, suppressing a sob. "By our laws . . . I am free to choose whomever I should wed. 'Tis only that before . . . I wanted so desperately to gain mine father's favor!"

"And now?" Elienor prodded.

"And now . . . now I know I must follow mine heart! I cannot allow mine babe to be born and never know his sire! Mine father—" Tears pooled at her eyes and spilled over her lashes. "Mine father needs must understand," she said sadly, as though she doubted he would.

"And if he will not?"

"Then there will be nought I can do to remedy it. I know only that I must do what I must," Nissa contended. And then her expression grew anxious. "Y . . . you've not told him?" she asked apprehensively, and then she rushed on. "You've not told Alarik that I was the one to lead you to the *kirken*?" Her voice was fearful, hopeful.

Elienor shook her head.

It seemed to Elienor that Nissa's expression brightened suddenly. "Will . . . will you tell him?" she asked hesitantly.

Faced with the optimistic look in Nissa's eyes, Elienor knew she could not refuse the request. She shook her head. "I'll not," she yielded.

Crying out in relief, Nissa buried her face into her hands and wept. Elienor watched a moment, feeling awkward with the unexpected show of emotion, and then reached out to touch Nissa's arm. Nissa lifted her face, her brows drawing together. "Why?" she asked in bewilderment. "Why would you not tell him? After all I've done to you, Elienor?"

Elienor shrugged and shook her head. "For Alarik," she revealed softly. "Because Bjorn is his brother . . . for the nephew he might not know otherwise . . . and because it seems to mean so much to you," she proffered.

"And to Bjorn!" Nissa assured, her lips quivering. "He wishes so much to make things right betwixt himself and Alarik!"

Elienor nodded. "And where is Alarik now?" she asked once more. "I . . . I need to see him." She did, desperately. More than aught else, she needed to behold him with her own eyes, needed proof that he yet lived—that this was not part of some cruel dream, that by some twist of fate, she would awaken and find herself alone. The last she recalled was her flight through the air as she'd hurled herself against him.

"Oh, but Elienor! Do you think you should seek him out so soon? You've only just awoke. Mayhap . . . mayhap it would be best if you waited until he returned."

"Nay!" Elienor whispered fervently, and it was her turn to be despairing. "Nay, Nissa . . . I must see him! I *must*!"

In that instant, a look of profound understanding passed between the two, and Nissa nodded. "Then I shall lead you to him," she relented, and with a tentative smile, she proceeded at once to help Elienor rise from the bed.

Alarik had slept not at all throughout the night. Dark shadows rimmed his steely eyes, a silent testimony to his inner turmoil. In his heart there was an emptiness that made him feel more vulnerable then he'd ever thought conceivable—all these years he'd mistakenly assumed love, itself, rendered a man impotent. Now he knew better ... 'twas not love, at all, but *fear* of loving that was the true weakness, for by it he'd lost everything.

Kneeling at the altar, he thought of Elienor lying so still within his bed and his gut twisted. He'd never done such a thing as pray ere now, for the old gods were not invoked in such a manner. Nevertheless ... he felt the need to attempt the strange ritual ... for Elienor's sake—for his sake!

The door had been left ajar.

During Elienor's absence, the roof had been erected, and the little building was now shadowy within. Still ... she could see well enough to make out the figure kneeling before the altar.

With Nissa supporting her, Elienor halted silently in the portal of the *kirken*. Her heart pounded within her breast at the sight before her. Stunned, she broke free of Nissa and leaned upon the door frame for support. She turned and motioned for Nissa to leave her, and then her gaze was drawn again, like metal to a lodestone, to the curious sight within.

Never had she seen Alarik pray ... and though he did so awkwardly, his sincerity was evident in his every gesture. Still, to her surprise, she found it changed nothing. Nothing, at all. She shook her head, bewildered, for in truth she felt the same for him now as she had moments before.

She loved him recklessly.

Alarik sensed the presence well before he heard the footsteps enter the *kirken*, but didn't bother to pause, nor did he conceal his prayers. He cared not who spied him at it now, for he'd kept his convictions to himself much too long. Mayhap, had he been more convincing, Olav might have changed his tactics. Mayhap he would have softened? And mayhap not, he acknowledged ruefully.

Only when he'd concluded did he turn, his brows drawn together in displeasure, expecting to find either Bjorn or Brother Vernay observing him, and was stunned to find neither. His shadowed eyes widened at the sight that greeted him. Elienor, in all her tattered glory. His heart quickened. "Elienor?" he croaked. He surged clumsily to his feet, lack of sleep making his body unwieldy.

For the longest moment neither spoke.

Elienor's eyes filled with unshed tears. "You are," she asked, swallowing the knot that formed in her throat, "truly here?" And he was, for his presence dominated the small *kirken*. She touched her own face, as though to touch his, assuring herself that the moment was real.

"Aye," he replied hoarsely. His arms ached to hold her, but he dared not move lest she prove to be nought more than an illusion. He was afeared to blink lest she vanish before his eyes. He tried to read her in the dim light but couldn't; her emotions were hidden to him by the glare of the sun in his eyes. Even as he determined she was real, he stood rooted to the spot, loathing himself for all that had befallen her since taking her from Francia, certain that she despised him for it.

Yet his eyes beckoned her.

Elienor attempted to take a step forward and swayed weakly. She braced herself upon the door frame, and in that moment, Odin himself couldn't have kept Alarik from her. He moved forward swiftly to claim her, and Elienor's breath caught as he swept her into his arms. A low cry was torn from his lips as his mouth brushed her brow, her nose, her mouth . . .

Elienor's heart skipped its normal beat. Looking up into his dark, smoldering eyes, she could only think how glad she was to be within his arms again—how glad she was to see him alive. She wanted him to hold her this way always . . .

"Shhhh . . . don't cry," Alarik soothed, his voice husky. "*Nei*, Elienor . . ." He placed his forehead to hers, and swore, "I shall make everything aright—everything!" And with that, he withdrew the leather neckband from about his neck and pressed her uncle's ring into her palm. " 'Tis yours," he revealed grimly. "I . . ." He swallowed. "I took it from Olav," he said without censure. The time for petty jealousies was past. Nought mattered now but Elienor's happiness—not even the accursed reason for which she'd gifted Olav the ring to begin with. He couldn't care any longer.

Unclasping her palm, Elienor stared in bewilderment at the ring, recalling the moment she'd given it to Olav, and then in succession . . . Olav's face as he'd released the serpent prow and descended into the water. "I . . ." Her voice faltered. "He was to have returned it to my uncle," she revealed somberly. Her violet eyes lifted to his. "H . . . he promised he would speak to you . . . that you might send me back to Francia . . . to my uncle . . ." She shook her head and averted her gaze suddenly. Alarik released her, freeing her from his embrace.

Elienor felt the separation acutely.

He lifted her chin with a finger, the shadows in his eyes deepening. His silver eyes pierced her. "And is that still your desire?" he whispered hoarsely. His fingers went to the scar at her temple, tracing the fine line. Though it was long healed now, it was a raw reminder of the suffering she'd endured at his hands.

Elienor said nothing, could not speak, for her heart lodged in her throat. Tears welled in her eyes.

And in her silence, Alarik heard what he most feared. The lump in his throat thickened. "Then . . . I shall grant you your freedom," he told her grimly, bending to kiss her scar. He'd sworn to do so, he reminded himself, and he would comply—no matter what it cost him!

Tears coursed down Elienor's cheeks. Life was so unfair! Now, when at last she wished to remain with him, could surrender herself with an open heart and soul, he would discard her so easily? "And will you also restore to me my heart?" she asked him, unable to stifle the note of bitter hysteria that invaded her soul.

Alarik shook his head, unwilling to mistake her words, unwilling to hope, only to lose her all over again. "Your heart?" he asked softly, his heart hammering. His gaze never wavered, afeared to miss even the slightest shift in her expression.

"Aye!" Elienor cried in outrage, "My heart! for as surely as you stole me away from Francia, so, too, did you seize it away!"

A muscle ticked in Alarik's jaw as he drew her back into his arms. "God—Elienor!" Afeared that he was somehow dreaming, he merely held her, unable to end the moment, unable to speak again for fear that he'd misunderstood. More than aught else he wanted her happy, but he wanted *her* more than life itself! He would give everything he held to see her look at him with adoration in her beautiful violet eyes.

"I . . . I love you!" she cried out, and then stiffened within his embrace, revealing to Alarik that she'd not intended to voice the endearment. Giddy relief unlike any he'd ever known jolted through him at her declaration. How he loved her impetuous tongue! A gratified smile curved his lips, but he said nothing as he savored the truth of the feelings she'd disclosed to him.

Regretting the foolish love words, Elienor cursed herself a thousand times for a fool! When would she ever learn to master her traitorous tongue? Did she think he would simply lay down his heart and vow his love in return? How foolish she was to hope that he would. He was a Viking leader—she nothing more than his French whore! He a noble chieftain—she nothing but a measly—alas, but she could not even claim the church for her own, for she no longer came to them a pure bride of Christ. In their eyes she was soiled! In an attempt to salvage her pride, she told him, "I meant nothing . . ."

"Elienor," he broke in, his voice gruff. "Do you wish to know what I've prayed for?" He held her possessively, as though to loosen his hold upon her was to lose her.

For the longest instant, Elienor could not find her voice. As long as he held her thus, she could almost believe he wanted her still. "What . . . what did you pray for?"

He answered her question with a question of his own. "Is it not your custom to ask your God to bless a marriage ere its union?"

Elienor's eyes misted. She shrugged at his question, fighting tears. Losing the effort to contain them, she closed her eyes. "You have decided to allow Bjorn and Nissa to wed?" she asked him in puzzlement, her tone anguished.

· *"That,"* he apprised her, swallowing the lump that appeared in his throat, "is not my decision to make, at all. Bjorn and Nissa *will* wed if 'tis their wish . . . though I have determined they may indeed remain at Gryting." Taking Elienor's free hand into his own, he charged, "Look at me, Elienor!" He waited until her violet eyes opened to meet his once more, and moved by the tears that flowed so freely down her ashen cheeks, he cupped her face within his callused palms, cradling it there, his touch more gentle than a tender babe's. "Shush," he hissed. "Don't cry, love!" he pleaded. "If you wish it, then I *will* send you back to Francia—if you wish it—but I beg you do not cry!"

Elienor tried desperately to suppress her sobs, but she could not. She buried her face into his warm, bare chest, unable to face the possibility that he would make her go! She couldn't bear it!

Alarik sank to his knees, seeing that her strength wavered. Kneeling before her, he urged her down upon her knees before him, and then bent to kiss her sorrow away. With every salty tear he kissed from her soft face, he felt his own uncertainty ebb. "Elienor," he whispered huskily, "I have asked *your* God . . . *my* God," he amended, testing the words, *"our* God . . . to bless *our* union— not Bjorn and Nissa's." Holding her face between his hands, he forced her to look into his eyes, and shook his head. "Tell me 'tis what you wish, as well! Tell me 'tis so!" he commanded, coming as close to pleading as he dared. 'Twas not in his blood to beg. If she refused him . . . then he would indeed release her. But he felt certain she'd not, for when she lifted her tear-stained face to his, every emotion she held in her heart was unveiled to him. 'Twas the look he'd waited so long to see.

"Y . . . you wish . . . you wish t . . . to wed . . . with . . . with me?"

Alarik nodded, smiling arrogantly now, knowing that her answer would be aye. But his jaw dropped as she broke away, surging to her feet and going to the altar. She fell to her knees before it.

"Elienor?"

Elienor heard the uncertainty in his voice and turned to look at him with misty eyes, gifting him with her most serene smile. "One more," she whispered, her voice breaking with joy, "One more . . . so that I too may ask the Lord to bless our union!" And she lowered her head to pray.

In mere seconds Alarik was on his feet. Filled with exhilaration, he lifted Elienor into his arms as though she weighed no more than a new born babe. He leaned eagerly to kiss her full upon the lips, thinking that it had been too long since he'd tasted of his little *Fransk*. And in his need to love her he went to lay her down upon the *kirken* floor, oblivious with the need to hold her, to love her.

"Not here!" Elienor screeched in consternation, laughing, sobbing. "Never here!" she told him.

Alarik grinned sheepishly and rose to his feet, bearing her toward the door . . . eager to get her into his bed, even if they did not more than sleep . . . his arms embracing her.

Elienor struggled to free herself. "Release me!" she demanded, and her eyes grew sober. "Let there be no doubts between us this time—allow me to go of my own will!"

Alarik halted abruptly, his expression suddenly grave. He shuddered as he looked deep into her eyes, and Elienor flushed as he allowed her to slide from his embrace. Her body melded against his, and she nearly ceased to breathe at the wicked sensations it roused within her.

"Do you feel I've forced you?" he asked gravely, as though suddenly unsure of himself.

The muted sunlight from the doorway bathed them both, and in that instant it was as though they were transported through time . . . and were again in the *kirken* in Francia. Only this time, it was *he* who could not see her face, *his* expression that was revealed by the light. "Nay," Elienor whispered, her heart rending at his forlorn appearance. "I only meant that I would go beside you—that all who see us will know I go willingly." Her eyes pleaded with him to understand.

Standing in the doorway, haloed by the sun, Elienor looked like an angel to him, but she was neither angel nor *Valkyr*, he knew. She was flesh and blood.

And she was his.

In that instant, Alarik's heart filled near to bursting. Thrusting a hand into her hair, he bent to brush his lips against her flushed cheek. "I . . . I love you, Elienor," he said, voicing the words for the first time in his life, his voice hoarse.

Elienor's heart soared, for it didn't take a seer to know he spoke true. He did love her, and she nearly cried out with the exhilarating sense of completion that burst through her in that instant. God help her, but for the first time in her life, she knew what it felt like to be cherished, for she was too young at her mother's death to recall her.

At long last. At long, long last. With a sigh, she allowed the ring she'd once held so tightly to slip forgotten from her fingers to the floor, not needing it any longer, for while it had once been her comfort, her family, it was no more.

Held so tenderly within Alarik's embrace, she had, at long last . . . come home.

Epilogue

"**M**ama! Mama! Tell us again of the vision . . . the one you first had of Papa!" a child's voice demanded. "Gunnar will not believe me!"

As Elienor swept into the *skali*, a throng of children rushed to surround her, led by her eldest daughter, Kirsten, who bore her mother's blue eyes and father's blond hair. All eyed her hopefully, and her own eyes lit with merriment as she glanced up to spy Nissa supervising the preparation of the tables for *nattver*. Upon Alva's passing, Nissa had quietly stepped into the task, taking her lessons from Alva. At Elienor's look, Nissa merely smiled, and shrugged, telling Elienor by that gesture that she'd been unable to sway the children from asking yet again.

Jesu! How many times would she be called upon to recount the tale? As it was, she felt she'd told it near a thousand times. Ahh, well . . . Alva *had* warned her, rest her soul. 'Twas simply that because it had been so long now since she'd had a single vision, she found herself e'er recounting the same tales. 'Twas a wonder no one ever seemed to tire of them. She sighed, capitulating.

"Very well." She smiled as she scanned the faces of her expectant audience, for among the children were her own two daughters: Kirsten and Dahlia. Along with them, Bjorn and Nissa's five, four girls, and their ever recalcitrant son, Gunnar. And the quiet lad who always lagged behind belonged to Sigurd and Clarisse.

Finding a suitable spot, Elienor adjusted her skirts and sat. And no sooner had she done so than her youngest daughter, Dahlia, scurried into her lap. After her came Mischief, eager as always. Her daughter shrieked happily, hugging the dog, and Elienor put her fingers to her lips, shushing her, for their infant son, Krossbyr, was fast asleep in their bedchamber, with Alarik watching over him. It never ceased to amaze Elienor how many hours he spent simply watching the babe.

"You didn't truly spy Uncle Alarik first in a dream!" Gunnar exclaimed.

Elienor merely smiled, for he said the same each time. Truthfully she was beginning to wonder if it was his ploy to persuade her to recount the tale yet again.

" 'Tis the truth she did," a deep voice resounded behind them. Elienor turned, startled to hear Alarik's voice so soon after putting the babe abed.

But she wasn't the only one startled by his unexpected appearance. Mischief bounded up, darting toward Alarik's boots. No longer a small pup, the big dog nearly toppled Alarik.

Elienor stifled a giggle.

The children laughed hysterically.

"Oh, Papa!" Kirsten exclaimed. " 'Tis as though he abhors you!"

"*Nei*," Alarik denied, frowning, refusing to believe that after all these years the mutt had still not grown to tolerate him at least. He bent to scratch Mischief's ears and the dog snapped at him, barely missing his fingers. The children

giggled again. Alarik's frown deepened. "Demon
hound!" he groused, and then his brows collided
further when Bjorn sauntered in along with Brother
Vernay in tow, the two of them ensconced in another
of their heated debates over which god, or gods,
were the true ones. Alarik suspected the argument
would be unending, for both men were resolute in
their beliefs. Mischief saw them and bounded after
them, leaping up excitedly, first upon Bjorn, and
then Vernay, lapping them with relish. "Ungrateful
beast," Alarik muttered beneath his breath.

Seeing his forsaken expression, Elienor urged
Dahlia from her lap and rose to embrace him.
"You are beloved!" she reminded him with a girlish
giggle.

And seeing their mother and father embracing,
their daughters rushed forth, each embracing one
of his legs. "We do love you Papa!" they announced
in unison, and Alarik once again sent a silent prayer
of gratitude heavenward that his warriors were not
present to view such a tender display. Never would
they let him forget it. Sigurd particularly.

Alarik and Bjorn shared a quick look, for Bjorn,
too, was burdened with his share of overly affection-
ate females, and then he released Elienor, bending
to lift both his daughters up into his arms. But as
each kissed his cheeks with their soft little lips, he
wondered in awe how he had ever felt himself too
manly for this. What could be more male, he asked
himself, arrogantly, then to be surrounded by the
females one loved?

"Papa?"

Alarik peered down at his youngest daughter.

"Did you know the first time you saw Mama
that she was the one?" Her eyes were bright with
the prospect. "Did you?"

He glanced briefly at the mother of his children, sharing a private look with her. He stifled a chuckle. "And did you ask your mother that question?" he wondered aloud, bouncing Dahlia.

"Yaaaaah!" his daughters shouted simultaneously.

He shook his head in an attempt to restore his hearing. "And what did she say?" He again glanced at his wife, smiling softly as he awaited their reply.

"She said aye!" Dahlia whispered enthusiastically in his ear.

"She said she knew when first she saw you!" Kirsten added.

Alarik cleared his throat, remembering the tale somewhat differently. Elienor shrugged, smiling coyly. "Then, aye," he relented, winking at Elienor, thinking suddenly that mayhap 'twas the truth after all. He grinned roguishly. "From the very first moment!" he told them, bending to restore his children to their feet. They clung to his neck a moment, and he pried them loose, straightening to look into his wife's beautiful violet eyes—as beautiful now as they'd been the day he'd first beheld her. His arms went out to seize her to him before she could flee. "From the very first," he said to her face, daring her to dispute him.

Elienor's eyes twinkled with mirth. She laughed. "From the very first," she acquiesced, returning an impish smile.

Across the *skali* Bjorn made a choking sound and looked to his own wife, but prudently said nothing.

Alarik ignored him, abruptly sweeping his wife up into his arms. She gave a little shriek as he hauled her toward their chamber, *their* chamber, he thought with a satisfied grin. With a little luck from Frey, he'd catch up to his younger brother yet, he vowed. "You lie very well, my love," he accused her, with a roguish grin.

Elienor merely smiled. "As do you, mine husband!" She wrapped her arms about his neck.

"What say you tell *me* the tale?" he asked her huskily.

Elienor giggled and nodded.

"But she hasn't told us the story yet, Uncle Alarik!" Gunnar protested, leaping up, giving his anxiousness away.

Alarik never heard the protest. He'd already shut the bedchamber door behind him.

"Odin's breath!" Gunnar exclaimed. "I didn't get to hear the story! And Uncle Alarik's already heard it! How oft must he hear the story?" he whined, and the *skali* erupted with peals of laughter, for *no one* had asked to hear the tale more than Gunnar Long-Ears had!

Author's Note

Olav Trygvason of Norway did in fact die much as I've depicted, though when he dove into the water, he went in alone, for Alarik and Elienor, alas, live only in my heart—and, I hope, in yours now as well! I've taken great pains to stay true to my research in that I've drawn Olav as best I saw him, and I even have gone so far as to include dialogue actually attributed to him by the *Heimskringla* (The lives of the Norse Kings), by Snorre Sturlason, edited by Erling Monsen, translated by A. H. Smith. But I have also taken incredible literary license with the circumstances surrounding the elusive battle of Svolde, as well as the battle itself. The truth remains, however, that Olav Trygvason of Norway *was* a zealous man who, while he may or may not have held to the "true faith," did oppress his people to such a degree that they felt they had no choice but to rise up against him. Some of those opposing him were Christian themselves (such as Svein Forkbeard), who resented Olav's ultimatums and iron fist. As for the rumors that he survived the battle, perhaps he did, but he never again returned to claim his throne or his lands. The remaining Scandinavian kings divided his kingdom among themselves, and it was said that those who took Olav's place also took the faith, though as long as they ruled over Norway they "let every man do as he would about holding Christianity."

Avon Romances—
the best in exceptional authors and unforgettable novels!

FOREVER HIS   Shelly Thacker
77035-0/$4.50 US/$5.50 Can

TOUCH ME WITH FIRE   Nicole Jordan
77279-5/$4.50 US/$5.50 Can

OUTLAW HEART   Samantha James
76936-0/$4.50 US/$5.50 Can

FLAME OF FURY   Sharon Green
76827-5/$4.50 US/$5.50 Can

DARK CHAMPION   Jo Beverley
76786-4/$4.50 US/$5.50 Can

BELOVED PRETENDER   Joan Van Nuys
77207-8/$4.50 US/$5.50 Can

PASSIONATE SURRENDER   Sheryl Sage
76684-1/$4.50 US/$5.50 Can

MASTER OF MY DREAMS   Danelle Harmon
77227-2/$4.50 US/$5.50 Can

OF THE NIGHT   Cara Miles
76453-9/$4.50 US/$5.50 Can

WIND ACROSS TEXAS   Donna Stephens
77273-6/$4.50 US/$5.50 Can